A Hex

for

Danger

Also by Esme Addison

Enchanted Bay Mysteries
A Spell for Trouble

A Hex
for
Danger

AN ENCHANTED BAY MYSTERY

Esme Addison

CROOKED
LANE

NEW YORK

Copyright © 2021 by Holloway LLC

Published in the United States by Crooked Lane Books, an imprint of The Quick Brown Fox & Company LLC.

Crooked Lane Books and its logo are trademarks of The Quick Brown Fox & Company LLC.

Library of Congress Catalog-in-Publication data available upon request.

ISBN (hardcover): 978-1-64385-586-8
ISBN (ebook): 978-1-64385-587-5

Cover illustration by Teresa Fasolino

Printed in the United States.

www.crookedlanebooks.com

Crooked Lane Books
34 West 27th St., 10th Floor
New York, NY 10001

First Edition: July 2021

10 9 8 7 6 5 4 3 2 1

To my family for their unconditional love
and continued support

Rodzina nie jest czymś ważnym. Jest wszystkim.
The family is not important. It is everything.

—A Polish proverb

Chapter One

"Coming through," called out a voice.

Lidia Sobieski descended the flight of stairs, her arms laden with a large wooden crate of bottles filled with herbal tea that clinked together as she made her way through the crowd of customers.

Alex rushed to meet her aunt on the landing and took the crate from her. Even though she was in her sixties, with her long dark hair laced with silver, and a gently lined face, Alex couldn't help but see her mother every time she looked at her.

"To the counter, dear," her aunt directed, then gave Alex a second glance. "You feeling okay?"

It was an unsettling feeling, the effect her aunt's appearance had on her. Her mother had died when she was seven, and the image she had of her in her mind was that of a favorite photograph. But it was a two-dimensional image, locked in time when her mother had been in her early thirties. But now, she could see what her mother may have looked like had she lived.

And Alex was getting used to it. Used to having lots of family around. Used to living in a small town where everyone knew who she was. She smiled. "Yes Ciocia Lidia, I feel great."

She placed the crate on the end of the counter while her aunt arched a dark eyebrow at her daughter Minka, who began grabbing the bottles and placing them in an ice-filled oak barrel. "Ever since word got out that we have ready-to-go bottles of our Keep Coolade herbal tea, we're been out of stock. And now I'm backordered." She exhaled in exasperation. "I've promised the mermaid festival committee that I would provide beverages for the unveiling of the mermaid mural in a few days."

The mermaid mural. Alex smiled. Bellamy Bay was proud of its mermaid heritage. The town was founded on the story that when Captain John Bellamy's ship landed in the area, there was already mermaids here. He'd written about it in his journals and told anyone with ears about his discovery. Of course, no one believed it was true; however, the town used the mermaid story as a fun marketing ploy that culminated in an annual summer festival that continued to attract mermaid lovers from miles around.

"I gave Kamila several complimentary bottles to hand out on the boardwalk today," Lidia continued.

"That's right," Minka said. "She's got bike patrol duty today on the beach."

"Alex," Lidia began, her eagle eye scanning the shop, "the perfumes are getting low. Why don't you restock those and leave Minka to the teas? They're in the backroom on the table, ready to go."

"Of course," Alex said. After retrieving them from upstairs, she began refilling the wood shelves that were almost bare save for a couple of items. She enjoyed handling the beautiful crystal bottles of various shapes and jeweled-toned colors. Each glass was filled with handcrafted, enchanted scents—the one she was holding had been inspired by her mother and had rose, jasmine, and magnolia. The perfumes filled the air around Alex as she delicately placed each bottle in its place. After restocking for the better part of an hour, she decided to take a break.

Rising from her kneeling position, she stood, wiping her hands on her purple apron, and went to the front of the shop to gaze out of the large plate-glass windows. It was something she did several times a day, a nice reminder of her sweet new life. Since the onset of summer, the small town of a few thousand had exploded with tourists and summer residents. Main Street was packed with visitors shopping or on their way to the beach or just enjoying their time in the sun. She smiled, only a few months ago she'd been a visitor to this town.

But now she was home in the town of her mother's birth, a community about an hour east of Wilmington on the North Carolina coast. She spent all of her time with her aunt, cousins, and friends, some old, some new. And she couldn't be happier.

Her gaze went to the street lined with multicolored shops with jeweled-toned awnings, buildings that had been standing for over two hundred years. Her world now consisted of clean white sidewalks dotted with wrought iron benches, large pots of flowers, shade trees, and sea breezes. So much character, so much history packed in a small unassuming area, and she loved it—loved being a part of a small town with all of its eccentricities and quirks. *Like a parade,* she thought with a thrill of delight—*an actual small-town parade.*

She could still see the red, white, and blue confetti that littered the streets after last week's Fourth of July parade down the town's historic center. American flags had waved from every shop front, and Alex smiled, recalling how many locals and tourists alike had filled the downtown sidewalks to watch the local high school band march by along with fifteen or so other floats. Alex laughed, thinking about how her cousin Minka, who had joined her in the crush of people on the sidewalk, oohed and aahed over the participants in the parade like it was her first time seeing such an event.

"Excuse me, miss?" a customer said, tapping her on the shoulder, interrupting her reverie. "Those teas I've heard so much about?"

"Our Keep It Coolade?" Alex guessed. When the man nodded, she pointed him in the right direction with a smile.

Botanika, the herbal apothecary Alex worked at, was crowded with customers. It was one of the reasons it was so difficult to restock the shelves this morning. Too many people in the shop, but what a wonderful problem for a business to have. With a sigh of contentment, Aleksandra Daniels, or Alex as she was known to her family and friends, turned away from the window and begin making her way back to her shelves.

Still lost in thought, she marveled that only three months earlier she'd quit her job in Manhattan as a risk analyst at a Fortune 500 company, relocated down South, and begun working with her aunt Lidia in their family business. This was the same family—her mother's family—that her recently deceased father had forbade her to see. Twenty years had passed since she'd last spent a summer in Bellamy Bay, playing with her younger cousin, Minka, who helped her own mother run the family business, and Minka's older sister, Kamila, who was a police officer in town.

Of course, now she thought she understood why her father had been so reluctant for her to see them after her mother died. . . they had secrets, secrets he didn't want her to be a part of. "You can only believe in what you see," her father had told her over and over again. "Anything else is fairy tales."

But that was the thing . . . Once Alex finally returned to Bellamy Bay, she'd discovered that fairy tales were kind of true, and the world as she knew it was not as it seemed. For example, the world was made up of Magicals and Mundanes. Magicals were people who had certain abilities and powers, while Mundanes were your everyday garden-variety human. And Alex and her mother and aunt and cousins? Well, let's just say they weren't mundane—not by a long shot.

They were, in fact, descended from a real mermaid, the same one featured in Poland's famous myth about the Mermaid of Warsaw. Alex's mother's family had immigrated to North Carolina from Poland generations ago. But before she'd moved to Bellamy Bay, she'd never heard of that myth, and she certainly hadn't known she was descended from a mermaid.

Back at the shelves, she noticed the shelf was filled and the crate was gone.

I finished up, Minka telepathed to her. *I had a break at the counter.*

Alex looked around the shop and saw her cousin grinning at her from behind the register. She was ringing up a customer and having a telepathic conversation with Alex at the same time. *Now that,* Alex thought, *takes skill.*

Minka, who was a couple years younger than her, wore her curly brown hair pulled up in a high ponytail and accented with a blue ribbon that matched her blue shop apron. She had a heart-shaped faced that gave her a wide-eyed look of innocence, and she could always be relied upon to provide positivity and good vibrations.

Thanks, Mink.

Alex went to the back of the shop, where, on a bar that ran half the length of the back brick wall, they kept ready-to-serve, ice-cold pitchers of herbal tea for the customers. They constantly needed refilling, and it had been almost an hour since she'd last looked at them. Two out of the four pitchers were empty, so she grabbed them and headed to the back room, where they could be refreshed from reserves in the refrigerator located there. As she made her way to the back, she saw a group of preteen girls in Bellamy Bay mermaid T-shirts, and with strands of pink and blue glittery mermaid hair mixed into their own, and stifled a laugh.

If they only knew, she thought with a smile.

She still remembered the evening her aunt had sat her down with her cousins and explained the secret of her heritage and the myth at the center of it all. The *Syrenka Warszawska,* or the Mermaid of Warsaw, her aunt began, a legend, though of course it was true:

Many, many generations ago, maybe as far back as the twelfth century, in the village that would eventually be known as Warsaw, a trio of fisherman noticed that whenever they went fishing, the waves were stronger than normal, their nets were always getting tangled, and their fish were set free. At night they watched the Vistula River, to discover and perhaps trap the source of their frustration, and discovered a beautiful syrenka, *a mermaid, was the culprit. They captured her, but she enchanted them with her singing, and they set her free. But then a wealthy merchant trapped her and placed her in a cage, with plans to profit from her uniqueness. The fishermen heard her pleas for help and helped her to escape. She was so grateful for their kindness that she vowed to use her magical abilities to protect the city and its people.*

The mermaid's image has been on the Warsaw coat of arms since at least the sixteenth century, and statues of her stood all over Warsaw, with a shield and sword to represent her fierce protectiveness. Her aunt had explained that although the myth ended there, the Mermaid of Warsaw's story did not. She went on to find love and have children, who in turn did the same. Over time, they lost their ability to shapeshift from Mer to human form, and most left Poland to explore the world and live in other countries.

Pitchers filled once again, Alex carried both crystal containers back into the main room of the shop and set them down on the bar.

It still sounded crazy to Alex, and she had to pinch herself at times to make sure she wasn't dreaming. Only the reality wasn't like the cartoons and movies. None of the women in the Sobieski family had fins or spent time living in the sea or sunning themselves on large rocks while singing songs. It was a lot more rational and reasonable than that.

Instead, the Sobieski women had two legs, just like a Mundane. They *were* all strong swimmers, but because Alex's mother had inexplicably drowned in Bellamy Bay when Alex was a child, she herself steered clear of the water. They could heal themselves—and others—which was an amazingly helpful ability to have. They sent telepathic thoughts to other Magicals and could will Mundanes to do things—if they were okay with that type of manipulation—and, oh yeah, she could totally influence the weather and command water and any sort of moisture, really. She was still learning all of the various terms and history—and techniques.

There was a council that regulated the use of magic in the community, punished Magical lawbreakers in ways a Mundane court could not and determined the proper percentage of black magic that could be practiced annually. The Council also maintained a list: Spells for Trouble that were forbidden to be practiced. And they established ethical good neighbor guidelines that Magicals were recommended to follow, like never reading the minds of others, even though you could. Or never making someone do something against their freewill.

It was, in fact, a lot to process and remember, and Alex wasn't always good at it, but she was, if nothing else, persistent. And if her aunt Lidia and cousins could do it, so could she. What she wasn't so sure about was keeping the secrets. It was hard. A challenge—and one she didn't enjoy.

Having a policeman for a father, she'd found life easier if she was honest and always told the truth. Now, her entire life was a lie. She was keeping things from her boyfriend, Jack, who was a detective; her friend Pepper, who was an inquisitive journalist; and all of the town folk generally. The burden to lie to almost everyone she cared about wore on her. But it was necessary. Her aunt had made that very clear to her, when she shared that many years ago their great-aunt had been killed when a witch hunter came to town hunting Magicals. So secrecy was imperative.

T-shirts that screamed that mermaids lived in town seemed like the opposite of discretion. But then again, maybe it was brilliant. After all, their Mermaid heritage was hidden in plain sight. And the town's people—did they know that mermaids lived among them? Did they know that Magicals were a thing? Not exactly. They knew that the Sobieski women were a little different—but most couldn't put their finger on it, while a few others point blank said they were witches.

Aunt Lidia had explained that the women in their family had always been known as healers—it was their role in the community, the way they earned a living. Back in the 1700s, when the town was first founded, they'd healed people from various diseases and attended successful births where both mother and child should have perished. They did practically everything but raise people from the dead, and that ironically enough was the genesis of the term "witch." Disgruntled customers, grieving widows, desperate mothers, and others began calling them witches when they couldn't perform miracles, do the impossible. And the term had stuck.

Witch was a term that Aunt Lidia didn't like. *In fact, she categorically denied it.* Just as Minka embraced it. They weren't witches—they were mermaid descents Aunt Lidia insisted. However, they lived in a patriarchal society that deemed all women with powers to be witches.

But they were magical. *They could enchant . . . things.*

Alex surveyed the shops, as always finding immense pleasure at the variety of items they made and sold to the community. Botanika offered many kinds of herbal remedies, bath and body products, tisanes, candles, and the like. And while some were . . . Mundane, many were not. Aunt Lidia and Minka enchanted some of the products for added effect and benefits. For example, though a peppermint tea could naturally help a sore throat simply because it is scientifically proven to have antibacterial, antiviral, and anti-inflammatory properties, an enchanted peppermint tea, filled with the intention to heal any issues in one's respiratory system while bolstering their immune system, compelled customers to sing the praises of the shop and return time and time again, or buy online if they weren't local to the area.

Whatever the case, Alex knew she came from a long line of strong, independent, talented women, and she found inspiration in that knowledge.

Alex looked around, searching for something to fill or fix. It wouldn't do for her *ciocia,* her aunt, to see her holding up the wall, twiddling her thumbs. Maybe she should start on the online orders. About ten had come in overnight, and she'd need to pull the orders from the shelf, pack them up, and—

And then everything stopped.

Alex looked around curiously. The lights in the shop went out. The playlist of music stopped playing. The air-conditioning ceased flowing. People were staring at darkened cell phones. Cars stopped in the middle of the road and the world—or Bellamy Bay at least—was suddenly silent.

From across the room, Minka found her cousin. Eyes wide, she telepathed, *What's going on?*

I don't know, Alex responded. She raced to the front door and then stumbled as a wave of dizziness encompassed her. She stood where she was, trying to blink away the fuzzy feeling. It was a heavy oppressive feeling that dulled her senses while also making her feel nauseous and like if she walked, she might tumble to the ground. Trying to find her bearings, she grabbed onto the door, flung it open, and stepped out on Main Street, blinking into the bright sunlight.

Pushing back the urge to vomit, she looked up and down the street, seeing nothing amiss. Everything seemed fine, but something was seriously wrong in Bellamy Bay.

Chapter Two

The nausea was gone, but Alex's head still ached.

She clutched at her temples, wondering where the pain had come from. She had never been one for migraines. Then she remembered that she could heal herself, that she could make headaches go away with a few uttered words and intent. Leaning against the brick wall of the shop, she spoke words of healing to herself until the pain and dizziness subsided.

But Alex wasn't the only one who was in need of healing. Pedestrians everywhere were bent over, holding their heads. A few moments passed, and then they weren't. The wave of lightheadedness and vertigo that had swept through the town had apparently lifted.

Downtown was eerily quiet. People were stepping out of their cars, appearing slightly dazed and absolutely confused.

And then car horns begin to blare, and engines turned back on. Music spilled onto the streets. One driver, then two, and then all of them returned to their cars. Alex went to the shop. Corrine Baily Rae was singing again, the cool air from the air conditioner filled the shop, and the lights turned on.

"What just happened?" Lidia joined her on the street, her face pinched in concern.

"Not sure." Alex gazed around her, a feeling of uneasiness settling over her. "But whatever it was, it's over now."

"Power outage," Minka suggested as she joined them, grabbing Alex's hand and gently squeezing it. "Something with the nuclear power plant in Wilmington?"

"I certainly hope not," Pepper said, out of breath as she jogged toward them as fast as she could, wearing a light blue day dress and heels. Her bright red hair was pulled up into a topknot, and her fair complexion, covered in freckles, glistened with sweat.

Lidia scowled at her daughter and then Pepper. "I think we'd all be dead if there was a problem with the nuclear plant. Don't you agree?"

Minka gulped, avoiding her mother's stern gaze. "Right."

Pepper offered Lidia a quick smile before looking at Alex. "What just happened?"

"No one knows," Alex said.

Ever the journalist, with recorder in hand, Pepper grinned at Alex. "This could be my biggest story to date! Bigger than the murder of Randy Bennet." She sighed dramatically.

Pepper, who was a reporter for the local newspaper, the *Bellamy Bay Bugler*, was always on the hunt for a story. And Pepper, whose last name was Bellamy, was the daughter of the mayor and a descendant of the town's founder. Despite that privileged beginning, she still hustled for a story like her life depended on it.

"What if the networks pick my story up? I could be interviewed. Maybe asked to join someone's team as a television reporter." She fairly swooned. "I'll be back. I need to get some first-person accounts of what just transpired."

Minka stared into the distance, a frown developing on her face.

And Alex noticed. "What's wrong, Mink?"

She shook her head. "Just hoping this is not another case of the military destroying the environment." She turned to look at her cousin. "We've been discussing Camp Malveaux during our Bellamy Bay Preservation Society meetings. We—mostly me—are concerned about the proximity of the military base to our beaches. They're only forty-five miles east of here."

"What does that have to do with what happened?"

"In my research, I read that even though military bases may be good for local economies, they're not so great for the environment, with their weapons testing, pollutants, and spilled oils. Maybe they've done something to make people sick. Not sure what would account for the outage, though."

"Enough speculation," Aunt Lidia snapped, and began ticking off ingredients. "Let's make a tea. We'll need gingko biloba, ginger, butcher's broom, cayenne, wild indigo, mistletoe, skullcap, and black cohosh. For the vertigo and dizziness." She looked at Minka. "Got that?"

"Yes ma'am," Minka said, and hurried into the shop.

* * *

In just an hour, the shop was almost back to normal. Tourists and locals alike didn't know what to make of what had happened earlier. However, Bellamy Bay appeared to have recovered, and customers trickled into the store while all the tea Aunt Lidia had prepared was gone. She stood behind the counter, eyes narrowed as she surveyed the shop floor. "I knew the tea would be a good idea. Looks like most everyone has recovered from their symptoms." She looked at Minka and Alex. "How are you two feeling?"

"Exhausted," Minka said.

"Same," Alex confirmed.

"It certainly was a strange occurrence." Lydia said. "Mayor Bellamy personally called every member of the local business owner's association to assure us that everything was fine in town and under control."

"Was it the nearby military base?"

Lidia shot her daughter an amused look. "Put your protest posters away. The mayor specifically stated it had nothing to do with the base."

Minka frowned for a moment, then brightened. "I wonder if the Bizarre Bellamy Bay blogger will cover this? If something strange is going on in town, he'll cover it and get to the truth of it."

"I don't know about that site, dear. Hard to believe what's on it sometimes. For example, he posted that there is a monster lurking in Bellamy Bay's maritime forest. Nonsense. I'd know if such a creature exists. And it doesn't."

Alex could care less about monsters and blogs. She wanted to make sure her family was okay. "Has anyone heard from Kamila today?"

"We communicated as soon as this thing happened," Minka said, tapping her right temple. "And she's okay. She was at the beach when it happened. She said a few remote-control airplanes and drones just fell out of the sky. But no one was hurt."

"I wonder if this event will affect my plans with Jack tonight? He may have to work."

Minka wiggled her eyebrows at Alex. "That's right. You have a date with the handsome detective."

"I'll text him to confirm." Alex glanced at a clock on the wall. "With everything going on, I forgot to ask If I could leave a few minutes early to go home to shower and change."

Minka laughed. "You mean you don't want to show up in your work clothes?"

Alex tugged at her ponytail. "I need to wash my hair." She looked down at her clothes. "And put on something not covered in beeswax and essential oils."

"Get out of here." Lidia nodded and smiled "Have some fun."

Alex stood, untying the apron from around her neck. She didn't need to be told twice.

* * *

Ninety minutes later, Alex arrived at Bread & Putter, a golf-themed gastro pub that specialized in Scottish food and whiskey. After a long, hot shower, she felt renewed. She'd blown out her long dark hair so that it fanned around her shoulders. She wasn't much for makeup, but she'd added a bronzer to her cheeks, to emphasize her summer tan; a pinkish-nude lip gloss; and black mascara and liner that would really accentuate her green eyes.

They'd agreed to meet at what was essentially a fancy sports bar so she wasn't too dressed up. Dark rinse jeans, high-heeled sandals, and a white lacy top that showed off her tanned shoulders completed her look.

Located on Maple Street, a road that ran parallel to Main Street, the sports bar was located in an old building with a white stone front, large plate-glass windows, and blue and green tartan awnings. It was a two-story building that had a cigar room on the second floor.

She'd been here a few times with Jack. It was one of his favorite places to eat, with its dark wood and leather furnishings, framed photos of golfing greats on the walls, plus the accoutrements of golf hung up as decorations. Large televisions spanned the room, with most on golfing games being played around the world, though there was one television on a 24/7 news channel.

She spotted Jack at a corner booth, and her lips automatically rose in a smile. It was hard not to smile at a handsome man with deep dimples. With chiseled features, a square jaw, a bronzed complexion that came from living at the beach in the summer, and beautiful blue eyes fringed with long lashes, he was undeniably attractive. He rose to his six-foot-one height when he saw her approaching, and greeted her with a warm hug. He was casual in khaki pants, a collared denim shirt with the sleeves rolled up, and a braided leather belt, and Alex was glad she hadn't gone too dressy with her wardrobe choices.

They'd met very soon after Alex had moved to town. He'd bumped into her while he was jogging and she was walking her German shepherd, Athena. They'd bonded over both being transplanted New Yorkers in town, then developed a friendship that had become something more.

She could feel the muscles in his arms as he wrapped them around her for a tight embrace. He gave the best hugs, Alex thought with a sigh. She pressed her face against the hard muscles of his chest and breathed in his fresh summery scent.

"Hey, you," he said, grinning when they parted.

She slid into the leather seat across from him. "Hi yourself. So how was your day?"

"Busy. A body was found today. On the edge of town in some woods. The maritime forest? Some college kids drinking in the woods found him. So, there's that." He picked up a roll and tore it in half.

"Want to talk about it?"

He spread a pat of soft butter on his bread and looked at her. "There's not much to discuss. He's unidentified at this point— Caucasian male, probably early thirties. Dressed like he'd just left work. We're hoping there are dental records somewhere. But I don't want to talk about it," he said with finality. "No work at dinner. You know the rule."

She gave him a knowing look. "You're tense. I wish you'd let me give you a calming tea blend to drink. It would really help with—"

He groaned good-naturedly. "You know how I feel about that hocus-pocus stuff. When we first met, I made my feelings clear on the topic. I don't mind that you work at an apothecary and think herbs and lotions can really help people, but please don't push me to try something I'm not comfortable with. I've got a prescription for sleep meds if I need to relax."

Alex studied him for a moment, noting the stubborn angle of his jaw. "Okay. Just trying to help." Her gaze bounced around the room as she tried to find a way to change the subject, and it landed on a television showing the latest international news. People dying. War being raged. She looked at Jack. "Do you ever get tired of it, working in law enforcement? Putting away the bad guys?"

"No, it never gets old." Jack chuckled. "I can't believe you even have to ask."

"I use to wonder the same thing about my dad. It never ends, and it takes a toll."

"You're right. It's a never-ending job, and it can and does negatively affect marriages, family . . . But men like your father and me, we don't get tired of it. If anything, it's what we're meant to do, how we're wired."

Alex laughed. "My father used to say that it was his lot in life to ensure justice always triumphed. And that he had accepted that a long time ago and that I would have to do the same. Accept what life has given me."

Jack reached for the second half of his roll. "And do you accept what life has given you?

Alex thought of her life. Her mother had died when she was young. Her father had recently passed away. And she was a mermaid, whatever that meant. She'd accepted a long time ago that she didn't have a mother. She was still trying to accept the fact that her father was gone. But her being descended from mermaids? That was still a work in progress.

And while she was happy that she had reconnected with her mother's side of the family, she didn't love the fact that the world she'd thought she lived in didn't exist. It was an ephemeral creation in which magic existed. Her father has raised her to believe that such things weren't real. And it had been a lie. Her father had lied to her her entire life, and that realization stung.

So no, she didn't quite accept the fact that she was a mermaid living in a magical world.

Jack watched her for a moment. "It's written all over your face." He leaned back in chair, pushing the bread basket away. "You'll never find happiness until you truly accept yourself."

She couldn't help but grin. "Thanks, Yoda."

Jack laughed. "Just sayin'."

Alex sat back to the dining room, and when Jack's attention focused on something over her shoulder, she turned to follow his gaze.

It was Dylan. *Also a Magical.* So yeah, the Sobieski women weren't the only ones in town with . . . abilities. There were a few others who'd settled the area when Alex's ancestors had. Dylan Wesley, CEO of his family's company, and member of the wealthy, important, and influential Wesley family was a bit of a thorn in Alex's side.

She bit her bottom lip as she watched him guide a tall, curvaceous woman to a table in the center of the room.

"That guy certainly lives a charmed life," Jack commented with a grin. "CEO of a million-dollar company, sports cars for every day of the week, and always with the flavor of the week on his arm."

When she'd first moved to town, Alex had met Dylan and been surprised to discover they had known each other as children, played together when she'd visited for the summer. As adults they had a very strong attraction to each other, one that Dylan wanted to explore. But Dylan, who was a self-professed nonpracticing Magical like Kamila, seemed to evoke magic when it suited him, and in ways that upset Alex's otherwise orderly life.

Being with him left her feeling unmoored, wanting to take chances and act spontaneously. After her mother had drowned, she'd lived her life as cautiously as possible, even becoming a risk analyst because she was good at evaluating risks and recommending ways to mitigate them. Dylan was the opposite of safe.

Jack was more her speed. Steady. Reliable. Just like her father had been. First a police detective, then a police chief, her father had died six months ago from complications of the heart. Jack reminded her very much of her father, and she knew that if they'd had the opportunity to meet, he would've like Jack. She could not say the same for Dylan.

Alex looked at Jack. "You're not doing so bad yourself, Mr. Frazier."

He leaned in, grabbed both her hands, and brought them to his lips. "You're right about that, Miss Daniels. I don't have the million dollars, but I certainly have the beautiful woman."

At five feet five, and with an athletic yet feminine physique honed by almost daily jogs, Alex knew that men generally found her attractive, but it was still wonderful to hear—especially when it came from her boyfriend. A zing of happiness bounced around her belly at the thought, at the sound of the word. *Boyfriend.* It was still a new thing. She hadn't had a steady guy in a couple of years—too busy with work and tired of the kinds of guys she was meeting. So being in a relationship felt strange . . . but nice.

She gazed into his eyes, grateful that she'd met Jack. Though they'd butted heads when she'd tried to prove her aunt wasn't guilty of a murder when Jack had arrested her, there was also a connection, a mutual attraction that was slowly growing into more. They'd been seeing a lot of each other in the past three months. She glanced at Dylan, who noticed her at the same moment, and he inclined his head toward her in greeting.

Tall and deeply tanned, he had dark hair, darker eyes and elegantly defined features reminiscent of a male runway model. He dressed like one too.

The woman with him threw her head back in an uninhibited laugh that immediately annoyed Alex.

The last time she'd seen Dylan, he'd asked her to give their relationship a chance. And she'd flatly turned him down. She gave Dylan another glance. He was leaning forward, saying something amazingly funny. Either that or his date was just a flirt. She was certainly a beauty, with lush brown hair that glistened with red highlights in the dim light of the gastropub. Her hair fell in waves past her shoulders, making her look like a heroine on one of those bodice ripper romances.

She had full round features that gave her face a seductive slant. Her dress was a flimsy, gauzy bright teal-blue with fluttery cap sleeves, gathered under her ribcage in the empire style, showcasing deep cleavage, with the skirt skimming her body and pooling at her feet. The effect was creative and artsy, and Alex immediately felt clunky and unattractive in her jeans and simple white blouse.

Another musical laugh from Dylan's date. *Really?* Dylan was that funny? He'd never been that funny with her. Ugh. What was she saying? She stopped herself. She did not want to be with Dylan. She wanted Jack.

Dylan caught her eye, but she ignored him, instead leaning forward and planting a kiss on Jack's lips, whose eyes widened as he leaned back with a satisfied smile. "You must really love golf," he quipped.

"Something like that." She snuck another look at Dylan and was gratified to see a red tinge to his suntanned cheeks.

Alex focused on her dinner. The meatloaf was delicious, filled with local onions and mushrooms, and she'd almost finished her entrée when the woman with Dylan dramatically waved an arm covered in bracelets of brightly colored crystals. A sob escaped her lips, and she pointed to one of the screens on the wall. One of the few on a news station.

Alex hadn't been paying attention to the news feed, but it appeared they were covering a tidal wave that had hit mainland Japan.

The woman bowed her head and covered her eyes while Dylan went to the bartender and spoke briefly to him. The bartender picked up a remote and changed the channel.

Alex watched as the woman raised her head, removed the fingers covering her eyes, and glanced at the screen. And she smiled approvingly. *What was that about?* Alex wondered.

The waitress arrived and swapped out their finished dishes for an impossibly large slice of apple pie smelling of cinnamon and paired with a large scoop of vanilla ice cream artistically covered in bourbon sauce. They both grabbed forks and dug in. Alex closed her eyes and moaned in delight while Jack raised his eyebrows, watching her.

"That good?"

She grinned. "Oh yeah."

He took his own bite and nodded. "So good," he agreed, and for a moment they ate in companionable silence.

When they were done, Alex pushed her plate back. "Did you discover any more about the outage after you left the shop this morning?"

"Yeah. Word came from somewhere on high that there was a glitch with the power grid. Nothing to investigate further or be concerned about."

Even the cell phones? "What about—"

But Jack's look silenced her. And then he smiled.

Alex gazed at him thoughtfully. "Well, that's that."

They enjoyed the rest of their meal, updating each other on the past few days. When they left, Alex cast a glance over her shoulder at Dylan. He was watching her, which for some reason made her smile.

Not being physically around Dylan had been beneficial in helping Alex to keep him off her mind. But now, seeing him tonight, she realized that she still had feelings for him. Not love—she'd never been in love—but an attraction still the same. Didn't mean she would act on it, but it surprised and disappointed her to know that as into Jack as she was, she still felt something for Dylan. She didn't want the attraction to be there. Not after he'd used black magic a few months ago to scare her off investigating a murder that implicated her aunt and involved his family.

Since moving to Bellamy Bay, Alex had borrowed Minka's Prius, because, coming from New York City, she didn't own a car. She was still using it. Minka didn't mind, and Alex kept the tank full of gas and the car cleaned, and she'd promised to help with any maintenance bills that came up until she decided what to do about transportation. They stood next to the car now, her leaning against it like she was in high school, Jack standing so near she could smell the notes of sea salt and lemon in his cologne.

Sighing, she leaned in for a hug.

He held her close. "I had a nice time tonight," he said.

"I did too." She pulled back slightly, her gaze falling to his lips. He moved forward, planting a kiss on her mouth.

They stayed that way for a moment before Alex pulled away.

"See you soon?" he said, a look of contentment spreading across his face.

"Of course." And she was still smiling as she drove away.

*   *   *

Alex stood in the doorway of her aunt's home. A seafoam-green Queen Anne style with cream trim and black shutters and roof, the historic home was surrounded by rows of purple tulips that ran alongside the wraparound porch, with orange and yellow daffodils leading up the brick walk to the front door.

Her home for the foreseeable future. Alex had made herself comfortable in the same house her mother had grown up in. Clearly decorated with love, the house featured bright uplifting colors, hardwood floors that always shined and smelled of lemon oil, furniture that was freshly dusted, and bright white walls. Vases of fresh flowers from the garden out back decorated and perfumed the foyers with clean, sweet-smelling scents. Antique nautical maps, framed in burnished copper, lined the hallways, and trays of decorative sea glass glittered blue and green in the sunlight.

Alex's dog, Athena, who was almost three years old, jumped up on her hind legs to greet her with a wagging tail. Full-grown, with a glossy coat of brownish-black fur, the sweet dog had become hers when her father became sick and could no longer care for Athena.

She took a few moments to rub her head and neck, and pepper her with kisses. Then, she kicked off her shoes and placed them in the hall closet, and wandered into the kitchen to see who was there. In this house, someone was always in the kitchen.

Much like the other areas in the home, the kitchen was a bright cheery space filled with large windows that let in sunlight. With white glass-front cabinets, gleaming stainless-steel appliances, and lemon-yellow accents, the kitchen's modernity was a striking contrast to the historic character of the home. A large wooden table filled the eat-in kitchen and was the focal point of the room—when the stove wasn't in use, of course.

Alex groaned with pleasure when the smells of sugar and butter reached her nose. Her aunt had been baking something. Minka appeared with a plate of cookies. "Have one?"

With a rueful grin, Alex had to say no to the *kolaczki*, a Polish cookie made with a delicious cream cheese dough and filled with pureed fruit sprinkled with powdered sugar—it was one of her favorite treats.

"But they're raspberry," Minka said in surprise. "From the backyard. How can you resist?" she teased.

"No way. I just shared a slice of apple pie with Jack that was the size of my head." She laughed. "It was so good, though."

"Bread & Putter," Minka said knowingly. "Their portion sizes are ridiculous, but that's why people love it." Minka set the plate on the table. "Tea then? Our Sweet Dreams blend?"

"Sounds perfect right about now. Thanks."

She sat down and watched as her cousin, wearing fuzzy pink pants and a white tank top with pink polka dots, heated up a kettle. She grinned when Minka's shoes came into view. Bedroom slippers, they were large fluffy shoes made to look like pink elephants.

A moment later, Athena stood and walked into the hallway. Alex watched her movements.

Minka noticed too. "Oh, that's probably Kamila. She said she'd stop by tonight for dessert."

There was the sound of a key turning in the front door lock, and Kamila entered the kitchen, with Athena trailing her. Still dressed in her summer police uniform of navy-blue shorts and light blue polo shirt with the Bellamy Bay Police Department logo on the pocket, she grinned at them. A couple inches taller than Alex, she had a physique that made it clear she went to the gym—every day—paired with attractive girl-next-door looks, with straight, shoulder-length, caramel-blonde hair and light blue eyes.

She snagged a cookie from the plate and ate it, then grabbed another one. She was looking at Alex. "Okay if I give this to Athena? She's doing a great job of not begging right now."

Alex laughed. Her girl was well trained and sat at her feet with her head resting on her paws. She was between her chair and Kamila's and didn't beg for food like most dogs, but her eyes were certainly tracking the movements of every cookie that left the plate. "Go ahead, and then tell her she's a good girl for not asking."

Kamila did so and allowed Athena to eat the cookie from her hand.

Alex looked at Kamila. "Learn anything about what happened today with the outage?"

Both hands on her hips, Minka looked puzzled. "Honestly I thought it was something hinky with the moon. It's full tonight and for the next few days. It's the absolute best time to cast spells, by the way." Minka directed this to Alex, who laughed. "If you're taking notes."

"Let's not have Magical school right now, please."

Minka faked a scowl at her sister. "Anyway, my point is crazy things can happen then. It's been scientifically proven that the moon effects people, nature, events."

Kamila gave her a sister a "get serious" look. "Far as we know, just a good old-fashioned power outage."

Alex's brows knitted together. "That also made cell phones stop working . . . temporarily?"

Minka moved to a window, pushing the curtains aside to stare into the night sky. The moon was full. Luminous and milky white, it almost lit up the sky. "Probably, but still . . ." She looked over her shoulders at her family. "It's not a bad idea to be on the lookout for strange things."

Chapter Three

Alex spent all morning filling candles and gazed at the collection of jars full of locally sourced beeswax with satisfaction. In honor of the upcoming festival, she'd challenged herself to create a candle that evoked mermaids. If it turned out well, it would be the official souvenir of the event.

None of her friends or coworkers in New York would believe that she was proficient at candle making, but after many training sessions with her aunt, she felt comfortable doing it by herself.

The clean, crisp scents of ocean, air . . . and cotton candy and raspberries hung heavy in the air, and six rows of creamy white candles flecked with pink metallic flakes were cooling in the backroom when she heard the front door jingle. This would be their first customer of the day. Wiping her hands on her apron, she stepped onto the main floor and saw a very pretty woman bent over a candle, inhaling its scent.

"Hey, Celeste. What brings you to Botanika today?"

At the sound of Alex's voice, Celeste righted herself and grinned at her. "My mother wanted me to make sure you all were coming to dinner tonight. And I have a little shopping to do on my lunch break." She waved a piece of paper at Alex. "I have a list."

"Kamila is working, Minka has a date, so it will just be me and Aunt Lidia tonight."

"Great. I'll let my mom know. Come hungry. She makes a *lot* of food."

Alex laughed. "Noted. Now let's see what we can do about that list of yours." Alex rounded the counter and took the paper from her friend.

Alex had met Celeste at Coffee O' Clock, the coffee shop down the street that she probably frequented too often. She'd been an MBA student then, working part-time as a barista. With Celeste's mother, Josephine, being Lidia's best friend and the town being so small, they'd continued to run into each other, even when Celeste left the coffee shop and started a new job. Along with Jack and Pepper, Alex counted Celeste as another friend she'd made in Bellamy Bay.

About the same height as Alex, with a svelte dancer's build, Celeste was twenty-three, with long dark hair, a caramel complexion, a sprinkling of freckles on her nose, wide-set hazel eyes, and full lips. She wore black pumps and a chic summer skirt suit in light gray, with a violet shell underneath.

Alex grabbed a basket and began moving around the shop floor, looking for the items on her list. She looked over her shoulder at Celeste, who was sniffing a rose-colored bar of soap. "How are things at Wesley Inc.?"

Celeste put the bar down and picked up a green one instead. "Amazing. Literally my dream job."

"That's wonderful that they hired you right out of grad school."

"I got lucky, that's for sure."

"I don't know about luck. You graduated from the MBA program at Bellamy College magna cum laude and obviously impressed Dylan and Tegan so much when you did your internship that they approved your application for their junior executive program. I think that was all you."

Celeste made a self-deprecating face. "Oh, you're right. I worked my butt off." She laughed good-naturedly. She picked up three of the green bars and showed them to Alex. "I'm getting these. I need a good detoxing soap. And it smells like cucumber and melon—so, refreshing. I love chlorella and spirulina in my morning smoothies, and now it will be in my soap." She moved to the counter. "Anything *special* done to the soap I should know about?"

By "special," Celeste meant enchanting. Like Alex, Celeste was also a Magical.

Alex grinned, then lowered her voice. "The ones with the blue marbling have been charmed to remove any negative energy from the body."

"Oh yeah, I need that." She replaced two green bars with two that had blue streaks and handed them to Alex.

"You've got negativity in your life?"

Celeste laughed. "It's nothing."

"Okay. So, what are you doing in your new job?"

"I'm working in a new division headed by Mr. Wesley."

"And what are you doing?"

"I can't say. I had to sign an NDA—that's a nondisclosure agreement—and get a top-secret government clearance. It's all very hush-hush but exciting." She grimaced. "But I can't talk about it. Sorry."

Alex could feel the tension coming from Celeste even as she smiled, and wondered why her question vexed Celeste so. Now she was dying to know what Dylan was working on. But of course, she wasn't talking to him. And now Celeste was fidgeting and probably hoping she'd stop asking questions.

"How are things with your new guy?"

"I don't know what it is about him," she said with a dreamy look on his face. "I just want to be with him all the time."

Alex tried not to make a face. For some reason, she didn't think the former history professor turned museum director was the right man for Celeste, but she faked a smile. "You two are serious, huh?"

A goofy grin spread across her face. "I think so. And you'll get to see him this week at the unveiling of the mural."

Alex nodded. As part of the mermaid festival, a famous artist had been brought to town to paint a mural, commemorating the town's heritage, on the side of the welcome center located in the park. "Speaking of the festival, I finished my candles."

"That's great. I can't wait to see your handiwork."

"They're still cooling." Alex laughed. "But I'm bringing them to the festival planning meeting. If they make Pepper think of mermaids, I'll be happy."

She watched as Celeste moved around the shop. "See anything else you want? Or are you ready to check out?"

Celeste turned to look at her, her eyes bright with interest. "Did you get everything on my list?"

Alex checked. Fresh verbena. Basil. Anise. Dried seaweed. Crushed oyster pearl. "You're in luck. We have everything you need."

"Awesome." She paid for her purchases and chatted while Alex packaged everything up. "Between you and me, I'm a little nervous about representing Wesley Inc. on the festival planning meeting committee."

Alex shot her a reassuring grin. "You'll be fine. Didn't you say you and your mom have always helped out?"

"Yes, but this year is the first time I'll be reporting back to Tegan. Of course, that was always Bryn's job . . ."

Alex waved a hand. "Please don't mention Dylan's sister. Why isn't Tegan representing the Wesley family?"

"She thought Lidia would be there and you know how those two don't get along. But now it's even worse. Tegan holds Lidia responsible for sending her daughter away."

Alex snorted. "Bryn Wesley killed two men just so she could make a land deal. She's responsible for where she is right now. And all to impress her mother and hopefully get a promotion?"

Celeste hesitated. "Well, I think there was a little more to the story than that."

"What do you mean? I thought Bryn went on a killing spree so she could make a CEO of Wesley."

Celeste glanced around, then lowered her voice. "I am not supposed to tell you or anyone this, but I know I can trust you."

"Of course," Alex said. "Tell me."

"Bryn thought that The Warsaw Shield might be hiding on the Old Wesley property. That's the real reason she wanted it, and she thought it held a value beyond being an artifact worth preserving for the Magical community."

"What possible use could a mermaid's shield have outside of being featured in a Magical museum?" Alex chuckled. *If that's even a thing.* "All it did was block things, right?"

Celeste gave Alex a knowing look. "No, it is supposedly much more than a defensive tool. Let's just say it has *protective* abilities."

Alex thought for a moment. "Oh . . ." she said, finally understanding, though not fully. "You mean it's . . . a weapon?" She thought for a moment. "What did she want to do with it?" She remembered the nearby Marine base and the weapons testing that bothered Minka. "Sell it to the military?"

Celeste lifted an eyebrow. "Let's just say she wanted to sell it to somebody." She mimed zipping up her lips and throwing away the key. "But you didn't hear it from me."

*   *   *

Celeste's parents lived two streets away from the beach, in a neighborhood of vibrantly colored homes built on stilts. Josephine's home was a bright yellow, with palm trees in the yard along with several species of tropical flowers providing bright pops of magenta, lavender, and blue.

Driving over in Lidia's little red sedan, Alex held a bottle of white wine on her lap. When they arrived, Josephine welcomed them inside her home, which was airy with an open floor plan, and decorated in white, sand, and ocean blue.

The woman, who had a complexion a few shades darker than Celeste's, had a warm honeyed skin tone and thick dark brown hair of a naturally curly texture that was pulled into a bun accentuating her oval face and high cheekbones. Her eyes were a golden maple syrup brown, and her mouth, wide and full, offered a sincere grin. Alex immediately felt comforted and instinctively knew she was a soothing foil for her aunt's hot temper.

Alex handed her the hostess gift. "It's nice to see you again, Josephine. Thank you for the invitation."

"It's high time I had you over. Welcome. Celeste just called— she's on her way." Josephine gave Alex a tight hug and then waved her into the house.

Lidia gave her friend a hug too. "When is Nate coming home? I swear I haven't seen that husband of yours in almost a year."

Josephine smiled wearily. "He's been in Singapore since January, for work."

"Bronson certainly is keeping him busy at Carolina Shipping."

Josephine gave Lidia a rueful look. "Ever since he became VP of Logistics, he's been abroad on assignment. I hope he'll be home in time for Christmas."

"I'm here!" Celeste sang out as she walked in behind Alex and Lidia. She was still dressed for work. "I had so much to do at the office, I didn't think I'd be able to get away before eight. But I made it." She sniffed the air. "And I'm starving."

* * *

They sat down to dinner, with large serving bowls set out family style. Scents of garlic, onion, and thyme wafted around the cozy dining area, and Alex's stomach rumbled in response.

"It all looks delicious," Alex said as she sat beside Celeste at the table. "What's on the menu—Southern food?"

Celeste had shrugged out of her suit jacket to reveal a silk tank underneath. She pointed at one bowl: "Not exactly. Rice and beans here." And at another: "Stewed chicken there. My mother makes it spicy, so, you've been warned." She reached forward and ladled a large amount of the dish into her bowl. "And this is vegetable stew."

"It has a wonderful coconut base," Lidia added. "Simply marvelous."

Alex looked at Celeste. "I see why you said come hungry." She turned back to the table to see Lidia placing a drumstick on her plate. "I seriously hope there's no dessert."

Josephine chuckled. "I do love Southern food. I was born and raised here after all. But you may not know my great-grandmother was from Haiti. She is a descendant of the Polish-Haitian community there. Have you heard of them?"

Alex looked confused, but Lidia only smiled knowingly while Josephine explained. "You didn't know you were getting a history lesson with dinner, did you?" She laughed. "When Napoleon was trying to quell a rebellion in Saint-Domingue, in which he hoped to bring slavery back to Haiti, he brought in a legion of Polish soldiers who'd enlisted in the French army with the hopes that the French government would help them get their country back from the Third Partition."

Alex nodded, knowing that during that time, the Kingdom of Prussia and the Russian Empire had divvied up the county of Poland between themselves, and the actual state of Poland no longer existed.

"When the Polish soldiers saw that the Haitians were fighting for their independence, much like they hoped to do, they realized they were on the wrong side of the war."

Lidia smiled at her best friend. "And they joined the Haitians in their fight against the French oppressors."

Josephine laughed. "Lidia loves this story. Many of the surviving soldiers stayed on the island. One of those soldiers was a descendant of the Mermaid of Warsaw, a very brave warrior, a Merman. And he married a local girl who was a high priestess to Mami Wata. Known on the island as a true water witch." She smiled. "The rest is Magical history."

Alex looked first at Josephine and then at Celeste. "So you're . . . half mermaid . . . half water witch?"

Celeste exchanged knowing glances with her mother. "Yeah. Kinda cool, huh?"

"Wow. Yes, very cool."

"Great-great-grandmother moved to Bellamy Bay because she'd heard from some sailors on her island that there were mermaids here. For whatever reason, she wanted to leave her home, but I supposed she still wanted to be around family. She went to the Outer Banks first and then landed here, where she met your ancestor

Zofia. They talked, shared histories and realized they were distantly related. Third or fourth cousins." She looked at Alex. "We're almost kin."

"Not 'almost,'" Lidia said in firm tone. "We *are*. Your ancestor's name is listed in our written history. Josephine and I are second cousins five times removed, which makes you—"

"Family," Alex finished for her. She reached out and squeezed Celeste's hand. "No wonder I liked you the first time we met." Alex looked at Celeste with new eyes.

* * *

After dinner, Josephine and Lidia were in the craft room, and Celeste and Alex sat on the large deck in cushioned patio chairs, taking in the view, glasses of lemonade in hand. A large umbrella provided shade for them and the leaves of the numerous plants that decorated the area rustled in the slight breeze.

"I think I can hear the crash of the waves from here," Alex commented.

Smiling, Celeste nodded. "And when the sky is clear, you can see the ocean between those houses." She pointed to the two rows of homes directly across the street from them.

Alex squinted her eyes, then laughed. "Yes, I see the water." She sipped her beverage. Then took another sip. "What is this? I thought it was just lemonade with mint leaves."

"Refreshing, right?" Celeste took a big swallow before continuing. "It has the addition of fresh vanilla, sugar, and a little sea salt. My granmè Fleur used to make it for us. A little taste of home, she'd say." She held the glass up to the sun and smiled as the sunlight sparkled behind the yellow liquid. "This is what summer tastes like to me."

"Must've been nice growing up this close to the beach."

"The best. I can't imagine not living near the water. Especially for our kind, it's so calming and energizing." She glanced at Alex. "But you didn't grow up near the water, right?"

Alex shook her head. "No. And now, I'm wondering if that's why I felt so . . . I don't know—unsure?—no, *unstable* most of my childhood. I've always had this feeling of anxiety that I've lived with, this feeling that something bad is just about to happen. I thought it was because my mother died and my father was always working, always in danger, you know?"

Celeste patted her arm. "I'm sorry. I must sound like a spoiled brat."

"Not at all. You have family, friends . . . My life started off great too, but, well, my father did the best he could. He was a wonderful father." A sudden wave of sadness washed over her, a fresh feeling of grief for her late father and the mother she could barely remember brought tears to her eyes. "It would be nice to think that living by the beach would've made me feel better but I doubt it."

Celeste leaned forward. "Well, you've got your Aunt Lidia and Minka and Kamila. And you've got me." She laughed self-consciously. "I've always wanted a big sister. Someone that could look out for me, and we could talk about boys." She stopped and rolled her eyes. "Sorry, that's silly. I'm an adult and—"

"No, it's not stupid. I've *always* wanted more family. I used to watch TV shows where there were tons of siblings, and I'd imagine being the middle kid." She laughed. "Now, I'm feeling silly, but I would've loved to have had a little sister."

They grinned at each other.

Celeste finished her drink and settled into her chair sighing contently. "I've got a great boyfriend and an amazing job and now the big sister I've always wanted. This is turning out to be the best summer ever."

"I agree." Alex said, thinking of the family she was fortunate to have reconnected with, her newfound passion for herbal remedies . . . and Jack. This year was turning out pretty well for her too.

*　*　*

Aunt Lidia came into the shop at noon. It was her day to sleep in if she desired. In reality, she used the time to get up as normal, clean the house, and cook dinner for the coming evening. "I've made and frozen enough pierogi to get us through the summer," she declared when she entered the shop. Her hair was pulled back into a loose French braid, and she wore sandals, light blue capris, and a white blouse. She looked refreshed and ready for a day of work.

Alex laughed. "Oh good. I was worried there wouldn't be enough. What kinds did you make?"

"All of your favorites, *kwiatuszki*," her aunt said, using the Polish word for "flower."

The Sobieski family had been in America for generations, but Aunt Lidia still liked to use a few Polish words here and there. And because her mother had done the same thing, Alex knew what most of them meant.

"Potato, cheese, and onion, and wild mushroom with caramelized onion."

"Yum." Alex licked her lips, already tasting the flaky crust. "I'll definitely be home in time for dinner tonight."

Lidia went into the back room, set down her purse, and came out with a big smile. "Your festival candles look and smell wonderful, Aleksandra. I'm very proud of you." She went behind the counter and sat on a stool there. Lidia's gaze swept the area, landing on a piece of paper. She picked it up. "What's this?"

Alex glanced at the list. "Celeste was in here earlier. That was her shopping list. I guess I forgot to toss it in the trash can."

"That's strange." Lidia frowned as she read the list. "Did she say what she was using the ingredients for?"

"No. Why? Is something wrong?"

"Maybe not." Lidia was still scowling at the paper. "I just hope she's not up to no good."

Alex laughed. "Celeste?"

Lidia arched an eyebrow. "Her mother's a little worried about her and that man she's seeing."

"I'll see her later today at the festival planning meeting. Should I ask her anything?"

Lidia folded up the paper and slid it into her pocket. "No, it's fine. I'll see Josephine this week, and I'll mention it. She will know if it's anything important."

* * *

It's another glorious day in Bellamy Bay, Alex thought as she walked the few blocks from Botanika to the town hall. The sun shone bright, the air smelled of sea salt, and everyone she came into contact with was happy. And why not? They were at the beach. And it was summer.

Smiling, she turned the corner and faced the town hall building, a large imposing brick structure with Roman-style columns, surrounded by a large green space. Locals commonly used it to play Frisbee, soak up the sun, or have picnics. She'd been there before a few times for various reasons, so she knew the conference room was on the second floor. She waved at the receptionist before bounding up the stairs. She was excited to be on the mermaid festival planning committee and happy to truly be a part of the Bellamy Bay community.

When she opened the door, she was greeted by Minka and Celeste, who stood in the back of the room, chatting beside a table of refreshments. She looked around the room and found a case of her candles in small, clear glass jars had already been delivered. Smiling, she set one out at each chair and lit it. The room quickly bloomed with a fresh, sweet scent.

Pepper held a stack of papers and was placing one at each chair, making sure to avoid the flame of the candles. Three other women made up the planning committee.

Pepper hurried to finish and sat down beside Alex just as the woman banged a gavel on the podium. Alex smiled at her. "How are you?"

With a sigh, she sank into her leather chair. "My mother is running this—what do you think?"

Alex gave the woman named Cressida, all chignon and prim, starched dress, a second glance.

She raised a thin eyebrow at Pepper, who obediently stopped talking. "I am bringing the first meeting of the Bellamy Bay Mermaid Festival planning committee to order," Cressida called out, all smiles now. "As you know, this will be my tenth year heading up the committee, and I'm looking for another successful event that will bring plenty of tourism dollars to our beloved town. Every year our committee includes members of the founding families and local business owners. This year I'm happy to welcome two new members to the group, Alex Daniels and Yuko Pemberton. Yuko is a co-owner, along with her husband, of Sushi Y'all."

There was a light smattering of applause, and Yuko inclined her head toward Alex with a smile. "Nice to meet you." Yuko was a petite woman, probably in her sixties but with a round youthful face, milky complexion, dark brown eyes, and shoulder-length black hair that was parted in the middle.

Ah, Alex thought. The Southern-Japanese fusion restaurant she and Jack had been meaning to attend but had never quite made it to yet. "I can't wait to visit your restaurant. I've heard great things about the food."

"Yuko will be heading up the teams of volunteers. This year we have twenty-five. I'd like fifty in total." Cressida glanced at Yuko. "It's summer and people want to play. Not volunteer. You have your work cut out for you."

Cressida looked at Alex and her candles. "Very pretty," she commented. "You'll all note the candles before you. These are to be the official candle of the festival. We'll be placing the festival logo on the candle and selling them at the festival market and the gift center." She took a moment to sniff. "I don't know what mermaids are supposed to smell like—fish and seaweed maybe?" She wrinkled her nose. "But they should sell very well and make a nice festival souvenir."

Are they enchanted? Celeste telepathed to Alex.

No, Alex responded. *I still haven't quite learned that technique.*

Cressida invited Minka to the podium, and Minka jumped up, bubbling with energy. "Hey guys," she began. "As you may know, I'm heading up the arts and crafts for the festival this year. And I've come up with an amazing list of activities for the kids." She referred to a printout she had with her. "They'll be a mermaid-themed face-painting booth in the park on Friday and Saturday, a mermaid-themed slime craft, and a do-it-yourself mermaid-themed jewelry craft with seashells. Tiaras anyone?" She grinned around the room. "Also, a puppet show at the library, recreating the founding of the town, and an event where the kids can make papier-mâché swords and shields, just like the Mermaid of Warsaw had."

She clapped her hands together. "Does that sound amazing or what?"

"Swords and shields," Cressida began thoughtfully. "Doesn't that sound a little violent? Children today are already exposed to too much violence."

"What do you mean?" Minka stood up straighter. "Those were the Mermaid of Warsaw's tools. What she's known for. How can we have a festival celebrating her life if we don't have her sword or shield? Have you been to Poland, seen the statues? There is no mermaid without her weapons."

"We're not precisely celebrating *only* her—it's all mermaids. It's the idea of—the *tradition* of—mermaids. Most of them didn't have weapons."

Minka scrunched up her face. "No, this is about the Mermaid of Warsaw specifically and her descendants. At least that's the founding story we're celebrating. And the one Captain Bellamy wrote about in his journal."

There was a slow clap in the doorway, and all eyes turned toward the sound. Alex saw the beautiful woman who'd shared dinner with Dylan, standing there in a flowing white dress that both hid and accentuated her curvaceous figure. Her expressive brown eyes gleamed.

"I love the passion you have for the Mermaid of Warsaw. *Brava.*" She moved into the room and gave a hug to Minka, who looked both surprised and happy by the support. A fragrant cloud of sweet orange, bright cherry, and spicy clove filled the room. Even though Alex didn't want to like her, the woman had a vibrant energy that was infectious. She was the artist. Alex wondered how she'd connected with Dylan and if they were an item.

When she moved away from the doorway, Alex saw Dylan was standing there, dressed in a gray summer suit and crisp white shirt opened at the collar. He stepped in and greeted everyone in his elegant Southern drawl. Her heart began to pound. Something about him always made her catch her breath. She looked away quickly and saw Minka giving her a knowing grin.

"I see you all have met our muralist?" Dylan grinned, giving Cressida a one-armed hug. "This is Neve Ryland. She's been in town for a few weeks, working on the painting that no one has been able to see." He chuckled. "Not even me."

Alex knew that a large tent had been erected around the mural so that the artist could paint undisturbed, rain or shine. It had been the talk of the town. What was she doing under there? What would the mural look like? Alex was also eager to see the final product.

Everyone, including Alex, clapped while Cressida shooed Minka back to her seat. She pretended to pout, saying, "You've ruined my surprise, Dylan. But yes, everyone, this is Neve Ryland, the celebrated artist of mythological subjects."

"And also a writer and researcher," Neve chirped with an infectious grin. "And I think *not* including the Mermaid of Warsaw's shield and sword in the festival—even as a papier-mâché craft—is a mistake."

"My goodness," Cressida said, looking a little flustered. "It's not like that sword and shield really existed. We are all talking about a myth."

Neve laughed. "Are we?" Her grin widened. "I wrote my dissertation on the possibility of mythological weapons."

Frowning, Cressida sniffed. "We all know the stories this town were founded on are made up, which means the Mermaid of Warsaw didn't really exist, nor did her shield or sword." She laughed. "I mean, really."

The glint in Neve's eyes was unmistakably challenging. "I happen to believe that the Mermaid of Warsaw was real, and so was her—"

"And that's why we selected Neve," Dylan rushed to interrupt her. "For her passion and knowledge and grand imagination. She's perfect for painting our mural, is she not Cressida?"

Cressida pursed her lips but didn't respond.

Dylan moved beside the artist, placing his arm around her. "Wesley Inc. is cosponsoring her participation in the festival."

So, Alex thought, *it's business then?* They certainly seemed chummy for professional reasons. She was beautiful, he was handsome. Alex wondered if it would stay platonic—not that it was any of her concern.

"I am an expert on mythology, with a special interest in female iconography in world myth. My dissertation included research on the Mermaid of Warsaw. I've read everything published about her." Neve stepped to the podium, forcing Cressida to move to the side, an exasperated expression on her face. Neve looked at Minka as she spoke. "And we absolutely have to have swords and shields at the festivals. We want little girls to feel the empowerment that the Mermaid of Warsaw must've felt when she protected her town." She shot Cressida a look of admonishment. "They weren't weapons of war; they were tools of peace." She held up her hand like she was giving praise in church. "The Mermaid of Warsaw was a powerful agent of change, of good, and we're going to honor her."

Minka rose from her seat, clapping loudly. "And I am here for it!" she said.

Alex took a breath. This woman was certainly a force, and Alex wanted to speak to her and find out all Neve knew about Alex's ancestor.

Neve's eyes fell on the candles. "From Botanika?" She found Alex and smiled.

Alex nodded. "Yes, I made them in honor of the Mermaid of Warsaw. I'd be happy to give you one."

Eyes bright with enchantment, she moved toward the closest one. "May I smell one? I've heard your candles have the ability to practically transport you by scent alone." Neve set her folder down before her, and leaned over the candle, breathing deeply of the fragrance. "Makes me think of the sea and the wind and—" Suddenly, the flame of the candle seemed to spark and leap into the air and toward Neve. She jumped back in surprise, her cry of astonishment filling the room.

Alex watched in horror, as the spark fell on a folder in front of her, erupting into a small fire.

Chapter Four

Alex jumped up and ran to the fire extinguisher mounted on the wall beside the door.

Her father had taught her as a teenage how to use one. *PASS*, he'd told her. *Pull* the pin. *Aim* at the fire. *Squeeze* the lever. *Sweep* the lever from side to side. She did it all now, a blur of action. The fire was out within moments, even before a fire alarm could sound.

The room was stunned into silence, and then Cressida began bustling about giving orders: Pepper, to clear out the burned paper and charred candle; Minka, to wipe down the tables; Celeste, to open the windows. Josephine had gone to find the custodian, and Yuko had extinguished the flames on the remaining candles—just in case.

Alex went to Neve, her eyes filled with remorse. "I am so sorry. Are you okay?"

"Yes, of course." She said, her smile shaky but present. "But if I hadn't jumped out of the way . . ."

Dylan was at her side, a steady arm around her shoulders. "You were never in any harm. I assure you. If Alex hadn't put the fire out, I would've."

Cressida clapped her hands, glancing at the white foam covering the table. "Let's take a thirty-minute break to finish cleanup and then we'll wrap things up." She went to Alex, her face grim. "I appreciate your quick work just now. But if you hadn't made faulty candles, none of this would've happened. Perhaps it's back to the drawing board for you?"

Celeste had finished opening the windows, and a slight breeze lifted the remaining smell of smoke from the room. She came to Alex's side. "I don't think this is Alex's fault. The other candles are fine. Maybe it was just a freak accident."

"Sounds like a town lawsuit waiting to happen." Cressida bristled. "No thank you. We'll drop the branded candles for this year."

Celeste frowned, then glanced at Alex. "Sorry.

"It's not your fault. Maybe the candles are bad—the wicks or something."

*   *   *

After the break and once the room was clean and sorted, the meeting resumed, and Neve returned to calmly discussing the inspiration behind her painting. Despite the accident, Alex was still excited about the festival and looking forward to speaking with Neve.

I can't wait to pick her brain about mermaids.

Alex sent the thought to Celeste, then looked at her with a wide grin. *She sounds amazing,* she continued. But she was surprised to see that Celeste's brow was knitted and her nose wrinkled. *What's wrong?*

Celeste rolled her eyes. *She's working with Jasper at the museum. All he can talk about is how amazing she is. I'm over it.*

Oh, Alex said leaning back against her chair. *Sorry.*

It's fine. Celeste made another face, and her mother turned to look at her as if she was sending her daughter a message about minding her manners.

46

Neve's gaze swept across the room, seeming to land on Alex, but maybe she just imagined it. "I personally want to invite you all to the unveiling of the finished mural in the park tomorrow. I hope you'll all join me at noon for art and some enchanting herbal tea." She gave Alex another look—this time she was certain. "I've heard wonderful things about the teas at the local apothecary. Can't wait to try them."

She must know I work at Botanika, Alex thought. *Maybe that's why it feels like she's talking to me personally.*

Neve regarded everyone in the room with a warm gaze. "Well, I'll leave you ladies to it then. Dylan is giving me the grand tour."

Alex couldn't help herself. "Where are you going next?"

"The old Wesley property. I hear it's beautiful."

Alex shot Dylan an interested look. Many generations ago that land had been the Wesley homestead, but when witch hunters burned the house to the ground, the family had sold the property and moved to their current location on the peninsula. But thanks to his murderous sister, the property was back in the Wesley portfolio.

* * *

After they left, Cressida called Josephine to the podium to discuss the town's marketing efforts for the festival. As the director of Tourism for the town of Bellamy Bay, she was also coordinating the social media, advertising, and marketing efforts for the festival.

After Josephine finished her presentation, Alex looked around the group, wondering how she could help on the committee. She raised her hand and asked Cressida the question.

Cressida glanced at her paperwork and then nodded. "You'll be in charge of vendors. We have a list of previous vendors you can work with—confirm that they are attending, send them their welcome packages, and answer any questions they may have. Day of the festival, you'll be on point for making sure everyone is set up and ready to begin selling at nine am sharp."

Cressida continued on until the agenda was completed. Celeste was in charge of wrangling all of the food trucks and culinary vendors. "And Celeste, since you're dating the director of the museum, I understand you'll also be updating us on the exhibit he and Neve are curating for the event?"

Celeste nodded. "That's right." Her mother shot her a disapproving look.

"As usual, the party at the lighthouse keeper's cottage is always sponsored by Botanika and Wesley, Inc.," Cressida said. "This year Celeste and Minka will be heading up the plans for this event, since both Lidia and Tegan are conspicuously missing." She gave both Celeste and Minka pointed looks.

"We're on it." Minka assured.

"We intend to make this truly a magical event." Celeste winked at Alex. *And I mean really magical!* she telepathed.

"We've decided on a theme," Minka declared. "Under the sea!"

Cressida's lips twisted like she'd bitten into a lemon. "How original."

"Just you wait." Minka's grin widened. "It's going to have the best decorations, the most delicious food—"

"I get it." Cressida waved a hand. "Just make sure everything goes as planned." Taking a deep breath, she looked at everyone. "You have your marching orders. I'll see you ladies again in a week. Next time, the meeting will be at my house, and we'll have tea."

* * *

It was a perfect day in the park. Humidity was low, the sun bright and clear, and the ocean breeze was constant. The park that anchored the downtown area of Bellamy Bay was filled with tourists waiting for the unveiling of the mural. A wall, part of the town's welcome center located opposite the famous mermaid fountain, was covered by a huge tan tarp. The mural had to be at least nine feet high and eighteen feet wide. There was a festive feeling in the air, with ice-cream and cotton candy vendors, lemonade and iced coffee carts, and mermaid-themed balloons floating in the air.

Today, the unveiling of the mural was the kickoff of the annual summer mermaid festival, a monthlong event that would continue with a reception and exhibit at the museum the next night, events at the bookstore, and more parties before culminating in an outdoor fair ending on Saturday.

Botanika had a table at the event, and Minka would be manning the booth. Pepper was moving through the crowd with her recorder and microphone. Kamila strode the perimeter in mirrored sunglasses, her sidearm hanging from her waist. She didn't see Jack but assumed he'd appear. Eventually.

Alex saw Celeste, her arm looped through her boyfriend Jasper's. About ten or so years older than Celeste, Jasper was tall and lean, with short hair, cropped on the sides but with a shock of thick dark blond hair that fell over one eye. He was constantly tossing that lock of hair off his forehead, and the hair and the gesture reminded Alex of a smug 1990s boy band member—the one that couldn't sing or dance, but who was self-assured in the knowledge that he was the best looking in the group and knew it. The ridiculously floppy hair contrasted with round glasses that perched at the end of a long supercilious nose, giving him an appropriately cute professorial look.

Alex had never seen him without brightly colored suspenders and a bow tie, an affection that seemed absurd to her. Now, even outside at the park, he wore navy-blue boat shorts, leather flip-flops, a crisp white oxford shirt with the sleeves rolled up, suspenders—cherry red, and the aforementioned bow tie—also bright red.

She tried not to roll her eyes when Celeste caught her watching them and waved. She waved back before moving toward the front of the crowd. The mayor stepped to the microphone to welcome everyone to the town, officially kick off the festival, and initiate the unveiling of the mural. Mayor Bronson Bellamy, Pepper's father, was short and squat, but powerfully built, with a friendly square face, pale skin exploding with freckles, a full head of red hair, and the exuberantly boisterous demeanor of a politician always trying to win over a voter.

Dylan was turning the microphone on and handing it to Neve, who wore a magenta sundress, with her heavy hair piled up in a cloud of dreamy waves, her sunglasses resting on top of her head. Her cheeks were flushed with excitement, or maybe it was just a little extra sun—Alex couldn't tell. And she carried a few pages of notes in her hands.

The microphone squealed as Dylan adjusted the height for Neve. A banner on the bottom of the stage they stood on flapped in the breeze, announcing the mural's sponsors: Wesley Inc. and Leviathan Industries. Dylan grinned at the crowd, introduced himself, and then gave the microphone to Neve.

"You guys," she began, her face shining with enthusiasm, "I am so honored to be here to share in your celebration of all things mermaid!" There was a light smattering of applause led by Minka, who had come out of the Botanika booth for a better look. "I want to thank Wesley Inc."—she paused, looking at Dylan with adoration—"and Montgomery Blue of Leviathan Industries." She shielded her eyes from the bright sun and peered into the crowd, then waved at a tall man in sunglasses, with a deep tan and a full head of dark graying hair. He waved back before disappearing into the crowd.

A shy one, Alex thought of the man. *He mustn't like the limelight.* She turned back to the stage.

"I've worked with Jasper Collins, the director of the Bellamy Bay Museum of History, to curate an exhibit at the museum on the town's mermaids that begins with the local Native Americans' account of the mermaids from ancient to modern times. His knowledge was invaluable and helped inspire my choice of subjects for the mural."

She found Celeste's boyfriend in the crowd and threw him a kiss. "Thank you, Jasper."

He inclined his head in a courtly manner. But Celeste, who was holding on to him even tighter, wore a pinched expression on her face.

A sudden breeze kicked up, swirling around the park, causing several pages of Neve's paper to fly about. Dylan ran around gathering them up for her.

What is he—her errand boy? Alex wondered in exasperation. *And where's Jack?* She looked around the park. He'd promised to join her.

Neve took a moment to arrange her papers before beginning, smile still in place. "This small town is rich in history, and I hope I have done justice to Bellamy Bay, the history and most importantly, the mermaids who founded this town."

She does believe! she heard Minka say in her thoughts. Alex turned to look at her cousin, who had her hands clasped at her chest. She wasn't sure if she should share in the excitement or not. They didn't want people to know mermaids were real, right?

She turned back to Neve, who had stepped off the platform and approached the mural. She gave the crowd a cheeky grin over her shoulder and ripped the tarp away like she was a hostess on a game show.

A hush went over the gathering as everyone took in the big, colorful painting. It was done in a photorealistic style, the images looking like flesh-and-blood people you would see at the coffee shop or bookstore, only they were about nine feet high.

"Don't be shy!" Neve called out, "Come closer. Tell me what you think."

The crowd moved forward, cell phones out, taking photos. Alex stared at the painting and swallowed. The setting of the mural was the sea, a wide expanse of waves with no horizon in sight. The central figure was a mermaid, clearly the Mermaid of Warsaw, holding her sword and shield. Her skin was pale, and her hair, long, dark, and voluminous, covering her bare chest, was wet, as if she'd just come up from deep within the sea. She wore a come-hither expression that contrasted with a determined gleam in her green eyes.

Minka came up behind Alex and touched her shoulder lightly. "It's beautiful," she said in reverent tones. "Majestic. Fierce . . ."

Kamila joined them, taking her sunglasses off and squinting at the painting. "Is it a battle scene?" She pointed to a Greek god who stood proudly on the helm of a small ship rushing toward the mermaid. He was tall, tanned, and muscled, with a glistening helmet over a cap of short, curly dark hair and a clean-shaven face, and he had a spear and shield, though both were held slackly at his sides.

Pepper appeared, snapping a few photographs of the mural before answering. "I thought Neve was supposed to include our family's Viking heritage. Why are there no Vikings in this mural?"

Speaking of Neve . . . Alex searched the area, wanting to talk to her. Instead her gaze landed on Celeste, this time holding hands with Jasper while he spoke to Neve and Dylan. Alex had never seen Celeste quite so clingy. She'd have to ask her if everything was okay with their relationship. A moment later Celeste and Jasper had joined their group while Kamila was still trying to figure the painting out. Finally, she gave up. "I've got to walk the perimeter. I'll see you guys later."

Alex and Minka turned back to study the painting. The smell of paint, still fresh, tickled Alex's nose.

Neve gauged the expressions on the faces in the group and smiled. "What does everyone think?"

Jasper was the first to speak, his eyes still on the painting. "I feel like it's missing something."

Neve followed his gaze back to the painting. "Really?"

"I don't understand why he's there," Pepper interrupted, pointing at the militant figure.

"Oh, him." Neve smiled. "That's Ares."

"The god of war." Jasper folded his arms across his chest, an unreadable expression on his face. "A rather handsome fellow."

"Exactly," Neve said, as if she were a teacher complimenting a student in class.

"But what does that have to do with our town?" Pepper asked, her recorder out.

Neve glanced around the group. "Anyone?"

"Perhaps he represents the challenges the mermaid had to face to get here?" Minka offered.

Pepper inched forward, her forehead wrinkled in bewilderment. "I don't understand art," she whispered to Alex.

"Well, I think it's beautiful," Minka said. "It's the perfect addition to our town."

"It's very Instagrammable," Celeste said, straightening a bit but still holding Jasper's hand. "I was just telling my mother your painting will help market the town to a younger demographic. We'll have to come up with an official hashtag for the mural."

The mayor joined their growing group, winking at Pepper as he did. "You did a fantastic job, Ms. Ryland." His voice boomed, ricocheting around the park. "Just fantastic."

"Thank you. I'm very proud of it. It's my best work to date. And I've painted many mythological subjects." Dylan joined the group, and she wrapped an arm around his shoulder. "And this guy helped make it possible."

Dylan pushed away the praise with a wave of his hand. "The museum is hosting a reception for Neve tonight. I hope you will attend?"

A murmur of agreement went through the crowd.

Neve playfully punched Jasper on the shoulder. "Everything ready at the museum?"

He laughed. "Shipshape, ma'am."

Smiling, Alex turned to ask Celeste what she'd be wearing for the event, but was surprised to see her shooting daggers at the artist.

What the heck was that about? she wanted to know.

Minka rushed back to the tent when she saw people queuing up for tea, while Alex stared at the Mermaid of Warsaw, wondering what she'd really looked like. A strong gust of wind rushed through the park, lifting Alex's hair and causing her eyes to water. She heard a yelp of shock. She turned to see that a leftover can of blue paint, the color of the ocean on the mural, had overturned, splattering over Neve's dress and then leaking into the grass and all over Neve's high-heeled sandals.

Dylan was nearby, and the artist grabbed his arm for balance as she stepped out of the paint and tossed her shoes off.

For a minute, Alex thought back to another time, when she'd been with Dylan. She was barefoot on the beach, and he'd just saved her life. She pushed the thought away, watching as Neve laughed at her ruined clothes and shoes.

"My goodness," she began, "I've almost caught on fire and now this. I've been having the worst luck lately," she told Dylan as they walked away. "If I were the superstitious type, I'd think I'd been cursed."

Chapter Five

An hour after the unveiling of the mural, the park was still filled with tourists.

Alex had taken over the tent while Minka headed back to the store. Aunt Lidia and Josephine were taking a walk, and Alex was inventorying the remaining tea blends and candles set out before her, when she noticed Neve approaching her.

"You changed clothes," Alex observed.

"Dylan ran to the B&B I'm staying at and brought me this." She looked down at her clothes, this time a blue sundress with a wide red belt and matching heels. "And all so I could stay here and see you."

Dylan, again, Alex thought to herself. *Maybe there was something going on between them.*

"I've been dying to talk to you," Neve said when she stepped under the tent, fanning herself. "I've heard so much about you, your family, and your highly effective herbal remedies." She eyed Alex slyly and then grinned. "I've done a lot of research on mermaids. Research that has brought me to Bellamy Bay. And I've learned some amazing things. One of which you really need to know about."

"Me?" Alex glanced around before settling into her chair. "Like?"

"It goes without saying, this is a secret." Neve lowered her voice as an adult woman dressed in a pink mermaid costume passed by. "But mermaids are real."

Alex looked at the costumed woman and then at Neve. "You know the mermaid bit is just to bring in tourists, right?"

"I know, I know—it sounds unbelievable, right? But it's not fairy-tale stuff, it's plain science. There are scientists researching something they're calling 'the mermaid gene.'"

Alex shook her head and opened her mouth to say something but couldn't find the words.

"They think they've found genetic proof that there are humans with genetic markers that give them the ability to stay underwater for long periods of time and swim at super speeds for long distances."

"That wouldn't make them mermaids—super-human maybe."

"There's more," Neve said, moving closer and lowering her voice. "I'm no scientist, so I'm not the best person to explain this, but it is a fact that humans evolved from a fish-type ancestor, possibly the ancient lung fish. Did you know that the zebra fish shares seventy percent of its protein-coding DNA with humans?"

Wordlessly, Alex shook her head.

"Or that human embryos have tails and gills? And the thinking is that fifty or sixty thousand years ago there was this fish that evolved into a fish-human with the ability to shapeshift between forms, and then it evolved into the human as we know it, with no ability to shift at all. It's not as far-fetched as you'd think."

Alex glanced around, making sure no one was in earshot. "Companies are actually researching this?"

Neve nodded. "And interbreeding with humans caused the fish-human type to almost die out, but the ones that remained were revered as gods and goddesses. Like the Mermaid of Warsaw?" She frowned. "Until they were not. But now the true fish-human hybrids have died out, but some remaining humans still have fish DNA."

Alex swallowed the lump in her throat. "Making them genetic mermaids."

"Yes!" Neve said excitedly. "Isn't that amazing?"

Alex nodded her head slowly, working through what she was hearing. Wondering if it made sense. And could there possibly be an explanation for her and her family's abilities? "How did you hear this?"

" I did a mural for a company that creates medicines based on DNA in RTP."

Alex nodded. "I just learned about the Research Triangle Park in the local paper. It's an area with several universities and high-tech research and development companies, right?"

"That's right. And I've been lucky enough to find a few art patrons there. One of the geneticists there had a crush on me, and we went out for drinks. Honestly, I was just trying to get him drunk so I could get more information." Neve laughed lightly. "He was hoping to take me home"—she rolled her eyes—"so he told me things that he shouldn't have. Namely, that while researching another project, they'd stumbled onto a genetic marker for what they were somewhat humorously calling 'the mermaid gene.' After all this time, it's still around. Can you imagine?"

The news made Alex feel a little dizzy, but she focused on Neve. "No, I can't."

Neve looked over her shoulder before continuing. "The research, which is ongoing, is of interest to many people. The guy told me they've even started a database of people who may have the gene."

"A database?"

"Yes, they'll eventually want to find the people that have these markers, and probably study them."

Alex frowned. "I'm not sure that sounds benevolent. Who have you told?"

"No one,"

Yet. Alex thought she heard the unspoken word. And then she understood. "You're keeping this from someone?"

Neve grimaced. "When I'm on assignment, sometimes I find things, things of importance, and I share that information with my employers."

"Who do you work for? I thought you were an artist?"

"I am, but . . ." Alex saw bands of tension tighten Neve's face and realized she was in serious conflict with herself. "The organization I work for is powerful, and my challenge is to determine who should know what. Who is good, who is bad. How will that knowledge be used."

Alex ran a hand through her hair. *They were talking about art, right?* But it didn't seem like Neve was talking about murals.

"It's a heavy burden at times. Sometimes, I wish I could unknow things."

"When you're traveling around painting these murals, are you always hoping to glean information from your hosts?"

Neve's face lit up. "No, not always. Sometimes it's just about the painting, the artistic expression. And that's when I'm at my happiest. Take your mermaid festival, for example. I was so honored to be asked to come and create a mural for your town. And to have the opportunity to meet you."

Alex wasn't sure how to take this woman. She was an artist— and what? A fact finder? A researcher? To what end? "As fascinating as this sounds, why are you discussing this with me?"

"I was able to sneak a peek at the database. It's still early days, but your aunt was listed. So was your cousin Kamila. I can only assume you and Minka are part of this. You have the gene, don't you?"

Eyes wide, Alex looked around the park. No one was within earshot, no one could possibly know what they were discussing, and yet Alex was absolutely terrified.

Neve reached out and grabbed her hand. "You don't have to worry! Your secret is safe with me." A look of admiration filled her eyes. "It is such an honor to meet you, Alex. My life's work has been about documenting people like you, through art."

But Alex did not feel reassured. She gently pulled her hand away. "I don't know what you're talking about, okay? I'm just a regular person with normal DNA."

A mischievous grin played on Neve's lips. "I get it. You can't confirm it, right? There's like a club? With rules?" Alex frowned, rising from her chair. "How does the gene express itself? It has to be more than strong swimming and breathing underwater. Can you do hydrokinesis—influence water with your mind? I've heard that might be a possibility."

Hydrokinesis: so that's what it was called, Alex thought to herself. "Neve, I appreciate your enthusiasm for the mural, but it ends there. Neither me nor anyone in my family is who you think we are, and I would appreciate it if you would keep this information to yourself."

A dark look crossed the woman's face. "You don't get it, do you? We need to help each other. The best way to keep your family safe is if it's not a secret." She waved her hand around the park. "Isn't that what you're doing now—hiding in plain sight?"

"I really don't think making this information public would help anyone. And even if the mermaid gene is real—and I'm not saying I believe that's true—where would the danger come from?" *She couldn't know about witch hunters, could she?* "And why is there a database?"

Neve's eyes stretched wide with disbelief. "Governments, militaries, pharmaceutical companies—they'd all love to map a genetic mermaid's genome and understand how they can monetize it. They'd take something beautiful and destroy it if they could."

Alex stared at the woman.

Neve leaned forward. "If people found out that mermaids were, in fact, not a fairy tale, and that someone like the Mermaid Of Warsaw had been real, there would be people who would want to worship them like the goddesses of yore, but there would also be people that would try to find her descendants and prevent them from—" She paused as Alex greeted two women who stopped by the table and browsed through a group of bath salts, then left. "The Mermaid of Warsaw had a sword and shield for a reason."

Alex nodded, impatient for her to continue. "Okay?"

"I believe the Mermaid of Warsaw was an amazing human hybrid, one of a group of similar mythological beings that helped protect our world. And because of her genetic gifts, she was meant to help protect the seas and the coast—that was her domain after all—and any and everything that came from it."

"You've lost me," Alex said, frustrated.

"Don't you understand? You're in danger. Your family is in danger. Maybe not today or tomorrow, but eventually. In my own way, I'm trying to help you."

"How? What are you doing?"

"I have two choices. I can tell everyone what I know. Or no one. Right now, I'm keeping what I know to myself, and it's harder than you'd think."

Alex shrank back from her intensity, both fascinated and horrified by what she was hearing. "You fear for your life too, don't you?"

Neve's smile belied the warning in her eyes. "People who know things always do. Such research may begin with the best of intentions, but somehow bad people get a hold of it, and the next thing you know, it's a weapon to deter and suppress." She shuddered. "But it's not too late. We can fight this. *You* can fight this, but I need your help."

"Me? How can I possibly help you?" Alex looked over Neve's shoulder and saw her aunt fast approaching. Neve followed her gaze and stopped talking.

"Hot one today," Aunt Lidia said as she joined Alex behind the table. Lidia smiled at the woman. "Welcome to our little tent. You're the artist, yes?"

Neve stood up straighter, her smile bright. "I am. And I was just asking about the best product to try."

"Hmm . . ." Lidia nodded, giving the woman an assessing gaze, then smiled. "I have just the thing for you." She ducked under the table and retrieved a canister of tea, handing it to Neve. "On the house. For your beautiful painting. My friend and I were just looking at it."

"Thank you." Neve took the gift and inspected the label. "Very sweet of you."

Lidia patted her arm gently. "One to two cups daily for the foreseeable future. If you need more, you can order online." She handed Neve a business card from her apron pocket. "Here—our website is on it."

"I can't wait to try it." Then Neve glanced at the delicate watch on her wrist. "I have to go. Another meeting. But I'll be at the museum's reception tonight. You'll both be there?"

"I have another engagement." Lidia said.

"But I'll be there." Alex nodded. "I wouldn't miss it."

Neve reached out and took Alex's hand in her own. "Find me later on in the evening, and we'll talk more. I have so much more to tell you."

* * *

Jack wouldn't be able to attend the reception.

At least not on time. But he promised to swing by after his shift ended. Alex was disappointed, but she understood. Her father had often called her to say he couldn't make the dinner she'd prepared for him because of work. She got it. Police work never ended. And what he was doing was important, but still . . . She hoped he could make it before the event ended. She'd just spend the time with friends and family. She turned to Minka, who sat in the driver's seat of her car and smiled. "Ready?"

"Let's go!"

They stepped out of the car, linked arms, and headed for the museum. A medium-sized brick building that used to be a train depot for a now defunct train line, it was picturesque with its peaked green roof and black wrought iron fencing.

With her normally wavy hair flat-ironed for the night, smoky eyes, glossy nude lips, and her favorite little black dress, paired with sparkly silver heels, Alex felt desirable. It had been a while since she'd really dressed up.

*   *   *

The museum, usually staid and austere, was filled with patrons chatting, holding glasses of wine, and eating heavy hors d'oeuvres. A tuxedo-wearing trio played soft jazz from a corner, and the lights were dimmed for the night. Shimmery silver and pale blue balloons filled with metallic confetti floated in the air, creating an ethereal ambience.

Alex had only been to the museum once, she was embarrassed to say, and that was only to drop off brochures for the shop.

Now, as she walked around the main hall of the museum, she saw that there were many interesting exhibits on the history of her adopted home. Some featured the Algonquians, the Native

American tribe who had lived in the area first; they had been followed by English colonists, then immigrants from other countries,
the enslaved community, and the prominent industries of naval
supplies and fishing. There were pictorials of Bellamy Bay during
the Revolutionary and Civil Wars, Reconstruction, both World
Wars, and more.

Minka tapped her on the shoulder. "There's so much stuff here.
It's been a while since I've visited. Looks like Celeste's boyfriend has
really expanded the exhibits."

"What was here before?"

"Mostly shipping history, pirate stuff—which was cool—and
all of the military history."

"What military history?"

"Oh, um . . . the U.S. Navy took over the city after World War
II and used it for missile testing and stuff." She pulled a blasé expression. "Boring." She moved to another exhibit. "Ooh, look. Sea
turtles."

Alex glanced at the exhibit, which showcased the areas of the
island marked as a nature preserve, as well as a timeline for when
preservation efforts by the Wesley family began on the island.

Minka waved at a group across the room and turned to Alex. "I
see some of my friends from the Preservation Society. I want to say
hi." Minka shimmied her shoulders. "Be right back."

Alex shooed her way with a smile, then looked toward the
source of a melodious laugh in the room. It was Neve, surrounded
by a group of men in suits, all rapt with interest.

And why not? Neve was stunning in a silky white sheath that
revealed one shoulder and highlighted her voluptuous figure. And
Dylan was at her side. Solicitous. Fawning.

Alex grabbed a glass of white wine from a passing waiter. But
also with Neve were Jasper, Mayor Bellamy, and two other men.

Alex recognized one, the other festival sponsor. He appeared to be in his early fifties. He was taller and broader than either Jack or Dylan, with a powerful frame dressed casually in a silk shirt, linen pants, and loafers with no socks. What was his name? *Montgomery Blue.*

He caught her looking at him and grinned. Alex took in his intelligent dark eyes, olive complexion, and thick dark hair full of gray streaks. She smiled back, wondering why a chill had just traveled up her spine. She looked away quickly to Neve, who was directly beside him.

Neve wiggled her fingers at her in greeting. Alex waved back, eager to finish their discussion. She searched the room, wondering where Celeste was, then spotted her in a small group, talking to—Tegan. Alex hesitated, not wanting to join that group, but also wanting to be social. She was aware that she was standing alone at a party. Tegan and Celeste were joined by Tobias Winston, her aunt Lidia's friend and attorney, and Pepper. She moved through the room to join the group.

Celeste smiled at her when she arrived, and the small circle widened to include her. "Having fun?"

Alex nodded.

Celeste looked festive, wearing a party dress in deep violet, with a sequined tank top bodice and a tulle mini dress that fell mid-thigh. A large tote, silver and sparkly, hung on her shoulder.

What's in the bag? Alex telepathed to Celeste with a curious grin.

Celeste smiled. *Oh, this and that.*

Greeting everyone before turning to Dylan's mother, Alex couldn't quite make her mouth form a smile. So she said hello and quickly brought her glass of wine to her mouth.

Tegan's icy-blue eyes glittered, but she didn't smile either, though her lips twitched in response. "Aleksandra." She inclined her head. "Where's Lidia?" This time her red lips split into a hard, expectant smile. "I thought she'd be here."

Alex assessed the woman and almost laughed. Like Tegan actually *hoped* to see her aunt. Coldly beautiful, Tegan had pale bloodless skin, sharp features, and sleek dark hair styled into a bob that grazed her shoulders. She wore a royal blue pantsuit and heels that made her tower over Alex by several inches. A necklace of blood-red jewels clung to her throat.

Alex wouldn't tell her the truth: that she'd asked her aunt to attend, and Lidia had stated rather passionately that she wouldn't go anywhere "that woman"—Tegan—was. She smiled at Dylan's mother. "She's busy."

Tegan sniffed in response before turning to Tobias. "As I was saying, I couldn't be prouder of my boy. He's taking Wesley Inc. to new places."

Tobias, a short man with glasses and a round face, grinned. "Dylan's always been a smart one. I'm not surprised."

Alex glanced at Celeste and then Tegan with interest. "What has Dylan done?"

"Only closed the biggest deal in our company's history." She exchanged glances with Celeste. "Isn't that right, dear?"

Celeste preened under Tegan's gaze. "That's right, Mrs. Wesley."

Alex shot her friend an amused glance, wondering how she'd gotten on the right side of Tegan.

Pepper perked up and leaned in. "Any details you can share?"

Celeste opened her mouth to speak, but Tegan beat her to the point. "No." Her voice was firm. "Certainly not for you."

"Oh." Pepper laughed, though it was a bit forced. "Okay." She looked around the room, and Alex followed her gaze, seeing Cressida, Josephine, and Yuko huddled in a corner, probably discussing the festival.

"Well," Pepper said, "I've got to mingle and get a few comments for the paper."

When Alex turned back to Tegan and Celeste, she was surprised to see Dylan standing there. He smelled spicy and sweet, of tobacco and leather. A heady mix. A strange mix. But it was intoxicating, and she had to stop herself from closing her eyes, leaning toward him, and inhaling. Instead, she cursed Jack for the millionth time for not being with her when she needed him.

Where is he anyway?

Dylan was handsome, as usual, in a white blazer, crisp white shirt with blue pin stripes, and blue dress pants. He looked like he was about to go yachting. He smiled at the group. "What did I miss?"

Celeste grinned. "Your mother was just singing your praises."

"Oh, that?" He shrugged nonchalantly. "Just another acquisition."

Tegan patted her son on his cheek and smiled indulgently. "If you say so, dear." She took Tobias's arm. "Montgomery looks bored talking to the mayor. Let's save him, shall we?"

Alex turned once again to look at the man who was cosponsoring the festival. He was watching her, or at least it seemed that way to her. He inclined his head, and Alex felt strongly that he wanted to speak to her. But about what? She had no business with him.

Tobias bowed toward Alex. "Tell your aunt she was missed tonight."

Tegan rolled her eyes and placed her arm through his, leading him away.

Dylan filled the silence with a laugh. "My mother."

"So, your big deal?" Alex prodded.

He shoved his hands into his pockets. "Can't say much until it's publicly announced." He noticed Alex's glass was empty and took it from her, placing it on a passing waiter's tray. "Another?"

Alex shook her head. "No, thank you." She needed to keep her wits about her. She would talk with Neve later, and she wanted—needed—to be clearheaded. She turned to Celeste. "This super-secret, hush-hush big deal . . . you're working on it too?"

Celeste nodded with a grin.

Dylan chuckled. "All I can tell you is that it will take our company to the next level."

Alex laughed. "I thought you already were at that level."

The mayor was making his rounds, shaking hands and laughing boisterously like a tiny hurricane. He stopped by their group and engaged Dylan in a conversation about having Wesley sponsor a new initiative, when another man joined them. This man, who had been at Dylan's side earlier when he was with Neve, smiled by way of greeting.

He was a few inches shorter than Dylan's six foot two, fit and with a full but neatly trimmed brown beard that covered a tanned face. He had gray eyes that contrasted with thick dark eyebrows and a cap of cropped brown curls. He wore a baby-blue summer suit with an open-collared pale blue shirt underneath. Although the mayor continued to monopolize Dylan's time, the newcomer introduced himself to Alex.

"I'm Bryce. Greenberg." He winked at Celeste, who smiled politely in return. "We've met in passing." He handed Alex his business card.

She took it without reading it. "New in town?"

He nodded but stopped when there was another peal of laughter from Neve.

"She's having a good time," Alex observed.

Celeste exhaled loudly. "Why doesn't she just leave town? The mural is done."

Alex looked from Celeste to Neve in surprise, and then saw that Neve had a hand on Jasper's arm—and that he seemed quite pleased with the attention.

"Excuse me while I get my boyfriend." Celeste took a deep, hopefully calming breath before stalking across the room.

"Well now," Bryce said with an amused grin, "are we about to see a catfight?"

She looked at him. "That's not nice. She's obviously upset."

"I know." His cheeks turned pink. "I was just trying to lighten the mood."

Bryce continued to chat with her, but Alex was more interested in what Celeste was doing. She analyzed her body language, noting the clenched fists and the tight set of her jaw. And the more Jasper talked to Neve, the more upset Celeste seemed to get.

Bryce asked her something, and she asked him to repeat himself.

"I asked you what brought you to town. I can tell from your lack of a Southern accent that you're not from around here."

"Oh . . . sorry." She told him briefly how she'd come to be in town, but stopped when she saw something she couldn't quite believe. The roof directly over Neve had begun to drip water. Only a little bit, but enough for Neve to notice, pat her hair, and step out of the way. And Celeste had done it! Alex couldn't be sure, but the determined look on Celeste's face and a slight twitch of her fingers . . .

I saw that, Alex sent to Celeste.

Saw what? Celeste asked, her tone innocent, even telepathically.

You know what, Alex said.

There was a pause and then Celeste replied, *I just want her to leave town. That's all.*

Behave, Alex admonished. *This type of behavior is beneath you.*

Meanwhile, Bryce was still talking. "Dylan mentioned that you work at the apothecary in town. You'll have to tell me about it sometime."

Alex looked at the man. Was he trying to pick her up or just making conversation? He was cute, but she wasn't interested. She gave him a tight smile. "Sure."

She kept her eye on Celeste, who grabbed Jasper by the hand, indicating that he should follow her. Which he did. They went down a hall marked "Staff Only," and Alex turned back to Bryce. But he was already gone, probably fed up with her lack of engagement.

She looked down at the card in her hand. It read "Bryce Greenberg, CEO/Founder Tarheel Defense. Protecting the peace . . . so you don't have to."

Huh, Alex thought as she scanned the room and found Bryce at Dylan's side. They were deep in conversation while Tegan, flanked by Tobias and Montgomery, looked on approvingly. Alex reread the card. It had a Greensboro, North Carolina, address. *Never heard of him or his business,* she thought with a shrug. And placed the card in her purse.

When Celeste didn't return after a few minutes, Alex was concerned. Despite the sign that read "Staff Only," she walked down the hall and heard voices. Celeste was yelling, and it sounded like Jasper was trying to calm her down. They were in Jasper's office, with the door shut. Alex rested her forehead against the cool wall, eyes closed, trying to hear what was being said.

Clearly, Celeste thought more was going on between Neve and Jasper. And then Alex heard a smacking sound and a gasp. Had Celeste slapped Jasper? The door flew open, and Celeste ran down the hall and back to the reception, without looking backward, without seeing Alex standing there. Several museum patrons were standing by and had clearly heard at least part of the argument.

Alex returned to the reception, hoping to find Celeste. She needed to talk to her, big sister to little sister. No way did she need to be acting this way over a man. But a quick scan of the room showed Celeste was nowhere to be found. *Maybe she went outside to calm down,* Alex thought.

Certainly, she needed to cool off.

* * *

Two hours into the reception, the night was broken up by more speeches from the mayor, who thanked Jasper for hosting the event, and Wesley Inc. and Leviathan Industries for sponsoring the muralist and festival.

Alex had waited all night to find a moment alone with Neve. But the most popular woman in the room had held court all night. *Maybe I can speak to her after the mayor's acknowledgments,* Alex thought.

She was also more than a little curious to chat with Montgomery. He'd seemed interested in her, and she wanted to know why. She'd looked for him earlier but couldn't find him. Now he was standing in the back of the room with Dylan.

Alex faced the front as the mayor called out to Neve to join him onstage to take the proverbial bow, but he couldn't find her. Chuckling, the mayor said she must be in the powder room and asked the gathered group to please offer their gratitude for the mural when they saw her.

The crowd applauded, and the mayor directed everyone to return to enjoying the food and drink. Alex still hadn't had a chance to talk to Celeste. She hoped her friend was okay. She didn't see her. Or Jasper. Perhaps they were talking, and hopefully resolving their issues. And then she saw her, making her way through the crowd and back toward Jasper's office. Alex made to follow her, when a hand grabbed her from behind.

It was Minka, finally returned from chatting with her friends. "I got an earful from the Preservation Society."

Alex grinned. "What have you just volunteered for?" She tried to keep her eye on Celeste, but she disappeared down the hallway, so Alex turned back to her cousin.

Minka's eyebrows shot up, and she lowered her voice to a whisper. "Maybe a protest."

"Of what?" Minka had Alex's full attention now. She'd find Celeste after the party.

"Leviathan Industries."

"You mean the company donating thousands of dollars for our mermaid festival?"

Minka shook her head ruefully. "The very same. A member of the society discovered that Leviathan makes their money in deep sea mining. What if that's why they're here? What if that's why they're donating money to our festival? So the mayor will approve mining off our coasts?" Minka's voice rose in panic, and Alex could tell the group had done their work riling her up.

Alex searched the room, looking for the CEO of Leviathan Industries. First, she found Jasper, his bow tie crooked. He was speaking to Cressida. Then she found him—Montgomery Blue. He was talking to the mayor, and he looked quite friendly. She and Minka exchanged glances. "I'm sure—"

A shriek pierced the room, and the violinist, surprised by the noise, made a screeching noise with his bow.

There was a moment of eerie silence, and then everyone turned to look toward the source of the scream.

The fast gait of heels clicking on tile could be heard in the silence.

Someone was running.

And then Celeste appeared at the end of the "Staff Only" hall, her hands slick with something wet and bright red.

Eyes stretched with fear, she looked around the room. "Someone call 911. There's been a murder!"

Chapter Six

J ack finally made an appearance.

But Alex couldn't dwell on how relieved she was that he'd made it. After discovering a body, Celeste needed her. After the police had been called, and her hands washed of blood, Celeste sat with her hands covering her face. Someone had wrapped a suit jacket around her shoulders while she cried uncontrollably.

Alex had wanted to run down that hall and see who was hurt and if she could help in any way, but it had been Dylan who grabbed her by the shoulders, sat her down beside Celeste, and told her not to move, that she didn't want to see what was behind that door.

It was Bryce and he who walked down the hall and discovered that Neve was the victim. He'd returned after a moment to tell her and Celeste that there was nothing to be done. She'd been found in Jasper's office, lying on the floor, blood spilling from her wound. It appeared that someone had smashed a heavy object against her head and left her. She was dead, and there was nothing Mundane or Magical to be done.

Alex was numb, her arm around Celeste's shoulders. She wasn't sure what to think. Neve was dead? The woman who'd promised to tell her things she needed to know? And Celeste? Had she done it?

Alex couldn't unsee the woman's bloodied hands, and she was afraid to ask. Afraid to hear the answer. So she said nothing, just held Celeste when she curled into her arms and cried.

After the crime scene techs arrived, and the area was blocked off, fingerprints were being taken, and security footage had been recovered, Jack approached them. He took Alex's hand and gestured for her to follow him to a quiet corner.

"Coroner's on the way. You okay?"

She nodded, unable to speak. Then shook her head. "I'm not sure. I'd just met her, but we were supposed to talk tonight. She was just here and alive . . ." Her voice trailed off, and she realized tears were rolling down her cheeks.

Jack used his thumbs to gently wipe the tears away. "I'm sorry this happened, but we will find out who did it." He looked around the museum. "No one is leaving until everyone provides a statement and we check alibis."

She shivered involuntarily, and he rubbed her bare arms to warm her.

"I know you're observant. Did you see anything I should be aware of?"

Alex gulped, wondering what she should say. She didn't know who'd done it, but she certainly knew who'd had motive and possibly opportunity. Where had Celeste been when Neve was attacked? No, she couldn't divulge anything she knew to Jack, not until she knew for herself that Celeste wasn't involved. "I didn't see anything."

He peered into her eyes and rubbed her cheek tenderly with a finger. "It's my job to know when people are lying," he said, his voice low. "Remember?"

Sighing inwardly, Alex gritted her teeth. Like her father, who'd been a police detective before he made chief, Jack prided himself on being able to assess a person's honesty based on body language, years of experience and good ol' instinct. She didn't want to lie to him, but she had to for Celeste's sake. "I didn't see anything, Jack."

His gaze was penetrating as he stared into her eyes. And then he blinked. "Okay. I believe you."

But he was lying. She'd learned a lot from her father too. And she could see in in his eyes. He didn't believe her either. They were both lying.

And that wasn't good.

* * *

Police officers were stationed at each exit, and the visitors were lined up to provide their names, contact information, and location during the time of murder. Celeste had found the body, so Jack was beginning with her first. Alex had asked Celeste if she wanted her to stay with her, and Celeste had agreed.

Jack had set up in another staff office for interviews. He sat behind the desk, leaning forward, recorder on and pen hovering over paper.

Alex sat on the other side of the desk and beside Celeste, holding her hand. She gave her an encouraging smile. "Tell him what you told me."

Celeste took a deep shuddering breath before she began. "I was looking for Jasper, and I didn't see him in the exhibits area, so I thought I'd check his office."

Jack nodded. "Okay."

Celeste glanced at Alex before going on. "I knocked on his door. There was no answer. So I opened it, walked inside, and saw her—Neve—on the floor." She heaved like she might throw up, covering her mouth just in case. But she didn't, just gave Alex a sickly smile. "At first, I thought she was just hurt, so I ran to her and lifted her head up—"

"That's how you got blood all over your hands?" Jack asked. Celeste nodded, unable to speak. Jack's face was grim. "First time seeing a dead body, I imagine?" She nodded again and looked at Alex, hopelessness washing over her face.

Alex squeezed her hand reassuringly.

"And you cleaned your hands?" he asked her.

Celeste looked at me, eyes wide. But she nodded. "They were—I was—" She stopped as a wave of nausea seemed to rock her.

"Where were you before you decided to go look for Mr. Collins?"

"Um . . . here and there, moving around the museum, talking to people, looking at exhibits . . . I went outside for air for a time."

Jack nodded, taking notes as she spoke. "Did you argue with your boyfriend earlier today?" He looked up then, one eyebrow raised.

Celeste looked at Alex.

Alex telepathed, *Just tell him the truth. If you didn't do it, you have nothing to fear.*

But instead, her eyes widened as if she had everything to fear.

Uh-oh, Alex thought.

Celeste turned to Jack, her cheeks trembling with the effort to smile. "Someone told you?"

He referred to his notes. "Several witnesses recalled you getting upset with your boyfriend about his relationship with the deceased. And at least one person overheard you arguing?" His gaze sharpened. "Do you have anything else to add?"

She shook her head. "It's all true." Her voice thickened with emotion. "But I didn't—I wouldn't . . . *kill* her. I'd kill *him* maybe." She laughed harshly. "But not her."

Don't say things like that, Alex sent to her. *Jack doesn't have the best sense of humor during investigations.*

"You'll need to account for your time tonight. The officer at the door will take your statement."

"Of course," Celeste said, beginning to rise.

As she did, Alex noticed her heels for the first time. They were encrusted with dirt. Why were her heels covered in soil?

Jack caught the direction of her eyes and looked down too, with only a twitch of his eyebrow as indication that he noticed.

Alex took a deep breath, hoping it was nothing.

"Why are you shoes dirty?" he asked, pointing to her heels.

She laughed, though nothing was funny. "I told you. I went outside for some air." She smiled at him, almost looking relieved. "Are we done?"

"Just one moment," Jack said. "Do you have reason to believe Jasper was having an intimate relationship with the victim?" He narrowed his eyes, waiting.

Celeste looked at Alex, her face transformed into an expression of pain as she returned Jack's gaze. "Maybe. I don't know. I hope not."

"Are you done with her? She's had a big shock tonight. I'd like to get her home."

"Of course. But, Miss Thomas, please don't leave town. We'll probably need to speak again."

With one arm around her shoulder for support, Alex guided Celeste out of the room. She looked over her shoulder to Jack, who was watching their progress down the hallway. And then she heard Jack call to an officer: "Get Jasper Collins in here!"

* * *

A Hex for Danger

Once Alex had asked Minka to take Celeste home, she permitted herself a moment to breathe. Many patrons had been allowed to leave after talking to the police, and the museum wasn't as crowded.

She loitered by the crime scene, wondering what she could see. When the police officer guarding the door stepped away, she poked her head into the office. There was a desk piled high with papers, folders, and books. Walls covered in framed degrees, a few photographs of Jasper with others, a globe on a back table, and souvenirs from trips around the world. White fingerprint powder covered every flat service, and yellow police tape crisscrossed the threshold.

Alex saw an outline of where Neve's body had fallen. She appeared to have been standing on the side of the desk where Jasper sat before she was assailed. Alex gazed around the room, wondering what had happened.

There was a tap on her shoulder, and she jumped.

"You can't be here," Kamila said, her face somber.

"I know—I just wanted a look around."

Her cousin crossed the tape and looked at Alex from the other side. "There's nothing you can do here. Go home. Get some rest. I'll stop by in the morning with an update."

"Sure, okay." Alex backed away from the scene, still not believing Neve had been murdered. She bumped into Pepper, whose face lit up.

"Can you believe my luck! I'm the only representative of the media here. If I can get the scoop on this—"

"Pepper," Alex admonished her, placing a steadying hand on her arm. "Surely you're not happy there's been a second murder in Bellamy Bay?"

"Of course not, but someone has to tell the story. And why not me? It's my job after all. And actually, this makes three since you've been here. There's a John Doe who was found a few days ago. But it doesn't seem very interesting. Just some software engineer who partied too hard—a drug overdose I think."

Alex thought for a moment. "Jack mentioned that to me. At the time, the victim was still unidentified. But a drug overdose? Why was he in the woods?"

Pepper shrugged. "Maybe whoever he was partying with got scared and dumped the body. But there's no glamour to that story. Former frat boy ODs. His wife came to the newspaper office, wanting us to do a story about how the police weren't doing enough. She also told me that the day after he died, she discovered his laptop was missing. But I followed up with Jack, and he said that either she's lying about the missing laptop to get them to make the case more than an overdose, or it's unrelated."

A bored expression crossed Pepper's face. "Sounds like Jack is doing everything right. She's just upset everyone knows she was married to a drug addict. He probably sold his laptop for money. Who knows?" She shook her head. "But this artist murder? There's going to be a lot of interest."

Alex wrinkled her nose. "About that. I was wondering if—"

A gasp escaped Pepper's glossy lips. "You want to work together, don't you?"

Alex hesitated, recalling how suspicious Pepper had been about her family's past when she first moved to town, then relented. "Against my better judgement... yes. You're . . . tenacious. And you have resources I don't have, so yeah, let's work together. I have a feeling Jack is going to try and pin this on another person I care about.

"No way." Pepper's eyes glittered with enthusiasm. She could barely hide her excitement. "When do we get started?"

"Tomorrow morning. Kamila is going to stop by and tell us what she knows. And you'll have had time to get background on Neve, right?"

"Definitely."

"Let's meet at Coffee O'Clock, share notes, and figure out who our suspects are."

Chapter Seven

As promised, Kamila stopped by her mother's home early in the morning.

Lidia had prepared a cast-iron pan full of fried potatoes and sautéed onions fresh from her vegetable and herb garden that curled alongside the back of the house. The entrée was paired with softly scrambled eggs seasoned with dill, parsley, and thyme. The enticing scent of roasted coffee beans met Alex as she descended from the stairs. And she gratefully accepted a mug from Minka, who joined her at the table.

"How did you sleep?" Lidia asked her as she doled out plates of food.

Alex sipped her coffee before speaking. "Not very well. I couldn't stop thinking of Neve." *And of Celeste,* she wanted to add, but didn't. She and that girl were going to have a talk, and soon. *But first, coffee.* She ignored her food and drank the rich brew, allowing it to slowly pull her out of her morning brain fog.

"It was awful," she finally said. "Thank goodness, Dylan stopped me from seeing her, so I can remember her as I last saw her—beautiful and full of life."

Lidia looked sad, her eyes cast downward. "This is just between you and me, girls. But Neve was pregnant. I sensed it when she came in the shop."

Alex thought back to the gift her aunt gave the artist. "The tea?"

"It was a blend of nettle leaf, red raspberry leaf, milky oat tops, and rose hips. It's our Magical Mama blend and helps support a healthy pregnancy. She was with child—it was so soon I don't even know if *she* knew. But I could sense the beginning of a second aura around her belly. Not every Magical can see that, but I was trained in midwifery many moons ago."

Alex picked up her fork, digging into her potatoes. "I wonder who the father was." And she also wondered if Celeste knew.

Minka looked queasy and poked at her eggs with her fork. "Whoever he was, maybe he killed her? A lover's spat?"

Athena jumped up, barking, and Alex heard the front door open and the light tread of Kamila's athletic shoes. "I was hoping I wouldn't miss breakfast," she said with a grin. "Hey, Mom. Anything for me?"

"Of course." Lidia stood and went to the stove to make her oldest daughter a plate.

Kamila, dressed in her bicycle patrol uniform, joined the table and began eating as soon as the plate was put before her. "Sorry, guys. I'm famished." She looked at Alex. "I had a kickboxing workout at the gym before my shift and then had a call first thing."

"What kind of call," Minka asked, pouring herself more orange juice.

"B&E—breaking and entering. The coroner's office."

"That's strange." Alex commented. "What's in there but dead bodies?"

Kamila laughed. "Not the body storage area—his actual office. You know, where his desk and computer are? It had been rifled through like somebody was looking for something."

"Was anything missing?"

"Not that he could tell. But nothing of importance is kept there. All files are digitized. And anything found on bodies is sent to the police station."

Minka looked at the clock on the wall. "I'm meeting Celeste at the lighthouse today. We're talking to the florist and caterer for the party." She shot her sister a look. "She's not in any trouble is she, because she found the body?"

Finished with eating, Kamila pushed her plate away and stood, empty coffee mug in hand. "This is all in the family, of course."

"Of course," Alex responded immediately, and her aunt and Minka nodded.

"Detective Frazier is taking a very hard look at Celeste." Kamila poured more coffee in her cup and returned to the table.

"What? No." Minka's eyebrows shot up. "She's our friend. And I need her for party planning. Why are they focusing on her?"

"The coroner thinks Neve died between eight thirty and nine pm, based on witness accounts of when she was last seen, the few security feeds the museum has, and a physical examination." She shrugged. "And why Celeste? Well, for starters, she can't account for her time during that period."

"Anyone else?" Alex asked, wondering if—no, hoping against hope that there were other suspects.

"There are a few other people who don't have alibis. Detective Frazier will be investigating them. But none of them have a motive as compelling as Celeste's," Kamila replied.

Alex sank in her chair.

"Like who?" Lidia asked, looking at Alex in concern.

"An out-of-town friend of Dylan's named Bryce Greenberg, Montgomery Blue—the head of Leviathan Industries, and Jasper Collins. But Jack says the evidence will probably show that Celeste did it." She grimaced when Minka gasped. "Sorry, I know she's our distant cousin, but when you find the body, and everyone knows you accused your boyfriend of sleeping with the victim *and* you slapped him—well, it doesn't look good."

Minka's face drooped with sadness. "That slap shows she's prone to violence?"

"Something like that." Kamila nodded.

"This is the Randy Bennett case all over again," Alex said straightening in her seat. "I know he's by the book. I know he follows the evidence, but he doesn't know Celeste like we all do." She looked around the room, and Lidia nodded. "She didn't do this. She's emotional and impetuous, but she's not a . . ." Alex couldn't bring herself to say the word.

But Kamila could. "Murderer? It may take some time, but Detective Frazier will figure it out."

Minka's hands balled into fists. "I know Jack's a nice guy and *very* cute, but how can you say that? How can you trust him? Remember what he did to our mother."

"Calm down." Kamila said. "Have some tea. He's just doing his job. And if it hadn't been our mother, I would've thought he was doing the right thing too. Mom did look guilty. And now, so does Celeste. It'll all shake out in the end."

But Alex wasn't so sure. She knew firsthand how stubborn and persistent Jack could be.

Kamila took one look at the expression on her face. "What is it, Alex?"

Alex looked around the table, and finally at Kamila. "If he's not going to look at other suspects, we have to. Will you help?"

"I'm not doing anything illegal." Kamila snorted.

Alex leaned forward. "No one is asking you to."

Kamila drained her coffee cup as she stood. "Let's see what Jack does first, and where the evidence leads. If it seems like he's going down the wrong path, maybe I'll help."

"This needs to be done quickly, before he arrests Celeste for something she didn't do," Alex persisted.

"Did she tell you she didn't do it?" Kamila leveled her cop stare at her, and Alex suppressed the urge to flinch.

She swallowed. "I haven't asked her."

Kamila raised her eyebrows as she looked at Alex. "That's the best I can do." Then she smiled, cop face gone.

After Kamila left, Alex checked the clock on the wall. "I need to meet someone."

* * *

As promised, Alex texted Pepper and asked her to meet for coffee. She walked the few blocks from the shop to the café, Athena bounding in front of her. The sun was directly overhead, beaming down clear yellow light; the sky was blue and cloudless; and the scent of the blue and purple hydrangeas planted alongside the sidewalk fragranced her walk.

When she reached the shop, she patted Athena on her head, attached her leash to the bike rack outside, and told her to be a good girl. Athena stood at attention for a moment, then lay down with her head between her paws.

Alex pushed open the bright red door and was immediately assailed with the scent of coffee beans. Pale birchwood floors, brick walls painted white, and large framed black and white photos of coffee plantations and their farmers created a warm hipster vibe. The café was filled with morning coffee drinkers. Alex saw

Pepper in a back corner, sipping something from a large white mug.

She waved and headed for the line, where, when her turn came, she requested a golden latte, a frothy milky drink mixed with turmeric, cinnamon, pepper, and ginger. Once she received her drink, she wound her way through the tables and slid into the booth across from Pepper. A yellow legal pad and several ink pens were set before her. She raised an eyebrow when she saw Alex's drink.

"Aren't we being healthy?"

Alex laughed. "Aunt Lidia says it helps the body process stress and anxiety, among other benefits, so why not." She took a tentative sip because it was clearly very hot, with steam rising from the mug. "And I like the taste."

Pepper gave the beverage a skeptical look. "I'll stick with my coffee, thanks. What did you find out from your cop cousin?"

Alex shared what she knew and then looked at Pepper expectantly. "What did you find out?"

"Using public records and the internet, I discovered that Neve Ryland was an only child. She grew up in Maryland, went to Johns Hopkins and double-majored in art history and mythological studies before completing a master's degree and a PhD in mythology."

Alex leaned forward. "She mentioned she wrote a paper on mythological weapons. I'd love to read it. Was it published anywhere?"

"Yes," Pepper said, checking her notes. "In the *Journal of Slavic Mythological Studies* about ten years ago. I tried to access it online, but apparently you can only find it in the print version."

"Make a note that we need to try and get that, please."

Pepper nodded as she wrote down her notes.

"She owned a townhouse in Washington, DC, that she rarely lived in because of her extensive traveling. She was staying at the

B&B in town and had been here for the past three weeks working on the mural."

"Any boyfriends? Past husbands?"

"Not that I could find." She picked up her cell phone, swiped and type for a minute, and shared the screen with Alex. "There's also a lot of information on her website." Pepper opened another tab, and an animated header cycled through Neve's most recent paintings. "I've read through it, and nothing jumps out at me." She clicked on the "Events" tab. "She traveled a lot, worked with a lot of corporations." She clicked on a "Murals" page that gave more detail about each painting Neve had done, the inspiration behind it, and the companies who'd sponsored the painting.

"I'll go through this tonight and see what I can find. Thanks, Pepper—this is all good stuff."

Pepper shrugged. "I wish there was more. Nothing screamed 'murderer,' at least not yet."

"No, it's good. It's a start." Then Alex shared the list of reception attendees who didn't have an alibi. "We'll have to speak to each one and find out if they had a relationship with Neve, some history or any reason to want to kill her."

Pepper shifted uncomfortably in her seat and played with her coffee cup.

"What is it? Is there something else?"

"I saw Celeste arguing with Neve in the park a week back or so. I didn't think too much about it. I know Celeste works for Wesley now, and they're sponsoring it, so maybe they were arguing about the direction of the painting or something . . . but now Celeste is on the no-alibi list." She grimaced. "Maybe I should tell the police."

"No," Alex said a bit too quickly. "Let me . . . I'll talk to her first. And if there's anything there, I'll tell Jack." She finished her drink and stood. "I'm going to check out the B&B, see if Neve left anything in her room that could be useful, maybe talk to the owner and see if he knows anything. And then I'll start talking with everyone on the list."

"And me?"

"Keep digging into Neve's past. There has to be something there we can use to break this case. And let's reconvene later in the week."

"Don't forget about our next festival planning meeting. At my parent's house this time. We can talk after."

On her way back to the shop, Alex called Celeste's cell phone. She needed to speak with her ASAP. The phone rang and eventually went to voicemail. Alex left a message, letting Celeste know that they needed to talk, that she wanted to make sure she was okay, and was she free for coffee later?

*   *   *

With Minka managing the shop, it was a perfect time for Alex to stop by the B&B, located a few blocks from the shop. Like Manhattan, downtown Bellamy Bay was pedestrian friendly, and she loved that she could walk everywhere she wanted to go, especially when the weather was nice.

She approached the B&B and hoped the front desk attendant would agree to let her search Neve's room. Black antique lampposts lined the brick path to a sweeping front porch dotted with black rocking chairs. The house itself was a large, three-story, white Victorian with gray trim, and the spacious front yard, exploding with a riot of blooms in yellow, red, and orange, was surrounded by a low wrought iron fence. A big brass pineapple decorated the door as well as the door mat.

The owner of the Seaside B&B, a man Alex had seen around town but never spoken to, greeted her from behind a wood counter when she entered the reception area, a space of oak paneling, dark blue carpet, and beach-themed wall decorations. The remnants of a full cooked breakfast scented the air. The foyer was lovely, and she imagined that Neve had probably really enjoyed staying at the house.

"Hi," she said in a cheery voice. "My name is Alex Daniels—I'm Lidia Sobieski's niece?" She'd discovered the best way to introduce herself in town was by referencing her aunt, whom everyone seemed to know and respect.

"Of course," the man, tall and lanky, probably in his late sixties, said with an easy grin. Mostly bald, with bushy eyebrows, brown eyes, and a large nose over thin lips, he smiled at her. His name tag read "Carson MacInnes, Proprietor."

"Clearly you're related," he said. "The hair, the shape of the eyes . . . I know her from our business association. What can I do for you?"

Great. This was the response she'd hoped for. "Mr. MacInness—"

"Please. Call me Mac—everyone does."

"Mac . . . my friend Neve Ryland stayed here—"

He groaned. "Such a sad story. Who would do such a thing?"

"I know, right? I was hoping to look around her room and see if she left anything that could help me figure that out."

He gave her a speculative look. "Are you a police officer like your cousin?" He grinned. "She's a feisty one."

"No. . . but I am helping out."

"Well, a friend—or family member of Lidia's is a friend to me. Not sure how much help it will be, but I can show you the artist's room." He came around the corner. "Right this way."

Alex followed him as he made small talk with her about the weather.

"You know, that artist was a real nice lady. Last time she was here, it was colder, and I told her she needed to come in the summer to see the town at its best. You remember that cold snap we had in May?"

Alex nodded, remembering the week in the beginning of May when everyone had needed to put light jackets on.

He chuckled. "I'm glad she took me up on my suggestion and came back—" He stopped, frowned, stumbling over his words. "Not to get killed, but to see the area when it was nice and warm . . . well, you know what I mean."

Alex patted his arm. "I know what you mean, Mac."

They went up one flight of stairs, turned right, and stopped at a large room at the end of the hall. The door had been left open, and police tape barred the entrance. Mac held the tape up and gestured for Alex to follow. She stepped inside and looked around. The room was beautiful and spacious, with a king-size platform bed in the center of the room. Four large posts dominated the bed, which was covered in a rich brocade burgundy comforter set and shams with gold tassels. There was an antique desk, an old wardrobe, a tall bureau, and a nightstand holding a brightly colored Tiffany lamp.

"As you can see, the police have already been here and thoroughly searched. Fortunately, they took care not to break anything. All antiques here. This was my grandmother's family home, you know."

"No, I didn't know that." Alex smiled, looking around the room. "It's lovely." An old-fashioned phone ring could be heard in the distance, and Mac stepped outside the room.

"I better take that. Be right back."

She waited for him to leave, then pulled a pair of latex gloves from her purse, the ones they used at the shop when working with lye to make soap. She opened drawers, peeked under the bed, opened the wardrobe, and searched the en suite bathroom. The police had been thorough. There was nothing left to be found.

She peeled off her gloves, placing them back in her purse, and returned to the front desk. Mac was just ending his phone call.

"Find anything?"

"Unfortunately, no."

"Hmm," he rubbed the gray whiskers on his chin, his bushy eyebrows knitted together in thought. "You know, Ms. Ryland left her sketchbook in the dining hall during breakfast the day she died. I was going to give it to her the next time I saw her. I doubt the police will want it. I flipped through it." He made a face. "Just a bunch of strange drawings." He retrieved a leather portfolio from behind the counter. "Would you like it?"

"Of course." The clock on the wall behind him chimed, and Alex realized she'd lost track of time. She needed to get back to the shop to relieve Minka.

Alex left without opening the book. She'd take a look at it later. With her head down as she texted Minka to let her know she'd be ten minutes late, she bumped into a man entering the B&B.

"Oh, sorry!" She looked up to see Bryce Greenberg grinning down at her.

"Where's the fire, Ms. Daniels?"

She laughed. "Late for work, that's all."

His eyes twinkled as a quizzical look appeared on his face. "What are you doing here?"

"Just running an errand."

He nodded, and his gaze fell to the portfolio in her hand, although he didn't say anything.

Alex's mind filled with questions and possibilities. He'd been staying at the same B&B as Neve. Surely, they'd have met over breakfast or in the hallways. What was their connection?

"How are you taking the news about Neve?"

He frowned and rocked back on his heels. "Ms. Ryland? It's horrible, of course."

"Did you know her well?"

"We talked during the evening wine-and-cheese reception."

Alex nodded, noting that he was neatly sidestepping her questions. "And you'd never met her before coming to town?"

A slow smile dawned on his face. "I'm beginning to feel like I'm being interrogated, Ms. Daniels."

"Sorry. I'm just curious about what happened. That's all. But since we're on the subject, what were you doing at eight thirty pm last night?" She smiled, hoping to soften her words. "If you don't mind."

He chuckled. "Wow. You *are* interrogating me. I have nothing to hide. Dylan and I stepped outside to get some fresh air and talk business."

"You're in town because of Dylan?"

"We're friends from college. We went to Duke University together. You have my card. Give me a call and we can talk herbs." He continued past her into the inn.

When Bryce was gone, Alex opened the sketchbook and was surprised to see a pocket on the backside cover. A sealed plastic sandwich bag was pushed to the bottom of the pocket. Alex pulled the bag out and looked inside. There was a scrap of paper with an address on it folded over multiple times so small that the small square could fit in the palm of Alex's hand.

Alex recognized the address as the old location of Bellamy Bay Realty, with Dylan's name and cell phone number. She needed to speak with him. She recalled him saying that he and Neve were going to tour the property. Why had Neve left this here? Was it an accident? Or meant for someone to pick up?

As Alex made her way back to the apothecary, she thought about Bryce. He seemed like a nice guy. And probably not the murderer. She'd confirm his alibi with Dylan so she could remove him from her list of suspects.

* * *

When Minka returned on her lunch break, Alex waited for her to slip her apron back on and step behind the counter before asking whether she'd mind if Alex left again. She explained that she wanted to stop by Wesley Inc. and talk to Dylan.

Minka's face was grim. "Anything to help solve this case, Alex. That's why you're going? You're investigating?"

"Yeah, I am. I texted Dylan when you were out, and he said he would be leaving town hall after a meeting, and we could talk. And I also want to learn more about his friend Bryce."

"Let me know what you find out."

* * *

Alex headed for the park and checked her phone. No messages from Celeste. She put the phone away and was suddenly aware of her appearance. As she approached the courtyard, she wished she'd dressed slightly better than jeans, athletic shoes, and the shop T-shirt. But it couldn't be helped, and besides she didn't want Dylan to be attracted to her anyway. Regardless, she pulled her hair out of its ponytail holder, shaking it out and running her fingers through it a few times before entering the park proper.

She passed the mermaid fountain and paused when she saw the mural. Stacks of flower bouquets, candles, and stuffed animals were set at the base, an impromptu memorial to the artist.

"She wasn't here in town long but she made quite an impact, didn't she?"

Alex turned around to see Dylan with a couple of to-go cups of sweet tea from a nearby beverage cart. Something about him called to her, made her want to wrap her arms around him and hold him tight, but she blinked it away. She was with Jack, she reminded herself. Alex took a cup. "Thank you."

He gestured toward a bench set directly across from the mural. "Want to sit?" Alex nodded and they both sat, gazing at the mural for a moment and sipping their drinks in silence.

"This is not how I planned for this event to go," he said quietly. "When I invited her to come to town."

His sadness was palpable, and if things hadn't been so awkward between them, she would've given him a hug. But she didn't want him to take the display of affection the wrong way. "You feel some-what responsible."

He nodded.

"You couldn't have known . . . it's not your fault." He gazed at the mural in front of them without comment. "Hopefully the police will find out who is responsible."

This time he looked at her, a hint of a smile on his face. "You're not mounting your own investigation like you did with Randy Bennett?"

She smiled and shook her head. "I'd rather not say."

"Because your boyfriend wouldn't be pleased."

She sipped on her tea and ignored his question. But she could feel the weight of his stare.

"When you called me, you said you had something to show me?"

Alex set her cup down and retrieved the bag from her purse. She told him how and where she'd found it. She handed him the address first. "Look familiar?"

"This is my family's old homestead."

"Why did Neve want a tour of that land?"

"Inspiration for the mural?" He shrugged. "There are scenic views there."

"You two spent a lot of time together. What did you talk about?"

"The usual stuff, but she wanted to know if any proof of the Mermaid of Warsaw's actual existence had surfaced in town."

"Like what?"

"Undeniable proof." He laughed. "Her sword, her shield."

"And has it? Bryn thought it was buried on your grounds. Any luck on finding either?"

"Not yet." He turned to look at the mural before speaking. "What do you think?"

Alex looked at the mural and considered his question. But first she had one of her own. "How'd you find her?"

"Referral from a friend."

She could see the recent events weighed heavily on him. "It's beautiful. It's thought provoking and now with it being her last work, famous."

Dylan stood. "Yes. That's what I thought too."

Alex also stood, and they began walking, when she stopped in front of the mermaid fountain. "Your friend Bryce . . . he said he was with you when Neve was killed."

His jaw tightened. "Yes, so?"

"Just trying to account for everyone at the reception and their whereabouts."

"It's like I thought. You are investigating."

She gave him a direct look. "You're his alibi, and he's yours. Anyone else see you two at that time?"

"Really? I'm on your list of suspects too? Again." He chuckled and shook his head in disbelief. "Sometimes, Aleksandra Daniels, you're just too much."

"No, I don't think—I just needed to . . ." But he'd already stood and begun walking off.

And Alex was left staring at the mermaid fountain.

Chapter Eight

When Alex returned to the shop, she saw Kamila leaning against the counter, talking to Minka.

"You returned just in time," Minka said. "Kam was just giving me an update on the case. And then you can share what you know."

Kamila gave Alex a hard look. "I hope you're not doing what I think you're doing. Detective Frazier won't like it."

Alex's smile was enigmatic. "I was just out for a stroll." She wrapped an apron around her waist. "What do you have for us?"

"We're still looking for the weapon. It's nowhere on the premises, that's for sure."

"Any idea what it is?" Minka asked, lowering her voice.

Alex shook her head. "No one is sure except to say that it was hard and heavy and possibly organic in nature."

"Organic, like a piece of wood—"

"Or a brick or rock or something," she said grimly. "Yeah. Savage, right? There's also no clear security footage showing the director's office."

"But there's cameras all over the museum—I've seen them," Minka protested.

"Yeah. Near the exhibits, but not for the offices."

Kamila's phone chimed with a text. She read the message and groaned.

"What's wrong?" Alex asked, nudging her shoulder.

"It's the wife of the man who OD'ed in the woods. She's been calling the station every day, asking for updates."

"Poor woman," Alex said. "I'm sure handling the death is difficult, but to know it was because of drugs . . ."

Kamila shrugged. "People should remember to 'just say no' to drugs. You know? Alright, the mean streets of Bellamy Bay are calling. I gotta go."

*   *   *

With Kamila gone and Minka in the backroom, the shop floor was quiet. Alex checked her phone. Nothing from Celeste. She was beginning to think her friend was avoiding her. Alex knew that she was probably at work and very busy, but it wasn't like her not to respond.

Shaking her head, she opened up her laptop and went to a search window. Celeste couldn't have murdered Neve, and the best way to prove that was to find the person who actually had done it. Beginning with Jack's list of those who didn't have alibis. First up was Dylan's friend. She wanted to learn more about Bryce Greenberg.

Alex retrieved his business card and typed in the website of his company. An image of an American flag rippling in a gentle breeze appeared. She clicked on the "About" page and then "Tarheel Defense Team," and saw a glossy headshot of Bryce. The bio underneath said he was originally from Charlotte, North Carolina, had an MBA, and was an officer in the US Army before taking over the company his father had founded a couple decades earlier.

She clicked around and saw that Pepper was right: he had numerous contracts with the Department of Defense, though the specifics of the contracts were not stated. A quick search online revealed that Bryce didn't have any social media accounts, and she couldn't find any connection between him and Neve.

Sighing, Alex closed the laptop. She'd have to talk to Bryce in person. Maybe she'd have better luck then.

* * *

After dinner, Alex took a long, hot shower using the Sweet Dreams soap bar from the shop, changed into a soft T-shirt and pajama bottoms, and hopped onto her bed. Athena leaped up alongside her, taking a few moments to get comfortable as she circled the bed, finally coming to rest with her nose nuzzling Alex's legs. Alex opened her laptop and went to Neve's website. She had some research to do.

She looked at the artist's list of previous scheduled appearances. Neve had led a busy life, traveling often for painting assignments, staying in towns for a month or so at a time, and apparently being wined and dined by her sponsors as well as local politicians and celebrities, if the photographs were any indication.

Under "Recent Murals" were three beautiful images created by Neve in the past year. A mural of Poseidon welding his trident over rolling waves; the Norse god, Thor, holding his hammer, and another of a languidly beautiful Asian woman holding several jewels. It was clear that Neve had been fascinated with mythological deities beyond the Mermaid of Warsaw.

Each mural had been painted in a different city: Poseidon and his trident in Boston, Watasumi's Tide Jewels in Honolulu, Thor in St. Cloud. Alex couldn't discern a pattern beyond the theme of mythology.

She opened her eyes and texted Pepper, telling her about the findings on Neve's website, and asked her for help researching the paintings. When Pepper asked what she hoped to find, Alex could only tell her she didn't know. Just to check, please.

After Pepper responded that she was on it, Alex decided to call Celeste. Drinking her tea, she dialed the number and wasn't surprised when it went straight to voicemail. She went back to her laptop and searched for Neve's website. Her scroll was endless, and the effects of the Sweet Dream soap and the Calm Down tea were making it impossible for Alex to keep her eyes open. She was just about to nod off, when her head snapped up.

She was staring at a picture of Neve. She was in a gallery or museum, standing with a crowd of people wearing evening wear and holding drinks. Jasper was in the row behind her, and while his grin was wide for the camera, his gaze was on the back of her head.

Jasper had lied. He had known Neve.

Chapter Nine

Today was Alex's turn to open up Botanika.

The clock had just chimed nine, and she'd just unlocked the front door when Pepper bustled into the store.

"Heard the latest?"

"Good morning to you too." Alex grinned. She reached behind her to turn on the low mood music that always played in the store.

Pepper moved around the shop, restlessly smelling items from the new candle table. "Remember that big news Tegan Wesley was so closemouthed about?" Alex nodded. "Well, it was posted on Twitter this morning. Wesley Inc. purchased four companies." She rattled off the names of the companies. "Apparently about two thousand employees will lose their jobs. And really random industries—I don't understand Dylan's strategy. But anyway, one company specializes in language studies, one creates new source materials for industry, and—"

"Wait," Alex interrupted. "What was the last company you just named?"

"Tarheel Defense. Why? Ring a bell?"

"Yes. It's Bryce Greenberg's company. And Dylan just acquired it. That doesn't sound like real estate development. What does Tarheel Defense do exactly?"

Pepper's eyes widened. "I've heard of them. Last year, I researched an article dealing with Camp Malveaux and they were one of the companies involved. "They are a veteran-owned company with some major contracts with the Department of Defense. They make weapons, I believe."

"Since when has Wesley been in the business of war?"

Pepper shrugged. "Who knows? And I'll take these." She held up several bars of pink and purple soap and handed them to Alex. "Anyway, my dad says it will be good for the town. Bring more jobs."

"This must be the top-secret thing Celeste is working on." Speaking of which, Celeste had never called her back. She thought, not enjoying the feeling of foreboding churning in her stomach.

Pepper took her shopping bag. "I've got my research intern looking into Neve's past commission. I also gave him the name of everyone on Jack's list, and he can see if there's a match with her prior sponsors. It's probably a wild goose chase, but we'll see."

"Thanks, Pepper. I appreciate it. Say, listen . . . have you heard your father talking about doing business with Leviathan Industries?" Pepper gave her a blank look, so Alex continued. "Minka heard that it's a sea mining company, and she's concerned that he's interested in getting your father's permission to mine off the coast of Bellamy Bay."

"I know that Mr. Blue has been out with my father for drinks and golf a few times, but I can't imagine my father every agreeing to let someone harm our coast in that manner. His family founded this town. He loves it—he wouldn't want to see it destroyed."

"Of course. I just wondered . . ."

"I can ask, of course, but I'm certain Mr. Blue is only in town for the festival and nothing more."

* * *

Later that night, after a busy day at the shop, Alex made herself a cup of matcha and lemongrass tea before heading to her bedroom. She called Celeste again, but her phone went straight to voicemail. Now Alex knew Celeste was avoiding her. She'd left another message expressing her concern for her and telling her it was urgent that they speak, that Jack considered her a suspect—all information she explicitly did not want to share in a message, but desperately needed to relay. Resolved that she'd said all that she could in a three-minute message, she set her phone down and looked around the room, her gaze falling on the portfolio Mac had given her.

She retrieved it from her dresser, sat in a chair, and began flipping through it. She sipped her tea, then froze when she saw the first image. And then the second. And the third. She was shocked to find horrific images of war and devastation. One image after another was a colorful, chaotic scene of death.

Alex had been expecting mermaids and gods, but this was disturbing. What would cause Neve to create such horrible images? She went to her laptop and returned to Neve's website, searching for her paintings again. She found them and clicked through all the images. There was nothing that compared to the violent sketches in the portfolio.

She returned to her laptop and searched on "Wesley Inc. and pharmaceuticals" and came up with nothing. She did the same for "Leviathan" and was left with no hits. Then she searched "Tarheel Defense" and found something: an old *Carolina Business News* article discussing the two divisions of Tarheel Defense: Pro-Tek and Bio-Tek, it's bioweaponry arm.

She stared at the screen. How had she missed this during her first search? Here was a connection. Bryce owned a company that created pharmaceuticals and biological organisms and viruses as weapons. And Dylan had purchased it? Was this the same company that Neve had mentioned in reference to the mermaid gene?

She searched for Neve's name along with "Bio-Tek" and got several hits. Eighteen months ago, Neve had created a small mural inside the cafeteria of the Bio-Tek campus. Bryce was the CEO of that company. He might want to keep Neve quiet about something she'd learned. Finally, someone besides Celeste with a potential motive. And Bryce had lied. He had to have known Neve before he arrived in town.

* * *

The next day after work, Alex went home for a quick shower, and she and Minka drove to Pepper's parents' home to attend a social gathering for the mermaid festival event planners and sponsors. Minka had explained that it was mostly social, but some business would be covered.

Alex was looking forward to the party, not because of the festival but because she wanted to show Pepper Neve's drawings and finally get the chance to corner Celeste.

The Bellamys lived in a large white Greek Revival home with towering columns, black shutters, and a portico. The property was only a few blocks away from downtown and was one of several large historic estates built by the town's founders. Alex and Minka parked on the street and were greeted by Pepper, who wore a fancy yellow party dress with a boat collar, butterfly sleeves, and a sash around the waist.

"Don't laugh," she muttered as she ushered Alex inside. "My mother made me dress up."

A waiter in formal attire hovered in the background, providing cold drinks, tea sandwiches, and delicate pastries. The group, including Yuko, Josephine, and Celeste, were already seated when Alex arrived. She hadn't gotten the memo that the attire was Southern tea party, but fortunately she'd dressed somewhat appropriately in white capris, heeled sandals, and a blouse.

She tried to catch Celeste's eye, but her friend was busy looking at her notes. Alex telepathed her instead. *We need to talk.*

Celeste looked up and smiled at her. *Sure. Later.*

And Alex relaxed. Maybe it was her imagination, and Celeste wasn't avoiding her.

During the course of the meeting, Pepper's father stepped in to say hello. Montgomery Blue was with him, and Minka frowned.

Don't do it, Alex telepathed to her cousin. But it was too late.

"Mayor," she began, "are you and Mr. Blue discussing mining off our coast?"

The men looked at each other, and the mayor gave Minka a wide grin. "We did just return from a meeting over steak and whiskey," he said, chuckling. "And we were talking business, but no, of course we weren't discussing disturbing the beauty of our beaches. I know that people are talking, but I want to assuage any concerns you or anyone may have. Montgomery and I are talking about collaborating on a few civic-minded projects, but nothing related to mining." He pressed a hand to his heart. "I love this land. My great-great-grandfather founded our town two hundred years ago, making a treaty with the local Native Americans and . . ."

Pepper leaned toward Minka, muttering, "Why did you ask him about this? He'll talk for hours about how much he loves the land."

Montgomery stepped forward. "I'm fortunate enough to have made a lot of money in my life." He shrugged. "I just want to give back in a meaningful way. My company has a nongovernmental organization that's done good works, but we can do more."

His gaze touched everyone in the room, and Alex could feel the silky, soothing effect of his words. "After spending time in this beautiful community, I know helping you all preserve the pristine beauty of your beaches and sea life is the right thing to do. And besides, I would never do anything the citizens of Bellamy Bay didn't want." He smiled, his gaze falling on Minka. "You're a member of the local preservation society, yes?"

Minka glanced at Alex in surprise. "I am. I'm the secretary, actually, and very involved."

"Perfect. You and I should schedule some time to chat. You're just the kind of person I'm looking for to join my organization." His grin widened. "We all want to save the world, don't we?"

"Of course." Minka nodded, somehow clearly smitten with the man. "I'd love to talk preservation. It's my favorite topic, second only to herbs."

But Alex was concerned. She wasn't sure why, but she was. Montgomery didn't have an alibi for Neve's murder, for starters. She needed to speak to him. He turned to look at her, almost as if he'd heard her thoughts and smiled at her. A little taken aback, Alex returned the smile. She'd probably been staring at him, and he'd felt her gaze on him. She looked away, feeling embarrassed.

After the gathering broke up, Alex saw Montgomery at the mayor's side. And then Bronson excused himself. *Now is my chance,* she thought to herself.

She approached him and stuck out her hand. "Alex Daniels. Nice to meet you."

He took the proffered hand and gave it a firm shake. "Montgomery Blue. And I know who you are."

"You do?"

"You're one of the Sobieski clan."

"That's right." Alex felt a little off-balance under his piercing gaze. "How are you finding our town?"

"It's lovely. And might be perfect for what I have in mind."

Alex couldn't bite her tongue fast enough. "Mining?"

"You people have a one-track mind." He chuckled. "No, I'm interested in buying a beach home. I'm looking at Ocracoke, Bald Head Island, and here."

"Ah. That's why you want to save our beaches. Sorry, you had to come when we had a murder. Did you know Neve Ryland?"

He chuckled, his dark eyes gleaming with amusement. "I've heard about you and your sleuthing. On the case, are we?"

She noted that he hadn't answered her question.

"I'm familiar with her work. Her loss will be felt in the art community, I'm sure." He glanced toward the mayor, who looked up and waved him over. "If you'll excuse me?"

Well, that went nowhere, Alex thought, sighing. Then she looked around to find Celeste, who was standing by a dessert table, selecting mini-pastries from a beautiful tiered silver tray. She went to her, smiling. "How are you? We haven't talked since—"

"Please don't remind me," Celeste said as she took her saucer of petit fours and moved to a chair. Alex followed, sitting beside her.

"Maybe you should talk to someone, if you don't want to talk to me, about what happened. About what you saw?"

Celeste closed her eyes, a pained expression on her face, and shook her head. "That's the thing. I don't want to talk about it."

"Are you sure? I'm here for you if—"

"Look, I got all of your messages. And I appreciate your concern. But I don't want to talk about it. And that's final." Her voice was firm as she turned to Alex with a hard look. "Please." She softened her voice. "I just want to forget it happened."

Alex placed a hand on her arm. "You know Jack thinks you did it. Where were you between eight thirty and nine pm?"

"I went outside."

Alex groaned. "Alone?"

"Yes. I know it looks bad, but I just needed some fresh air. Can you just leave this alone, please?"

Alex crossed her arms. "You know me better than that, right?"

Celeste rolled her eyes then nodded. "I'd just confronted Jasper about Neve. He said it was nothing, that I was imagining things. I didn't believe him. I was upset, I needed to calm down, so I went to the gardens in the back of the museum and sat on a bench by the statue of Captain Bellamy. It's by the little pond and just . . . It was a full moon, okay? It's appealing the way the moonlight glistens off the water. It was calming for me."

"And no one saw you out there? Nobody can vouch for your whereabouts?"

"I wanted to be alone," Celeste repeated, her voice firm. "No one was there."

"I'm afraid Jack is going to try to blame this on you. If you know anything that could help your case, you need to—"

Celeste stood abruptly. "There's nothing that can prove my innocence. In fact, it's probably the opposite."

"What do you mean?"

"Just forget it." Celeste set her plate on a nearby table, grabbed her purse, said her goodbyes to everyone, and left without another word to Alex.

Alex stared after her wondering why she was acting so strange. Almost acting like she was… guilty.

After Celeste stormed of, Alex went to the coatroom, where she'd stored her purse and the portfolio, and retrieved the leather-bound book. She gestured for Pepper to join her, and they stepped onto the porch together.

"This is the portfolio I was telling you about."

Pepper leaned over her shoulder with interest. "Oh right, the weird sketches."

They were more than just sketches, though. They were full-color drawings so bright, so vivid that they were garish in the depictions they portrayed. Alex begin to flip through the pages. "What do you think?"

Pepper put a hand to her mouth. "Oh my. What am I looking at here?"

"Not sure. It seems to be mythological in nature. Gods reigning down destruction on the mortals?"

"Neve was such a positive ray of light. Why on earth would she draw such . . . darkness? It's just horrible." Pepper looked away, pained, and then returned. "Let me see more."

Alex had just flipped to another page when Yuko stepped onto the porch, closed her eyes, and took a deep breath. When she opened them, she saw Alex smiling at her, and she laughed.

"Sorry, these types of meetings masquerading as tea parties are so tedious. I just need some air."

"Of course," Alex said. "We all do."

Yuko came closer. "What are you two looking at?"

"Just some drawings," Alex said quickly, trying to close the portfolio.

But Pepper was too quick for her. "This is Neve Ryland's work. Pretty gruesome. Take a look."

"Poor woman," Yuko began. "After she came to town, she made me think I should have a mural created in the restaurant. Something—" She glanced down at the artwork. "Oh." She stopped and frowned at the pages. "Well, not like this. I was thinking cherry blossoms, pineapples, kudzu, and scuppernongs." Lines creased her forehead. "I know about this . . ." She looked at the women. "Do you know what you're looking at?"

Pepper shook her head. "Not at all."

"My father used to tell me this story. It's about a Japanese sea god who used magical gems to control the tides." She laughed. "It's a fantastic story of dragons and sea gods that terrified me when I was younger. In fact, I used to tell my son the same story. But instead of frightening him, I think it made him join the Marines like his father did." A fond smile moved fleeting over her lips. "He's always wanted to slay a dragon."

* * *

After work, Alex was sitting at a table for two at Sushi Ya'll.

Jack texted her when she and Minka were on their way home from the meeting. He wanted to meet for dinner, and she had agreed, suggesting Yuko's restaurant. Once seated, they took a moment to look at the menu of items that fused down-home Southern entrées with Japanese delicacies. After the waitress took their order, Jack asked Alex about the festival planning. She gave him an update and then asked him about the case.

The waitress brought their drinks, bubble sweet tea—a mixture of black tea, sugar, lemon juice, milk, and tapioca pearls—for Alex and a cold bottle of Japanese beer for Jack. Jack sipped at his beverage. "I'm afraid you're not going to like it."

"Celeste?"

"Yes. I've reviewed footage from around town. And we found something very surprising."

"What?"

He hesitated before bringing the bottle to his lips. "I used facial recognition software to find all of the video with Neve on it, and in several locations Celeste is also there. Apparently, Celeste was following Neve. She can be seen in several clips, skulking in the background."

"Skulking?" Alex scoffed. "Really?" He nodded. "Can't it just be an odd coincidence?"

"Celeste thought Neve was having an affair with Jasper Collins, right? And she was angry enough, emotional enough, to slap him."

"Yes." Alex pressed her lips into a grim line. "So why haven't you brought her in for more questioning? Or arrested her."

"Don't worry. I will. I'm just compiling more evidence, so when I talk to her, she'll see the futility of her situation and just cave."

Alex couldn't hide the look of anger and disgust on her face. She pushed away from the table, rising. "You're doing it again," she said, her voice low but insistent. "You're going after someone I care about." She looked around the restaurant, saw that customers were watching her. "I need some air. I'll just—I'll be back." She hurried to the reception area, which was thankfully empty.

A moment later, Jack appeared. His lips were pressed in a grim line, and the lines between his eyebrows were deep. He took a step toward her. "Alex, I'm sorry. I know you and Celeste are close. But I'm just following the evidence. I'm just doing my job. You know that."

Alex shook her head, pushing away his outstretched hand. "Did you know Celeste and I are cousins? Distantly but still. She's family. My entire life it was just me and my dad. Do you know how lonely I felt?" Jack began to shake his head, to open his mouth to say something, but she interrupted him. "And then I came to Bellamy Bay and I have so much family, so much love. I've never experienced anything like it. I just want to protect them, to protect what I've found." Her nose began to smart, her eyes filling with tears—angry tears. She wiped them away. "And then there's *you*, always you trying to take away the people I love."

Gently, he grabbed her by both arms and brought her close to him forcing her to look into his eyes. "Alex, I promise you it's not like that. I'm not trying to hurt you. I'm not after your family. All I want to do is keep this town safe. I want to keep you safe. Protect you."

Alex remained tense for a moment, but his calm voice and steady demeanor soothed her, and she relaxed in his grasp, her anger gone as quickly as it appeared.

He caressed her cheek, one finger outlining her lips. "I care so much about you, even if you can't see that."

She closed her eyes, pressing her forehead against his chest for a moment. "I'm sorry. I didn't mean to—I know you're doing your job. It just feels so personal. And I have this compulsion to *do* something." She pulled back, looking up at him, taking in his sincere gaze. She knew his sentiments were heartfelt. She'd grown up around men like him—her father, his friends. Men who just wanted to do the right thing no matter what. Sighing, she mustered a smile for his benefit. "I get it. Serving justice is important to you. It was the same with my father."

He gave her a tired look. "I'm glad you understand. It's not always fun, but I do sleep well at night, knowing I'm on the right side of things." He watched her for a moment. "You okay?" She nodded and he smiled. "How about we return to our meal then?"

Moments later they were back at their table, and the waitress brought their food. Alex had ordered the fried chicken sushi rolls with a side of tempura bread and butter pickles, and groaned when she saw all of the food.

"This is too much. You're going to have to help me—with the pickles at least."

He chuckled, glancing at his own curry rice dish with sweet potatoes, buttered corn, honey carrots, and a side of fried chicken yakitori in a vinegar-based BBQ sauce. "I don't even know what bread and butter pickles are."

"They're just sweet and spicy instead of sour and flavored with dill. Aunt Lidia cans her own and they're delicious."

"Give me good ol' dill. But I'll live dangerously and try one."

Alex pushed her plate toward him, lifted up a golden-fried chip, and took a bite after a quick inspection. His eyes widened and he moaned in satisfaction. "Wow. These are good." He forked several more and put them on his plate.

Alex laughed. "Told you."

They ate in compatible silence, and Alex tried not to think about how much trouble Celeste was in. But then Jasper entered the restaurant, standing at the take-out counter. She stood, excusing herself.

Jack looked toward the entrance and shook his head. "Alex," he said in a warning voice.

"I'm just going to say hello."

Jack pushed his plate away and wiped his mouth with his napkin. "Right."

Alex smiled, hoping she looked friendly as she approached Jasper. He was just paying for his order when she arrived at the counter. "Hi, Jasper, how are you?"

"As well as I can be, considering someone I worked closely with was bludgeoned in my office." He glanced over her shoulder at Jack and raised an eyebrow. "Has your boyfriend found the culprit? Please tell me he's at least making headway."

"Jack doesn't discuss his investigations with me." She gave him a curious look. "But since you brought it up . . . any idea who did it?"

His hand tightened on his brown bag. "No. Why should I?"

"Neve was found in your office for starters. And Celeste seems to think that you had a relationship with her. Did you?"

A look of indignation disturbed his refined features. "Of course not. She asked me if she could use my office to make a private call, and I agreed."

"A call. She wasn't meeting someone there?"

"Not to my knowledge, no." He frowned, taking in her expression. "You don't believe me, do you?"

"You've really upset Celeste, and now she's mixed up in this murder investigation—"

"Because of me, you think?" He cleared his throat. "I had nothing to do with Neve's murder."

"Celeste is my friend. And I'm going to help her if I can."

A look of scorn twisted his features for a moment before he smiled at her. "I heard you fancy yourself a detective." He chuckled. "Good luck with that." He held up his bag. "I've been tasked with bringing dinner for me and Celeste. She's been craving sweet potato pie mochi, I dare not disappoint."

At the word "craving," Alex thought of Neve and her impending pregnancy. "Any idea who Neve was dating in the past few months?"

His jaw tightened. "No, not all. In fact, to my knowledge, she wasn't seeing anyone. Her schedule would've made that difficult." He fixed an inquisitive gaze on her. "Why would you ask that?"

"Oh, no reason." She looked over her shoulder. "One more question, if you don't mind."

He gave her a peevish look. "What is it?"

"Did you know Neve before she came to town?"

He didn't blink, and his eyes looked directly into her own. "No."

"I better get back to my dinner date as well."

His smile was perfunctory. "Good night, then."

Alex was on her way back to the table when she bumped into Yuko, who was staring worriedly at her phone.

"Hey, everything okay?"

The woman looked up, automatically smiling. "How was your meal? Everything okay there?"

Alex nodded.

Yuko's gaze went back to her phone, and her eyes were filled with concerned. "Sorry, it's my family in Okinawa. A horrible tidal wave hit the island a week ago, and now it seems another is on its way."

"That's horrible. I hope your family will be okay."

"Yes, I'm sure they'll be fine. My father says the Chinese government is behind it."

"Behind what—the tidal wave? How is that even possible? It's nature."

"I'm not sure. They're clever. Motivated. Maybe they've invented something that causes seismic activity, enough to create a tidal wave."

Alex shot her a dubious look.

"In other news," Yuko continued, "the battle over the Senkaku Islands is heating up again."

Alex knew from watching the news that the ownership of the islands in the East China sea was in dispute, with Japan claiming ownership while both China and Taiwan insisted it belonged to them. After the discovery of oil under the island a few decades back, a cold war of sorts had developed between the countries.

"Apparently, while the mainland was dealing with the aftermath of the tidal wave, Chinese soldiers took up positions on the island, and now they won't leave." She shrugged. "I'm sorry—it's a very old problem these islands." She wiped away a tear. "Thank you for coming. Come again soon."

By the time Alex made it back to her table, Jack was finishing up a call. He eyed her for a moment before speaking. "You'll be interested to know that forensics came in, and we think Neve was hit in the head with some sort of rock. Two blows to the side of her head. Flecks of a rare mineral were found in her wounds. It's so rare that our techs couldn't identify it. They've sent it off to a lab in Raleigh for advanced tests."

Alex sipped her tea. "No one just carries a rock around with them. It had to have already been in Jasper's office, don't you think?" Jack shrugged. "Someone picked up something already in Jasper's office and in an argument hit her with it. So maybe it wasn't premeditated. It has the hallmarks of a crime of passion, right?"

"Yeah, like a jealous girlfriend who was confronting her boyfriend's lover."

"Jasper just spoke to me about Neve. There's a photo of the two of them together on her website that says otherwise."

Jack shrugged. "Sorry, Alex. He may be a liar, but he doesn't have motive. At least none that I've found."

Panic bloomed in Alex's chest. There had to be another suspect. "Do you know if Neve was seeing anyone in town? Did you see her with anyone else on that footage?"

"You know I shouldn't be sharing this with you, but she did spend a lot of time with Jasper, but also Dylan Wesley . . . and Montgomery Blue."

"Montgomery?"

He nodded. "But Dylan and Montgomery brought her to town, so it's not strange that they were together. Honestly, same for Jasper Collins. She was working with him on the museum exhibit."

Alex's stomach took a dive. "We're back to Celeste?"

"Pretty much."

"How long before you bring her in."

"Why? What are you going to do?"

Alex was going to try to find another suspect, that's what. But she couldn't tell him that. She understood that he had a job to do, but she had one as well: protecting those she loved. She gave him a noncommittal look in response.

"Means, motive, and opportunity," Jack said. "As the daughter of a former detective, you know how it goes. Celeste has motive—jealousy, well established by the video of her stalking the victim and the argument and slap that many people, including you, overheard at the museum."

Alex wanted to cover her ears with her hands, but he wasn't done.

"She does not have an alibi for the time that Neve was murdered. So, there's opportunity. Physical evidence already places her at the scene of the crime."

"I know," Alex said, frowning. "I know . . ." She exhaled loudly. "So . . . the rock?"

"Yeah. I learned my lesson with your aunt. I don't want to bring in the wrong person, so I'm waiting, hoping we can find the murder weapon that will hopefully have Celeste's fingerprints on it."

"Not hopefully," Alex insisted.

"You know what I mean."

"What about Jasper Collins? Does he have an alibi? If it was something from his office, his fingerprints would be on it. Maybe he was having an affair with her and wanted to keep her quiet once Celeste found out. How can you say for certain that it's Celeste, but not him?"

"I've thought of that too. If Celeste didn't already look guilty as sin, he'd be my number-one suspect."

Alex stared off into the distance.

Jack groaned. "I don't like that look."

She returned her gaze to him. "What look?"

"The look that says you think you can do my job better than me."

"Have you considered that there could be another motive?"

Anger shadowed his face. "No." He ran a hand through his hair. "You know something I don't?"

Alex played with her napkin for a moment, wondering how she could tell him about the mermaid gene and how Neve felt her life could be in danger. "Neve told me she learned something from one of the companies she worked for that could've put her life in jeopardy. A sort of corporate secret."

"You're talking about industrial espionage. Any proof of this?"

"No, not yet," she said firmly.

He rolled his eyes. "Great. I've just given you your mission, haven't I?"

She gave him an innocent look. "No. I'll just let you do your job." She smiled sweetly and patted his hand. "Sounds like you're on the right track."

He was annoyed—Alex could tell by the way his jaw was set. She paid the bill, and he left the tip and walked her to Minka's car.

"Stay out of it, Alex."

She faked a smile for his benefit. "How long before you arrest Celeste?"

"Alex, don't be like this."

"How long?"

"A few days. Maybe a week. Waiting on more forensic reports and hopefully for my officers to find the weapon."

"You're going to search Celeste's home, aren't you?" Alex said. Jack crossed his arms over his chest and looked at her. "Don't worry, I'll find you another suspect," she added.

"Alex," he called to her, but she'd already jumped into her car, slammed the door, and revved the engine.

*　*　*

The next morning, Alex asked her aunt if she could have the day off. She needed to find Jack a suspect—any suspect. First, she'd begin with Bryce.

Alex greeted Mac when she entered the Seaside B&B. He was seated behind the reception counter, reading the paper.

"Morning," he replied, as he set the paper down carefully, folding it back in order.

Alex glanced down at the newspaper and then turned it around to read an article on the bottom of the page. There was a black and white headshot of a man in his mid-forties, smiling into the camera. Clean-cut. Glasses. Nice friendly smile. The headline stated, *"Recent Software Engineer's Death Still Unsolved."*

Mac followed her gaze and frowned. "A shame, isn't it. By all accounts, he was an upstanding citizen with a good job, decent friends, and a normal life."

"But it was a drug overdose, right?"

He shook his head. "It's sad. Left behind a wife and kid. The article says none of his friends, family, or coworkers knew him to have a drug problem."

"That is strange. But Detective Frazier is on the case." She smiled. "He'll figure it out soon."

"Yes, that and the lady painter too." He eyed her curiously. "What can I do for ya?"

She looked around the reception area. "Any chance that Bryce Greenberg is in his room?"

He pointed down the hall. "He's eating breakfast."

"Thank you. If you don't mind, I'll just pop in and say hello?" Mac nodded, already returning to his paper.

Alex went to the dining room and saw a long table full of family-style served dishes.

Bryce was sitting at a side table, his plate heaped with eggs, bacon, and fried potatoes. "You're back. Join me?"

Alex poured herself a cup of coffee. She sat with Bryce and wondered the best way to get her questions answered.

"You're ready to talk herbs?" he asked, grinning.

"Sure," she said, and decided that if they talked about herbal remedies, she could steer the conversation toward his biotech company. "What's your interest?"

He drained his cup of coffee and set it down. "Actually, business. My company has a pharmaceutical division—Bio-Tek. Our research team is constantly looking to nature for new product ideas."

Alex almost choked on her coffee. He'd brought the subject up for her. She covered up her surprise by coughing.

"You okay?" he asked, lines curving around his eyes as he smiled at her.

"Yes, I'm fine." She looked at him. "We have more in common than I thought."

He nodded. "Yeah. That's why I wanted to talk to you. In fact, Dylan said I should make a point of talking to you. I'd love to get a closer look at some of your products. Dylan told me how popular and effective they are."

"Your company was recently acquired by Wesley Inc., correct?"

"Correct."

"Why?"

Doing his best Godfather impression, with the accompanying face and hand gestures, he said in a gravelly voice, "Dylan made me an offer I couldn't refuse."

"Dylan always seems to get what he wants." Alex laughed.

He winked at her. "Almost."

"What was the deal? If you don't mind me asking?"

"Triple the worth of the company, a position on the board, and a vice president position within Wesley Inc."

"For their new division."

"That's right."

"And this new division's focus?"

"Defense."

"Against?"" Alex asked.

"Against all enemies, foreign and domestic."

"And that includes pharmaceuticals."

His lips moved into an impressed moue. "Wow. You don't stop do you?"

"Let's just say I'm motivated to find the truth."

"So you'll help me figure this out?" She gave him a pointed look, and he nodded. "Wesley acquired both divisions . . . for security?"

"I'm sure you know that biological products can be used as weapons."

"Is that what you're producing?"

He wagged a finger at her, amusement in his eyes. "I didn't say that."

"But you didn't say you weren't." Why was he being so obtuse? It was almost as if he was hiding something. She felt like she was past the point of being impolite with him, but she couldn't stop. "Why did Dylan buy a group of companies only to shut them down, but then keep yours open, dissolved into Wesley?"

Bryce shrugged. "You'll have to ask him that."

Alex focused on her mug, considering what she'd just learned. Dylan was up to something again. She remembered the mermaid gene. "Are you also working on genetic-based solutions?"

He lowered his voice. "Where did you hear that?"

"Around." He looked skeptical, so she tried again. "Online. I've been reading the business trades lately. Speculation mostly."

He rubbed a hand over his stubble beard. "Shouldn't be any speculation. All of our employees sign NDAs. But I can say that

122

medicines based on individual DNA is the next big thing in my line of work."

It was possible his company worked on the mermaid gene. But also possible it was a company she'd never heard of . . . Was there a connection with Neve? *There has to be,* Alex mused to herself.

"Did Neve Ryland paint a mural for your company in Greensboro?" Alex held her breath waiting for the answer.

"No."

She exhaled in irritation. She was getting nowhere with this case.

"It was in Morrisville, actually. Our Bio-Tek campus is separate."

She tried to hide her surprise. There was a connection. He did know Neve. Morrisville, Alex knew, was a suburb of Raleigh and Durham, and part of Research Triangle Park. Bio-Tek had to be the company researching the so-called mermaid gene.

"What was the subject of the mural?"

He eyed her for a moment, then smiled. "Mermaids."

Chapter Ten

Alex covered up her surprise with a cough.

"The ocean environment is integral to our research," Bryce explained. "I wanted a mural that reflected our focus." He stood. "I'm getting more coffee. Would you like some?"

"Yes, please." Alex watched Bryce as he stood at the coffee bar, wondering if he was capable of murder. He had a motive—keeping Neve quiet. Surely he had the means. He was a healthy, able-bodied man capable of overpowering a woman. But would he have done it in such a manner? The brutality of the crime smacked of passion and impulse, and Bryce just didn't seem the type. Of course, appearances could be deceiving.

He grinned at her over his shoulder. "Decaf or regular?"

"Regular," Alex said, still distracted by her thoughts. *Did he have opportunity? Where was he when the crime was committed?*

Bryce returned with a fresh cup of coffee. "Thank you," she said, smiling up at him. She poured cream from a small silver pitcher into her mug and stirred. "I'd love to hear more about your genetic research. It sounds very interesting."

"I can talk shop all day long, but I am limited by the NDAs I've signed with our government partners. What do you want to know?"

"Obviously, I have mermaids on the brain," she began lightly. "What with the mermaid festival planning and all. I'd love to know what a mermaid mural has to do with your research."

"We're working on a series of products—still in the research stage—based on marine life, algae, coral . . . things that could be used to help create cures and therapies for cancer, Alzheimer's . . . I thought a mural of a mermaid under the sea would be a fun way to highlight our work."

"Have you made any interesting discoveries experimenting with sea life?"

His eyes glittered. "Perhaps."

She suppressed a groan. *More ambiguity.* "Anything you can discuss?"

"I could, but I'd have to kill you." He raised one eyebrow, his expression bland. And then he dissolved into laughter. "I love saying that. Never gets old."

Alex stared at him, not sure how to respond. But then she cracked a smile. "You're kidding?"

"Of course. I mean, yeah, I'm working for a government agency and I can't discuss it. But I wouldn't kill—" He stopped, smile sliding off his face for a moment. "Oh, you're good." He leaned back in his chair. "Wow." He fiddled with his coffee cup. "I didn't kill her, if that's what you're wondering."

Alex didn't feel like lying, so she just smiled at him. "But she did paint a mural for your company. Did you brief her on your work to help . . . inspire her painting?"

He frowned slightly, as if he was trying to suss out her meaning. "Not me personally, but one of my employees did. He was enamored with her, if I recall." He chuckled. "Why do you ask?"

"So she didn't know the details of your project?"

His frown deepened. "She shouldn't have, no. And there's no way she could have . . ." He lowered his voice, a look of concern on his features. "Did she tell you something?"

"Of course not. She mentioned that she had to sign a nondisclosure agreement."

His face cleared. "Oh yeah, our confidentially agreements are rock solid. When you sign a Pro-Tek NDA, you're agreeing to take our secrets to your grave." He stopped and looked at her, realizing what he'd said, and smiled. "You know what I mean."

"Right." She stood, picking up her dishes. "I better get going, but I've enjoyed our conversation. I'll see you around."

He winked at her. "Not if I see you first."

He was joking, but Alex's stomach flip-flopped a bit. Bryce had motive and means. But had he had opportunity? She had to talk to Dylan and see if his alibi was rock-solid.

*   *   *

Alex stood at the reception desk for Wesley Inc. She asked to see Dylan, and the young woman in a blue blazer told her she'd call him down.

Alex walked around the lobby, taking in the various pieces of artwork on the walls, when she heard a group of footsteps and animated talking. She turned to see a group of young people in smart suits, heels, and spit-shined loafers, crossing the lobby. Celeste was in the group, Alex noted. She moved toward the group and called to her.

Her friend was all smiles and looking professional in a fitted two-piece skirt suit. She stopped when she saw Alex, the friendly expression sliding off her face. "What are you doing here?"

"Don't worry—I'm not here to interrogate you. I'm here to see Dylan."

Celeste relaxed a bit. "Discussing me?" Alex shook her head. "Then what?"

"Totally unrelated to you. But you and I do need to talk later. I'm worried about you."

Celeste lowered her voice, grin still in place. "I'm worried about me too. But I don't want you and Mr. Wesley discussing the investigation, if that's what you're planning. This is my job. I've worked hard to be here, and I don't want to lose it. Don't ruin it for me, *please.*"

Shocked, Alex stared at her. "Celeste Thomas, I'm not trying to ruin anything. I'm trying to *help* you."

Celeste gave her a worried look but nodded. "I know. I'm sorry. I'm on edge, okay. New job. A boyfriend I can't trust. And a murder investigation. I'm trying to hold it all together, that's all. I really want to impress the Wesleys, Alex."

"And you're doing a great job. I understand—no more talk about the investigation, okay?" Celeste nodded, a look of gratitude on her face. She looked over Alex's shoulder. "Here comes Mr. Wesley."

Alex watched her join the group, and they went to the elevator together.

Dylan greeted her with a warm smile. "To what do I owe the pleasure?"

"I hope you don't mind, but I have some questions."

His smile stayed in place. "Don't you always?"

She smiled at him. "Indulge me."

He shook his head as a slow grin appeared on his face. "What do you want to know?"

"I heard that you've purchased four companies, one of which is Tarheel Defense."

"Yes. So?"

"Do you really need four more companies?"

He laughed. "It's business."

"Those poor people. All out of work. So, you're a corporate raider now. Dylan, I'm surprised."

His grin wasn't a happy one. "Why, you think I'm better than that?"

Alex ignored his question. "What about the employees who will lose their jobs."

"They've all been well compensated and have access to job placement resources. Some will come work for Wesley." His gaze sharpened. "Is this really why you came to see me?"

"You're leaving Pro-Tek and Bio-Tek open. Why? Because it's your friend's company?"

"Let's take a walk on the grounds." He led her though a back entrance, and they were in a beautiful park-like landscape with lush green grass, strategically placed trees, bright flowers, and walking paths. Employees dressed down in athletic gear were walking and running the paths. Outdoor equipment like chin bars and monkey bars spotted the run trails. Some staff had laptops on picnic tables, and a few people swung in hammocks, reading books. It was certainly a forward-thinking campus.

He stopped in front of a wrought iron bench beside a rock-lined creek and indicated that she should sit.

Trees provided shade, though dappled sunlight still fell all around them, and the scent of honeysuckle and lilac perfumed the air. The Wesley campus was beautiful and peaceful, and Alex could see why Celeste enjoyed working there.

"Bryce called and told me you tracked him down and cross-examined him over eggs and bacon this morning."

"That's not exactly how it happened. He wanted to talk herbs."

A gentle smile played on his lips, but his voice had an edge. "I don't appreciate you grilling my friends."

But Alex ignored his tone and returned his smile with one of her own. "He said he was with you when Neve was killed. Is that true? Are you his alibi?"

Dylan gazed at the greenery around him. "Not exactly."

Aha! Alex thought. *I knew it.* "Tell me."

He dipped his head downward. "It doesn't mean anything, but we stepped outside to talk business. It was loud inside, so I went to the porch." He shrugged. "While we were outside, I got a call and asked for privacy. He said no problem, told me he'd walk around to the gardens to give me privacy."

"Why didn't he go back inside?"

"I don't know. Probably the crowds. He was never what you'd call a social butterfly," Dylan laughed. "But after college he joined the army and was deployed a few times overseas. When he came back, he just didn't like being in crowds. I didn't ask why. So, it wasn't weird that he didn't want to go back inside."

"But you don't know."

"No, I don't. But I know him. I've known him for years. He's not a murderer. People who spend their life trying to discover new medicines to end pain and suffering don't usually go around killing people."

"And you've also recently acquired his company and brought him into Wesley Inc. You certainly don't need the bad press . . . You lied to protect him?"

"Sure." He stood. "I didn't tell the whole truth. But he didn't do it. I doubt he had time."

"That's not for you to determine." Alex's voice rose slightly. "Did you know Celeste is considered the number-one suspect?" She snapped her mouth close. She hadn't meant to say that.

His eyes widened. "No, I didn't know that. Because . . . ?"

"Because you gave your friend an alibi, for starters. Will you let Jack know?"

He stood. "I need to talk to Bryce first. But yes, I will."

"When?"

"Soon."

"Because you want to help Celeste?"

"Because I want to do the right thing."

And Alex exhaled. Maybe now Jack would begin to look at someone else and give her more time to find Neve's killer.

* * *

Alex had time before she had to be at the apothecary, so she headed to the coffee shop. After ordering a blueberry biscuit and a large latte with an extra shot of espresso, she settled at a table in the back of the room and began typing on her laptop. She needed to find out more about Bryce.

She knew that the secret Neve had found out about was the mermaid gene, but she needed more information.

She found several articles profiling Bryce as an up-and-coming businessman, a couple detailing his takeover of the business, a few from his time in the army.

She tried to find anything on the mermaid gene, but all she could find were references to *The Little Mermaid*. Maybe it wasn't even real. Maybe Neve had made it up so she could make her discussions more interesting. And then, Alex found something. It was small and on an unassuming blog called *Bizarre Bellamy Bay— where life is stranger than fiction.*

There were no images or bright colors. The blog looked like something from the late 1990s, but there were archives going back ten years, cataloging the strange goings-on in a small town with apparently over ten thousand followers. Alex vaguely remembered hearing about this blog—maybe from Minka?

The post in question, titled "Are Mermaids Real?," stated that a trusted insider source had provided information on many occasion, told the blogger that there was a company who believed in mermaids, believed they'd found a series of gene mutations that made up what they were calling the "mermaid gene." And those genes had been narrowed down to Bellamy Bay, among a few other places. The blogger ended the post with the thought-provoking question: *Well, readers. Is this fact or fiction?*

Alex read through the hundreds of comments and saw that, although a few commenters expressed skepticism, and at least one commenter wondered if the mermaid festival celebrated a true mermaid heritage, most readers believed it was science and wanted to know the characteristics of a person with the gene. Laughing and shaking her head in wonder, she continued to skim.

Who are these people who simply believe without proof? she thought to herself. She had proof, and sometimes she still had a hard time believing.

Alex looked at archives and saw that the blogger normally added a post once a week on Mondays, and that had been the schedule for years. She wondered why he hadn't posted anything in the last two weeks. She tried to find contact information for the blog owner. Maybe this person had more information to share. Did they even know Neve had been murdered? If they did, maybe they thought they were in danger as well. Maybe Neve had told the blogger who she was afraid of.

Alex quickly typed up a message expressing interest in talking further and offering new information about their mutual friend sharing the mermaid tip. She hit "Send" and hoped for the best. But this was definitely the proof Alex needed, showing that Neve had been killed for spilled secrets. Only she couldn't tell Jack, could she? He wouldn't believe it.

Could she tell Dylan? He'd purchased Tarheel Defense—didn't that mean he was somehow involved?

No, she'd have to handle this herself.

* * *

Alex looked up and saw Pepper walking past the window. She trotted to the front door and waved her in.

"I was just thinking about you," the journalist said, entering the shop. She sniffed the air. "The coffee smells so good, and I could use a cup. *And* I found something you ought to see."

"Great. Join me." Alex pointed to her table.

After Pepper placed and received her order, she returned to the table, set up her laptop and turned it around to face Alex. Several tabs were open, the first of which was a local Boston newspaper article detailing the latest artwork by Neve. The accompanying photo showed her standing beside several men and women—and Jasper Collins.

"Wow," Alex breathed. "The plot thickens." She wondered if Celeste was on to something when she thought those two had been seeing each other. And Jasper had lied—blatantly lied to her face—when he told her he didn't know Neve before she came to town. Why would he lie unless he had something to hide?

"But wait, there's more," Pepper said in the voice of cheesy late-night commercial narrator. She clicked on the next tab. This time it was an article from a Honolulu art blog featuring a reception for Neve at a pineapple plantation.

Alex skimmed the article and inhaled sharply. "This event was sponsored by Leviathan Industries." She turned to look at Pepper and they both spoke at the same time.

"Montgomery Blue."

Chapter Eleven

"We have three definite suspects," Alex said. "Bryce Greenberg, Jasper Collins, and Montgomery Blue." She explained Bryce's lack of alibi and possible motive without going into details about the mermaid gene.

Pepper took notes on everything and then looked up, her pupils dilated. "Industrial espionage. This is exciting."

"So now, I need to talk to Jasper and Montgomery, find out exactly what they're relationship with Neve was."

"I wonder if she was in a relationship with one of these men?" Pepper mused as she chewed on her pen.

And she was pregnant, Alex thought to herself. Did the father of her child kill her for some reason? Jasper seemed like the most probable candidate. She needed to find out from Celeste exactly why she thought they'd been having an affair.

"We should take a harder look at Jasper Collins." And then a thought occurred to Alex. "When you get back to work, can you check your archives for any photographs of Jasper's office?"

"Sure, I can check. What are we looking for?"

"I'm not sure. But something that could've been used as a murder weapon."

Pepper scribbled something on her notepad, then stood, beginning to pack up. "Sure. I can do that. I have a deadline for an article I'm working on, so it may not be until tomorrow. Can it wait that long?"

"Sure. I guess Jack won't arrest Celeste by tomorrow. I have another question for you. Have you ever heard of a blog called *Bizarre Bellamy Bay*?"

Pepper snorted out a laugh. "Yeah, sure—the ramblings of some sci-fi enthusiast who lives in his mother's basement."

Alex wasn't sure that assessment was far off, but still, at least some of the information on the blog was based in truth. "Any idea who's writing it?"

Pepper screwed up her face. "Not a real journalist, that's for sure," she scoffed. "Thanks to the internet, anyone thinks they can be a reporter. But it's not true. I have degrees in journalism. I interned with the biggest paper in Atlanta before I returned here, and have researched and reported on tons of events. I'm the real deal, while this person is afraid to show his face."

Alex eyed Pepper curiously. She seemed very worked up by this blogger. Almost artificially so. "You're not the blogger, are you?"

Laughter sputtered from Pepper's lips. "Who, me? Of course not. That blogger is practically a fiction writer. I want to win a Pulitzer one day."

"But he gets scoops, doesn't he? People come to him with big stories. I know you want that for yourself. What aren't you telling me?"

"Okay." She exhaled loudly. "When I first heard about this blogger, I thought I could find out who was behind it, and make a name for myself."

"And?"

"And I investigated and came up with nothing. I couldn't find out anything. It was almost like they didn't actually exist."

"Well, of course they exist. Just because you—"

"I'm good at my job. I did everything right. I should've been able to find him—it bothers me, okay?" Pepper crossed her arms over her chest. "I couldn't find this stupid blogger, sitting in his underwear in the dark, writing about aliens in his mother's basement."

"Maybe I can help you."

Pepper's green eyes brightened. "Two heads are better than one?" Alex nodded. "And I take the credit, I get the scoop?"

Alex rolled her eyes good-naturedly. "Sure, Pepper. I just want to find out who the blogger is and talk. They may have some insight into something I'm looking into."

"What could you possibly be looking into that's related to the *Bizarre Bellamy Bay* blogger?" Pepper stared at Alex expectantly and then grinned. "Let me guess—you're not at liberty to say?"

"Something like that."

"I have a file. I'll find it for you, okay?"

Trying not show her excitement, Alex nodded.

Pepper pushed her phone into her purse. "Okay, now I'm really leaving. We'll talk soon."

Pepper left the shop, and Alex stayed to finish her latte.

* * *

It was a little after noon, and the sun was at its zenith. There were a million things running through her mind, and Alex couldn't think. Whenever she had what her dad called "monkey mind," a term he'd learned when he began practicing meditation for stress, she ran.

After a quick stop at home, where she changed into her running gear, added a baseball cap to protect her face, and picked up Athena, she began running toward the beach.

She was already anticipating the calming rhythmic sound of the waves crashing on the surf. She didn't listen to music when she ran, instead preferring to hear the sounds of the sea gulls overhead, the splash of the water as it hit the beach, and the whir of the breeze. She ran past downtown, past the police station, and onto the road that ran parallel to the beach. When she came upon a wooden stair that took her up a dune and down to the beach, she stopped for a breather. For her and Athena too, who had been bounding alongside her the entire time.

Instead of running on the boardwalk, she wanted to jog on the sand. She took her shoes off and placed them under the stairs, took a deep breath and took off, Athena's leash in hand. While she ran, Athena was good about staying focused on the run and not on the sand crabs scuttling on the sand. They ran uninterrupted for a mile before Alex stopped, hands on knees. There was no one around, so Alex took Athena's leash off and let her play in the water. The dog ran to and from the water as it ebbed in and out.

And Alex watched her dog with a smile, always enjoying watching her play at the beach. Athena stopped dashing about and looked at Alex from about twenty-five yards away, her ears perked up. "What is it, girl?" Alex murmured to herself, knowing her dog couldn't hear her. But then Athena turned away and went back to tugging on a piece of driftwood she'd claimed.

Alex began walking again, stopping to stretch out her legs and arms, rolling her neck around when the hair on the back of her neck stood on end. She turned around but didn't see anything. But she did have the distinct feeling that she should retrieve Athena and head back home. It was around two pm but the stretch of beach she was on was deserted. Now that she thought about it, that was strange. Just two hundred feet away she could see the beach was packed with tourists.

She stopped and stared down the expanse of beach. *Something is wrong*, she thought as a lump formed in her throat. Her feet felt rooted to the sand, but a voice inside her screamed, *Leave. Leave now.* Smiling and speaking in soothing tones so she wouldn't spook Athena, she grabbed the leash, attached it to Athena's collar, and began running the way she came, toward the staircase and her shoes.

She heard Athena's low growl first, and then something cold and invisible smacked against her. She moaned on impact. It didn't hurt exactly, more stung as she felt an icy slipperiness wrap around her body. She couldn't breathe. She could blink her eyes, but not much otherwise.

She was frozen in mid-step, with one arm and leg raised in mid-stride, other knee bent. Something, some kind of energy prevented her from moving. She struggled against the invisible bonds, but nothing happened. Alex looked down to see straps of glowing blue energy wrapped around her body. And then she remembered: Bryn had used the same technique to immobilize Stephanie Bennet before Alex had found and saved her.

A Magical was here.

Again, she struggled against the restraints as Athena ran around her in circles, her bark deep and forceful. *What. The. Heck.* How could she get out of this? And who was doing this? She was frozen in place, when she heard a voice in her head. It was telepathic, but she could tell it was male, and its tone was low and insistent.

Stop your investigation before you get hurt.

Alex looked down at Athena, who was going wild, ears up, growling and prancing around, her eyes stretched wide and the whites extra bright, like she could see an intruder about to break into a house. But no one was there—at least no one that Alex could see. She tried to keep calm and breathe deeply. And remember her abilities. Remember her training. She was a Magical too. She wasn't helpless against whoever this was. This coward who was obviously using a spell for trouble to hide his appearance, a cloaking spell.

Who are you? she sent back.

The invisible restraints somehow tightened even more around her.

Stop asking questions and you won't get hurt.

She'd never been taught how to get out of this—whatever it was. That would have to be corrected immediately. She tried sending various thoughts to the person. But they were invisible, so where to direct the energy? She tried to send the intention to free herself through her body—but nothing. She tried to imagine herself running free on the beach—but nothing. Her mind raced for a solution. She hadn't been raised as a Magical—it wasn't fair. Nothing came naturally to her. What was she supposed to do?

Athena. Athena could sense the person. Could she see him? Smell him? Feel him? She looked at her beautiful dog, crouched low and growling. And sent her thoughts: *Where is he, Athena? Where is the bad man? Show me!* She didn't know if it would work. Would Athena pick up on the telepathy? And if so, would she understand? Of course, if she could hear it, she could understand. Dogs understood commands. She knew how to sit and roll over and get her leash.

She watched as Athena stopped her frantic activity, though she kept the low growl going and she trotted purposely about twenty-feet away from Alex and stopped, her barking high and her tail wagging. He was there, invisible but there. Desperate to do something, an idea came to mind, as ridiculous as it at first seemed. She called on the moisture in the sand around Athena to rise up and cover the man so she could see him.

Unbelievably, the sand floated up and began landing on something, sticking to it, and in seconds the vague shape of a man took form. Finally, she could see her enemy. *Good girl!* She sent to Athena, who barked in response. *Free me. Let me go.* She sent her thoughts to the sand figure, and her bonds released, the cold slippery feeling sliding off her like icy water. She shook herself off like Athena might do and, with raised hands, flung her own energy at him, thinking, *Stop! Freeze!*

And for a moment, the sand covering the man-shaped form actually crystalized into ice, but then he broke free of the ice sculpture, and the sand form crumbled, and he must've taken off running, because Athena took off in chase, barking and scaring a flock of birds resting on the beach, with Alex behind her. And then Athena stopped and began walking in circles.

Alex caught up with her, panting. She rubbed her head, nuzzling her face with her own. "Good girl. You went after the bad guy. You're a good girl."

Alex stood, staring down the expanse of the beach. Whoever he was, he was gone. But he was a Magical. And he'd warned her to stop investigating the case. Which meant she was close to revealing the truth. And nothing about this case was as it seemed.

What did magic have to do with this case?

When Alex and Athena returned home, she gave her dog a large bowl of water and a peanut butter doggie treat for being so protective and willing to do battle with an invisible foe. Then she headed upstairs to shower and change. She'd heard voices downstairs, but she wasn't ready to face anyone just yet. She was tired, a little freaked out about the attack, and angry with herself for not being able to do a better job of protecting herself.

After a nap, Alex called Kamila and told her what happened. Kamila was both a Magical— nonpracticing —and a police officer, so she seemed like the best person to call. She told Alex she'd come by after work for dinner with the family, and they could discuss it.

Alex wanted to keep investigating, but frankly, the attack had shaken her. She made herself a cup of Calm Down tea and lay down to take a nap.

After what seemed like only a few moments, a light tap on the door woke Alex. She looked up to see her aunt Lidia poking her head into the room.

"Hello, sleepyhead. Sleuthing made you tired?"

Laughing, Alex sat up. "I guess so."

"No worries. I heard you had an interesting day. Are you okay?"

"Kamila told you?"

Aunt Lidia nodded. "She told me and Minka. We're concerned, of course. But it seems like you handled yourself well."

"Could've been better." Alex she explained how inadequate she felt and how she wanted to better understand how to defend herself against all Magical techniques.

"It will come in time. You've just discovered who you are. We don't want to overwhelm you."

"I don't like being at a disadvantage."

Lidia smiled at her niece. "And that's exactly why you'll get better. Minka will teach you a few tricks after dinner."

*   *   *

During dinner, Alex explained to everyone in detail what happened.

Kamila rubbed her hands together. "I was really hoping this case had no Magical elements to it. The investigation just got that much harder."

"Well, it does, and we're trying to figure it out—as a family," Minka said, her jaw jutting out stubbornly, "whether you're on board or not."

Alex laughed at Minka's expression, but Kamila only frowned, her cop face firmly in place. She waited a beat and then grinned. "Well, if we're going to do this, it's best we go whole hog with it. Fill me in."

Minka looked relieved and glanced at Alex. "It's your show. You want to start?"

Nodding, Alex updated everyone on Bryce's lack of alibi and possible motivation. She decided not to tell them about the mermaid gene, because why get everyone upset for no reason if she didn't have to? But she did share the information about Jasper.

"Next steps?" Minka prompted.

"I'll talk to Jasper tomorrow," Alex said, "and figure out a way to speak to Montgomery."

"Sounds like a plan, ladies," Lidia said. "Let's have dessert and coffee. And then Minka is going to teach Alex how to break free from a Magical vise. Once it's explained, you'll realize just how easy it is."

Minka nodded and snapped her finger. "Yeah, just like that."

* * *

Minka led Alex to the backyard and whipped her hand around like she was holding an invisible lasso. Alex was immediately wrapped up in a tight cold vise. Minka giggled. "I know how to do this, but I've never used it. It's kind of fun, actually." She grinned at Alex, who tried unsuccessfully to wiggle out of the energetic grip.

She walked around Alex in a circle, as if she were giving a college lecture. "The vise is created by the energy we use to create our magic. You send the intent to the source of your energy, which for us is usually, for lack of a better word, our heart or heart chakra, and fling your hands like so"—she demonstrated with her own hands—"in the direction you want to trap."

"And how do I get out of this?" Alex said, not enjoying the cold slippery feeling that pulsated around her.

"It's not impossible to break free, but it does require a real burst of energy and focus. You have to essentially deconstruct the energy holding you prisoner, using your mind to visualize the particles separating and then being pushed apart." She stopped. "Go ahead, try it."

Alex took a deep breath and looked down at the glowing blue ropes of energy that crisscrossed her body. She did the visualization as her cousin instructed, and began to feel a loosening of the vise, but lost it when she realized she was doing it.

"Try not to try," Minka said. "I know, that's easier said than done. Take several deep breaths and slow your heart down as much as possible. You want to conserve as much energy as possible going to your bodily functions, so you can exert it externally."

"When did you learn this?"

"I was fourteen, and I practiced for a year until I got it right."

"So, what makes you think I'm going to pick it up in a matter of minutes."

"Because you're a natural and have the same power your mother had, or so mom says. While I have to try harder and practice to be just as good."

When Alex had first arrived to town and discovered she was a Magical, her family told her that, as a child, she had used her magic to make the water in the backyard fountain jump into the air in intricate swirls and loops. And Alex couldn't remember it. None of it. Not practicing magic or ever having knowledge of it—and it bothered her. "Maybe if someone hadn't wiped my childhood memories, I'd be better at this now because it wouldn't be brand new."

Minka bit her lip. "We surmised it had to be your mom or dad, right?"

Alex frowned. "I know. And I guess I can understand why they did it, but it doesn't make my life easier now. It makes me feel like I can't trust my memories of them. I mean, they were good people, right?"

"Of course they were. Try again," Minka suggested, her eyes bright with hope.

"Alright." Alex tried again, this time taking several deep breaths. She closed her eyes and did the visualization until she felt the coldness slide off her body and her limbs were free. She shook her arms out. "I did it."

"See. Told you."

"Okay. And how do I do it to somebody else."

"Same way you conjure water from anything." Minka looked around, raised her hand over a flower and watched as the moisture rose from the blossom until the vibrant pink turned brown and the succulent petals dried out, flaked, and fell to the ground. "Sorry, flower," Minka said to the plant.

"Gather energy from around you—I mean—it's everywhere and in everything—the water, plants, people . . . Combine it into ropes and then add the intention to hold tight and *voila*—you've got it. Try on me."

Alex tried several times with no luck. She stared at her hands, wiggled her fingers, and then looked at her cousin. "You don't feel anything?"

Minka pretended to inspect her nails. "Nope. Nothing. Nada." She grinned. "Try again. Remember. Try, don't try."

Alex tried several more times before throwing her hands up and huffing in frustration. "I can't do it. I don't understand the technique."

Minka wrapped an arm around her cousin. "At least you know how to break free, right?" Alex nodded. "So, baby steps. Practice energy gathering—just try to create a ball of energy and make it bounce around. Once you master that, we'll go to the next step."

Alex rolled her eyes, feeling like a failure. She didn't enjoy this feeling. Her father had raised her to be good at everything or at least to strive to be good. Shoulders slumped, she followed her cousin into the house.

Chapter Twelve

The next morning, Jack stopped by the shop, a tense look on his face.

He stood in front of the counter and handed Alex a to-go cup of coffee. "Spring in Paris. Your favorite."

Alex opened the cap and breathed in the scents of coffee mixed with lavender syrup and cinnamon, a lovely concoction Celeste had created for her when she worked at Coffee O'Clock. "Thank you. I was just wishing I had a cup of coffee."

His forehead creased as he looked at Alex. "You weren't going to tell me you were attacked at the beach?"

Alex took a sip of the coffee before responding. "I suppose Kamila filled you in?"

His nod was terse, his voice gruff. "Are you okay?"

A band of tension spread across her shoulders, and she was reminded of the times when she'd kept things from her father, anything that might upset or stress him out. Working in law enforcement, she knew he constantly worried, and she'd never wanted to add to his problems. Not as a child or a teenager. And she found that she felt that way with Jack. She cleared her throat and smiled at him. "I'm fine. Don't worry about me. You have enough on your shoulders."

"I can't *not* worry about you, Alex." He wore a pained expression on his face. "You don't want to give a statement? Did you get a look at the attacker? Did he or she say anything to you?"

"I told Kamila everything. I believe it was a man, but I didn't get a good view of him, and he told me to stop investigating the case."

"And will you listen?" He crossed his arms over his chest. "That's two people telling you to butt out. Me. And this guy, whoever he is. I don't appreciate his methods, but we do share the same sentiment."

Alex sipped her coffee. "I'll take it under consideration. Have you found another suspect besides Celeste?"

"Not yet. But there are a few pieces of news on that front. Bryce Greenberg came forward to say that he didn't have an alibi for at least part of the time in question. So, I'll be giving him a closer look."

Alex looked up from her coffee cup with interest. "That's something."

Jack nodded. "Forensics came back on the weapon. It's a mineral called ozite. It's very rare, and only one company in the world mines it."

Alex knew immediately. "Leviathan Industries?"

"Yes. And I won't ask how you know that."

"So now you're going to talk to Montgomery?"

Jack exhaled slowly, shaking his head. "I don't want to discuss this with you, Alex."

"This only confirms my suspicion that Neve and Montgomery had a preexisting relationship too. Maybe he's the father of her child, maybe—" Alex stopped talking when she realized what she'd said.

Jack's mouth dropped open. "How do you know about that? We've purposely kept that information out of the media."

Alex grimaced. "Neve came into the shop, and Ciocia Lidia guessed . . ."

"She guessed, huh? Alex, I can't speculate with you. You know that." He leaned forward, both hands on the counter between them. "I hope you'll keep that information to yourself? It may be useful in finding the murderer."

"Of course, Jack." She reached for his hand and patted it. "You can trust me . . . I actually have information to share with *you*." She told him about Neve's website. "Both Jasper and Montgomery have ties to Neve. That's got to mean something. When you talk to Montgomery and Jasper, can I sit in?'

"Absolutely not." His tone was firm, but then he softened his voice. "But I'll let you know if I learn anything that absolves Celeste, okay?"

"Sure." Alex said, glad she'd already made plans to talk to Jasper. And then Montgomery would be next on her list.

He glanced at his watch. "I have to go, but if you have any more trouble, I want to be the first person you call. Got it?"

Distracted, Alex nodded, still thinking about what she'd ask Jasper.

He looked up from his watch and stared at her for a moment, his gaze intense. "I don't think you do."

"What?" Alex blinked, focused on the way his blue eyes went smoky when he was not angry. But something . . .

"Don't call 911," he continued. "Don't call your cousin. Call *me*."

Surprised by the passion simmering in his eyes, she nodded. "Yes, of course. I promise."

He leaned over the counter and placed a kiss on her lips. His mouth was warm, his kiss urgent. "Thank you."

* * *

When Minka came in to relieve Alex for her lunch break, Alex told her she'd made an appointment with Jasper and would be back soon.

Alex walked the few blocks to the museum. It was still early, and there weren't many people visiting. Alex spoke to the receptionist, who told her Jasper would be out shortly. In the meantime, she was welcome to look at the exhibits. She wandered around the main room, stopping to look at a history of ship building in the town. Captain Bellamy's business had started off small, exploded with each war when ships were needed, and they'd received several government contracts and then turned to commercial shipping in the seventies.

Jasper appeared at the end of the staff-only hallway. "Ms. Daniels, if you'll follow me to my office."

Alex was looking forward to getting answers from Jasper, but she was hesitant to join him in his office. After all, a murder had occurred there.

Jasper noticed her reluctance, his face grim. "Don't worry. The office has been thoroughly cleaned. You'd never know a woman died in there."

He was so unemotional about what happened, Alex mused. She had a hard time imagining him committing a crime of passion.

Once in his office, Jasper settled in a chair behind his desk while Alex sat in a chair across from him. She gazed around the space, wondering if there were any clues to be found. It looked the same as the night of the reception, and she was sure if there had been anything to be discovered, Jack and his team would've done so.

"You want to discuss the history of mermaids in Bellamy Bay. It's a very interesting topic. Historically, many sailors reported seeing mermaids, and those reports were taken at face value. Like

148

Christopher Columbus, Henry Hudson of Hudson River fame, and Captain John Smith of Jamestown. The Columbus and Smith sightings were in the Caribbean."

Caribbean mermaids. Alex smiled at the thought, thinking of Celeste and her heritage. "That's all very interesting, but I really wanted to talk to you about your relationship with Neve."

Jasper sat back in his chair, face drawn with disdain. "I have nothing to hide. What do you want to know?"

"Did you know Neve before she arrived in town?"

"You've already asked me that." He gazed at her for a moment. "Neve and I met in Boston. I traveled in art and history circles there and was invited to an event celebrating her latest work. We met and discovered we had similar interests."

"Why did you lie about your relationship when I asked you earlier?"

He chuckled. "Because it might implicate me in a murder."

What does Celeste see in this guy? Alex wondered to herself. She narrowed her eyes, unable to disguise her suspicion. "You stayed in touch?"

"Infrequently. She traveled a lot, so it made staying in contact difficult. An e-mail here and there."

"You must've been pleased when you discovered she was coming to town."

"I was. And it was a complete surprise. She didn't know I'd moved from Boston, and I didn't know the festival had invited her down. When Dylan told me, it was pleasant indeed."

"Why did Celeste think you were having an affair?"

He shifted uncomfortably in his seat. "I'm not sure. I've given her no reason to feel insecure. She's gorgeous, she's smart . . . I try to be as attentive as possible with her. But I did spend a lot of time with Neve. It was professional only, honest." He held up a hand like he was taking an oath. "But she and I could talk about things. It was easy with us."

"And you talked about mermaids?" Alex's cell phone chimed with a new message, but she ignored it.

"Among other things. Mythology is—was—a special interest for both of us."

Jasper's desk phone rang, and he excused himself to take the call, with an apologetic grin and holding up a finger.

Alex nodded and retrieved her own phone to check messages. There was one from Pepper.

Found a few photographs of Jasper's office from an interview the paper did when he first took over the museum position. Tell me if you see what I see.

Alex looked at an image of Jasper smiling proudly behind his desk. She zoomed in and moved the image around, looking at items in his office. There was a laptop. Stacks of papers. Folders. Books. Pen holder . . . A grayish hunk of rock polished to a high shine.

Bingo.

As her heart pounded in her chest, she glanced up at Jasper, who was talking to someone about a shipping order for shelves and not paying her any attention. She texted back, *Send this to Jack and tell him Jasper needs to be questioned ASAP. If the murder weapon was his paperweight, did he tell the police it was missing? If he didn't, why not?*

Because he's guilty that why, Pepper texted back.

Gulping, Alex put the phone away and tried not to stare. Was she alone in a room with a murderer? Was Celeste dating a killer?

Jasper placed the phone down. "Sorry about that. I ordered oak shelves, and they want to send me pine. *Idiots.*" He chuckled. "Where were we? Ah yes, mermaids. Would you like for me to show you the exhibit?"

"Why don't you have an alibi for the time Neve was killed?" She couldn't help herself. As interested as she was in the mermaid history of the town, she had more pressing questions to ask. And she wanted to get them out before Jack arrived. *If* he arrived.

"Ah. I see. You don't actually care about the exhibits." He frowned at her. "I've already gone over this with the detective. I was going about the business of managing the reception. I have no idea what time it was when I was running around." He shrugged. "I could guess that I was on the main floor, but I could've been outside on the grounds, seeing about fairy lights in the garden that went out, or I could've been in the kitchen, discussing how the waiters were passing out more red wine when the patrons wanted white." He sniffed. "It is summer after all."

Alex frowned at his frivolous attitude. "Did you happen to see Celeste when you were outside? Or Dylan? Or Bryce? They were all there at some point."

"No. But it was a busy night."

There was the sound of footsteps in the hallway, and Jack appeared. Alex sighed in relief.

When he saw her, he pasted a small polite smile on his face. "Alex," he began in painstaking tones, "I didn't know I'd see you here." He nodded curtly at Jasper, who watched with amusement. "Can we speak privately for a moment?"

"Hi," she said enthusiastically. "Of course. Let's talk." She took him by the arm and pulled him into the hallway, closing the door behind her. "I'm the one who told Pepper to search the paper's archives for a photo," she began in low tones. "And I'm the one who told her to send it to you."

"I already had someone searching the newspaper's archives, only we were waiting for the original photos to be developed and sent to us. They should arrive tomorrow. I would've seen this."

Alex handed him her phone with the image of the rock on Jasper's deck. "Well, you're seeing it now. I should be here when you talk to him."

"Every time you interfere with my investigation you're putting yourself in harm's way," he whispered. "Do you understand that?"

"I'm sorry." She wrapped her arms around his waist and pulled him close, hoping she looked suitably contrite. "I just want to help. And I can take care of myself."

He gazed into her hopeful eyes until his face softened into a reluctant smile. "It's very hard to say no to you, Alex." He looked toward the ceiling with a "why me?" expression. "Fine. Don't say a word. Not one word."

He opened the door and stepped into the room. "Mr. Collins, may I speak with you?"

Jasper nodded and gestured him in.

When the door was closed, Jack shoved Alex's phone under Jasper's nose. "What's this?"

Alex stood in the back, near a bookshelf, trying to make herself invisible, while Jasper peered at the image of the ozite on his desk.

To Alex's surprise, his mouth dropped open in a gasp of delight. "My paperweight. Have you found it? It went missing the night of . . ." Realization dawned on him, and he looked up, eyes wide with fear. First at Jack, then Alex, and then back to Jack. "You don't think that—"

Jack watched him skeptically. "Yeah, we think it might be the murder weapon."

Impulsively, Alex reached into his mind to see images of Neve flying through his brain. Him talking to her, her talking to him. Her smiling. Her laughing. Him watching her paint. He certainly had a lot of memories of her. Celeste had been right to be concerned. But she didn't see him killing her. She wanted to delve deeper into his mind. Maybe the actual murder was buried deep. But there were the ethics and morality of using magic to consider.

She didn't necessarily feel okay about what she was doing. It was so invasive. She wouldn't want someone reading her mind, seeing her deepest thoughts. This was the issue that bothered Kamila, the reason she wouldn't practice. But this was also a murder investigation, and shouldn't she use every tool available to her?

Just one more deep dive, she promised herself. She turned back to Jasper, trying to see further into his mind. Again, all she saw was him enjoying his time with Neve. It was almost like she was viewing a loop of memories, the same ones kept appearing over and over again. And she could sense, almost feel his emotions for her. The memories were infused with affection. He'd cared deeply for her.

Jasper turned to look at her curiously.

And she took a breath. Could he sense what she was doing? She immediately retreated from his thoughts, blushing at potentially being caught snooping in his memories.

"Why are you staring at me like that?" Jasper said.

"Sorry," she said quickly. "I was just wondering about the paperweight. It's interesting."

"It was a gift from Neve. She was appreciative that we'd brought her here to paint the mural."

Alex blanched. Neve had been killed with her own gift? How horrible.

"And where is it?" Jack asked.

"I'm not sure. It disappeared that night."

"Why didn't you report it missing?" Jack's pen hovered over his pad as he stared at Jasper.

"Well, for one, it's just a rock. I thought it had been moved while the police searched the office and would eventually turn up. Sorry."

"What was the paperweight made of?" Jack asked.

"I'm not sure."

"Your office window was unlocked the night of the murder. Who knew you kept it open?" Jack continued. Jasper shrugged and Jack moved to the window and looked outside. The museum gardens, with a coiling brick path and wooden benches, were directly behind the office. Fairy lights still hung from the trees, waiting to be taken down. "Anyone could've come in from the garden and left the same way, which would account for why we didn't see anyone enter or exit the office on the security footage."

He turned and glared at Jasper, as if he was purposely holding back information. "Who knew Neve was going to your office to use the phone? Who did you tell? Who overheard you?"

"I don't know," Jasper said, his voice rising in alarm.

"I'll need a list of visitors to your office for the past two weeks. Results of the fingerprinting came in, and I need to eliminate anyone who was here for legitimate reasons." He pinned Jasper with a stare so hard, Jasper flinched, looking away. "You can give it to the officer outside." Jack moved toward the door. "Don't leave town."

"Not planning on it," Jasper said with a weak grin.

*   *   *

Outside the museum, Alex stood beside Jack's truck, a large, shiny blue Ford F150. "What do you think? You believe him?"

Jack glanced back at the museum. "Neve died in his office, his paperweight was the murder weapon, and he can't account for his whereabouts when she died."

"Why not take Celeste off your suspect list and arrest him?" Alex asked. "You brought in my aunt with much less."

"And I learned from my mistake. I was wrong and I let her go. This time when I make the arrest, I want it to stick. No do-overs," he said, glancing at Alex. "I know you don't want to hear it, but Celeste is hiding something."

Alex sighed. Because she knew that much at least was true. But still, she couldn't have done it.

"The evidence just keeps stacking up against her."

"There's more?"

He nodded. "Yeah, I'm afraid so. And that's all I'm going to say on that topic."

Alex ran a hand through her hair, frustrated. "How many suspects do I need to hand you before you realize Celeste isn't involved?"

Eyebrows knitted together, Jack gazed at her. "I'm just doing my job. You know that. Celeste still has more motive than anyone else in town. You know that Neve was pregnant. She was obviously seeing someone—maybe Jasper. Until I find compelling evidence to the contrary . . ." He stopped when he saw the worry and frustration in Alex's eyes and put a gentle hand on her arm. "That's not a challenge for you by the way. That doesn't mean try harder, investigate more. Or place yourself in jeopardy."

Alex opened her mouth to speak but he leaned toward her, pulling her close, and silenced her with a kiss.

Her eyes fluttered in surprise and then closed as she felt herself softening, tenderness and longing for something more flowing through her, warming her heart. She leaned in to accept the kiss, to kiss him back. When she opened her eyes and looked into his, she found his gaze to be unreadable.

"Leave the investigation to me. Please."

Alex didn't respond. She was pleased that he'd kissed her; it was nice. Actually, it felt wonderful, but was he kissing her because he cared or because he wanted her to shut her up? To stop meddling?

"Do you want a ride back into town?"

Alex shook her head. "It's nice out. I'll walk."

"Alright." He opened his door, then looked back at her. "You sure?"

Alex nodded. "I'm sure." And she began walking back to town.

Chapter Thirteen

When Alex returned to the shop to give Minka her lunch break, her cousin's cheeks were pink with excitement.

"Montgomery Blue called the shop, looking for me, when you were out. He wants to get together to discuss preservation opportunities with me. We're meeting for coffee. Will you come with?"

"Sure, of course," Alex agreed, not wanting Minka to be alone with the man. "Actually, why not just invite him to the house for dinner? We can all meet him."

"That's a great idea. I'll make the arrangements. And let you know when it's happening."

*   *   *

After Minka left on her lunch break, Alex texted Pepper and asked her if she minded stopping by on her lunch break, then told her that she'd talked to Jasper and one of the minerals Leviathan Industries mined had come up. She wondered if the paper had a dossier on Leviathan or the mineral, ozite. Alex was pleasantly surprised when Pepper responded that she'd interviewed a professor of mineralogy at Bellamy College in the past and had some information to share.

*   *   *

Thirty minutes later, Pepper was in the shop with a folder in hand.

"It's an interesting mineral," Pepper said in greeting. The first recorded usage of it was by Native American tribes along the coast of North Carolina who used it to ward off bad spirits. You can find statues and pendants made of it in several history museums in the state and beyond.

"It's usually black, gray, or greenish. It's only found in a few places in the world, off the coast of North Carolina and in certain places in the Baltic Sea."

"That is rare."

"Yeah, and Montgomery is mining it," Pepper said with raised eyebrows. "Leviathan is the only company that has access to it."

"What is it used for? And why does he have a monopoly on it?"

"I think he just happened to find a use for it first and put the resources in place to get it. As far as minerals go, it's spectacular. It has high magnetic susceptibilities because of the high concentrations of iron and manganese in it. The mineral comes in a variety of the colors I mentioned, but the rarest of them all is called dragon ozite. It's a bright green on the outside with a shockingly orange-red color inside, and it's found off the coast of New Bern in mines dating back to prehistoric times."

"Wow . . ." Alex shook her head. "Does he have a background in science?"

"No. He's strictly a businessman, but I know he's got teams of scientists and geologists working for him."

"I know a little about mineral use in industry," Alex said. "I had a cell phone company as a client in the past. So, I know certain rare earth minerals are used in making cell phones and laptops. Why is he mining ozite, and who's buying it?"

"Military contracts, I think," Pepper said. "I did some digging and found that his company is developing a new type of tank impervious to directed-energy weapons."

Alex exhaled in frustration. "I don't know anything about weapons."

"Maybe you can find someone who served in the military?"

"Yeah. Maybe. Thanks, Pepper. That was very helpful."

* * *

The day at the shop had been uneventful but steady with customers. Alex was in the middle of restocking candles when the front door-bell jingled.

"This is where the magic happens," Bryce said as he entered Botanika.

Alex looked up from her work. She stood, heaving a box of candles off a shelf as she did. "Hi, Bryce. How are you?"

His eyes lit up as he took in the shop. He walked around, picking up items and reading labels. "This place is fantastic," he said, and then took a deep breath. "It smells so vibrant and healthy." He laughed. "And I'm fine, thank you."

Alex set the case down and went to the checkout counter, her conversation with Pepper still fresh in her mind. She'd mentioned that Alex should talk to someone in the military about directed-energy weapons. Hadn't Dylan said Bryce had served?

"Were you in the armed forces?"

An amused look crossed his face. "You've been talking to Dylan about me?"

She shrugged. "Not really, but it did come up. What branch?"

"Army."

"What did you do?"

His lips quirked up. "Air and Missile Defense. Why?"

"Oh, no reason," she said nonchalantly. "What can you tell me about directed-energy weapons?"

An eyebrow raised. "That's certainly random. Well, ironically enough, it's one of my areas of specialization."

What are the odds? Alex wondered to herself.

"What do you want to know?"

"I'm not sure," Alex confessed. "It seems like they may figure in Neve's death somehow, and I'm just trying to work it all out. The mineral ozite may also play a role in this. Do you know anything about ozite?"

"It's very rare."

"I've heard. And only Leviathan Industries mines it."

"Where did you hear about it?"

"Came up in the murder investigation. Did you work with it in the army?"

"No. But some of my team at Pro-Tek have. We buy it from Leviathan and are testing it for a variety of possible uses in weaponry. Many companies are doing that in a race to create the next big advancement in weaponry."

"I heard Montgomery was using it to make a new kind of tank."

Bryce snorted. "Tanks are anachronistic. Only a civilian would believe that lie."

"Directed-energy weapons are the wave of the future?"

"The future is now in that case. But yeah, you could say that.'"

"What are they exactly?"

"It's a ranged weapon that damages its target with highly focused energy, like laser, microwave, and particle beams."

Alex rubbed her temples. "In laymen's terms, please?"

He laughed. "Okay. Ever seen *Star Trek*?"

She nodded, recalling with a smile how often she'd watched the reruns of the original television show with her father. Captain

Kirk's kind and compassionate nature had reminded her of her father, and in fact he kind of looked like him in photographs she'd seen of him in his thirties.

"Think about the guns they had—the phasers?"

"Okay. Yeah?"

"Take the ray of energy that came out of the gun and multiply it by a million. Bigger gun, stronger beam of energy. That's what I'm talking about. And the potential applications of this technology are limitless. That's the Barney version," he said, grinning. "As simplified as possible. How is this possibly related to Neve's murder?"

Alex wasn't sure how much she should say to Bryce. He really did seem like a nice guy, but he also had motive, means, and opportunity. She was treading on dangerous ground if she revealed the corporate espionage angle because that was the same motive he would have had for killing Neve. But—and it was a big but—if he was the killer, talking about Montgomery might make him feel like she wasn't on his trail and maybe, just maybe, he'd slip up and say the wrong thing.

"Neve might have learned some company secrets while working for Leviathan in Hawaii, and maybe she told the wrong person and was killed because of it."

Bryce lowered his voice to a whisper. "I've met Montgomery a few times. I can't see him getting his hands dirty killing someone."

"I know—he's the type that would just pay someone to do it. What would you do if you were him—if you wanted to get rid of someone because they knew too much, as the saying goes, but you didn't want to do it yourself?"

He rubbed a hand across his beard. "I'd find someone close to her, someone she trusted but someone who could be blackmailed into doing the deed."

Alex stared off into the distance. "That's good. Very good, Bryce." But she was also alarmed. Was this what Bryce had done? "But who was close to her in town? She didn't live here."

"Dylan, me, Jasper . . . we all knew her in some capacity."

"Right," Alex said, and tried not to look worried. "How is it that Leviathan has a monopoly on ozite?"

"The story is that only Montgomery knows where it's located, somewhere off the coast of Russia, but it's an old family secret, one that only he knows."

"But also found off the coast of North Carolina?"

Bryce shrugged.

Alex thought for a moment. "Montgomery is Russian?"

"I'm not sure. Certainly he's spent a lot of time there for business purposes. That's been documented in the business trades."

"Maybe Neve discovered the location of the ozite, and Montgomery had her killed because he was afraid she'd tell someone. Or perhaps she did tell someone, and that was her punishment? But who would she tell?"

He stared at her. "A competing company seeking their own access to the mineral?

Like Bryce's Tarheel Defense with its two divisions? Alex gnawed nervously on her bottom lip. Was he admitting to something right now, right here?

But he only laughed. "It's an interesting theory. How to prove it?"

"I don't know." She shifted uncomfortably behind the counter. Why was he being so forthright with her? Was it because he planned on killing her too? Alex turned to check on a customer by the perfumes. Maybe she was just getting paranoid, but Bryce seemed guiltier to her by the minute. After a few moments, she returned to the counter, where he was still waiting for her.

"I actually stopped by here for a reason," he began. "Two reasons. First, I wanted to thank you. Dylan urged me to tell the police the full truth about my whereabouts when the murder occurred. He didn't name names, but I know he'd only listen to you about something like this."

"What do you mean?"

"He cares a lot about you. He talks about you all the time, how he screwed things up, how he wishes he could go back in time and fix his mistakes . . . I knew it had to be you that told him to tell the truth."

Alex wasn't sure what to say. Was he happy he'd been forced to tell the truth or only pretending? Or was he secretly planning his revenge?

"And second, I have something to share with you about the night of the murder . . ."

Alex gazed at him expectantly, wondering if this was the moment he confessed he was the killer and then dragged her into the backroom and bashed a—

"It's about your friend Celeste."

Startled out of her reverie, she stared at him. *"What?"*

"Yeah." He nodded.

And her stomach sank. But then hope fluttered in her chest. If he'd been in the garden when she was, maybe he could provide an alibi for her, and she for him. "You saw her?"

"She was doing what I can only describe as"—he leaned over the counter and lowered his voice—"dancing with the devil in the pale moonlight."

Alex squinted at him. *Batman references?* "I don't understand what you're saying."

"She was by a small pool of water with her arms outstretched to the sky—to the full moon—barefoot, dancing and chanting. She had some odd items at her feet—trinkets and such. They were shiny, glittering in the moonlight. I couldn't get a close look . . ." He nodded. "Yeah."

To his credit, Alex thought, he looked very confused.

"Is your friend a—a witch or something?" He held up both palms in a placating gesture. "No judgment—everyone does their own things, you know. I've dated a hot Wiccan or two in my time, so . . ."

Alex groaned. *Oh, Celeste, what were you up to?* And then another thought occurred to her. "Did you tell the police this?"

"Oh yeah. The detective? He was very interested."

I'll bet, Alex thought. "What time was this?"

"Maybe seven thirty or eight?"

Celeste would've still had time to commit the murder—at least in Jack's eyes. No wonder he wasn't about to remove Celeste from his list.

And Celeste! What had she been thinking?

After Bryce left and there was a break in the customer flow, Alex called Celeste. Her call went straight to voicemail.

When Alex closed down the shop for the evening, she texted Pepper and asked her if they could meet at the wine bar down the street for a little happy-hour discussion. Pepper agreed, telling her she'd be there as soon as she submitted an article she was working on. Alex asked Minka if she wanted to join them, but she declined, saying she had a date with her television.

At six thirty, most of the shops on Main Street were closed. The sky was still sunny, streaked with fluffy white clouds and patches of aquamarine sky. Head down, Alex began texting Pepper, telling her she was about to arrive, when she almost bumped into a woman.

"Oh, I'm sorry," Alex said as she peered into the face of a young woman with pale skin and dark circles under big, red-rimmed gray eyes.

The woman offered a weak smile. "It's fine. You didn't see me." Her voice cracked. "No one sees me."

Alex placed her phone in her purse and looked at the woman. "Are you okay?"

The woman shook her head. "Not really. I've just come from the police station." A mixture of despair and disgust passed over her face. "My husband died, and the detective in charge has decided he died of a drug overdose, when Chris never did drugs." Her voice rose almost hysterically for a moment, but then she took a deep breath. "We had kale smoothies for breakfast and chia bowls for lunch. Does that sound like the type of man who would put drugs in his body?"

This was the wife Kamila had mentioned, the one who didn't believe her husband had died the way the authorities said. "I'm so sorry for your loss—" Alex began, but the woman cut her off.

"Everyone is sorry," she said, her voice breaking into a sob. "But no one is sorry enough to do something about it."

"What do you think happened?"

"It doesn't matter. That police detective is the one who should be asking me this question and then listening to my answer. But he won't. It was not death by accidental drug overdose." She shook her head. "If the police won't help me, who will?" Her eyes filled with tears again, and she swiped at her eyes.

Alex felt helpless to comfort the woman. She dug into her purse and pulled out a card for the apothecary. Smiling, she said, "My name is Alex and I work at Botanika." She pointed in the general direction of the store. "It's not much, but we have teas and things that may help with your stress." Her words felt entirely too inadequate for the moment, but the woman took the card anyway.

"I'm sorry to bother you. You're a stranger, and here I am spilling my guts to you on the street." She waved the card at her.

"Thanks, I guess?" She whirled around and hurried in the opposite direction without another word.

Alex stared after her, wondering if Jack was indeed doing everything he could for her. She knew firsthand that when Jack came to a determination, he stuck with it unless he was forced to see otherwise. He'd done it with her aunt, and now he was doing it with Celeste. She'd have to ask him about this case, too, the next time she saw him.

She turned to the bar, and when she opened the door, she was greeted by low salsa music and the murmur of customers grouped at tables in the darkly lit room. There was a small dance floor, and a few couples joyfully moved to the rhythm of the music, twirling around with perfectly syncopated steps.

She turned toward the dining area. The air was fragrant with smells Alex couldn't identify, but her stomach growled in response. She sat at the bar and reviewed a tall, laminated menu, finally deciding on a small plate of appetizers she could share with Pepper, and a Chilean sauvignon blanc.

A few moments later Pepper arrived, and she immediately ordered a glass of wine.

Alex indicated to the waiter that they'd like some sparkling water too, then pushed the charcuterie board toward Pepper. "These are for us to share." Alex selected a cube of brie and fig and chewed on it thoughtfully.

Pepper ate several slices of aged cheddar and soppressata salami. "I'm starving. I just realized I haven't eaten since noon," she complained. "My mom is freaking out because there's a murderer on the loose with the festival about to happen, and of course my dad's not happy."

Grateful for the "in," Alex said. "Speaking of your father, did you know Montgomery Blue is using your father as his alibi?"

Pepper gasped. "My dad? I know they spent time together that night, but . . ." Her brow wrinkled. "He really shouldn't drag my father into a murder investigation. I know my dad wants to run for senator someday." She pulled out her phone. "Let's get to the bottom of this, shall we?" She texted a message, waited for a response. Screwed up her face.

"Gross, Dad," she muttered to herself. Texted again and then put her phone up. Laughing, she shook her head. "He says he had a bout of diarrhea brought on by those mini key lime tarts they were serving." Alex nodded. "He was in the bathroom at eight thirty and for about twenty minutes after."

"You're right, that is gross and TMI, but it shows that Montgomery lied. He couldn't have been with your dad if he was in the bathroom."

"Now Montgomery has opportunity."

"But not motive."

"Oh, I forgot," Pepper said, fishing into her tote bag. She held up a manila folder. "My notes on the *Bizarre Bellamy Bay* blogger."

Alex moved closer. "What did you find?"

Pepper spread the folder on the bar to reveal several pages of typewritten notes. "The first thing I did was use some of my connections to locate the blogger's IP address."

"And?"

"Nada. He uses a VPN—that's a virtual private network—to hide his location. He appears to be in Europe, Asia, and a bunch of other places. Then, I sent him an e-mail with a fake tip."

"Was there a response?"

"Yes. But it was very guarded. He didn't give any identifying information about himself. And after he checked out my tip, he told me it was inaccurate and never contacted me again. Even though I tried."

"What did you tell him?"

Pepper laughed. "I've seen some really crazy things on that blog, like there's a company creating a material that can block magical powers, like Kryptonite but for witches, I guess? Which is ridiculous since there's no such thing as magic, so obviously that one is made up. I made up an equally silly idea. Two actually. First, I said I'd seen a UFO behind the lighthouse, and then I told him there was a werewolf in the maritime forest, and then asked him if we could meet to discuss it. It took him like twenty-four hours to figure out I was full of it—on both accounts." Pepper handed Alex pages. "This is the e-mail exchange."

Alex gave the papers a cursory look. "Anything else?"

"I was able to interview one of the blog commenters who said he'd talked to the blogger on the phone a few times. And he confirmed that the blogger is a he, that he's very interested in the paranormal activity in town, and that he had contacts in high places that leaked him information."

"I wonder how he got those contacts?"

Pepper shrugged. "He said after he started blogging, people just started contacting him, people who were able to confirm their positions in intelligence, the military, government, and corporations. I guess people who are sworn to secrecy about things they really want to share. Anyway, I was really excited about meeting him, until it went nowhere."

"I sent another e-mail. If he contacts me, I'll let you know."

"What makes you think he'll take you any more seriously than he did me?" Pepper assessed her friend for a moment, then gasped. "You have real information to share?"

"Maybe."

"Hold that thought," Pepper said, standing up. "Nature calls."

Alex sipped on her replenished glass of wine and gazed around the room while Pepper excused herself to the restroom. As Alex's eyes adapted to the dark, she blinked when she saw someone she thought she recognized. *Jasper.* He looked miserable at a table as he nursed a drink. Montgomery sat with him, his face composed, his body language relaxed.

She picked up her phone and called Jack. "You'll never guess who I'm looking at right now."

"Hello to you too." He chuckled. "Who?"

"Jasper. And he's inside that new wine bar downtown—"

"With?"

"Montgomery Blue."

Jack was silent for a moment. "Anything else?"

"No," Alex said, a tad frustrated. "But they're both on your suspect list—"

"No, they're both on *your* suspect list."

"You're telling me you don't want to know what they were talking about? Why they're meeting?"

"No. And I definitely don't want you finding out for me." He paused a beat. "Understood?"

"I'm sorry, you're breaking up," she lied, and then hung up. A feeling of anxiety tightened her chest. She thought she was a pretty good liar when she needed to be, but it didn't mean she enjoyed it.

Pepper returned and sat down. "What did I miss?"

Alex quickly got her up to speed on the two men. "I know it's a small town, and they're both involved in the festival, but is it more than that? Jasper looks really upset. I'm just dying to know what Montgomery could possibly be saying to him."

"Oooh. Sneaky," Pepper said. "I can totally help you. I'm going to pretend to take a closer look at the artwork near their table, and see if I can listen in."

Pepper finished her wine and stood. "Here I go," she whispered with a wicked grin.

"Wait," Alex said, wondering if Pepper had too much wine. Pepper was already threading her way through the room.

Alex waited impatiently as Pepper pretended to talk on the phone while she gazed at a painting of a vineyard near their table. A few moments later, she returned and sat down.

"Well, Jasper's upset and Montgomery is consoling him."

Alex gazed at the two. Jasper's head was bowed while Montgomery looked slightly bored. "Anything else?"

Pepper shook her head. "They got really quiet when I came close."

Alex thanked her and called Jack back. "I got something."

"I thought I told you—"

But she ignored him and pressed on with her update. She knew that he wanted to hear it, even if he pretended that he didn't. She told him what Pepper heard, and then paused.

He finally responded. "Thanks."

She smiled. "You're welcome." And then she remembered her encounter with the grieving widow. "Have you wrapped up the OD case?"

"Yeah." His voice took on a wary tone. "Why?"

"Just wondering how you resolved it so quickly. Was it really cut-and-dried?"

"Where is this coming from? Don't tell me you don't have your hands full with the Neve Ryland case?"

Alex explained how she'd run into the wife of the OD victim and what she'd said to her.

Jack exhaled. "Evelyn Robinson. She's a teacher at the high school. Seems nice enough, but it's a sad case, and I feel for her—heck, we all do. But he was found with enough uppers in his system to kill three men. A clear-cut case after we found bottles of pills in his car.

"Evelyn said he's been working long hours and coming in on the weekends. She thought he was possibly using the drugs to stay awake, and she'd warned him about using them, but thought he was smart enough not to overdose on them. He was a normal guy with a normal job with normal friends. A wife. A kid. No pets. Nobody in his life that would want to murder him and make it look like an accidental overdose."

"You interviewed his wife, colleagues, and friends?"

Jack exhaled loudly into the phone. "I know how to do my job, Alex. I went to his home and spoke to the wife. I took a look around—no search or anything, just trying to get a feel for the guy. His wife showed me his home office; she was cooperative. It was filled with stacks of comic books, shelves of posable action figures . . . superheroes, Justice League and Marvel Universe characters. Apparently, he was a collector of that kind of stuff. You know the type— grown-up geek with money to buy toys." He laughed. "Posters from the Thor and Superman movies all over the place."

"But still—"

"He killed himself. Accidentally. And that's all there is to it."

Alex was silent.

"I'm just finishing up at work. Do you want me to swing by and drive you home?"

"No, I'm fine. I walked. And anyway, Pepper and I are hanging out."

"Yeah," Pepper sang into the phone, "we're having a girls' night out." She waved the bartender down to order more drinks and food.

"But come by the shop in the morning. I want to talk about Montgomery Blue."

"Oh, don't worry. I'll be there first thing. You and I need to have a talk."

Chapter Fourteen

The next morning in the shop, Alex was surprised to see her first customer.

It wasn't Jack.

It was Evelyn Robinson. She still looked unnaturally pale, like she'd been hiding in a dark room, crying for days. And considering that her husband had accidentally killed himself, she probably had been. Her brown hair, which Alex could tell had been cut into a chic chin-length bob with blunt-cut bangs, now hung limply, framing her oval face.

The front door opened again, and a teenage boy entered with a sullen expression on his face, hands jammed into the pockets of his faded black skinny jeans.

Evelyn held up the business card Alex had given her the night before. "I need something for anxiety," she said when she approached the counter. "My nerves are . . . bad." Her lips trembled, and Alex wondered if she would start crying right here on the shop floor.

"I have just the thing. One moment." She went to a shelf of jars filled with loose teas and began adding herbs from several glass jars into a sachet for her.

Evelyn followed her to the shelf. "Anything for grief? For the pain I'm feeling?" She looked back at the teenager and then at Alex. "That's my son, Tanner. Sixteen and angry with the world."

Alex paused and looked past the woman to her son. She smiled at the boy, who ignored her and crossed his arms over his T-shirt, black with a picture of ET and emblazoned with the words "Phone home?" from the famous movie.

"We don't have anything for grief specifically, but what I do have is ashwagandha, St. John's Wort, valerian, and lavender for anxiety and depression." She turned around and handed the bag to the woman. "Drink two to three cups beginning around five pm. By bedtime you should sleep soundly. And you need to sleep. I can tell you're not rested. The effects should carry over to the next day . . . you'll feel calmer, more relaxed."

Evelyn followed Alex to the counter. "How can I rest knowing that my husband's murderer is walking around free?"

Alex glanced at the teenager with alarm. Did he know what his mother thought? But he appeared not to have heard, or maybe he'd heard it all before and didn't care. Alex rang up the purchase, took Evelyn's money, and began counting her change.

"I talked to Detective Frazier about your case," she began in a low voice. "We're friends, and of course, while he didn't tell me anything confidential, he did tell me that the evidence clearly pointed to a determination of accidental death by overdose." She handed the woman her change. "Besides, who would want to kill your husband? By all accounts he had no enemies."

Evelyn's eyes shone with tears as she stared at Alex. "I heard about you. After we met last night, I looked up your store's website, and your name came up on a local blog. You found out who killed that man when the same detective who is ruining my life charged your aunt." Her eyes brightened. "Why can't you do the same for me?"

Alex paused, realizing what the woman was asking. She shook her head. "I really wish I could help you. But there's nothing to go on. No clues, no suspects."

"But you know the detective, right? You know how he is, like a dog with a bone even when he's on the right track." Evelyn looked furtively over her shoulder. "Look, I can—"

The front doorbell chimed, and Jack entered the shop, nodding at the teenager when he saw him.

Tanner glanced at Jack and scowled, finally speaking. "I'm going outside, Mom. The vibrations in here just tanked."

Jack's face was stony as the teenager rushed past him.

Evelyn barely acknowledged her son when he left, preferring to glare at Jack.

Alex turned back to the woman, placing her hand on her wrist. "What were you going to say?"

"Forget it. Nothing." She grabbed her bag and hurried out of the store.

Jack froze in place, not turning to look after Evelyn. A muscle on his jaw twitched. "What was that about?"

"She bought tea."

"Alright, I won't pry. And I also can't stay long—sorry. But you said you wanted to talk?"

"Right . . ." She told him about Montgomery's lack of an alibi.

Jack laughed. "The mayor was in the bathroom. Okay. You want me to confirm that with him?"

"Yes, I do." She shot him a look of incredulity. "Isn't that your job? Or should I do that for you?" She winced when she realized how acerbic she sounded. "Sorry."

"Clearly someone needs a hug." He went behind the counter and gathered her in his arms before she could protest, and held her for a moment. "See," he said, his lips against her hair. "This is why

I don't want you involved in my case. Besides the fact that it's not legal for you to do so, it wreaks havoc on our personal relationship. You see that, right?"

The store was empty for the moment, so Alex allowed herself to relax against his chest.

"That's what I wanted to talk about with you," he said, voice still gentle. "You've got to stay out of my case. Please. For us. For me. Just let me do my job."

Her arms were wrapped tight around his waist. He felt so good to her. Strong. Comforting. She really, really didn't want to upset him, to mess up their relationship, but . . . "I'm sorry. I just want to prove that Celeste didn't do this, that there are other viable suspects."

Alex could feel his body tense at the mention of Celeste's name. "What is it? What aren't you telling me about Celeste?" He gently pulled away from her and returned to the opposite side of the counter. The tenderness he'd displayed only a moment earlier was gone, and she knew she'd get nothing more on that topic. "Did you talk to Montgomery? Have you looked at Bryce Greenberg?"

He inhaled again, this time more slowly and deeply, as if he was counting to ten in his mind. "I think it will be better for us if we don't discuss the case further."

She leaned forward, elbows on the counter, chin in her hands, and gazed at him intently. "I'll take that as a yes. What did you find out? That both Bryce and Montgomery can't account for their whereabouts when Neve was killed?"

He gave her an inscrutable look but didn't comment.

"Or how about the fact that they both had preexisting relationships with her?"

Jack shook his head. "You're wasting your time. The evidence against Celeste is overwhelming. In fact—" He stopped himself.

"I've already said too much." He slapped the counter lightly. "I have to go."

*　*　*

Once Lidia arrived at the store, she sent Alex on an errand to the local farmers market. On her way there, she texted Pepper to ask a favor. The marketplace, on a grassy patch of land near the town park, operated every day from eight am to twelve pm during the summer. Her aunt needed fresh peaches and apples for desserts she'd be making in the coming days, and Alex had volunteered, wanting to get out in the sunshine and salty breeze.

The market was filled with locals and tourists alike, wandering through the four long rows of venders. There were freshly picked okra, black-eyed peas and green beans, local honey, and every in-season fruit one could think of. A basket from the shop swung from her arm as she stopped at one table and sampled a cube of melon, fresh basil at another, and a spoonful of tomato cobbler at a third. But she stopped when she heard someone behind her call her name.

She turned to see Montgomery coming toward her, a large iced coffee in his hand. *Well, well, speak of the devil . . .*

She stood still, waiting for him to reach her. She wanted to talk to him. When he came closer, Alex noticed a ring on the pinky finger of his left hand, a thicker than usual silver band with an oval crystal in the center, bright green with a black swirl in the center.

"We meet again." He grinned at her. "How are you?"

She returned the greeting, wondering if he had time to talk. She gestured toward his coffee. "That looks good. Where did you get it?"

"Walk with me and I'll buy you one."

She stared at him for a moment, wanting to get information from him, yet not really wanting to go with him. But there was something about him—yes, she did want to walk with him. He could probably help her. "You're offering me coffee?" She smiled. "What's the catch?"

"No catch."

"I understand you want to work with my cousin?"

"Ah yes, lovely, sweet Minka. She's such a bright ray of light, isn't she?" He grinned good-naturedly. "I can tell she wants to do good in the world, and I think I can use her. My foundation needs people like her, and if I do move to this area and open up a new office, I certainly want someone with her passion and drive to spearhead our efforts."

Alex gave him a closer look. He seemed sincere where Minka was concerned. She decided to relax a little. Maybe working with his foundation, whatever it was, would be good for Minka.

They walked the next aisle over, and Montgomery led her to a booth offering coffee beans grown in Ecuador but roasted in Swansboro, a small town about an hour east. She placed her order, he paid for the coffee, and they walked over to a bench and sat.

"I'd actually like to know more about you."

"What would you like to know?" he said in a gracious tone. "I'm an open book."

Alex wondered again at her luck. Here he was giving her the perfect opportunity to find out more about his past relationship with Neve without her appearing to pry. "First of all, I'd like to know how you knew Neve Ryland."

He rubbed his chin thoughtfully. "And how will that help you get to know me?"

"It will help me figure out if you're a killer, for one." She smiled at him as if she was joking. But she wasn't.

He laughed. "I'm game. I'm all for being eliminated from your little list of suspects."

Alex noted the condescending edge to his voice and knew he had zero concern about being a suspect. Was that because he was innocent or because he knew he would never get caught?

His gaze was penetrating but his voice lighthearted. "Does the detective know what you're doing? I hear you two are an item." He paused. "Of course he knows. And it's a problem." He chuckled.

"You're very observant."

"'Intuitive' would be a better word." He took a moment. "Neve painted a mural for one of our offices. I wouldn't have handled the logistics of the commission—I have a man for that." His smile was rueful. "What a talent."

"You've probably heard that the murder weapon was a hunk of ozite, the mineral that only your company mines."

He nodded. "Yes, that was unfortunate."

Alex hesitated. What was unfortunate? The murder? Or the use of his mined mineral as the weapon? As she looked at him, she realized that he was very hard to read. She wondered if she delved into his mind what she would see. Then immediately admonished herself for the thought. But then again, if he was a murder suspect like Jasper, wasn't it okay? Certainly, if she'd done it to Jasper, she could do it to Montgomery?

"How did Neve get the mineral, and why did she give it to Jasper?"

"I believe it's called regifting? Someone gets a gift and then—"

"I'm familiar."

"Right. Neve was a rare talent and a true beauty, inside and out. She was given that sample of ozite to represent that same rareness and beauty. It was at the reception for the mural she created for us. I think it was an inspired gift."

"When did you give her the gift? And where?"

"It wasn't from me exactly. One of my team. And maybe a year ago? Nine months maybe? I think it was at her Honolulu exhibit. It was a depiction of the Tide Jewels. Spectacular! Do you know the Japanese myth?"

"Actually, I do."

"I had her create a mural depicting the sea god, Watatsumi, for our offices there."

Alex nodded. "And she gave the mineral to Jasper."

"I suppose. Is regifting a crime?"

"No, but murder is, as you very well know."

"What possible reason could I have for wanting Neve dead?"

"That's what I'm trying to find out."

He was suddenly all serious, and Alex could swear the temperature dropped a few degrees. "Don't you think looking for a murderer is a bit . . . *risky?*"

"Perhaps," she agreed.

"Weren't you a risk analyst before you moved to town?" Alex nodded slowly, wondering why he seemed to know so much about her.

"I have a team of risk analysts on my payroll, and I know the types of tools they use to analyze risk. What would your risk analysis matrix say about the foolhardiness of your endeavor?"

She thought about his question but didn't say anything.

And he smiled. "I think if I consulted with my team of analysts, they'd tell you to stay out of it. You could get hurt," he said reasonably, as if he was suggesting she put on sunblock when she went to the beach. "Someone you love could get hurt."

Alex straightened in her chair. Oh, she was definitely going to search his memories. All bets were off. He had no idea who he was messing with, what she was capable of. She could command a wave of water to crash down on him if she wanted to. A feeling of power coursed through her body, and she could feel her face burning with anger. "Are you threatening me?"

Eyes wide, smile affable, he spread his hands placatingly. "Of course not, just a friendly tip."

She rose from her seat, tossing her unfinished coffee into a nearby trashcan. Taking a deep breath, and as softly as possible—in case he could sense what she was doing—she reached into his mind with her own—and stopped.

It would seem Montgomery had his own walls up. She was stopped cold just on the periphery of his mind. It was a cold, dark, cavernous space with absolutely nothing there. Not the normal Mundane thoughts of what to get at the grocery shop on the way home, no wondering if he left the iron plugged in—just nothing. And then a cold, sticky feeling began to permeate her own mind, as if she was being covered in something oily and gross. The feeling pushed at her until she was out of his mind and firmly back into her own.

She gasped once she was free of the feeling, almost as if she'd been deep underwater and had just broken free to the surface and inhaled fresh air.

His smile seemed sincere, but his eyes glinted like ice in the sunlight. "Are you okay, Alex?"

Nodding, but unable to speak, she stumbled backward and away from him. When she was several feet away, she looked back at him. He was still standing in the same spot, sipping on his iced coffee, watching her with a smile on his face.

* * *

By the time Alex was halfway back to the shop, she remembered that she hadn't purchased any fruit for her aunt. She stepped off the curb, almost walking in front of a slow-moving white SUV because she was distracted by the interaction with Montgomery. And they didn't even honk at her!

Southerners, she thought warmly, *were so polite.* She waved an apology toward the tinted windows and stepped back onto the curb. Should she go back to the market? She definitely didn't want to run into Montgomery again. And now he was coming to their house for dinner?

She did not want that man entering their home, but what could she say? She'd reached into his mind and found a slimy pit of nothingness there. Minka would be so disappointed; she'd been talking nonstop about her potential new role as saver of the earth. And her aunt? Well, she might listen. Aunt Lidia was so volatile at times, she wasn't sure what to expect with her.

No, better to keep her thoughts to herself until she had more reason to share them. Besides, maybe it was just her. Back to present matters, though. She'd left the market empty-handed. She needed to go back. Her aunt wanted apples and peaches, and she didn't want to explain why she'd returned without them.

She picked up her phone to call her aunt and let her know she'd be later than expected, when the phone rang in her hand. She looked down at the screen. It was an image of Celeste, smiling and holding a coffee cup, from her days as a part-time barista.

Alex picked up immediately. "What's up, Celeste?"

"Can you come to my house?" she cried into the phone. "Jack is here with his officers, and they're searching the place."

Chapter Fifteen

C eleste lived in the same neighborhood as Pepper, a historic row of townhouses that were all at least two hundred years old.

The homes were each uniquely designed and in an array of creamy pastel colors, with small patches of bright green yard curbed by wrought iron fences. Alex parked on the street in front of Celeste's house. It wasn't hard to find; it was the one with four police vehicles parked out in front.

As she made her way up the sidewalk to the door, Alex greeted several policemen that she knew. When she got to the door, she was barred from entrance by an officer she didn't know. Smiling at him, she sent him a thought. *Let me in. It's okay. You won't get in trouble.*

He grinned her at. "Come on in," he said as he stepped away from the door to her allow her entry. "Wait . . ." His brow furrowed at the words, and Alex hurried past before he realized what he'd done.

Celeste's home was attractive in its simplicity. A bright teal color with black shutters and a yard bursting with yellow tulips. Alex had never been to her home, but she knew the general area. The house, Alex recalled Celeste telling her, had been in the Thomas family for generations.

It was clear a search had taken place. The home, furnished with sleek Scandinavian-style furniture, was decorated in tones of warm cream and yellow with bright splashes of blue and coral for accent. But now furniture had been moved out of place, stacks of books lay on the floor, and cabinet doors had been opened.

Pepper stood in the middle of the room with a scowl on her face.

"Hey." Alex greeted, surprised to her there. "What's wrong?"

"I heard the search was happening on the scanner, so I rushed over, hoping to get the details. then the officers told me I had to leave." She exhaled loudly. "How can I do my job with all of these obstacles?"

"Sorry."

Pepper's eyebrows rose. "But you're here. A perk of dating the detective?" She looked around at the policemen moving about. "Maybe I should date a cop."

"Celeste asked for me. I'll give you an update later, I promise." Alex watched Pepper walk to her BMW and drive off.

"You came," Celeste said, stepping out of the kitchen. She rushed toward Alex, who hugged her.

"It will be okay. There's nothing here to find, right?"

Celeste shook her head slowly. "Nothing to implicate me in the murder, but—"

"What's this?" Jack strode down the stairs with a small cloth doll in his hand. It was female, with long brown hair made of yarn, a bright red cupid mouth, a beaded necklace around her neck, and a lacy white dress.

Celeste stiffened beside Alex. "It's a doll."

"I can see that." Jack crossed the few steps between Alex and Celeste to stand directly in front of them. "And I've also been to New Orleans enough times to know what this is. It's a voodoo doll. He exhaled loudly. "Is this supposed to be Neve?"

Celeste stood, arms crossed and her lips pressed into a hard line. "No."

Kamila came down the stairs, wearing plastic gloves and holding the large silver tote Celeste had carried the night of the party. She shot Celeste a "what the heck?" look before handing it to Jack. "Thought you might want to see this."

He raised an eyebrow, took the bag and opened it. He began fishing out the items, each enclosed in a little plastic bag.

Alex recognized them as the items Celeste had purchased at their store. Verbena. Anise. Seaweed. Crushed oyster.

Jack held each baggie up to the light. "Drugs?" He sniffed the bag holding a dried herb and shook his head. "No, this smells like lemons or . . .?" He looked at Alex, sighing. "Can you help?"

Alex crossed her arms over her chest. "Really? Now you want my input?"

He shrugged, looking only mildly embarrassed. "Yes, I need your help. Any idea what this is?"

She didn't have to look at the baggy. She knew. "Lemon verbena."

"And what is it traditionally used for?"

"Many things. In an oil it can help with muscle pain. As a scent it can uplift spirts—and it builds immunity. It can also be used in teas."

He gave Celeste a dark look. "You carry ingredients for tea in your purse? Or were you making a witches' brew the night Neve was killed?"

Celeste flinched as if she'd been hit.

"I don't understand, Celeste," Jack said. "Your parents are pillars of the community. You work at Wesley. You're a professional." Exhaling loudly, he gave the items back to Celeste. "Bag it up and put it in evidence."

"Yes, sir." Kamila glanced at me and then Celeste before sending us a thought. *Sorry. We had to search. I figured better me than someone else.* She gave Celeste a very worried look before leaving.

"Now the witness account of your strange behavior in the garden on the night of the crime makes sense, somewhat." Jack retrieved a plastic bag in his pocket, dropped the doll inside of it, sealed it, and handed it to Kamila. "Take this too."

Jack returned to Celeste, who looked close to tears, like she was barely holding it together. "Celeste Thomas," he began, his tone ominous.

Alex reached for Celeste's hand and squeezed it. *It will be okay. I'll be with you every step of the way.* Celeste closed her eyes, and squeezed her hand back in response.

"I'm placing you under arrest for the murder of Neve Ryland." He took a deep breath and refused to look Alex in the eyes. "If you promise not to resist and come with me quietly, I won't use handcuffs."

Tears silently rolled down Celeste's trembling cheeks as Alex looked on in horror.

"Jack, there has to be another way," Alex said, her voice rising in panic. "I know it looks bad but—" She couldn't say more because, well, it looked bad.

Celeste took a deep shuddering breath and then wiped the tears from her face and squared her shoulders. "It's okay, Alex."

Alex looked toward the door. Where was Tobias? He should be here by now. *Don't say anything to anyone until he gets here,* Alex reminded her telepathically.

Celeste nodded mutely as she followed Jack out the door.

Tobias appeared then, slightly out of breath, cheeks a little flushed. "My apologies. I was on a golf course with poor cellular service. As soon as I got your voicemail, I left. He's arresting her?" Tobias asked as he watched Jack guide Celeste toward his work vehicle, an unmarked sedan.

"Yes," Alex said.

He nodded. "I best get going. I'll see you at the station?"

Alex dipped her head in assent, unable to speak. It was the arrest of someone she cared about all over again. And Jack was doing the deed. She really liked him, but she wasn't sure how much more of this their relationship could stand.

* * *

Once at the police station, Celeste was fingerprinted and her mug shot taken. Alex sat in the waiting room, wondering what she could do. She'd called her aunt Lidia, who had in turn told Minka and called Celeste's mother, Josephine. Minka had to watch the shop, but Lidia was coming with Josephine. While Celeste was going through processing, Jack appeared in the waiting room, his face grim.

Alex rose from her chair, a frown on her own face. But before she could speak, Jack said, "Look, Alex, I know she's your friend. But the evidence is overwhelming. You see that right?"

"But she didn't do it. I just know it."

"More analysis of the crime scene came in. Her fingerprints are all over the office."

"She's dating Jasper. It was his office. She's probably been in there dozens of times."

He shook his head wearily. "I was able to convince a judge to issue a warrant to search her house. She was convinced. Motive. Means. Opportunity. Celeste has it all. And this voodoo stuff, this just makes it worse. Did you know about this?"

Alex rolled her eyes. "It's harmless."

"She had a voodoo doll of the victim."

"Yes, but if you don't believe in magic, how can you think that's evidence that Celeste is the killer?"

"I wouldn't arrest Celeste if there was only the doll, but add it to everything else . . . I'm sorry, I waited as long as I could. Please tell me you understand?"

Alex did. But it didn't help. "When can I see her?"

"After processing, she'll meet with her attorney. After that you can see her briefly."

"Will you give her house arrest like you did Aunt Lidia?"

"I was able to get that for your aunt because she was older and didn't appear to be a flight risk with all of her family here, and her business."

"All of Celeste's family is here. Her job is here—what the heck? There's no difference."

"The victim was hit in the head with a rock twice. It's brutal. The citizens of Bellamy Bay are going to want the person who did that off the streets and safely locked away."

"Bryce Greenberg thought Neve was sharing company secrets. And Neve was killed in Jasper Collin's office with his own paperweight!"

"That's enough, Alex. We've been through all of this."

"No, it's not nearly enough if you think you've arrested the right person. And don't forget Montgomery Blue. He doesn't have an alibi. He has a connection to the murder weapon, and he knew Neve before he came to town."

"Bryce and Montgomery are nonstarters. Jasper Collins is only a person of interest, but even he doesn't look as good for this as Celeste. She has opportunity and means, and everyone in town knows she has motive. I have to go. An officer will let you know when you can see her."

Alex stared as the heavy metal door closed behind Jack and locked into place. She sat alone with her phone, doing internet researches on her three suspects, hoping to find something—anything—to move the case in another direction, when finally an officer appeared in the waiting room. "You can see her now, ma'am."

Alex hurried behind the policeman and walked down several stark white hallways. The air was frigid, and she wondered if that was by design. The policeman stopped in front of a locked door with a small rectangular window on it. Alex could see Celeste sitting alone, her eyes red and her cheeks tear stained.

He opened the door. "You've got ten minutes. No touching."

Alex waited for the door to slam shut, then sat down across from Celeste. "You okay?"

Celeste tried to smile, gesturing toward the Styrofoam cup of coffee before her. "The coffee is better than I expected. TV shows make you think the coffee in police stations will be disgusting, but it's okay." She picked up the cup and inspected it. "The cream is powdered, so that's gross." She bit her lip, and another tear rolled down her face. "I'm trying to be strong. Can you tell?"

Alex smiled encouragingly. "You're doing great. What did Tobias say?"

She lowered her voice. "That it doesn't look good. That everyone thinks I did it. That everyone thinks I was jealous of her—and I was." She set the cup down. "And that I killed her because Jasper was seeing her when he was supposed to only be seeing me. And he was." She laughed through her tears. "I totally get why Jack arrested me. I mean, how could he not?"

"But you have the truth on your side," Alex said. "You're innocent. You didn't do this, and that eventually will come out."

Celeste looked down, and a tear rolled down her cheek and splashed onto the table. "Don't waste your time. Jack thinks he's found the right person. So be it."

Alex frowned. "It's not like you to be so defeated. I know it looks bad, you in the garden during the reception, the argument with Jasper, the doll—tell me, are you covering for Jasper?" When Celeste didn't answer, Alex pressed on. "I know you're innocent. And if you're covering for him, why don't you want to fight this?"

"No." She shook her head, face still downcast. "He didn't do this."

Celeste raised her head and looked at Alex, tears glistening in her eyes. Looked at her like there was something she wanted to tell her.

But then the door behind Alex ground open with a loud metallic sound.

"Time," yelled the police officer as he stepped into the room. And he stood there staring at them both until Alex hustled out of her chair.

She tried to give Celeste an encouraging look. When she went back to the waiting room, she found Josephine and her aunt there. They both stood when she entered.

"How is she?" Josephine asked, a look of fear darkening her eyes.

"She's okay," Alex said.

Josephine gave Lidia a puzzled look. "I thought I'd taken care of this mess."

Lidia wrapped an arm around her friend's shoulder. "We'll figure it out."

"I have to run down a few clues," Alex said, itching to leave. To help. To *do* something. "Time has run out, and if I can't prove to Jack that Celeste is innocent . . ."

Josephine forced a smile, but her cheeks trembled with the effort. "Go on, then. Celeste and I appreciate anything you can do. That girl . . ."

* * *

Alex began walking home, when her phone rang.

It was Pepper.

Hey," Alex said, her fingers tightening around the phone. "Please tell me you found something to help Celeste."

"Yes, I think you'll find it most interesting."

There was a pause while Pepper attached a file and then sent it in a text. At the sound of the chime, Alex put Pepper on speaker and looked at the image. It was a screenshot of Bryn Wesley's Instagram account. The image was dated for the previous year. It showed her on a yacht, fashionably thin, dressed in a designer dress. Her dark hair hung in a precise cut around her haughty face, and her eyes were arrogant as usual. She leaned against the railing while Montgomery stood beside her, dressed in all white and holding a glass of a brightly colored liquid.

Bryn Wesley and Montgomery Blue? What does it mean?

"How did you even find this?" Alex said, after a moment.

"I was researching Jasper's feed, and something just told me to check on Dylan's and then Bryn's. Of course, her feed hasn't been updated since she went away—where is she again?"

"Kansas, I think. Or Missouri maybe? What does the post say?"

"Just that they're partying off the coast of Greece."

"Nice work, Pepper. I wonder if Dylan is aware."

"No problem. I'll keep digging. By the way, I got that information you asked for. I'll text it to you." There was a moment of silence, and then Alex's phone chimed with the incoming text.

"Got it," Alex said. "Thank you. I'll let you know what I find out, if anything."

*   *   *

When Alex arrived home, she entered the house and took a moment to kneel in front of Athena, covering her with kisses and giving her a good rubbing. Athena lovingly nuzzled her head on Alex's legs and then they walked into the kitchen together.

Minka was at the counter, tossing a salad in a large wooden bowl. "You're just in time. It's my famous strawberry summer salad. Goat cheese from the local dairy. Want some?"

Alex sat at the table, sighing. "Thanks, but I don't have an appetite at the moment."

"I'll make some tea," Minka said and then went about the task with efficiency while Alex explained what Jack had been up to.

Minka pouted. "First mom, now Celeste. If I didn't know better, I'd think he had it out for our family."

"I'm sure he thinks he's doing the right thing. But, I'm not going to let him ruin Celeste's life in the pursuit of justice. I have another cousin, more family to get to know." She sat on the edge of her chair. "And I'm going to do what I can to help her."

Minka handed Alex a cup of tea that smelled of lemongrass. "Here you go."

Alex thanked her cousin, and was about to take a sip, but stopped. "You know what else bothers me about Jack? His stubbornness. Take this case in the news. The software engineer? I've talked to the wife a couple times, and she thinks he's got it wrong, and now she's got me wondering too."

Minka joined Alex at the table with her salad. "What are you thinking?"

"Well, he was wrong about Ciocia Lidia. And I know he's wrong about Celeste. He's probably wrong about the software engineer case too. I kind of want to prove to him that if he could be wrong about that case, he might be wrong about Celeste's. Make sense?"

Minka ate a few bites of her salad. "This is not going to help your relationship with Jack."

"I know, but what can I do? How many times can I watch the man I'm with investigate people I care about?"

Minka chewed thoughtfully for a moment, her eyes on Alex. "Do you think you're trying to sabotage things with Jack?"

Alex's eyes widened, her mouth flew open. "*Minka,* why would you say that?"

Color flooded Minka's cheeks, but her gaze was steady. "Honestly?" Alex nodded. "I just wonder why you're with him. I've yet to really see chemistry between you two."

Alex frowned, lines appearing on her forehead. "We have chemistry. Especially lately, he's been more . . . affectionate with me."

Minka gave her cousin a knowing look. "What about Dylan?"

Alex looked away but Minka reached across the table and grabbed her hand. "Am I wrong?"

Alex fiddled with her cup. "Jack is good for me. He's good and decent and predictable, but in a good way. Do you know what I mean?"

"Of course, I do." Minka squeezed Alex's hand before letting go. "And he's the exact opposite of Dylan. Right?"

"I feel out of control when I'm with Dylan." Alex said, feeling like she was complaining. "I don't like that feeling."

"And when you're with Jack?"

"I don't feel like I'm risking anything. He's safe. Reliable. What you see is what you get with him, even if he's a bitter pill at times with his stubbornness and self-righteousness."

"And just a little bit boring? You're okay with that?"

"Yes, that's exactly what I want, what I *need* in my life. Stability. Dependability. And I like him a lot. You know that."

"If you say so." Minka pushed her empty salad bowl away. "What will you do about this other case?"

"I don't know. Part of me doesn't want to get involved. Let the police do their job and all that. But then I know Jack, and he's already called the case." Alex stared into her teacup for a moment before looking at her cousin. "Maybe I start with the man's workplace?"

Standing, Minka found her keys on a side counter and tossed them to Alex. "I'm sure you know what you're doing."

* * *

After taking a quick shower and changing into something more presentable than her shop attire, Alex drove to the small office park that Chris Robinson had worked at. A cursory internet search revealed the man's place of employment and the name of his supervisor, who'd been quoted in a news article about the death. She wasn't sure what she'd find, but Evelyn had been right about one thing. Alex had solved the murder of Randy Bennett, and she could do it again. Especially if it helped Jack see that he was wrong about Celeste. She sent Evelyn a brief text telling her she'd look into the case and keep her updated.

* * *

When Alex arrived at the office park, featuring a trio of brick buildings around a circular driveway and courtyard, she was greeted by a landscaped campus filled with flowers, picnic tables, and a gazebo. Alex parked in the lot behind the building, and passed a small sign declaring the park was overseen by Wesley Inc.'s Property Management division. *No surprise there,* Alex thought. If it wasn't owned by the Bellamys in this town, it was owned by Dylan and his family.

She parked and followed the path to a glass entrance at the back of the building, checked the floor directory in the lobby, and stepped into the elevator. She got off on the top floor and was immediately confronted with a large, three-dimensional red sign that read "BLIPPO." Alex signed the guestbook and told the receptionist she was there to see Aaron Ashley. She'd fibbed and said she was from the property management company and wanted to survey random supervisors for a quality-of-life survey. She'd made that up on her way over, and she hoped it was believable.

Boldly, Alex held up her business card to the woman. "My card?" The young woman shook her head, and after a cursory glance at Alex's chic pants and blouse ensemble, she didn't even bat an eye and buzzed her through two large doors, giving her directions on how to find Aaron.

It was after four, and many of the desks were empty, with a few people working at standing desks or sitting on bright orange stabilizing chairs. Inspirational quotes by famous visionaries decorated the wall, and there was an old-fashioned popcorn machine full of freshly popped corn. The tantalizing butter smell floated on the air as Alex passed a Ping-Pong table and an old-school arcade game before finding the office in question.

The door was open, but she knocked anyway. "Mr. Ashley?" Her grin was big and welcoming.

The man, in his early fifties and with a receding hairline sat behind a desk. He stood and automatically stuck out a hand. "Aaron Ashley. Nice to meet you." He gestured toward a leather chair on the other side of his desk. "Kiera said you were with Wesley?"

Alex only smiled in response. Better to keep things vague, but to the point. "I understand that you were Chris Robinson's boss?"

He leaned back in chair, frown lines appearing on his forehead. "That's correct."

"I just wanted to follow up with a few questions. Can you give your impressions of Chris?"

Aaron looked confused. "I've already talked to the police."

"Just doing our due diligence." Alex smiled. "Want to make sure this event doesn't impact the quality of life for the rest of the staff." She retrieved a pen and pad from her tote bag and affected a concerned expression. "How is everyone taking the news?"

The expression on the man's face relaxed. "We're okay. Everyone is surprised. Chris was a nice guy. A hard worker. No one suspected of him using drugs."

"Not even something for energy? I heard that he was burning the midnight oil working late into the night and on weekends?"

Aaron laughed. "Where'd you hear that? Quite the opposite actually."

Alex hoped she hid the look of surprise on her face. Hadn't Evelyn said her husband had been working overtime?

"In fact, it's a running joke here. If you're packed up and ready to leave at 4:59 pm . . . you were pulling a Chris Robinson. And as far as coming here on the weekend? Not Chris."

"You're sure?"

"I have to review logs of after-hours and weekend visitors for our department on Monday as part of a security protocol. He's never been here on a weekend."

But Evelyn had said that's where he was. Had he lied to his wife? Maybe he had kept secrets after all. "What can you tell me about Chris's personal life?"

He eyed her cagily. "Not much. He was very private. A wife. A kid. A picture of his son on his desk. He was really proud of his boy's grades and his interests. Said he would probably follow in his footsteps."

"And become an engineer?"

He shrugged. "Sure."

"What did you think of his wife?"

"Saw her at Christmas parties. She was always real quiet and unhappy looking until she had a glass or two of eggnog, know what I mean? And then she was all over Chris, trying to get him on the dance floor."

"Did Chris ever discuss his personal life in the office?"

"Not that I know of, but he was big on current events, though." He chuckled. "Always the one at the watercooler stirring things up with the latest podcast he listened to or saw on Twitter—you know the type."

Alex asked a few more questions to support her ruse of doing a survey and then thanked him for his time. Relieved, she stood. She must be a better actress than she thought.

He walked her to the elevator. "No problem. And tell the big-wigs at Wesley there that we could use a new arcade game. We've all bested Pac Man. Maybe Donkey Kong?"

* * *

The next morning, after a long hot shower and her first cup of coffee, Alex settled into a comfortable chair and opened her laptop.

Her shift at the shop didn't begin until two pm, so she could enjoy a leisurely morning. First, she would check her messages, and then—she almost stopped breathing when she saw an e-mail notification float by on her screen.

It was the blogger.

She clicked on the e-mail and scanned it. He'd heard about what happened to Neve and had questions. Could they meet in person to talk? Alex looked up, amazed that, after what Pepper explained had happened to her, he wanted to meet. But she guessed it was because she had real information, and Pepper didn't.

Alex quickly responded that she could meet any time after six pm—he could just name the time and place. She stared at the screen, wondering how long it would take for a response to come in. It was instantaneous:

Tomorrow, nine pm in the park in front of the mural. Come alone.

Chapter Sixteen

Alex could barely contain her excitement. She would finally get to meet the elusive blogger that evening. Her morning off had seemed to creep by, even though she'd gone for a run on the beach and spent a few hours going over the case with Pepper. Finally, she'd decided to get dressed for work and head in early.

She had just reached the corner of Cypress Lane and Main Street when a red sports car slowed down beside her. She didn't have to look to know it was Dylan.

He grinned at her. "Hop in—I'll give you a ride."

Alex didn't even think about it. She needed to speak to him. "Thanks." He revved the engine before taking off. "Show-off," she said, and buckled her seat belt. "Where are we headed?"

"It's about lunchtime. If you don't have someplace to be, why not join me?" Alex nodded, and Dylan grinned. "I know just the place."

After they'd arrived at a humble sandwich shop, Alex discovered it was takeout only, a hole-in-the-wall place with the best sandwiches in town. She was surprised, knowing Dylan's champagne and caviar tastes. Alex found a picnic table in the shade while Dylan placed their orders. A few minutes later, he came back with two drinks and baskets with grilled hot dogs and fries. He tossed packets of ketchup, mayo, and vinegar onto the table.

"Wasn't sure how you eat your fries."

"Vinegar actually. Grew up with my dad always pouring vinegar over our fries, and I can't have it any other way." She glanced at his hot dog, covered in chili, slaw, mustard, and onions. "That looks interesting."

"Carolina style. Best in the world," he said, and took a huge bite.

Alex looked down at her own hotdog, covered in ketchup, mustard, onions, and sauerkraut, the closest she could get to the hot dogs she got from vendors on the streets of Manhattan. She also took a bite. It was good, but not the same. No matter—she was hungry.

"Is Montgomery Blue a friend of the family?"

Dylan opened several packets of ketchup and squirted it on his fries. "You could say that. Why do you ask?"

"I found a picture of him and Bryn together on her Instagram account from a year ago."

He sighed. "Why don't you leave well enough alone. Bryn can't hurt you."

Alex wiped her mouth with her paper napkin. Her hot dog was messy. "I'm just wondering why she was partying on a yacht with him. He knew Neve. There could be a connection."

He shifted uncomfortably in his seat. "Maybe they travel in the same circles Bryn has probably been photographed thousands of times at parties."

Alex didn't disagree, but still the connection bothered her. "Does Wesley Inc. have business with Leviathan?"

"Not officially, no." He took a long pull from his large to-go cup.

"What does that mean?"

"He'd like to do business with us. My mother would like it too."

"But you don't?"

"No. His moral compass is—well, I'm not sure he's got one, frankly."

"But you do?" He turned to her, hurt written all over his face. "Sorry," she rushed to say. "I didn't mean for that to come out the way it did." Alex distracted herself by inspecting her cup and hesitantly tasted it. Her eyes flew open with delight.

"Yes, you did." He pointed to her drink. "Like it?"

"Yes. What is it? A Coke with raspberry syrup?"

Laughing, he shook his head. "Cheerwine. It's a cherry-flavored cola made in North Carolina. One of the state's best exports."

"I've never heard of it, but I like it."

"Me too. It's what I'm drinking."

"But back to Montgomery . . ." She bit her lip, disliking the clunky transition. "I just find it interesting that you have an ethical bias against working with him. What is it?"

"You do realize that I don't have to tell you everything just because you ask?"

"I know you and Bryn didn't see eye to eye about how you ran Wesley. She must've had business with him."

"I didn't keep up with her. I used to try, but it was exhausting. I stopped. I only interfered when she tried to kill someone I cared about." He gave her a pointed look.

Alex looked away. He was not shy about making his feelings for her known. "Alright, let's talk about something you do know about. Pro-Tek. Bio-Tek."

"What about it?"

"What are you going to do with all of the research that Bryce's company has?"

"That's an oddly specific question. Bryce's company, now Wesley Defense Division business, is top secret, and unfortunately, darling, you're not cleared for it. Nor should you be."

"Was Neve cleared for this information? She worked for the company, was around the staff . . ."

"An artist with a top-secret clearance?" He laughed. "Not to my knowledge, no. What are you getting at?"

"I think something she learned at one of the companies she worked for, maybe Bio-Tek, got her killed. Maybe she told the wrong person?"

"Which would mean you think Bryce had a reason to kill her." He laughed. "Just because my sister was found guilty of murder—two actually—doesn't mean I make a habit of hanging around killers." He looked at her lunch. "You going to finish your fries?"

"No, I'm full. Take them." She pushed the red-and-white-checkered carton toward him.

Dylan chewed thoughtfully on a fry before speaking. "Did Neve tell you what secret she was keeping?"

Alex looked at him. He was so casual in his tone, but she sensed that her answer was important to him. "Between you and me, yes, she did."

He inhaled sharply, throwing down the piece of fry in his hand. "She signed NDAs. How could she talk?"

"You know about it too, then?" *The mermaid gene. The database.*

"Of course I do. It's my project, my find."

Surprised at his candor, Alex said, "What are you going to do with this information?" Had someone killed Neve on his behalf? Was it Bryce?

"Make sure it doesn't get in the wrong hands, for one."

Alex frowned. Was Dylan the one with a motive to kill Neve? But no . . . he had an alibi, and he wasn't a murderer. "And second?"

"Monetize it in a responsible way."

Monetize the research of the mermaid gene? Alex stared at him in disbelief. "But how can you—how could you? You don't see that as a kind of betrayal?" Alex stood, needing to think. Every time she thought she had Dylan pegged—this time as the good guy—he did something to prove her wrong.

"Absolutely not. I'd rather it be in my hands than those of a Mundane or a Magical who practices black magic."

"Like your mother? Like your sister? So, that's why Bryn was with Montgomery? She wanted to sell the information to him. To do god knows what with?"

"Probably. But I wouldn't let that happen. It's safe with me and within the confines of Wesley Inc."

"That's why you purchased Tarheel Defense."

"Yes. They already have the defense industry setup, connections, contracts. It makes our new division competitive at launch."

"You're going to sell this information to the government? To the military?"

"I don't know. We'll see. But I promise you, it will be done responsibly."

Alex snorted. "Responsibly my . . ." She shook her head. "You're not the only one without a moral compass, Dylan. You're more like Montgomery Blue than you'd care to admit."

Alex didn't understand the look of pain that flickered across his face. But then again, maybe she didn't really care. She began walking away from him as fast as she could.

"Alex, wait. You've got me all wrong."

"And by the way, the supervisor at Blippo at your office park wants a new video game. You might want to check into that."

"What?" He stared after her in confusion.

But Alex was in the wind. *No more of his lies,* she thought as she walked—almost ran—toward the shop.

No more.

* * *

By the time Alex arrived at Botanika, she was covered in sweat and still angry. She greeted her aunt with a tired wave. "I need Calm Down tea."

"What's his name?" Aunt Lidia said with a laugh. "And I'll put a hex on him, no questions asked!"

Alex stopped in her tracks and stared at her aunt for a moment. And then they both burst into laughter. "Dylan Wesley. *So* infuriating."

"Those Wesley men are," Lidia agreed, and she handed Alex a chilled bottle of tea from the barrel by the counter. "Drink up. You'll feel better." She grabbed her purse. "I'm meeting Josephine for lunch, and then we're heading over to the courthouse for Celeste's hearing. Minka's volunteered to watch the shop so you can join us. She'll be here in fifteen minutes."

After finishing the tea, Alex found an apron and wrapped it around her. "Perfect. I'll come down there as soon as she arrives."

Chapter Seventeen

B y the time the hearing was over, Celeste was free to go home. Well, not exactly free, but at least she wasn't locked up in a holding cell. The judge decided to be lenient with Celeste, considering her lack of criminal history, strong family ties, and the character reference provided by Dylan Wesley, along with his personal assurance that she would not leave town. Personal assurances aside, the judge determined that because of the severity of the case, a high bail was necessary.

Tegan Wesley herself agreed to pay the one-million-dollar bond, shocking everyone in the courtroom with her generosity. And once again, Alex wondered, not for the first time, why the Wesleys appeared to have taken Celeste under their wing. In this context, it was certainly helpful to have powerful friends, but not when they had a proclivity to practice black magic.

When the judge told Celeste she was free to go, her knees buckled, and she fell into a puddle of tears, but she left the courtroom, held up by her mother and Lidia. Alex was the first to congratulate her.

"I'm so happy you're free. This gives me more time to find the real killer."

Celeste gave her a tired look. "Thanks, Alex. I appreciate the support you've given me during this time, but really you don't have to—you know, try and find the killer. I'm sure Jack will figure it out soon enough."

Alex did a double take. "I know you're tired, but you sound so pessimistic. You didn't do this, and I'm going to prove it."

Celeste nodded. "Maybe I just need to take a shower and get some rest and eat some of my mother's food."

Josephine appeared at her daughter's side. "She's coming home with me tonight." She wrapped an arm around her. "I'm going to take good care of her, just like when she was little and not feeling well. Doctor Mom prescribes plenty of chicken stew."

Celeste turned into her mother's embrace. "Thanks, Mom. Some of your home cooking is exactly what I need right now."

Lidia squeezed her shoulder supportively. "I've got a basket of goodies with your name on it. Some lemon sandwich cookies with sweet lavender and blueberry filling, chamomile and raspberry scones, peppermint and tangerine bath salts. . . and a warming, spicy kava kava blend, all designed to help you relax, relieve your stress and anxiety, and lift your spirits."

Josephine smiled wearily. "Why don't you bring it over tomorrow? It's Saturday and the shop opens a bit later, right? I'll make breakfast."

"Sounds perfect." Lidia gave Josephine a comforting hug. "Minka is opening the shop tomorrow, so Alex and I will come."

*   *   *

After the courthouse, the Sobieskis went home to prepare for a very special guest. Montgomery Blue was coming for dinner. It seemed after no time at all before the front door was chiming, and Montgomery stood at the door, wearing a light blue dress shirt, gray pants, and outrageously shiny shoes. He held a bottle of vodka in his hands and grinned at Alex. "Good evening."

Alex looked at the bottle in his hand and noticed his ring, which glinted in the sunlight. She felt decidedly ill at ease with the night's dinner guest, but Minka wanted him there. And she was, she had to admit, interested in the plans his nonprofit had for the town, especially if they involved her cousin.

"Hello, Montgomery. Thank you for coming." Her gaze fell to the clear bottle with a silver label in his hands. "I see you've brought a gift."

He extended it to her. "Yes, some of the finest vodka ever made."

She glanced at the proffered bottle. "I'm not really a vodka drinker."

His smiled deepened. "But perhaps your aunt is?"

And as if his words bid her, Aunt Lidia appeared behind Alex and took the hostess gift. She handed the bottle to Alex. "Put this in the freezer, please."

Alex eyed him curiously. She turned to her aunt. "Of course," she said, happy to take her leave.

Aunt Lidia also turned to move into the house and then stopped when she observed that Montgomery still stood in the threshold, his large frame filling the space. "Are you just going to stand there letting all the flies in?" she asked, hand on her hip.

He inclined his head. "I'm waiting to be invited."

Lidia inhaled sharply and stared at him. "Are you now?" She assessed him for a moment before speaking. "Won't you please come in?"

"Gladly." He grinned and followed her to the formal dining room off the main hallway, and Lidia called her daughters to dinner.

*　　*　　*

As they sat around the table, Alex took in the antique furniture, lovingly cared for but too fancy for their informal gatherings over sweet tea and pierogis. The table in the eat-in kitchen, Alex realized, was her preference.

Lidia wiped her mouth with her napkin. "How's your food?" She gestured at his plate, which was full of fried chicken, cheddar and chive biscuits, and cucumber salad—a Sobieski family dinner staple in the summer time.

"Best fried chicken and biscuits I've had since moving to the South." He smiled.

"How are you going to prevent entire ecological communities on the seabed from being destroyed?" Minka asked, cutting to the chase. "How are you going to prevent deep sea heavy metals from being introduced into surface water and where sea creatures will be exposed to them?"

He held up a hand. "I have an entire team of ecologists who create recommendations to mitigate the risks to our environment and another team who writes them into policy, along with the governing standards overseeing our work—and we follow them. And I'd like for you to join my NGO representing Bellamy Bay and the local preservation society. We don't work just to preserve the ocean environment but also the coasts and the nearby towns affected."

But Alex gave him a knowing look. In preparation for his visit, she'd done more research on his company, particularly its charitable division. She wanted to be able to poke holes in his stated intentions, so Minka and Aunt Lidia could see through his pseudo-altruistic charm. She'd been inside his head, and although she hadn't seen anything, she'd felt enough to know there was something off where he was concerned. She just wondered if anyone, especially Aunt Lidia, who was very observant, would notice as well.

Alex dipped her fork into her salad. "What you actually do is set up a good works project in every town where you're doing mining—or whatever it is you do—to counter the bad things you're doing in the environment. Isn't that what you did in Boston? And in Hawaii? Brought in Neve to paint a pretty picture for the locals, and create some work of charity to assuage your corporate guilt?"

He nodded, not rising to her prickly bait. "Sure. Yes, we did do those things, but it's not quite as conniving as you'd have everyone believe. I want to give back to the communities I work in. It's a part of our mission statement. My mother instilled the beauty of art in me as a child. So, I have made sure that art is an integral part of our philanthropy. We don't just commission paintings; we commission statues, industrial art—whatever our group recommends and the town leadership agrees to."

"I love it," Minka said, reaching for her second biscuit. "Art should be free and everywhere. I commend you for including this in your plans."

Alex crossed her arms, finding no fault with his response.

"What else do you do? Besides commission public artworks?" Minka asked, her cheeks flushed with excitement.

Alex shot her cousin a worried look. She was beginning to suspect that Neve did other things for this NGO, namely, something that got her killed.

"We provide grants to local charitable organizations—something we plan on doing with the Bellamy Bay Preservation Society. How does twenty thousand dollars sound, free and clear?" He looked around the table.

"Like a bribe," Alex said.

"How about thirty?" He locked eyes with Minka. "Could you put that money to good use? Save some turtles, build new sand dunes?'

Minka's mouth dropped open, and she nodded, unable to speak.

But Lidia frowned. "Wesley Inc. already generously donates to the Society. Perhaps you could provide something else?"

"Yes, I'm aware that Wesley is a donor, but we'd like to do more. And yes, certainly we can do more than just provide money." He glanced at Minka. "Just tell me what you need."

"I'd have to think about it—go to the group, discuss your offer, and see what they come up with."

With pursed lips Aunt Lidia stood. "Who is ready for dessert?"

* * *

After cake and coffee was served, conversation moved to travels, with Montgomery sharing a childhood trip to Poland.

"It was a pilgrimage of sorts," he said, holding a forkful of *kremówka papieska*—papal cream cake, a square of flaky pastry with chilled egg custard between the layers, and covered in powdered sugar. "We went to Krakow to see the Wawel Castle." He took another bite of the cake and licked his lips. "May I say, this is the lightest, creamiest version of cream cake I've ever had."

"Quite the flatterer, aren't you," Lidia observed with a smile. "My mother's recipe. Glad you like it. So, what brought you to Poland?"

"We have family in the area. They've been there for a long, long time."

Kamila eyed him with interest. "The dragon was the coolest part of that trip." She looked at her mother. "Right, Mom?" She looked around the table. "We went there when I was, like, twelve, I think?"

Aunt Lidia nodded. "Yes, it's an interesting tale." She glanced at Alex, who looked confused. "Never heard of it, dear?"

"Sorry, no."

"May I?" Montgomery asked, then began when Aunt Lidia nodded. His lips spread into a wide grin. "Who doesn't love a good dragon tale?" He chuckled. "The Wawel dragon appeared during the reign of King Krakus, at which time he required weekly offerings of cattle. If the dragon did not receive his offerings, he'd find humans to eat in town. Of course, King Krakus wanted to protect his people, so he called on his two sons for help, Lech and Krakus II. They could not, however, defeat the creature by hand, so they came up with a trick.

"They fed him a calf skin stuffed with smoldering sulfur, causing his fiery death. Then the brothers argued about who deserved the honor for slaying the dragon. The older brother killed the younger brother, Krakus II, and told the others that the dragon had killed him. When Lech became king, his secret was revealed, and he got expelled from the country. The city Krakow was named in recognition of the brave and innocent Krakus."

"That's quite the story," Alex finally said. "Mermaids, dragons— I never knew Poland had such fanciful beginnings."

"The limestone cave is still there, the dragon's lair under Wawel Castle," Kamila enthused. "So cool. Bones of the dragon—some say not the dragon, but a dinosaur—are hanging in front of the Wavell Cathedral on the grounds."

A tight smile froze on Montgomery's face as he nodded. "Yes, they've been hanging there a long time."

Lidia examined Montgomery for a moment and then abruptly stood. "Anyone want more coffee?" Everyone but Alex indicated they wanted a second cup. Lidia nodded. "Alex, come help me?"

Once they were in the kitchen, Alex looked at her aunt. "What's going on?"

Lidia paused in her gathering of coffee supplies. "Something about him bothers me."

Alex nodded, watching her aunt measure out coffee grounds and pour them into a filter. "You feel it too? Good. It's not just me."

When the coffee began to brew, Lidia turned around with a troubled expression on her face.

Alex hesitated for only a moment before explaining what she'd felt when she'd tried to reach into his mind.

Lidia's laugh was harsh. "That's what you get when you go poking around where you don't belong. But that is interesting . . ." She looked at the door to the kitchen speculatively, as if she could see straight through it to the dining room. "And he is . . . not quite what he seems."

"I knew it. I knew I couldn't be the only one to sense something about him."

"Something besides him being a murder suspect."

"Yes," Alex whispered. "What are you thinking?"

"When Kamila mentioned the dragon—or dinosaur—bones hanging at Wavell Castle, I sensed a dip in his energy. A dive, really. It bothers him—a lot."

Alex turned to look in the direction of the dining room. "Why would he care about something like that?

"Perhaps it was a relation."

Alex gawked at her aunt, unable to tell if she was teasing or not.

"I think," she continued, "that he may belong to an exclusive club of sorts, but I don't want to say until I'm certain."

"What kind of club?"

"The kind that very wealthy, powerful men belong to, men who make decisions about our world. And they can successfully be taught to guard their thoughts."

She told her aunt how she'd seen Montgomery at the museum reception, looking quite chummy with Tegan.

"Figures," Lidia said with a sour set to her lips. "So, he's a friend of the Wesleys. That can't be good."

"We'll talk more about it when we don't have a dinner guest. For now, let's just be good hostesses, shall we?"

* * *

After dinner, Alex went to the park to meet with the blogger. She'd tucked her hair under a Yankees baseball cap and pulled it low on her face. She'd grabbed a pair of her aunt's drugstore reading glasses to further obscure her identity. A T-shirt, jeans, and tennis shoes completed her look. Alex slowly walked toward the mural. Even with tall, illuminated lamp posts lighting the way, there were still several areas obscured by the dark. At this late hour, the park was practically empty, with a lone man walking a dog at its far end. She suddenly wished she'd brought Athena, but the blogger had said come alone, and she assumed that meant without a dog too.

She rounded a corner, came face to face with the mural, and took the time to study it once more. She gazed at the Mermaid of Warsaw, who looked as if she had a secret. But what could—

And then she heard a noise behind her, like someone stepping on a twig. She whirled around but stopped when the person spoke.

"Don't turn around," a voice said. "I have a gun pointed at your back."

Alex's shoulder's tightened. "Why would you have a weapon? I'm here to talk."

The person made a choking sound, half-laugh, half-cry, and Alex quickly turned her head to catch a look. She saw a slight figure in a dark hoodie and sweatpants. The face was partially hidden by the hood and the shadows, but something about the voice sounded familiar. She indeed felt something sharp in her back, so she faced front, hands up.

"Why do you have a gun?"

"I'll ask the questions. How do you know Neve Ryland?" the hooded figure asked.

"She was a friend," Alex said, realizing all at once that the person behind her was a woman, trying to hide the timbre of her voice. The *Bizarre Bellamy Bay* blogger was a woman, not a man as Pepper's source had said.

"Friends don't kill friends," the woman said.

Alex almost turned around then. "I didn't kill her! I'm trying to find out who did."

"Neve told me only two people knew about the information she shared with the blog. The person who shared the information with her and the person who wanted her to keep it a secret. She told me she trusted the scientist, but . . ." Her voice trailed off as her works sunk in.

"You think I'm the person she feared?"

"Yeah, so that's why the gun. For protection. You e-mailed about Neve. Who else would know?" Alex began to shake her head, but the woman nudged her in the back again. "The killer, that's who. And now you're here to kill me. Tying up loose ends, making sure no one is left to talk." Her voice wavered a bit. "Start walking."

Frowning, Alex realized this woman really thought she was a threat and wanted to take her at gunpoint to another location, a more isolated spot. When she didn't walk fast enough, she felt the hard edges of the gun's barrel against the skin of her lower back. And she also realized the woman's hand was trembling. She almost stopped walking then—she could take her. What was she doing allowing this woman to intimidate her with a weapon? She could use the energetic hold Minka had taught her—if only she could remember how to do it exactly. But even if she did it wrong, it could give her the time she needed to wrestle the gun out of the woman's hand.

As she slowly walked, Alex looked around her. It was quiet, eerily quiet except for the row of American flags that waved on the breeze making quiet snapping sounds. She needed water. The mermaid fountain full of water that continuously flowed in a loop from the mermaid's hand to the seashell below, and back again. She took several deep breaths and brought droplets of the water to her until she could feel her palms sweating with moisture. She imagined herself creating a lasso from the water, and with hands outstretched, she turned around and watched in amazement as a glowing blue rope of energy extended from her hands and wrapped around the woman.

Holy cow! She'd done it. The gun, a small semi-automatic, fell from the woman's grip as the energy slithered around her body in a tight vise, and the woman screamed, "Who are you? *What* are you?"

"Hush," Alex admonished, looking around the now deserted park. "I'm not going to hurt you."

Alex walked toward the woman, slid off the hoodie set low over her forehead, and looked into her frightened brown eyes.

It was Evelyn Robinson.

Chapter Eighteen

"Evelyn, what are you doing here?" Frozen in place, with her arms tight at her sides, she could only stretch her eyes wide. "*What* are you?" she asked again, her voice thick with terror.

Alex held her hands out, keeping the bands around the woman in place. "I'm a friend. It's me, Alex Daniels from Botanika."

Evelyn blinked, staring at Alex, trying to see her under the baseball cap and glasses. She turned to look at the mermaid fountain and then back to Alex. "You're . . . one of them. Neve was right. Magicals. They are real and they're here in town."

"*I'm going to release you and you're not going to run.*" Alex spoke the works but she also realized she was sending the thought, telling—no, programming—the woman on her next course of action. "Do you understand?"

The woman nodded slowly, and Alex lowered her hands. The glowing strand of the vise disappeared, but Evelyn still stood rooted to the spot, her hands at her sides.

Alex took the baseball cap and glasses off. "See, it's me."

Tears flowed down the woman's face, and her shoulders began to shake. "Chris was the *Bizarre Bellamy* blogger, and someone killed him because of this"—she threw her hands wide, gesturing toward the mermaid fountain—"mermaid stuff." She wiped tears from her face.

"How do you know it had to do with mermaids? I saw the blog. He posted a lot of different things."

"Because he told me that Neve feared for her life and she wondered if she wasn't being lured to Bellamy Bay so someone could get rid of her. He also wondered if his life was in danger since he posted all of her tips."

"Wait. You knew Neve Ryland?" Alex asked.

"I never met her, but Chris mentioned her often. She'd been giving him information for years. And she was sure someone would eventually kill her to keep her quiet."

"She told your husband she thought she was being lured to town?" Fear crept up Alex's spine. "Who would want to kill her?"

"Someone who wanted to silence her. Someone who had the power to bring her to Bellamy Bay."

Alex's mind flipped through the information she'd compiled on the investigation. Who knew about the discovery? *Bryce.* Possibly Dylan. Who'd brought her to town? Dylan, on the recommendation of Bryce. Had Dylan unknowingly brought Neve to town so his college pal could kill her?

"Chris has been fascinated with science and all of its possibilities for years. When he first created that blog, I thought it was just a hobby, a bit of silliness. He's written about things he thought could be real for the fun of it. But eventually he told me that people reached out to him, people who knew things and were concerned about it being secret. Government whistleblowers, military personnel who had knowledge of crazy things being developed or discovered. They thought that if the information was out there, if it was public knowledge—even if it was on an anonymous blog, it might temper the results somehow."

"That's amazing that he was able to accomplish that."

Evelyn tried to move her body against the thought program Alex had created, but she was only able to slightly shift her shoulders. She looked at Alex helplessly. "Can you free me of your mind control or whatever it is you're doing? I promise I won't run or scream."

"Of course," Alex said, before sending the thought to the woman. "And sorry, I just had to be sure I could trust you."

Evelyn nodded. "No, I get it. You can never be too safe. I'm just relieved that I can discuss this with someone," she rushed out. "I couldn't tell anyone—not even my mother. Chris swore me to secrecy. But if you're one of them—it should be okay." Her shoulders slumped. "I'm so tired of keeping this to myself. I didn't think I could tell the police—who would believe me?"

"Even though it would've provided motive for someone to actually kill your husband."

Evelyn nodded. "When I saw your e-mail, I thought this was my chance to finally catch the killer. I was going to shoot you," she continued somewhat breathlessly. "Preferably in the shoulder—a flesh wound, as they say on television. And then call 911."

"Wait—you saw the e-mail? I thought his laptop was missing," Alex said, eyeing the woman with suspicion. "How can you access the blog? His e-mail accounts?"

"It was taken. It's still missing. But I discovered he had a backup of everything on Tanner's laptop. He created a profile—I guess to make sure no one could find his work—and it was all there."

"How did you break into the profile? I'm assuming it was password protected."

"Tanner had the password. Chris gave it to him for safekeeping. Those two were thick as thieves," she added with a sad smile. "So you're one of them? Neve wrote about them to Chris. Magicians?

No, Magicals I think they're called. He could believe a lot, but even he had a hard time believing there were people in town with magical abilities."

Alex felt odd admitting the truth about her heritage to this woman, this Mundane. So she said nothing at all. "The police think my friend killed Neve, but I know she didn't. It sounds like whoever killed Neve also killed your husband. If I find Neve's killer, I'll find your husband's. And I have a good idea who he is—I just have to find the proof."

For the first time ever, Alex saw hope in Evelyn's eyes. "What do you have? What do you know?"

"I don't want to say right now, not until I'm for sure," she hedged, not wanting to tell this grieving widow anything to get her hopes up.

"If I can help in anyway, just ask," Evelyn said. "I want to bring his killer to justice."

Alex studied the woman. "Is the blog closed now? Because—"

"No," she said firmly. "Chris would want it to continue. It was his passion, and now it will be mine. I teach science, so there is some interest on my part. No one knows about Chris. I'll just keep the blog running, as a sort of tribute to him."

"Okay. If you see anything of interest, you let me know, okay?" Evelyn nodded. "And hang in there. I'm going to find out who did this." Something occurred to Alex. "Do you know why Chris was in the woods? From what I've heard, it was off the beaten path."

"Knowing Chris, he was meeting a source. He was always on the lookout for the next big conspiracy-turned-truth. I think he was really hoping to scoop the alien invasion, because according to him that too is coming." Evelyn glanced toward her gun on the ground a few yards away from her. "You mind if I retrieve my gun?"

Alex looked at the weapon. "Where'd you get it from anyway?"

"It was Chris's just for house protection, you know?" She laughed sadly. "I'm not even sure how to use it. Chris was supposed to teach me, but he never got around to it."

Alex nodded, carefully picked up the gun and inspected it. Her father had taught her how to use and care for a gun when she was fourteen. She'd never had her own, though, or used one. But the gun felt comfortable in her hand, and she remembered everything her father had taught her. She released the magazine and pocketed the bullets, faced the barrel toward the ground, and pulled the slide back, then locked it. Another bullet flew out and landed on the ground. Alex stared at it for a moment, and looked at Evelyn handing her the gun, muzzle down. "There's no reason you should be walking around Bellamy Bay with a loaded gun."

Eyes wide, she stared at Alex. "There is if you believe your husband was killed." She placed the gun in her sweatshirt pocket, giving Alex a plaintive stare. "I have to protect myself—and my son. What if they come after us next?"

"The police need to know all of this so they can help you."

She nodded wearily. "I told them that Chris was meeting someone in the woods. Of course, they didn't believe me. I doubt they checked up on it."

"Okay . . ." Alex regarded Evelyn for a moment, wondering what she should do about the fact that a Mundane knew her secret. Unlike the rest of her family, she didn't know how to erase memories. Maybe she could get Minka or Kamila to do it later? They'd definitely have to teach her.

Evelyn smiled at her, the first time she'd really seen the woman look happy since they'd met. "You're worried I won't keep your secret. That you're a Magical? I cannot believe Neve was right about you. I mean Chris told me, but I didn't believe it. I thought she was just trying to entice him with bigger and better stories every time they talked. And they've been talking for years. I mean she's been giving him information for a while. I don't know how she did it—come up with her information—but she did."

Alex swallowed the lump in her throat. "Yeah." Her voice came out in a rough whisper. And she realized she was frightened of what this woman would do with the knowledge. She'd have to wipe this woman's memories, and soon.

But Evelyn shook her head. "Your secret is safe with me. I won't tell anyone." The look of gratitude on her face was immense. "I promise."

Chapter Nineteen

Despite being charged with murder, Alex was relieved to see that Celeste looked none the worse for wear.

Whatever that would look like, Alex amended. She just didn't want Celeste's effervescent personality dimmed by Jack's actions. Alex and her aunt Lidia had arrived as promised, bearing a huge basket of goodies designed to make Celeste feel better. Alex watched as she descended the stairs, looking fresh, if not rested, in a white T-shirt and running shorts. She was barefoot, her face free of makeup and her hair styled in double French braids.

She looks all of sixteen, Alex thought with a grin. She stepped forward and gave her a hug. "How're you doing?"

"Better now that I'm home." A smile was in place, but Alex could tell that Celeste was not doing well. The light that normally danced in her eyes was gone.

Lidia pushed the gift basket forward. "Welcome home, dear."

Celeste took the gift basket from Lidia and thanked her with air kisses.

"Come on, guys," Josephine said. "Breakfast is on the deck this morning."

The group sat at a patio table under an umbrella, and enjoyed freshly squeezed orange juice, buttermilk biscuits with local black-berry jam, sliced cantaloupe, and scrambled eggs with spicy peppers, onions, and tomatoes. A breeze lifted the heat; at eight thirty in the morning, the weather was still pleasant.

Before sitting down at the table, Josephine placed a large bowl of something tan and creamy and covered in a brown spice before her daughter.

Scents of cinnamon and anise floated toward Alex, who looked at the dish with interest. "Is that oatmeal?"

Celeste's face immediately lit up, and she gasped in delight. "It's plantain porridge," she explained, favoring Josephine with a look of gratitude. "My mother always made this for me when I was little and feeling sad, or just sick." She smiled at the memory, immediately dipping her spoon into the bowl for a taste. Celeste closed her eyes and sighed. "Thank you, *manman*."

Josephine's eye glowed with satisfaction. "I'm just happy to have you home, baby."

They finished breakfast, and although everyone was enjoying their meal and time together, it was clear to Alex that Celeste was still sad. She looked emotionally drained with a glum expression on her face. Josephine offered to show them the latest artwork her husband had sent her from his travels. Alex begged off, saying she wanted to speak to Celeste alone.

Josephine reached for Alex's hand. "I think that's a great idea. Maybe a talk with you will cheer her up. Lidia and I'll be inside."

Alex went to Celeste. "Let's have more iced coffee and then talk. Are you okay?"

"No, not really." Celeste returned to the table, and poured more coffee from a pitcher into Alex's glass and then her own. "But I've made my peace. I know I'm going to jail, I just hate what this will do to my parents." She added cream and sugar to her cup. "They're good decent people, respected in the community—and then there's me, their jail-bird daughter." She cupped her hands around her glass and took a sip.

"You know I found the real killer of Randy Bennett," Alex said. "And I can do the same for you. I just need a little more time. In fact, I have a really good idea who—"

"Alex. Stop. Just stop. Okay?" Celeste set her cup down with a loud clink. "There's something I have to tell you."

Alex's heart began to pound. She didn't like the warning look in Celeste's eyes. "What is it?"

"I appreciate everything you're doing for me—your belief in me, your willingness to track down Neve's murderer. But the truth of the matter is . . . What I'm trying to say is—" She stopped, tears beginning to fall from her eyes.

"What is it, Celeste? You can tell me anything. How bad can it be? I know that you were following Neve around town—you were caught on surveillance film."

Celeste's mouth dropped open. "You know about that?"

"Yes, I do. And so does Jack. What were you thinking? It's one of the reasons he thinks you did it."

"I told you. I was jealous. I've always been a little possessive with men, but I'm a Taurus, I have Haitian blood coursing through my veins, and the spirit of Mami Wata . . . It's to be expected." She shook her head. "But with Jasper it's been off the charts, and I don't know why." She took a breath. "There was something between Neve and Jasper—I just know it. And I wanted to find out what."

"And did you?"

She shook her head. "He would never come clean."

"I also know that you argued with Neve in the park."

Celeste covered her eyes with her hands and slumped in her seat.

"There were witnesses, and they also told the police," Alex continued." What was that about?"

"I just wanted her to tell me the truth about her relationship with Jasper."

"So you confronted her." Celeste nodded. "And what did she say?"

"That it wasn't what I thought. But I didn't believe her. Clearly, I didn't believe her."

A heavy silence filled the air between them. "You don't have to keep looking for Neve's killer," Celeste spoke, her voice hard and flat.

"How can you say that?" Alex said, leaning close when she saw that tears had filled Celeste's eyes. "I'm so close."

"Because," she continued, tears rolling down her face, "you've already found her." She wiped her face with a napkin. "You're looking at her . . . It's me."

"What? I don't understand. You—"

The sound of voices could be heard. Lidia and Josephine were on their way back to the deck.

"I killed Neve Ryland," she said, leaning in and lowering her voice, "and I'm going to go to jail for it."

Chapter Twenty

When Lidia and Josephine stepped onto the deck, they knew something was wrong.

"What's happened, Alex?" Lidia said, her concerned gaze on her niece.

But Alex couldn't speak. She was certain she had heard wrong. Surely, Celeste had not just confessed to murder. She shook her head slowly, trying to negate the words, but Celeste's tearstained face was all the proof she needed.

Josephine stared at her daughter. "Celeste, what's going on?"

"Mother, I'm sorry. I'm so so sorry, but I can't keep this to myself anymore." Taking a deep breath, she looked at Alex first and then at her mother. "I killed Neve Ryland."

Josephine collapsed into her seat while Lidia stared at Celeste, puzzled.

"Why do you say that, Celeste?" Lidia asked. "I've known you since you were a little girl. You wouldn't hurt a fly."

"But I did!" she rushed out. "I didn't want this to happen. I just wanted her to leave town, leave Jasper alone. So, I did something." Her voice lowered. "Twice actually."

Alex exchanged glances with her aunt. "What did you do?"

She swallowed hard. "I cast a . . . hex for danger." She glanced at her mother, who exchanged baffled looks with Lidia. "Just to cause her a little misfortune. You know, a candle flame sparking to scare her . . ."

"That was you?" Alex said, feeling just a little hurt. "You let me think—" She stopped, recalling other incidents. "The overturned paint at the park? That was you too?"

Celeste nodded. "I just made a little gust of wind." She glanced around the room, afraid to meet her mother's eyes. "I was angry."

"And of course I saw you make the roof leak at the museum."

Celeste gritted her teeth. "She wouldn't take her hands off him. You know how flirtatious she was. I just wanted her to leave town and never look back. But the problems I was causing were too little, of no consequence."

A haunted look darkened Celeste's eyes. "I'm not a fan of these types of spells—created to purposely harness negative energy and cause harm, and I know that by doing it I'm opening myself up to karmic repercussions and consequences—but I was desperate. And it seemed like the first hex I cast wasn't strong enough, so I thought I'd do it again. The night of the reception was a full moon." She looked at her mother askance.

"How could I resist? *A full moon?* It was the perfect time to recast the spell for a bigger bang, so to speak. And I didn't want to miss the party, so I put the items I'd need for the spell in my tote and slipped away to a quiet spot in the garden when no one was looking, and where no one could see me, and recast my hex for danger." Her voice cracked with emotion, and she struggled to continue.

"An hour later, Neve Ryland was dead." Her body heaved with sobs. "Because of me. Because of my stupid insecurities and jealousies." She lifted up her head and looked around the room. "And you know what makes all of this even worse?"

Alex was afraid to answer, but she spoke anyway. "What?"

"I don't even like Jasper anymore. I'm just so over him and his stupid floppy bangs and bow ties."

Alex would've laughed then if it all hadn't been so horrible. She didn't know what to say, so she said nothing. She looked at her aunt, who oddly enough had a smile on her face. She turned to Josephine, who also had a rather indulgent look on her face as she gazed on her daughter. "I think I'm missing something here. Can someone fill me in?" Alex finally said.

Josephine reached across the table and patted her daughter's arm. "I wish that you'd come to me sooner. I can't imagine the toll this type of secret has taken on you. The weight of this . . ."

"It's been hard, Mom. So hard. Just knowing that my actions caused all of this to happen. I took a life. And I'm going to spend the rest of my life paying for my mistakes." She sighed. "But I deserve it. I—"

Josephine patted her daughter hand. "Sweetheart, you didn't kill anyone."

"No, I did. I know it's hard to believe, but somehow, I caused this—"

"No," Lidia said, her voice stern and brooking no argument. "You didn't." She looked at Alex. "Remember when I found that list of items Celeste purchased at the shop?"

Alex nodded. "You were concerned. You wondered what Celeste was up to and said you'd talk to Josephine." She turned to look at her aunt's best friend. "And you did?"

"She did," Josephine confirmed, "and I paid Celeste a visit that evening. While she was preparing dinner for us, I did a little snooping of my own and found the items in her room. I knew exactly what she was up to. Oh, I didn't know who it was for, mind you, but I knew she was planning a little mischief for some unsuspecting person, so I did a little spell of my own." She chuckled. "Being half witch has its privileges."

Celeste's eyebrows shot up. "Mother, what did you do?"

Josephine eyed her daughter sharply. "I charmed every single one of those items so that they could only be used for good. So, if you asked them to work in something bad—"

"It wouldn't work," Celeste breathed. She jumped up and hugged her mother. "If what you say is true, then I didn't kill her. I wondered why my spell wasn't working." She laughed, giddy now. "I mean, I'm good at what I do! So, the bad things that were happening to her—"

"Were just bad things happening to her. Not your doing at all," Lidia said.

Celeste fell into her chair, relief slackening her features. "I didn't do it. I'm not a murderer." She laughed as tears continued to fall down her cheeks, but this time they were happy tears.

"You come from a long line of good women who heal, help, and protect. It's not in your DNA to do otherwise."

DNA, Alex thought with a start. *The mermaid gene.* Bryce Greenberg had to be the key to everything. She looked at Celeste, who finally had the old sparkle in her eye. Not quite up to its usual luster, but there all the same. "I have a really good idea who might be the killer. Do you all have time for me to bounce some ideas off you?"

Chapter
Twenty-One

After a long day of work, Lidia, Minka, and Alex were home and enjoying *szarlotka*—Polish apple pie. The rectangular glass dish of dessert sat in the center of the table, scenting the kitchen with butter and sugar.

Alex took her fork and pressed into the thick flaky crust of the square-cut pastry and took a bite. Flavors of cinnamon, apple, and powdered sugar exploded in her mouth, and she moaned in delight. "I think my mother used to make this."

Lidia nodded. "One of her favorites. I'll have to teach you the recipe." She took several sips of iced coffee. "Now, you were going to discuss Dylan's friend with us?"

Nodding, Alex explained all of her reasons for suspecting Bryce. "But that still leaves Jasper and Montgomery," she continued. "But honestly, as much as I dislike Montgomery, I think we have to remove him from consideration. Besides commissioning her to paint a mural, there's nothing linking Montgomery to Neve. No motive."

Athena barked and Kamila entered the house. "Not so fast guys," she said, having caught Alex's last remarks. "I hate to say it, but Montgomery might not be on the up and up."

Lidia watched her daughter as she washed her hands and then served herself a slice of pie and a cup of coffee before joining the family at the table.

"After our family dinner, I decided to look deeper into our guest's past." She shrugged. "If my little sis is going to be working for this guy, I need to know he's legit." She looked around the table and raised an eyebrow. "And he's not."

Minka sat up taller in her chair. "How do you know?"

"I had a friend on the force tail him for a couple of days. Unofficial and as a favor to me. Everything was normal except on the last day, when my friend followed him to a restaurant in town. He was on a call with someone, and they were discussing the images he had on the table before him."

"What kind of images?" Alex asked, wondering where this was going.

Kamila looked around the room. "My friend paid a waiter there to snap a few pics when he visited the table. They were satellite photos."

Alex stared at her cousin. How many ethics, morals, and laws had Kamila broken to get this information?

"I'll do whatever it takes to keep my family safe, okay?" Kamila looked at her cousin, clearly having heard her thoughts. "That guy had all my spidey senses tingling."

"He owns a mining company. It's probably just work related," Minka said, her voice hopeful.

Kamila pulled out her phone. "Take a look for yourself. Someone at work who owed me another favor enhanced them for me and identified them with geospatial software. Look familiar?"

Alex shrugged, squinting at the fuzzy images. "I don't know what I'm looking at."

"The software made a match with ninety-eight percent accuracy. It's the Wesleys' old homestead."

"Wow," Minka said. "I can't believe you were so sneaky!"

Kamila rolled her eyes in response to her sister's comment and showed everyone her screen. They could see black and white aerial images of land on the coast, with specific areas circled in red. "Montgomery Blue is clearly looking for something."

"That land . . . it's the same land Bryn killed for," Alex frowned. "Neve had the address for that location in her things at the B&B. Dylan said she wanted a tour. And now, Montgomery has satellite images of the same property. Are there minerals off the coast of the Wesley homestead?" She rubbed her temples. "Dylan told me he didn't want to work with Leviathan. But maybe he was trying to do something in secret."

Minka laughed. "Like you can mine in secret. Guess we're not removing Montgomery from our list." Then she sobered. "And I guess I'm not working for his super-awesome nonprofit."

"No," Alex said. "Not until we know if he's a murderer."

Minka huffed. "I can't do my part to help the planet until this case is closed. Alex, can't you solve this already?"

Alex gave her cousin a reassuring smile. "I'm doing my best, Mink." She turned to the rest of her family. "So, now we have a deeper connection between him and Neve. Were they working together?"

"Looks that way," Lidia said. "The question is, on what?"

"Bryn wanted that property, killed two people because she thought—the Wesleys thought—the Warsaw Shield was hidden on the property. And Pepper and I saw an Instagram post of Bryn and Montgomery on a yacht about a year or so ago. Dylan said he wanted to do business with the Wesleys, but so far he'd refused."

Kamila heaved a sigh as she stood. "What could connect Neve, Montgomery, and the Wesleys?"

Alex was thinking. Putting pieces together. Recalling memories, snatches of conversation . . . and then: "I have it," she said, looking at her family. "The thing that ties them together, That connects them, is the land."

"The land," Minka repeated. "I don't get it. How?"

"Not the land exactly. What's underneath it—or what could be hidden there."

"Oh," Lidia said, finally getting it. She nodded. "Well, I suppose that makes a kind of sense."

"Stop with the riddles already," Kamila exclaimed. "What is it?"

"The Mermaid of Warsaw's shield," Alex said. "The story goes that it's buried on the property somewhere. It's the reason Bryn's locked up right now . . . and maybe, just maybe, the reason Neve Ryland was killed."

"Wait, that doesn't make sense," Kamila said. "Nobody believes in mermaids. No one but Magicals know the Mermaid of Warsaw was real, and absolutely no one thinks the Warsaw Shield is real."

The room went quiet.

Kamila's eyebrows knitted together. "Do they?"

Minka bit her lip. "Neve did. I mean, she never came out and said it, but she researched myths, she painted them, she gave presentations on them. I have to think she believed in them just a little bit."

Now would be a great time to tell everyone about the mermaid gene, Alex thought to herself. But she just couldn't bring herself to share the information. She didn't want to worry her family, didn't want them to know that they could be in danger, especially if it all turned out to be nothing. For now, she'd keep the information to herself.

"Neve wasn't a Magical." Kamila said. "And neither is Montgomery. They can't know about the Warsaw Shield."

"Well," Lidia said quietly, "perhaps."

"Perhaps what?" Minka asked.

"Just a minute," Aunt Lidia said, heading for the library. "I'll be right back."

The women stared at each other in silence.

Minka looked at Alex. "Did you notice anything . . . Magical about Montgomery?"

Alex told them about how she felt when she tried to access his thoughts.

Lidia returned with a large book with soft, worn green leather. The family history, lovingly and methodically recorded by their ancestor. She flipped through the pages carefully. "Minka, dear, put on another pot of coffee, please. I think we're going to need it."

*   *   *

After coffee had been brewed and the table was cleared, Lidia set the book on the center of the table and gestured for everyone to come near.

Alex leaned close and read the words printed in perfect calligraphy, script she recognized as her great-great-grandmother Zofia's, on the top of one of the pages. "*Smok.* That's Polish for . . . what?"

"*Smok,*" Lidia said, "means dragon." She traced her finger over a black ink sketch. "My grandmother wrote about a historic order of Magicals who only practice black magic. Their only purpose is to create evil and increase chaos in the world." She read ahead and then shuddered. "Their motto"—she took a deep breath before continuing—"rule . . . through fear, terror, and discord."

"Holy cow," Minka exclaimed. "That's *so* low vibration."

Kamila's face twisted in revulsion. "Sounds like a modern-day terrorist group."

"Or maybe Bryn missed her calling," Alex joked.

But Lidia did not smile. "They are the reason the Council created the allowable rate of black magic to be used annually. There are different types of Magicals with different origins. Some are positively oriented and some . . . are not." Lidia looked around the room. "We're not all descended from the Mer."

Minka's mouth dropped open. "I've never heard this. I thought we were all of mermaid descent."

Kamila looked disturbed. "Their motto . . . it's not ruling they're interested in. It's repression and oppression . . . Who are these people?"

"There can be no good without evil," Aunt Lidia began. "Nor dark without light. Our world demands duality. Balance. There are people not so different from us who descended from"—a shadow crossed her face—"dragons."

"Crap," Kamila muttered. "And so the plot thickens."

"Wait, are you saying dragons are real?" Alex sputtered.

"As real as mermaids," Lidia answered. "Well, like real mermaids, dragons themselves no longer exist; however, they live on in some people just like mermaid genetics do. Dragon Descents—their technical name—command fire just like we command water, and as a general rule, they're angry and aggressive, though some are better at hiding it than others. Dragons shared an ancestor with mermaids, but we diverged eons ago."

"You're saying in addition to mermaids, dragons are also a thing?" Alex stood up, throwing up her hands. "I guess I can understand that mermaids are half human and they mated with humans—that makes a kind of sense. But dragons? How does that work? I mean . . . dragons?"

Lidia gave her niece a patient look. "Are you through, *moja droga*—my dear?"

Alex stopped pacing and sighed. "Yes, Ciocia."

"There are many stories about how the Dragon Descents were created." Lidia shrugged. "Who can know which one is correct?

Some people believe they are reptilian humanoids with the ability to shift from reptile to human form, possibly from a dinosaur ancestor that didn't go extinct. Others believe that fifty or sixty thousand years ago, certain humans were genetically modified, upgraded—or downgraded depending on your viewpoint—with dragon or reptile DNA."

"That sounds disgusting." Alex finally said.

"Whatever the case, these people have been around for thousands of years and are wholly driven by their reptilian brain, something we all have, by the way, while most non-Dragons are not. They can command fire just as we command water, and they have additional non-Mundane powers." Aunt Lidia smiled understandingly. "I know it's a lot, but you can't think that mermaids are the only game in town."

Scowling, Alex looked around the room at her cousins and her aunt before shaking her head. "I can't deal with this. I just want to be normal. I want our world to be normal."

"See?" Kamila said. "That's how I feel. Welcome to my world."

Alex closed her eyes for a moment, seeing her father's image. She looked at her aunt, at Minka and Kamila. "If I had followed my father's directions, I would still believe the world was normal, and I'd still think I was a Mundane. But I wouldn't have you guys."

"You can always choose not to practice." Kamila said. "It makes things slightly better."

But Minka couldn't stop smiling. "You guys, come on! Give it a rest. This is so-o-o cool. Dragons are cool. And it makes sense—there are a lot of dragons in Polish culture. I mean *a lot*."

Lidia shot her daughter an indulgent look. "I don't know about *cool*, but dragon myths are certainly prevalent. Only we know those myths are based in fact. Europe, Asia, Africa, the ancient Americas . . . In fact, many royal families claim to descend from dragons. It's the source of their power, the God-given right to rule. The Chinese royal family, the British royal family—look it up. I'm not making this stuff up."

Alex felt like her head was about to explode, but she needed to know more. "What does this have to do with Montgomery?"

Lidia sighed. "I had my suspicions about Montgomery when he refused to come into the house before he was invited."

Alex paused, remembering the moment. "He did stand at the threshold until you invited him in and he accepted . . . I didn't think there was anything weird about that at the time. Just that he had good manners."

"It reminded me of something." Aunt Lidia waved a hand dismissively. "But it could be nothing."

"Wait." Kamila snorted a laugh. "Isn't that wait-to-be-invited-in rule for vampires? And please don't tell me they're real too."

"No," Lidia said patiently, "there's no such thing as vampires as represented in books and the media. Some things really are just made up. Perhaps that rule was taken from the Dragon Descents. It's one of theirs. They have a lot of power and hardly any sort of ethical guidelines, but they do have that one. They can't make anyone do anything unless they want to. It's called"—she went back to the book and ran her finger down the page—"simply the law of free will. They can do all sorts of horrible things if the person they're being done to allows it."

"If that were true, nothing bad would ever happen. Who would knowingly bring bad things into their lives?"

"You'd be surprised," Lidia said. "For example, say Montgomery wants to do drilling on our coast, which could have horrible impacts to the environment, and the town council and the mayor and even the townspeople accept the idea in exchange for, say, funding for a new baseball stadium. He'll be doing bad things with the will of the people."

"That sounds like every politician ever," Kamila said with a smirk.

Lidia laughed. "There are many Dragon Descents in politics and in power in various ways. They are drawn to it, and people are drawn to them. They're sneaky and deceptive, but also good-looking, charismatic, charming people who get things done and easily get people to do what they want."

Lidia flipped through the book and pointed to a drawing.

Minka drew closer. "It's a ring." She inclined her head. "Looks like an eyeball," she said, squinting. "In the center, I mean."

Alex recalled seeing a ring like that rather recently. "Montgomery wears a ring. A green crystal with a black center."

Minka's eyebrows shot up, and she laughed. "Fraternity of the Dragons, maybe?"

"And there's what Alex told me happened when she tried to access his mind," Lidia added.

"Which was wrong," Kamila asserted. "But considering . . . maybe not." She frowned, trying to understand her own logic.

"Only Magicals can prohibit other Magicals from entering their minds." Lidia thought for a moment. "Or . . ."

"Or what?" everyone said at the same time. They looked at each other and burst into laughter.

"Or they could be taught the technique by a Magical." She shrugged at the women's skeptical expressions. "It can be learned, just like someone can learn how to pass a lie detector test."

"But what Magical would do that? Reveal themselves to a Mundane and then teach them one of our skills?"

"Anyone who is working in collaboration with Mundanes."

Magical collaborators? Was Montgomery working with the Wesleys? "But I thought this was a secret we had to take to our grave," Alex said, looking at her family members in shock. "Now you're saying that there are people who know about us?"

"There are people who have reason to come in contact with us, who know of our existence and are willing to be discreet about us if we help them."

"Help them how?" Alex asked, fascinated by the idea that there were Mundanes who knew about them. *Like Neve, before she died. And like Evelyn now,* she thought with a twinge of worry.

"People in power, those in the government. They know." She looked around the room. "And they keep it secret from the masses."

"Interesting," Alex murmured.

Lidia was poring through the book. "This section is intriguing. I've read this book many, many times, but I must confess I've skipped over this section, not being very interested in this group of people, although they are very much like us. 'Some choose to embrace their heritage while others abstain on ethical reasons,'" Lidia read, shooting Kamila a pointed look.

Lidia turned to a section filled with drawings of dragons and men and women with certain facial features, distinct jaw lines, chiseled features, seductive eyes . . . all attractive. "They can look like anyone, but they usually have fiery temperaments and issues with impulsivity. And a proclivity for black magic," she reminded them. "That's always a big indicator."

Minka looked worried. "We have to find out what Montgomery is up to, who he's working with—and all without him knowing."

"And I can't tell Jack any of this." Alex said. "He'd never believe me."

Chapter
Twenty-Two

After a long day at work, Alex took a shower and decided to head to the family library to complete more research. She had a glass of blackberry lemonade on the table beside her, and her laptop before her. There had to be something she was missing about this case.

She flipped through the portfolio again, staring at the horrific images of gods raining down fire and brimstone on the people below. People that were staring up at the sky in horror, people that were running in fear, and some that had their hands pressed together in prayer. Why would Neve create these sketches when she clearly loved mythology and the beautiful fanciful side of the stories?

She pulled up a photo of the mermaid mural and stared at it, wondering what it meant. And then she went to Neve's websites and looked at the murals she'd painted in Honolulu and Boston. Her phone rang, and grateful for the break, she answered. It was Pepper.

"Remember I had my intern looking into Neve's past? She found something kind of interesting. Every time she's had an art show in some town, there's been some sort of major break-in at certain facilities, or emergency drills."

Alex set her drink down, not sure she was understanding. "What do you mean?"

"During her show in Honolulu, there was an incident on one of the naval bases. The media later said that it was an emergency drill with crisis actors. In Boston, a bridge was shut down for half a day for some undisclosed reason."

Alex rested against the back of her seat. "There's a million reasons why those events could've occurred, none of which have to do with Neve."

"I know," Pepper said, a bit petulantly. "I just thought I would share it with you. My intern is a real go-getter, and she was excited to find this connection."

"No, I get it. It's interesting . . . maybe another piece of the puzzle." Alex thought for a moment. "She had a show here. And nothing happened."

Pepper was quiet for a moment. "We had the power outage."

"That's true, but that was just a power grid issue . . ."

"Okay," Pepper agreed. "That's all I got. Did you ever find anything about the blogger?"

Alex was silent, wondering what she could share and what she shouldn't. "I had a meeting planned, but they stood me up," she lied. "But if I find something out, I promise you'll be the first to know." And that was true. If Alex could find a way to give Pepper a scoop to help her career, she would.

After the call ended, Alex went back to the mural Neve had painted in Boston. It was a picture of Poseidon holding his infamous trident in the Mystic River—an odd place for a god of the sea to be. The Tobin Bridge was behind him. A man fished off a pier while a woman sat on a bench, reading a newspaper. Another man gazed at a tall public clock, on a black post, that had Roman numerals. The painting was so detailed that you could see the direction the hands were pointing. The colors were bright and the painting style realistic, as if Poseidon himself was flesh and blood instead of a creation of myth.

Alex clicked on the painting from Honolulu. The Japanese sea god, Watatsumi stood at the helm of a naval ship, with the sleek body of a young fit man, and the head of dragon. His chest was bare, and his arms were covered in kanji tattoos. He held several bright jewels in his hand while sailors could be seen on the deck, involved in various tasks running the ship. One was reading a newspaper, and another looked at his watch.

Alex went back to the mermaid painting. Unlike Neve's other paintings, it lacked the hallmarks of her work: someone reading a newspaper and someone looking at a clock.

Her phone chimed with an incoming text. It was Kamila. Her message said there might be security footage of the parking lot from the traffic light by the entrance. But, first, it would be difficult to get a look at it, and second, Alex better not tell anyone she was doing it, and third, Kamila loved her. Smiling, Alex placed the phone on the bed beside her.

A moment later she turned back to her screen, but her mind had turned to pudding. Frustrated with her efforts, Alex closed her laptop, when her phone rang again. It was Evelyn.

"I've been going through Chris's e-mails, and I found something you need to see. Let's meet at the coffee shop on Main."

"Sure," Alex agreed. "I'll see you soon."

Ten minutes later, Alex was enjoying an iced matcha latte in the back of the coffee shop. She assumed Evelyn wanted privacy, so she'd sit at the most private table she could find. Alex leaned forward when she was settled. "You have something to tell me?"

"Yes. I think I mentioned that whistleblowers contacted Chris?" Alex nodded. "I'm getting a better idea of what he did now, and he was privy to some really amazing information. I also discovered in those e-mails that in order for him to receive some information, he had to agree to post fake information."

"Why would he have to do that?"

"As explained in the e-mails, they wanted to make it harder for readers to know what was real and what was not. By giving Chris made-up stories along with the real ones, the revelations were hiding in plain sight."

"As a practice that's called disinformation," Alex commented. "Okay. I guess that makes a kind of sense. So, what you have to share with me is . . . what? Real or fake?"

"I'll let you be the judge of that. I did a search for more e-mails from Neve and hit the jackpot. She sent Chris a list of several weapons of the gods—what they do or, rather, how they can be converted to modern functions."

"What do you mean?"

She retrieved a small notebook from her purse and found a page of notes. "Well, take Thor's hammer, for example. It was apparently 'found'"—she used air quotes—"in St. Cloud, Minnesota, hidden in the Sauk River. Uses include manufacturing earthquakes, leveling great swaths of the earth, manipulating the weather and generating storms, creating universal sound baths—not sure what that is—and of course destroying anything it happened to smash into. Unfortunately, the hammer is useless without a pair of gloves that Thor used to activate the hammer. The search is still on for them. Ostensibly, the hammer had a wireless technology that matched with a GPS signal in the gloves that created the boomerang effect."

"Obviously, that's fake news. Thor didn't really exist." Alex laughed. "I've seen the movies, and I know who Thor is and how his infamous hammer works . . . but that's just made up. Foreign governments are not bidding on a mythological weapon."

Evelyn looked perplexed. "That's what I thought. But Neve also sent a list of potential customers for Thor's hammer, even without the glove, or gauntlet as it's known. Governments in Iran, North Korea, China, Russia. She wrote that it can be used in construction, demolition. Meteorology. This is government use. It's crazy stuff. There's a list like this for five different mythological items."

"If what you say is true, then most of this stuff is made up. I know what's going on."

"You do?"

"The mermaid gene is the real story, and this mythological weapon story is the disinformation. I mean, we know the gene has been discovered, and companies are working on it. But if you posted both of these items, your readers would be really hard pressed to figure out which one was real, if they didn't reject them both outright."

"Right." Evelyn's eyes teared up. "And this is why Chris was murdered. Because he put these ridiculous items on his blog." She picked up her coffee mug and stared into its depths. "I was really surprised when I got your text telling me you'd help me. You're the only person in this town who believes me. Any progress?"

"Nothing specific, but I did talk to your husband's boss."

Evelyn's eyebrows shot up. "You did?" She gulped. "What did he say? Anything helpful?"

"Just that Chris didn't stay late in the evenings or come in on Saturdays like you said." She winced at the expression on the woman's face. "I mean, if he wasn't at work, where was he? What was he doing?"

Evelyn shook her head. "I don't like what you're implying."

"I don't even know what I'm saying, okay? But I do think that if I can figure out what he was up to during that time, it may lead me to find out who really killed him."

"You think whoever he was meeting killed him."

Alex shrugged. "Maybe."

"How will you figure it out?"

"It's a long shot, but I'm trying to get a look at the security footage from the parking lot where Chris parked."

"The detective told me the camera was at the wrong angle, and it didn't see anything."

"There might be more footage. We'll see."

"From where? From whom?"

"I don't know all of the details." Alex regretted telling Evelyn any of this. The last thing she wanted to do was get Kamila in trouble. No matter how grateful Evelyn might be for the footage, she might accidentally tell someone how it had been obtained. Better to shut the conversation down now. She leaned forward. "Are you okay? Do you have family around here you can talk to if you need to?"

She shook her head. "My family's in Florida. His family is nearby, but we're not close. It's fine. I've been talking to a counselor, which helps with the grief. But not with the fact that everyone thinks he did this to himself." She choked back a sob.

"Just imagine the day when everyone knows the truth. It's coming and soon."

Evelyn smiled at her. "Thanks for that." She grabbed a napkin and blotted her face. "I better get going. I hope what I've told you is helpful." She left, and Alex watched her go, wondering what her next step should be.

As Alex backed out of the parking lot, she thought about the facts of the case—both cases. Seeing that Main Street was clogged with evening construction, she turned down an alley between the historic buildings and slowed when a cat darted across the street. Someone had killed both Neve *and* Chris Robinson. There couldn't be two killers in Bellamy Bay. It made sense that there was only one. Jasper didn't have a reason to kill both Neve *and* Chris. She stopped at a red light and was about to turn, her mind still whirling with possibilities. Who had the motive to kill them both? Montgomery? Or how about—

Crash!

The sound of metal filled Alex's ears, as her body was propelled forward. Frantically, she glanced at her rearview mirror and saw a white SUV behind her. It had hit her once and was backing up to slam her again.

Smash!

She was hit again. And this time the steering wheel was spinning in her hands, the tires skidding out of control.

And Alex was rushing headlong into oncoming traffic.

Chapter Twenty-Three

Hands gripping the steering wheel, and foot pressed on the brake, Alex held tight, trying to right the car, but it completed several 360s, ending up in the opposite direction before it stopped.

And everything inside the car was tossed around. Including Alex. She felt dizzy and her hands trembled as they clung to the steering wheel. There was loud honking and the screech of slamming breaks as several cars driving toward her swerved in the opposite lane, barely missing her. Adrenaline ricocheting in her chest, Alex looked over her shoulder and saw the SUV was still behind her. She pressed the gas pedal to the floor and moved to the side of the street while the SUV sped away from her.

What just happened?

Taking deep breaths, she willed her heart to stop racing and found her phone on the passenger side floor. She began to dial Kamila's number, then stopped. Jack wanted her to call him, but she didn't want him to know she'd gotten herself in trouble. No—no way she was calling him. She dialed her cousin and waited. The call went straight to voicemail. Tears of frustration crowded her eyes, and her heart still pounded. She waited a moment. Kamila did not return the call.

She dialed Jack's number but hesitated before she hit "Send." He would be angry, accuse her of meddling in the case. Well, she had been. She stared at the phone. Waiting. Hoping. Kamila didn't call back.

Sighing, she hit "Send."

With Minka's car being towed, Jack drove Alex home.

Her entire body ached. She was really going to feel it in the morning.

When Jack pulled into the driveway of her home, he turned the ignition off. He had been angry when he took the call and realized Alex had placed herself in danger again. And angrier when he saw the damage to Minka's car—clearly the driver had been going fast, and it was a wonder Alex hadn't gotten hurt. The only thing he'd said to her was "Thank you for calling me," and that was through clenched teeth. And then there were ten minutes of silence as he drove her home.

"Let's try this again," he said, his voice straining with the effort not to sound upset. "Where were you coming from?"

"The coffee shop."

"Who were you meeting?"

Alex hesitated. She didn't want to lie, but she also didn't want to tell him it was Evelyn Robinson. She bit her lip and looked out the window.

"You know, someone is trying to warn you off whatever it is you're doing. Is there something I should know?"

She looked at him, knowing that his anger masked concern. She reached for his hand. "I'm sorry I've worried you." She shifted in her seat and winced in pain.

Alarmed at her discomfort, Jack leaned toward her, touching her face. "Are you okay? I can still take you to the ER."

"No, I'm fine. I just need some aspirin and a good night's rest. Why don't you come in? I'll make you some coffee, feed you . . ."

She was embarrassed to say the incident had frightened her, and she wasn't quite ready for Jack to leave her.

Jack stared at the brightly lit house, warm gold light streamed from behind the curtained windows. "I'm not your aunt's favorite person."

"She's forgiven you for arresting her—you know that."

He glanced at the time display on his dashboard. "Before you called, I was in the middle of something. Unfortunately, I need to get back to it."

Alex stared at him. She wanted to ask him what was more important than her right now, but she couldn't get those particular words out. They sounded weak. Needy. She forced a smile. "You're on a stakeout or something?"

"I'm working." He kissed her on the cheek.

"The big party at the lighthouse is in two days. Will you be working then too?"

"Yeah." He shot her a rueful look. "But I really wish I could come. I hear it's kind of spectacular."

*   *   *

When Jack was gone, Alex opened the front door and was greeted by Athena, who stood up on her hind legs to welcome her. "Hey, girl, I missed you," she murmured into the fur of her neck.

Alex followed the sounds and found her aunt and both cousins munching on large bowls of buttered popcorn and watching a movie.

"I fed Athena and took her out," Minka said, her eyes glued to the screen. She turned to Alex and paused the television show when she saw her face. "What's wrong?"

"Someone hit the car, with me in it and on purpose." She looked at Minka. "Sorry. I'll take care of the damages. It was towed to the Wesley Auto Repair shop in town."

Minka shrugged. "You know I could care less about that car."

Kamila stood. "Jack took a report?"

Lidia joined them. "Are you hurt?"

"Jack took down the details for all the good it will do. The windows were tinted, the make generic, and I was too panicked to notice the license plate." Alex turned to her aunt. "And I'm fine." She tried to smile through the pain she was feeling in her shoulders and back.

"No stickers or decals on the vehicle?" Kamila continued. Alex shook her head. "Well, they'll have front-end damage to their vehicle, with Minka's car paint all over it. I'm sure Jack will notify repair shops in the area to be on the lookout." She put an arm around her. "You sure you're okay?"

"Shaken up but fine."

Lidia frowned but nodded. "I know exactly what you need. I'll start your bath with a strong blend of arnica and helichrysum in Epsom salts for any aches you may have or get in the morning."

After her bath and a glass of tea that Lidia had placed by her bedside, Alex felt a wave of fatigue wash over her. She was exhausted—but more determined than ever to find out who killed Neve and Chris. They were the same person, she was certain of it. And that same person had tried to scare her tonight. But she wouldn't be intimidated. She had been concerned for her family's safety because the killer knew who she was. But Aunt Lidia assured her that the protective spell she'd placed over the house and land would keep them safe.

Curled under her covers, she searched her phone for the photographs of Neve's murals, flipping through the three images from Honolulu, Boston, and St. Cloud. The similarities being the man and the watch, and the man with the newspaper. There'd been an emergency at each location . . . It was such an odd coincidence, it had to mean something. But there hadn't been an emergency in Bellamy Bay, and there wasn't a newspaper or clock in the mermaid mural. What did that mean?

* * *

The next morning, Alex woke up with sunlight streaming through the cracks in her curtains. Blinking, she rubbed her eyes, stretched, and sat up. She'd gone to bed thinking about Neve's paintings, and she'd woken up thinking about them. Her dreams suddenly came to her: images of flying newspapers and clocks had rained down her as she'd walked on the beach. And then it came to her. *The newspaper. The clock.* Pepper's intern had been on to something. She looked at the clock on her phone. Was it too early to text Pepper on a Sunday? It was seven thirty.

She sent Pepper a text, hoping she had her notifications turned off and would receive it when she woke up. Less than a second later, Pepper responded with the emoticon of a cup of coffee looking sleepy and holding a smaller cup of coffee. Great—she was up. Alex texted what she needed, and hoped Pepper had quick access to it.

She wandered downstairs and into the kitchen for coffee. Aunt Lidia was always up by five thirty and by now had probably made two pots of coffee. The aromatic scent of coffee beans wafted through the house, and she followed the smell to the counter, where she grabbed the biggest mug she could find and filled it up, topping it off with half and half. The house was quiet when she went back upstairs and to her room. She checked her phone and saw that Pepper had sent the information she needed to her e-mail address.

She opened her laptop, sat on her bed, and sipped her coffee as she waited for her e-mail account to load. She found Pepper's e-mail and clicked on the attachment, then compared the information to the pictures of Neve's murals.

Unbelievable.

She checked again to make sure she wasn't mistaken. But no, the dates and times matched. Alex sat up, drinking her coffee. In every single image, the date on the newspaper and the time on the clock matched the emergency event in the same town. It was almost as if Neve had painted clues into her murals to let someone know when and what time to create a diversion.

If only she had proof that any of the mythological weapons had actually been found. And if so, the time and date of those occurrences. If they matched the times and dates painted in Neve's murals, that would prove what Neve had been up to in town. Not just an artist after all. Then she'd just have to figure out who Neve's partner had been—a partner who killed her because she refused to share information.

Finished with her coffee, she went back downstairs. Now her aunt was at the stove, and she turned around with a smile.

"Good morning. Feeling better?"

"Yes, thanks. The bath and tea were just what I needed." Alex stopped to flex her arms and legs. "Actually, I feel better than ever." She eyed her aunt with suspicion. "Did you—"

Lidia chuckled. "I may have enhanced the bath salts with a little something. If I missed a spot, you can always heal yourself, you know."

"Right. I keep forgetting about my abilities." Alex laughed. "It's not quite second nature to me yet. Although the telepathy is handy. More convenient than texting."

Aunt Lidia laughed. "I suppose so. You need to eat. Kielbasa and scrambled eggs. Buttered bread from a loaf I baked yesterday." She made a shooing motion with her hand. "Now have a seat."

After her aunt served her food, along with a fresh cup of coffee, Alex reached for a slice of soft bread with just the right amount of crust. "Where's Minka?" she asked as she picked up her knife and spread butter on the bread.

"Sleeping in. She stayed up late watching a movie marathon. But Kamila should be stopping by." Athena barked. "And there she is, right on time." Aunt Lidia grinned as she set another plate of food on the table.

Kamila entered, greeting Alex and giving her mother a kiss on the cheek. She was in uniform, her sidearm at her waist. She looked at the breakfast table. "Yes! Kielbasa for breakfast. After the kick-boxing workout I had this morning, I need the protein."

She joined Alex at the table and began eating. "You feeling better?" she asked Alex.

"Good as new, thanks to one of Ciocia Lidia's special bath blends."

"You're welcome," Aunt Lidia called over her shoulder as she headed upstairs.

Kamila began to frown but stopped herself. "I guess if you're going to use magic, healing is the best use of the ability. I'm glad you're okay."

"Thanks." Alex gazed up the stairs, waiting until she heard her aunt's bedroom door close. "Hey, I've been meaning to ask you something. What's Jack working on? He's gone a lot more than he used to be. Is it just the two murder investigations?"

Kamila narrowed her eyes. "What are you worried about? Detective Frazier doesn't seem like the unfaithful type."

Alex blushed. "No, it's not that. He's just . . . busy. I haven't seen a lot of him this summer. And when I do, he's usually just coming from work."

Kamila rolled her eyes. "Don't be clingy. Guys don't like that."

"I'm not!" Alex laughed. "I promise you, it's—it's something else. Consider it my intuition. I just feel like there's something going on with him."

"Or Celeste is rubbing off on you." Kamila shrugged. "I'll keep an eye out. But I think you're seeing things that aren't there."

Embarrassed, Alex was eager to change the subject. "So, how's work been?"

"It's been pretty tame. Swung by the coroner's office for a look-see. Ever since that break-in, we're providing extra protection, just in case."

"Did you find out who broke in?"

"Not yet," Kamila said. "But I did hear something you may find of interest. I was shooting the breeze with the coroner, and he mentioned that he recovered a piece of paper in the victim's shoe."

"In his shoe?" Alex laughed. "What was on it?"

"I'm not sure. Oddly enough, he said he thought it might be a list of the deceased favorite superhero movies, I guess. With dates and times—I'm guessing show times."

"For the local movie theater?"

Kamila shrugged. "I don't know. I didn't want to appear too interested."

"Is there any way I can get my hands on that note?"

"The original is probably filed away in the evidence room at the station. I can't just walk in there for no reason and grab it for you."

"I could do a spell for trouble and make myself invisible," Alex suggested.

"And get in trouble with The Council." Kamila screwed up her face. "Trust me, you don't want that headache."

"I know. I would never . . . I'm just frustrated."

"Don't worry, cousin. I'll go in and take a picture of the list and send it to you."

"Really?" Alex stared at Kamila. "Is that legal?"

Kamila exhaled loudly, ignoring the question. "You can't show it to anyone, and you can't tell anyone how you found it. Got it?"

Alex nodded. "Got it." She cleared her throat, and Kamila raised an eyebrow. "What is it?"

"While I'm asking for favors . . ."

"Yeah?"

"What do you know about the area where Chris Robinson's body was found?"

She shrugged. "Not much. Well, in high school it used to be the place the kids hung out when they were skipping school. Back then there was a clearing for a small fire, and the kids—not me of course," she said, smirking, "would bring music and beer and soda and hot dogs for grilling, and just relax. There was a trail from that spot over some sand dunes that went straight to the beach."

"What was the appeal of that spot?" Alex asked.

"Close enough to public access parking but deep enough into the woods that no one could find you unless you knew where to park. And no security cameras for the lovebirds."

The perfect spot for Chris to meet a source—or someone pretending to be a source so they could kill him.

"I know what you're thinking," Kamila said. "And yes, Chris Robinson went to Bellamy Bay High School, so he'd know of the spot. He'd also know that the local druggies went there to get high in private."

Alex nodded. "Any luck with that security video I asked you about?"

"It does exist. Just clearing some red tape to get access to it. I've put in a lot of favors to help our family with this case, and while I'm happy I can do it, it doesn't make me feel good about myself. Either I'm a decent law-abiding person or I'm not."

Alex frowned. "Sorry, Kamila. I don't mean to put you in a difficult position. I'm sure Minka doesn't either."

"I know. It's not you, it's me. Really. I want to help, and I'm in a position to do so." She shrugged. "I don't want to push too hard on the security camera video, but I will check on that list for you." Kamila moved back from the table and set her dishes in the sink. "Tell Mom I had to leave. If I find anything, look out for my text."

Alex and Athena walked her to the door. "Thank you."

Kamila punched her lightly on her shoulder. "You better not get me in trouble," she joked.

* * *

Forty-five minutes later Alex got the text from Kamila. Back in her room, she read the list and shook her head. Jack had been wrong. Had he even read it? This wasn't a list of superhero movies. This was a list of mythological weapons, each with a date and time. If her hunch was right, each date and time would match the corresponding information relayed on the mural.

She opened up her laptop and made a chart with the name of each mural, the god or goddess painted, and the date and time. Then she compared it to the list. Each and every item was a match. Neve's murals weren't just paintings; they were clues, messages to her partner, whoever that person was, telling them where to find the mythological weapon and the time and place of the diversion to disguise the recovery. *Amazing.*

Neve had not just been an artist. She had implied as much when she'd stopped by Botanika, but Alex hadn't understood what she was really saying. Who was she? And who had *she worked for?*

And why did Chris have a list of found mythological weapons in his shoe when he died? Had he intended to give it to someone? Had he met someone in the woods as Alex suspected? And had that person killed him because he couldn't find the list? Who in town would want that list?

There are so many questions and not enough answers, Alex mused to herself. And the mermaid mural? Was that a part of something bigger or just a painting? Alex closed her eyes, rubbing her temples. No, that surely had to be just a painting, a part of the festivities. There was no clock, no newspaper, no clues that the mural was meant to be anything except a beautiful painting. Neve had said sometimes her assignments were just that—opportunities to paint. It was only occasionally that they weren't.

That night, Alex fell asleep with images of the gods flying through her mind.

Chapter Twenty-Four

To the Mundanes, the annual Magical Mermaid Ball was enchanting, but to the Magicals it was truly charmed.

Minka and Celeste worked on the party in secret, and Alex was excited to see what all the hullabaloo was about. Kamila had promised her it was an event not to be missed.

Partygoers had to be ferried over, so Alex found herself, wearing a burgundy party dress and matching heels, on a large white boat with a crowd of townsfolk. Even Aunt Lidia had joined her, beautiful with her hair upswept in a twist and her figure fashionable in a steel-gray sheath with pearls and black heels.

After a relatively smooth ride over, they disembarked and were greeted by a mini bus, usually reserved for tourists, that circled the island before depositing them at the cottage—actually a large one-story home that had been converted into a ballroom—and lighthouse for a tour.

"I hope I don't see Tegan here," Lidia murmured under her breath. "Her mere presence ruins my day."

"Let's focus on how much fun we're going to have," Alex said, wrapping an arm around her aunt. "You look fabulous, by the way." They joined the line moving into the cottage.

Her aunt's smile was tender. "You do too. Just like your mother when she was your age. She'd be so proud of you. I only wish she could've seen you all grown up."

The line moved through the foyer and into the ballroom. Alex paused midway and stared around her. It looked like they'd stepped into the ocean. The room was filled with a hazy blue that approximated water. But you couldn't feel it. The smell was clean and at turns salty and fresh. Schools of brightly colored fish swirled expertly around the guests without knocking into them. The ground below them was sand filled with seashells. Sea plants waved from the floor.

"What the—" Alex began, surprised that she could still talk as normal. Was this some sort of virtual reality? Or was she hallucinating?

A musical sound floated around them, a mix of wind chimes, beautiful flute, or maybe harp music and a base note, something like a cello or tuba—maybe whale calls? Alex couldn't tell, but it immediately calmed her and at the same time lifted her spirits.

Lidia shook her head. "The girls have really outdone themselves. This is magnificent." She took a deep breath and closed her eyes for a moment. "Doesn't this feel nice? This is the world we came from." She lifted her arms and did a single twirl.

Alex stared at her aunt, fascinated. She'd never seen Aunt Lidia behave so fancifully. "Yes, it does feel nice," she stammered, almost stepping on a conch shell, luminescent in color and swirled with pink and purple. But her foot simply went through it. It wasn't real, just a very accurate depiction.

A merman floated by—an actual man with a silvery tail tinged with a blue metallic color and a black bow tie around his neck held out a try of a blue bubbly beverage in champagne flutes. "Drink, ladies?" he asked with a wide grin. He was gorgeous, with dark brown skin, curly black hair, and a chiseled chest and arms. His pectoral muscles glittered with gold symbols—tattoos that looked like the mermaid language found on the family's crystal scrying bowl.

Alex blinked. She turned to her aunt. "Is this real? He looks so real." She turned to the merman before her aunt could respond. "Are you real?"

His grin widened, his voice musical with an accent she couldn't place. "I am a special effect created by Blippo, a local virtual reality and video game development company. Tonight's event is an example of advanced virtual reality technology." He waited for them to take their beverages before swimming away.

"So that's how Minka and Celeste are explaining this?" She turned in a circle taking it all in. "Virtual reality. And without any special glasses?"

Lidia laughed. "Provide a halfway plausible explanation, and Mundanes will believe anything after a drink or two." She shrugged. "Who understands how these technologies really work or their limitations? Science or magic, the results can be the same."

Alex looked around and saw a mermaid floating by in the distance. Her hair was silver-blonde, her tail pink, her chest covered in a bikini top made of seashells and seaweed. Silver symbols ran up and down her arms. "It's beautiful and magical, just like they said it would be."

The large room was slowly filling with partygoers who looked around them with wide eyes and open mouths. Alex caught sight of another merman, with long brown hair, a fair complexion, and a silvery-green tale.

"What do you think?" Minka squealed, coming up from behind Alex. "Is this amazing or what?" Minka was gorgeous in a shimmery chiffon dress of pink and lavender that swirled around her with the currents of water. It was all spaghetti straps and flouncy skirt. In her curls, she wore a sparkly silver tiara embedded with pink, purple, green, and blue crystals.

"You've outdone yourself," Lidia said with a proud expression on her face. "And that music?"

"It's the real sounds of the ocean—at least what Magicals hear," Celeste answered, joining them. "It's a vibration, Schumann resonance. You know the sound the earth emits, but underwater. The earth is alive, and it has its own music." She giggled. "The frequency, among other things, calms humans and provides stability for all of the sea creatures. Isn't it lovely?"

Celeste shone in a beautiful dress of yellow and lime green that fell to the floor—well, to the sand—and swirled around her feet. Her shoulders were bare, and the bodice was studded with sequins that were not unlike the mermaid's fins that floated around them. Her hair had been ironed flat into a curtain of black silk that hung down her back.

Alex took a sip of her drink and almost swooned. "What is this? It's delicious?"

Lidia laughed. "Don't you mean *magically* delicious."

Minka and Celeste exchanged knowing glances.

"What does it taste like?" Minka asked.

Alex took another sip and tried to identify the taste. "Cotton candy? Buttered popcorn . . . candy apples?" She laughed self-consciously. "But that doesn't make sense."

"Of course, it doesn't," Lidia said with a soft smile. "It must come from a memory."

Alex thought for a moment. "Yes. It does. One of the last memories I have of my mother. We all went to the state fair. And that's what I had: cotton candy, kettle corn, and candy apples." She laughed. "I got sick that night and threw up, but it was one of the best days of my life. Usually, my parents would never allow me to have so much sugar, but they did that day." She took another sip and nodded. "Yes, that's exactly what it is."

Minka nodded approvingly. "The beverages have been enchanted to taste like whatever you want it to taste like. Your best memory. Your favorite things."

"Plus, they've been enchanted to help suspend disbelief for the Mundanes, so they're less likely to question our magical creations line about special effects." She grinned. "At this party, you must drink the Kool-Aid."

Minka and Celeste high-fived each other and then dissolved into a fit of giggles.

"Hey guys," Pepper said as she joined them, drink in hand. "How's it going?"

They all greeted her, and Minka complimented her chartreuse-colored dress.

Alex saw Dylan enter the room, with his mother on his arm. Montgomery was behind them, and she wondered if they were together.

As if he could feel her looking at him, Dylan turned to look at her. He grinned and gave her a two-finger salute in greeting. She offered a polite smile and nod in return. Minka caught the exchange and lifted an eyebrow.

It's nothing. We're just . . . acquaintances, Alex told her telepathically. She finished her drink, and a mermaid immediately appeared to whisk it away for her.

Bunches of brightly colored tropical flowers floated on the currents around them, and when they did, the exquisite scent of orchids bloomed, filling the air. Celeste sighed, and Alex turned to follow her gaze. She was looking at Jasper, who was laughing at something Mayor Bellamy was saying while Cressida looked on.

Alex touched Celeste's arm slightly and moved away from the crowd. "How are things with you and Jasper?"

"I'm not sure. He's called me a bunch of times, but I don't think I'm interested anymore. This whole situation with Neve has really soured things for me, whether he was seeing her or not. And I still don't know the truth."

"You can definitely do better," Alex said with an encouraging smile. "Just give it time.

Bryce appeared at the entrance, eyes literally saucers as he took in the room. Dylan called to him, and Bryce joined his group. Alex watched as Dylan handed him a drink. She turned and saw Minka making her way to him, her tiara glistening against the shimmering of the waves.

Merfolk floated around carrying trays laden with heavy appetizers, and the buzz in the room increased as everyone began to eat and drink more. The music filled Alex's ears, and she felt almost drunk on happiness. Alex felt her cell phone vibrating in her purse.

She stepped out of the room—and the ocean—and took a moment to clear her mind and senses. She looked at the screen. It was Evelyn.

"Hey," Alex said. "Are you coming to the party? Practically the entire town is here."

"I was hoping I could find you," she said, relief flooding her voice. "I've been calling around trying to track you down."

Alex moved closer to the door of the cottage, placing a finger in her ear. "Is everything okay?"

"I'm not sure. Something interesting came through the blog contact form. I'm on the island. Can we meet by the lighthouse?"

"Of course. I'm stepping outside now." She moved away from the house and saw Evelyn waving at her from a distance. She followed Evelyn toward the lighthouse.

"It's lovely here," Evelyn said pointing to the tall, whitewashed structure with a bright red lantern room on top that matched the red roof of the otherwise white cottage standing a few hundred yards away from it.

"Have you been inside the lighthouse?" Evelyn asked. "It's really beautiful, and the view on top is amazing. I like to come up here and clear my head . . . Think of the good times with Chris." She smiled at Alex. "Come on. You're not going to believe what I've discovered. It's proof Chris didn't kill himself."

Alex followed Evelyn inside the lighthouse and paused when she looked at the spiraling staircase, ascending hundreds of yards skyward—and then at her high heels.

"You'll be fine," Evelyn said. "I promise, the view will be worth it."

After a few moments of walking in silence up the stairs, the women reached the top. And Evelyn was right: it was beautiful, and Alex was happy to take in the view. Especially after the headiness of the party. The water looked silver in the sunlight, shimmering in ripples—and there was something Alex had never seen before—an island in the bay. It was small and desolate. She'd never seen it from the beach.

"You're right, it was worth the hike in heels." She laughed, then turned to look out over the water. "I could take in this view for hours and not get tired of it." Her gaze went back to Evelyn, who had an odd expression on her face. She wore heels and a plain black dress, Alex noted. Her only jewelry was a simple necklace. "You're all dressed up. You look nice. Are you going to the party?"

Evelyn's lips twisted. "My husband just died. Do you think I should be living it up with a bunch of Magicals?"

The smile disappeared from Alex's lips. "Of course not. It's just, you're wearing a dress..."

"I'm in mourning. Remember?" Her voice rose, and Alex realized that Evelyn was angry. "My marriage was destroyed because of all of that abracadabra crap," she said, jabbing a finger toward the cottage. "Because of people like you." She pulled something out of her purse that glinted in the sunlight.

A gun, Alex recognized with a twinge of fear. "Why do you have —" And then it hit her—like a tidal wave actually. Evelyn had come that night to the park with a weapon, not to defend herself but to *kill* someone. *Because she is a murderer.*

The pieces fell together with horrible precision—click. Click. Click.

Mac telling her that Neve had been in Bellamy Bay two months before for a visit.

Both Ciocia Lidia and Jack saying Neve was six weeks pregnant.

Kamila sharing that the spot in the woods was a "lover's lane" and that Evelyn's husband had been meeting a source when he was killed.

The list in his shoe was for his source.

Why couldn't I have figured it all out a few minutes sooner? Alex thought to herself.

Alex took a step back, and then another, until her back was against the railing. She looked behind her, alarmed. Nowhere to go except over the edge to the ground below. "Your husband thought he was meeting with Neve that night in the woods."

"Of course, he did," she said. "It was, like, *their spot*. He never doubted for an instance that he was meeting her. Only when he arrived, it was me and not her." She laughed. "You can't imagine the look on his face when he saw me."

"How did you do it?"

"He's not the only one who's a wiz with a computer. I used an app that made it appear that I'd sent a text from her number. And of course, he came running."

"Neve wasn't just a source," Alex said. "You found out he was cheating on you. Why didn't you throw him out of your house and file for divorce?" Alex said, mind racing for a solution. What in her magic bag of tricks could she use to counter this woman?

"I loved him," she seethed. "I didn't want him to leave. And I gave him a choice. I said forget her and come back to me and Tanner." An angry tear slid down her face. "He refused! That jerk refused me—said he was starting over with her. She was pregnant, and they'd be a family." Her grip was so tight on the gun that her knuckles turned red. "We were already a family," she choked out. "How could he?"

Alex shook her head. "I don't know . . ."

"He said she was going to quit her job, and they were going to move far, far away from everything and everybody and start a new life together. Can you imagine how I felt?"

"No," Alex said, her eyes trained on the gun. "But I bet it was very painful for you."

"He tried to explain it to me. Can you believe that?"

Alex shook her head, thinking that had probably been a very stupid move.

"He told me that she was so beautiful and smart and interesting and adventurous, and they cared about the same things. This was supposed to make everything clear, since I *wasn't* beautiful or smart or interesting or adventurous—do you see what I mean? Like, what was I supposed to do with that explanation? Say, 'Oh, okay, I see you're upgrading.' And just leave with my tail between my knees? And that blog! That stupid, stupid blog of his. She'd been his source for years—years! They had that in common. I tried to fake an interest. I mean, sue me for not caring about aliens in the government and magical weapons and fairy tales that turn out to be true!"

Her shoulders heaved in a tortured sigh. "I shouldn't have had to compete with her. And did you see her? So beautiful. Her hair? My God—like a freaking shampoo commercial."

She steadied herself and held the gun out before her with two hands. "I had everything under control. I killed him in the most perfect way—I didn't leave a trace of how I did it. And you know how they always suspect the spouse?"

Alex nodded silently, eyes still on the barrel.

"I made sure to pester the police and the newspaper so much that there was *no way* they could ever suspect me, even if they did find out how he actually died. I'll admit, I was a little paranoid about someone thinking I did it. But when I found out you were dating the detective, I thought, how clever would it be if he heard from you that I was *also* bothering our local Nancy Drew about solving the case. You think I just happened to run into you outside that wine bar?"

"You were following me?"

She chuckled. They would never suspect me, not the way I was begging and pleading anyone and their mother to help me solve the case. And then that night at the coffee shop, you told me you might have security footage to look at—which meant you'd see me.

"Which created an entirely new set of problems for me." She sneered. "Now, I had to get you out of the way before you figured things out and connected Neve to Chris . . . to me." Evelyn closed her eyes for a moment and then opened them. "And now, I have to kill you just so there are no loose ends." She puffed out a breath in exasperation. "I'm actually tired of killing. This isn't who I am, you know? I'm a science teacher, for goodness sake."

"And the laptop wasn't really stolen?" Alex guessed.

"I tossed it at the dump. Couldn't have anyone seeing all of the love letter e-mails from Neve to Chris, could I? I read them and almost vomited."

"They would provide motive for you," Alex said. And motive for killing Neve too, she suddenly realized. "You hated Neve."

"Of course I did. She came to town a few months ago—I know because I rented an SUV and followed him and saw them meeting here—I knew it was their special spot. After work and on the weekends, he came here to see her. Picnics and wine in the woods. Really? He never did that romantic crap for me. He hates wine. But he drank it with her."

"Wait, you rented a vehicle? Let me guess—a white SUV with tinted windows? It was you that rammed my car?"

"I told you, I didn't want to kill you. I thought if I scared you off, you'd back off, but no, you're too nosy for your own good. I regret ever asking you for help. I would've been fine. The detective would've just closed the case."

"I'm sorry that you had to go through this. But you didn't have to kill him. You didn't have to kill Neve either. How did you, by the way? I didn't see you at the museum reception."

"No? I was there watching her laugh in all the men's faces, touching their arms, tossing her hair." She sneered. "She was such a flirt. That's why your friend thought her boyfriend was cheating on her, which, incidentally—he may very well have been."

"Jasper?"

"Yeah." She snorted out a laugh. "I saw the way he looked at her, the way he clung to her side. Made me sick to see how she acted. Like taking my husband wasn't enough."

Alex winced, seeing the pain in the woman's eyes. "This isn't the first time you've been cheated on?"

"What is it about me? Do I have a sign on my forehead? I'm a nice woman. I'm smart. I'm funny and I cook." She laughed. "Oh, do I cook. That's how I got the drugs in Chris's system. I crushed them up to a fine powder and mixed it up in his bone broth and reishi mushroom soup. He couldn't taste the difference.

"I put it in a thermos for him and he drank it on his way to meet his lover. By the time he got there, his heart was already racing, he had shortness of breath, and he probably had sweat pouring down his body. I'm sure he thought it was just eagerness to see her, but when I got there, I made sure he knew it was me who caused it."

Alex thought back to that night. Chris's body had been unidentified then. Neve wouldn't have known her lover and the father of her unborn child had died, which would explain why she was so happy and carefree. Alex felt sad for the woman, even if she had wrecked a not-so-happy home. She turned to Evelyn, cringing at the hatred she saw in her eyes. Killing Neve had certainly been a crime of passion—it was all there. The anger, the jealousy . . . Evelyn must've confronted Neve in Jasper's office, and . . . "I get that you were motivated to kill Neve. But to bludgeon her in the head with a paperweight? It was a vicious way to go."

"She deserved what happened to her. Just. Like. You. Do."

Alex was alarmed at the situation, but she wasn't exactly scared by this Mundane. She almost laughed but stopped herself; no need to escalate the situation. "I thought you said you didn't know how to use a gun."

"I lied."

"Even so, you're not going to kill me, Evelyn. If anything, *you* should be afraid."

Evelyn made a "get a load of this guy" face before her features twisted into anger. "You think you have the edge on me because you're a Magical?"

"Yes, I do."

Evelyn laughed and ran her fingers over her necklace, a string of crystal beads, black in color, with dark blue swirls. "Hit me with your best shot. If you don't, I'm going to kill you." Evelyn's smile was pleasant. "And if you do, I'm still going to kill you."

Without thinking, Alex flung all of her power at the woman's hand and watched, expecting to see the gun fly from her hands. It did not. She gasped. What had she done wrong? She tried again, flinging her hands before her. Nothing.

Evelyn laughed. "See? Your magic has nothing on me."

Alex looked at her hands, stretched her fingers, trying to discern the problem, as a ball of anxiety, tight and growing, expanded in her chest.

For some unexplainable reason, her magic no longer worked.

Chapter
Twenty-Five

"Clever, right?" Evelyn fingered the crystal beads around her neck.

Alex stared at the necklace, trying to discern what was so special about it. It looked like a string of blackish-blue pearls. Nothing more.

"I learned about it on Chris's blog. I thought it was one of his fake new items, but after I met you, I figured it was real. I contacted the company employee who shared the tip—and blackmailed him into sending me a sample. And I don't think he really minded since he'd just been laid off—the company is under new ownership, actually." She laughed. "It's pretty, right?"

Alex glanced at the necklace and nodded politely.

"I don't know how it works exactly, but this combination of crystals blocks the frequency and vibrations of your magic." She shrugged. "So now you are going to climb over this railing and jump. And then all of my problems will be solved."

Alex looked behind her. She didn't have time to process the fact that there was a substance able to block her magic. Did other Magicals know? She had to warn them. She sent Minka a message and waited. No response. That was magic; of course it didn't work.

It was at least three hundred yards down, not a fall she could survive. Not unless she could also fly. And unless she also had some bird DNA, she thought insanely—

"What are you waiting for!" Evelyn said, taking the gun and pointing it under her neck.

Now Alex was afraid. A killer was pointing a gun at the soft flesh of her skin, and she had no magical defenses. But no . . . wait, yes, she did have defenses. Maybe not magical, but she was fighting a Mundane. Fight magic with magic, but in a Mundane fight . . . Her daddy may have treated her like princess, but he had *not* raised a coward.

Her father had taught her self-defense, and she'd taken classes in college as her physical education credit. She knew that, first things first, she had to put space between them. And then she had to find something as a defensive weapon. She checked in her peripheral vision and saw the silver circular top of a trash can a few yards away. If she could grab that, she'd have a fighting chance, but first she had to get that gun out of Evelyn's hand.

She pasted a mask of defeat onto her face and looked at Evelyn. "Okay, okay, you got me. Without my magic, I've got nothing."

Evelyn grinned, and Alex pretended to turn around like she was going to climb over the railing, her right leg on the middle bar, but then she quickly whirled around. Holding on to the top rail for leverage, knee raised, she kicked her right leg directly into Evelyn's torso.

Contact!

Evelyn stumbled back, yelling in surprise. But she caught herself, didn't fall. However, it gave Alex just enough time to reach the trash can top and wield it like a shield before her. The woman lunged at her with a shriek, and there was a loud metallic clank as the gun made contact with the trash can lid. And again.

Finally, summoning all of her strength, she was able to use the trash can top to knock the gun out of Evelyn's hand.

Growling in rage, Evelyn reached down to her leg and up her dress a bit and pulled out a knife.

"A knife?" Alex breathed, hardly able to believe her eyes.

"I teach biology," Evelyn said. "Dissections? I'm good with a knife." She reached forward and Alex quickly blocked the jab with the trash can top.

Clang!

Another jab, and Alex stepped out of the way. "Where'd you learn how to fight with a knife?

Evelyn laughed. "I know—I'm pretty good, right? That's thanks to five years of sword lessons for Tanner. He grew up wanting to be a knight, and here I thought I was indulging him with a completely useless skill. I'd say it's coming in handy right about now." She jabbed again with the knife, and Alex blocked the thrust.

Alex looked into this woman's eyes, recognizing that Evelyn had lost her grip on reality somewhere between teaching high school science and discovering her husband had a secret baby on the way.

"Who do you think you are?" Evelyn shrieked. *"Captain America?* Put that shield down and fight me."

"Actually," Alex said as she hopped to the side, moving out of the way of another thrust, "more like the Mermaid of Warsaw." Something rushed through her body, close to adrenaline but stronger, more powerful. She might have lost her ability to practice magic for the moment, but she still had the DNA of a warrior in her body. And this schoolteacher who had killed her own husband *and* had bashed a beautiful, vivacious woman in the head, murdering her and her unborn child—would not be killing another.

She placed the garbage can in both hands and swung it like a bat at the woman's head. Once. Twice. The sound of contact against the side of Evelyn's head rang out like a bell, and she wobbled on her legs. The thin sheet metal of the top wasn't hard enough to cause real damage, but it could stun her. And it did. It was enough for Alex to push her down to the ground, then turn her over onto her stomach, with her own knee in Evelyn's lower back. She grabbed the woman's left hand and twisted it behind her, while the hand holding the knife still flailed around as Evelyn screamed.

Alex's father had also taught her about pressure points. The knife was still in Evelyn's hand, and Alex pressed her wrist to the ground and twisted it with a jerk, hearing a cracking sound. The knife fell out of her hand as Evelyn wailed in pain. Alex took her right hand and twisted it behind her back. Panting, she looked around, wondering how she was going to get this woman down the stairs.

She looked down at her clothes and laughed. She'd done all of this in a dress and heels.

The sound of shoes pounding against metallic stairs could be heard, and voices and police radios. Feeling relieved, Alex thought that help might be on the way.

Evelyn murmured, a mixture of pain and anger, with her face smashed into the ground. Alex saw the necklace glinting in the sunlight, and with one hand still holding the woman's wrists in place, reached for the necklace and was about to yank it off when Jack jumped up the last few steps and appeared on the landing in suit and tie.

His gun was drawn and pointed at Evelyn. "You okay?" he asked as his face turned from fear to disbelief. He took in the scene. "What happened here?"

"She tried to make me jump off the ledge at knifepoint. And I fought back."

"And won," he said in surprise. He gestured for Alex to remove her knee from Evelyn's back, which she did. And then he yanked the woman up off the ground and snapped handcuffs on her. She screamed in pain, and he looked shocked. "The cuffs aren't tight," he protested.

"I think I broke her wrist trying to get the knife out of her hand," Alex said as she rubbed at the bruises and nicks that ran up and down her arms. "How did you know?"

"We got some surprising results back from Neve's paternity test." He glanced at Evelyn, who hung her head in shame. "Chris Robinson was the father. And then Kamila called me and said I needed to take a look at the traffic cam video from the parking lot where Chris died—a request I denied, but in this case I'm glad she didn't listen."

"You saw Evelyn?"

"Not exactly. We saw a rented vehicle turning into the parking lot around the time Robinson was found. I ran the SUV's plates, and we got her name from the rental company. I tried calling you to let you know you'd been right to think there was more to the Chris Robinson case. I wanted to apologize. I couldn't get you. And then Kamila called me, saying she couldn't reach you, and she started demanding that I—"

Kamila came running up the stairs along with several uniformed police. "Sorry, we're late. I was on the ferry when I got Jack's call. And the rest sped over on a police boat." She threw a surprised look at Evelyn in handcuffs. "You good?" she asked Alex.

"I'm fine." She pointed toward the ground. "Evelyn had a gun, but I was able to knock it out of her hands."

Kamila retrieved the gun and looked at Alex, her brow furrowed.

Alex knew her cousin was trying to telepath with her and wasn't getting through. A guarded looked came over Kamila's face, and she looked around, trying to find the source of the blockage.

Alex touched her neck and then pointed to Evelyn when Jack looked away to give the officers orders to cordon off the area.

Kamila went to the woman and began to unclasp it, when Evelyn perked up, seemingly out of her coma of defeat. She looked at Alex and pointed a finger. "She's one of them!" she shrieked for all the world to hear.

Alex stopped breathing when Jack turned and looked at her. "What?"

"Her," Evelyn said again, tears running down her face. "She's a Magical. She has powers." Jack turned toward Alex, an uncertain look in his eyes.

Alex shrugged.

"I only stopped her because of my necklace," Evelyn was saying, a hysterical edge to her voice. "Don't let them take it away from me, or they'll be able to do things. She's probably not the only one. There's more. This town is filled with them."

Jack walked toward the woman and indicated that Kamila should continue taking it off. She did so and handed it to him. He opened his palm and stared at the string of black-blue spheres. "You think this is a magical necklace?"

"Yes," she blubbered through her tears. Her finger pointed at Alex again. "And she's got powers. She's a witch. She's a Magical. She's—"

Jack looked at an officer watching the proceedings with a smirk on his face. "Take her away, please. And make sure this"—he handed him the necklace—"goes into evidence." He turned back to the woman. "I know this is a strange town, but there's no such thing as magic. Not magical beans. And not magical jewelry. And the sooner you acknowledge that, the better off you'll be." He nodded toward the officer, who grabbed her by the handcuffs and helped her down the stairs.

Jack went to Alex, his hands in her hair, on her face, pushing her chin up to look at her neck. Gently grabbing her hands and inspecting her arms. "You're bleeding," he said, commenting on the scratches on her arms Evelyn had inflicted.

"And I scraped my knee," Alex offered with a grin, looking at her left leg. "But I think I'll be okay."

"No matter. We'll get that taken care of, promise." He pulled her into a tight hug, with his nose and mouth in her hair. He didn't say a word, and Alex was stunned at the intense waves of love and affection that swept over her. She relaxed against his chest, allowing herself to drown in the emotion.

She made eye contact with Kamila, who stood behind him. Her cousin shrugged, then cleared her throat. "I'll give you two a moment." She nodded at Jack, who only had eyes for Alex. "Sir."

* * *

When she was gone, Jack pulled her back, his gaze tender as he looked into her eyes. He didn't say anything and pressed his lips softly onto hers for a kiss that lasted for a very, very long time. When he was done, he held her again at arms' length and looked at her. "Let's get you to the hospital for a more thorough check. You may feel okay, but I want to be sure."

Alex was suddenly exhausted. "Okay. Whatever you say."

With his arm around her shoulders, he guided her down the stairs.

Alex was fine.

Three days had passed, and she'd spent some time at the hospital and was then sent home with a prescription for rest and ibuprofen. Of course, Aunt Lidia had taken over healing her wounds, soothing her mind and clearing her body and aura because she'd come into contact with a mineral blend capable of blocking her magic. The existence of this mineral mix caused concern for Lidia, who said she'd take it up with the Council.

The last event of the festival, the celebration in the park, would begin in a few days, and Alex was ready for it to be over. Like Kamila had predicted, she'd just about had her fill of mermaids.

But not yet.

She was in the park, with the sun shining down on her, and she sat on the bench directly across from the mural. Athena lay at her feet after a leisurely walk, and Alex had some reading to do. In front of the mural seemed like the appropriate place to read Neve's dissertation on the presence of mythological weapons in contemporary society. Pepper had finally been able to track down the thesis and had sent Alex a hard copy. She reached for her back sack and pulled out the yellow envelope that held the document.

But something still bothered her.

Although Evelyn pleaded guilty to her husband's murder, she emphatically stated that she hadn't killed Neve Ryland. And as Alex thought back to their fight, a lot had been said about Neve—that she deserved to die, that she'd probably been seeing Jasper as Celeste suspected, but Evelyn had never 'fessed up to killing her.

Someone had broken into the coroner's office. Evelyn had said she didn't do that, and Alex tended to believe her. After all, what would've been her motive? And Alex had been attacked by a Magical. Sure, the pieces lined up nicely, but Alex felt she was missing something.

What was it?

Before she could ponder all of the possible answers, her phone rang. It was Kamila.

"Hey," she said without preamble, "remember when you asked me about Jack? If he was working on anything else?"

"Yeah."

"Well, I overheard him at work. On the phone . . ."

"What did you hear?"

"Not sure exactly. But he is working on something, a special case, only it's not with the Bellamy PD. I had eyes on our chief, and Jack wasn't talking to him. That's all I got."

"Thanks for letting me know." Alex set the phone down, lost in thought. She'd known Jack was up to something. Now she just had to figure out what. Alex stopped musing when a shadow cast over her, and she saw a teenage boy wearing a sullen expression. He stopped short of her, hands jammed into the pockets of his khaki shorts, his gray eyes squinting in the sun.

It was Evelyn and Chris Robinson's son, Tanner Robinson, she realized. This time in a black T-shirt featuring Spock from the television show *Star Trek*. She smiled at him. "Hey there. How are you doing?"

Sighing, he stubbed the toe of his white Converses into the ground. Eyes on the ground, he spoke in low, shy tones. "Pretty good, considering my mom killed my dad, and then she goes and tries to kill a real live mermaid." He raised his eyes to meet Alex's. "You *are* a genetic mermaid, right?"

Alex stifled a gasp, but he only laughed, coming closer to her as he lowered his voice. "I know, okay?" He smirked, revealing the cocky smile that only a teenaged boy could produce. "I've helped my dad with his blog since I was eleven. I knew everything he knew, and he kept a running list of everyone he thought might be a Magical in town. He was grooming me to take it over one day—and that's what I'm going to do."

She assessed the teenager. "You're the *Bizarre Bellamy Bay* blogger now?"

His jaw jutted out. "Yeah, I can do it."

"So you're staying in town?"

"I'll be just down the road with my grandparents in Swansboro. Still close enough to keep my eye on things," he assured her. "It's what my father would've wanted."

Alex felt horrible for what the boy had been through, but hopeful his future would be better. "I'll be rooting for you. But this list . . . my name is on it?"

"Not exactly. Your aunt's and your mom's names were on it. Only makes sense that you'd be one too. And your cousins." He shrugged. "It's genetics. Don't worry—the list is in a safe place." He tapped his head. "I have a photographic memory, and my dad swore me to secrecy. I won't break my promise to him."

"I believe you," Alex said, feeling the sincerity emanating from the teen.

* * *

When he was gone, her gaze returned to the life-sized image of the Mermaid of Warsaw, and she couldn't help but wonder . . . Was Neve trying to tell her—or someone—something? Her murals told stories, after all. They held clues, and Alex still hadn't figured out what they were.

She felt unsettled. Alex took a swig from her water bottle and read through the paper. Neve argued the point that mythological weapons were real because the gods were real; that at one point myths had been believed as true histories, and the accounts were considered factual accounts of wars and battle and the personal and political intrigues among the entities in power. Descriptions of weapons, their abilities, and the results they produced were too detailed to simply be the results of storytellers around the world. No, Neve thought that somehow, someway, they were real.

And although the gods may have disappeared from our earthly realm, their weapons still existed and waited to be found. Neve explained how mythological weapons could now all be explained with science, some simple, some complex, and only explicable by off-planet technologies. She argued that soon companies would try to recreate and or reverse-engineer these advanced technologies for modern application.

Neve believed she'd found a way to locate them based on analysis of myths, examining local histories, reviewing current events in newspapers, and using satellite and other advanced technologies. She believed that these weapons, in the right hands, could be tools of peace, if they could be found and remained in the hands of men and women oriented positively.

She went on to list several mythological weapons that she believed were real, explaining how she'd discerned their probable location, how they had been used to suppress, but how they could also be used for good in contemporary society. She gave the general area where she thought they were located, along with her reasons.

She also made it clear that if it was ever proven that these weapons were real, they could never get in the hands of those who wished to oppress societies.

Alex closed the paper and stared at the mural. Neve had been an interesting woman. Brilliant. Imaginative. Intelligent. And Alex wished that she'd had more time to talk to her and learn all that she knew. Especially about the Mermaid of Warsaw.

Alex looked up at the mural. What if the painting wasn't just a painting, as she'd thought. The mural was missing the newspaper and the clock, a code hiding in plain sight for someone to see. A missed opportunity to retrieve something. But maybe Neve had found the Warsaw Shield, and instead of giving it to her partner, she'd taken the information to her grave. Hadn't she said she'd decided not to share what she knew?

Alex had assumed she'd meant information about the mermaid gene, but if mythological weapons were real, and she'd been touring the Wesley property that was rumored to hide the shield . . .

Neve had made it clear she considered herself in danger. And she'd come to Alex for help. Was there a clue to the killer in the mural? Neve had painted the mermaid prepared to battle the god of war. Ares, she knew from a one-off class on world mythology she'd taken as an undergrad, represented all that was bad about war and battle. Mars, the Roman counterpart was all shiny and beloved—bravery, valor, and patriotism. But not Ares. Almost the black sheep of the gods, to the Greeks Ares represented the lust for blood, the indiscriminate slaughter of men, the joy of the kill.

Did Ares represent the government? Or maybe the military? She put the paper back into her backpack and pulled out her phone to research Ares, something she hadn't done before. She skimmed the god's profile. Described as having a quick temper, being aggressive, and having unquenchable thirst for conflict, he was the son of Zeus and brother to Athena. Symbols associated with Ares were spears, shields, chariots, boars, dogs, vultures—

Alex stopped suddenly at one of the items on the list, and her breath caught in her throat. She looked at the mural and smiled. If she'd been looking for a clue from Neve, she'd found it. In plain sight, Neve had literally painted for all the world to see the person she feared the most. And Alex's heart broke just a little because she hadn't been able to figure it out in time to save her. But she could bring him to justice.

Standing, with Athena's leash in hand, she walked toward the mural, finally understanding what Neve had tried to tell her.

Neve had known her killer, and it wasn't Evelyn Robinson.

Chapter Twenty-Six

A lex would make sure Neve's killer was punished.

It was the least she could do for the woman who'd known her secrets and taken them to her grave. But first Alex needed answers, and because of the discreet nature of the subject, she'd handle it alone—or almost alone, and then she'd call Kamila.

There was one person who deserved answers more than she did, and that's who she called before approaching the building. That plus it never hurt to have backup, even though she was pretty sure she could handle this Mundane.

Alex left Athena outside, tied to a bicycle rack, while she entered the building. Her dog met her eye, and Alex could've sworn her German shepherd's look conveyed, *You got this? You sure you don't want me to come with you?* She planted a kiss on Athena's head and assured her she was fine.

The coolness of the building smacked against her skin as she navigated through the reception areas, the spacious rooms, and the hallway, heading to the offices.

He stood when she appeared, as if he'd been expecting her. And maybe he had.

As usual, she was annoyed by his appearance. "The mineral associated with the Greek god Ares," she said in greeting, "is jasper."

"Well, hello to you too." The museum director grinned at her. "I see you're feeling better after that vicious attack. It's all anyone can talk about in town. Won't you come in?" he said pleasantly. "And its red jasper, if we're being particular."

Alex noted with some distaste that today's bow tie and suspender combination was a lemon yellow. She stood at the door, looking around the office. "Not only did Neve not want to tell you where the Warsaw Shield was, but she didn't return your affections. That's what you argued about, the night of the reception."

The affable grin on his face disappeared.

She wasn't afraid of this Mundane. She entered his office and settled into a chair. "When did you know she wasn't going to help you?"

A scowl appeared on his face. He closed the door with a quiet snick before returning to his desk. His lips twisted in scorn. "When the mural was unveiled, I saw the date and time of the weapon acquisition hadn't been encoded in the painting. I knew something was wrong."

Alex thought back to that beautiful day in the park. Neve had asked everyone what they thought of the mural . . . and Jasper had responded first.

"I feel like it's missing something," he'd said. Not hiding his displeasure at all. And Alex felt sick, because it was on that day while they'd been at the park, enjoying the sunshine and drinking herbal tea, that Neve had signed her death warrant.

"She thought she'd go away with him, that blogger. And throw away everything we'd worked for." He turned away from her then, gazing out the window behind his desk. "She always shared her findings with me. Hawaii, Japan. Boston . . . It was her job, after all, to find things for me. But this time . . . this time she refused. I tried to get her to change her mind—that night of the reception. I begged her, reminded her of all we'd done together—the traveling, the artifacts we'd discovered—but she laughed at me."

"She didn't want you." His jaw tightened, and Alex knew she'd hit his weak spot, his emotional pressure point. "But you couldn't force her to love you back. The law of free will?"

"That law will be the death of me," he spit out angrily. "Of all of us."

"Without it, your power and influence would run unchecked. It practically almost is."

"Almost," he conceded, "but not quite." He looked pensive for a moment, stroking his chin, lost in thought. Then he locked eyes with Alex and chuckled. "She told me she'd rather die than help me again. So, I picked up my favorite paperweight, and, well . . . you know the rest." The cruelest of looks transformed his features into something hideous. His eyes were slits, his skin took on greenish tinge, and his tongue was long and forked. He was a shape-shifter?

Alex blinked, and the image was gone. Had she even seen it? She rubbed her eyes and took another look. He was all floppy blond hair and cocky grin. But fear coursed through her body. Jasper wasn't a Mundane. Wasn't a collaborator. It was he, not Montgomery, who was a *Smok*. A Dragon Descent.

A tremor ran up and down Alex's spine. She'd thought she could handle a Mundane, but she had no experience with a Dragon. Could she do this alone? Alex wanted to leave the office then, wanted to put space between him and this vile creature. He was disgusting. *A monster.*

He grinned when he saw the expression on her face. "What? She had it coming."

She wanted to wipe the smug look off his face, but she knew she'd need more than just his confession. "Where is the murder weapon?"

"You'll never find it. I tossed it into the sea from whence it came. From whence *I* came."

Alex recalled seeing Jasper's memories. There was no murder. No ill will toward Neve. "How did you—"

"I can control my thoughts," he answered before she could get the question out. "Thereby controlling what you see—or think you see." He laughed. "I knew exactly what you were doing, plundering through my thoughts and memories. Shame on you. And I thought you mermaids had ethics."

Alex almost felt sick. He was right. She shouldn't have done it, but in this case he deserved to have his thoughts read and laid bare . . . and much more. She narrowed her eyes, watching him as he stood and began to pace the room restlessly. "And your relationship with Celeste . . . you wanted intel on her work with Wesley. Were you reading her mind, accessing her top-secret thoughts?"

"I knew Dylan was searching for the shield. And when I was a professor at the college and discovered Celeste was an intern at Wesley, I simply worked my considerable *charms* on her, and a romance"—he rolled his eyes as he spoke the word—"was born. "Unfortunately, the information I gained from her was negligible." He gritted his teeth. "But I know that shield is here somewhere. And I'm not leaving until I find it."

"And you were going to just let Celeste go to jail for a crime you committed?"

He stared at her for a moment, like he didn't understand the question. "Someone had to. Why not?"

Dylan's words came back to her then: *Moral compass . . . lacking.* "And Montgomery Blue. Where does he fit in all of this?"

"Who, Monty? That fellow?" He chuckled. "He's very, very, very rich. And he's very helpful."

"But is he—"

"One of us? Part of the old gang?" He paused for dramatic effect. "He's a Mundane collaborator. He answers to me. Does *my* bidding. Like when I told him to help fund this small-town festival celebrating the *mermaid.*" Again, his mouth twisted on that last word. "So, I could get Neve here. I knew she'd been here earlier in the year, and she hadn't even stopped by to say hello." He thumped his chest. "You don't think that hurt?" His eyes flashed with anger. "I wanted to talk some sense into her. But apparently she had other plans. In hindsight"—he laughed, a hard and brittle sound—"I guess she was always *team mermaid.*"

He snorted, an ugly sound, and a curl of smoke floated out of one nostril. He turned and stared out his window. "It was obvious with that mural. She's been the bane of our existence—that Mermaid of Warsaw and her descendants. Do-gooders, all of you. We get rid of one, but you just keep coming back." He looked over his shoulder at her, his face contorted into a mask of scorn.

Get rid of one? Her mind was stuck on the words. Get rid of who? Her mother? *Wait. What?* More fear, slippery and icy cold tingled inside Alex.

"Always thwarting us at every point. Making it your business to check our power. Like you mermaids could ever triumph over Dragon Descents. We rule the world; you're just a fish in our oceans." He jabbed a finger toward the window. "Her mural wasn't just a message for you and your kind. It was a message for *me.* And when I saw it"—he returned to his desk, placing both palms on it, and leaning over it, he bared his teeth in a grin. "I knew I had to stop her before she did something stupid."

"And what did you do?" Alex prompted, knowing the narcissist in him couldn't wait to explain.

"When it was clear she wasn't going to tell me what she knew, I did a spell for trouble, made myself invisible and entered the coroner's office to find that blogger's personal effects. I thought that Neve had given him the location of the shield and other weapons. But I couldn't find it." His fists clenched at his sides. "We need that shield. It was made from our sacred mineral. She had no right to keep it from us." His hair fell into his eyes. "Did you know that a very long time ago, dragons—real dragons—protected sea caves where that mineral was found? But some sneaky Mer went and stole it from us and created that shield. Created a weapon to use against us!"

One of his fists came down hard on his desk, shaking his pen holder. "And she was worried what would happen if it fell in the wrong hands." His laugh was harsh. "I can't tell you how many destructive mythological weapons she's found for us, how much chaos she helped create. She never cared before."

"That's because she was pregnant," Alex said softly, "and I'm guessing she wanted her child to grow up in a world of peace."

Suddenly, the feeling of coldness slapped against her like a wave of cold water and wrapped around her. The sensation was frightening, and she felt like she was freezing and suffocating all at once.

"Don't. Mention. Her. Pregnancy. Again," he commanded in a choked voice.

Alex was rooted to her chair, recognizing the feeling. That coldness. That anger. It was the icy-hot feeling of his rage. And as he moved around the room, Alex could feel it licking at her body like a serpent's tongue flicking in and out. "It was you at the beach, slipping inside my head, trapping me in your vise."

"I tried to warn you," he said, a reasonable expression sliding over his features. And just like that, the icy grip disappeared. "I don't hate mermaids per se. Take your cousin Minka, for example. She's such a sweet, good, whimsical little creature." He smacked his lips like he was tasting something delicious, and Alex's face wrinkled in revulsion. "Those are my favorite types of mermaids. It's fun to turn them and watch them go."

"Turn them—what?"

"Turn them *bad*." He sneered at her. "And then there's the other type, the warrior princess mermaid who wants to kick butt and take names. Make the world a safer place for all the non-Dragon Descents. Mermaids like your aunt, your mother . . . you."

Alex leaned forward, her heart suddenly racing. *"My mother?"*

His eyebrows shot up in mock surprise. "Oh, right. She's dead, isn't she? Interesting, that."

Her throat tightened. "What do you know about it?"

He shrugged, sat back in his chair, suddenly relaxed.

And Alex was frustrated. At every turn, when she tried to get answers about her mother's death, she was stopped. She fought back tears—angry tears—frustrated tears. Not today. Not in front of Jasper.

"It's been nice talking to you, but I actually have work to do." He picked up a pen and wrote something on a pad. He looked up and pretended to be surprised she was still there. "Was there something more?"

"Do you think you're just going to get away with murdering Neve?"

His grin widened. "I think I already have. Your boyfriend charged that poor woman with two counts of murder. I am *so* glad she killed her husband. Saved me the trouble. He was on my to-do list, right after I finished with Neve. The wife has an abundance of motive, wouldn't you say? And I found security camera footage that places her at the museum the night in question, and I'm sure she doesn't have an alibi. Your boyfriend would like to see that, no?"

Alex really hated the conceited look in his eye. It reminded her of Montgomery. Of Bryn and Tegan. . . She looked at him. "You need to turn yourself in."

"Or what?" he said, a look of real interest on his face. "Who's going to make me?"

Just then the office door flew open. "I am," Minka said, with a fierce look on her face. She stepped inside the office.

"And me!" Celeste added, storming in, hands and arms waving around her, causing papers and framed photographs to whirl violently in the air before crashing to the floor. "How could you? I knew there was something up with you!"

Alex exhaled in relief. Celeste had made it, and brought along Minka. She quickly telepathed the biggest news to them: Jasper was a Dragon.

Minka stared at him. *OMG*, she responded. *Like fire breathing?*

When Jasper saw the rage burning in Celeste's eyes, the slick grin slid from his face. "Celeste, look—I'm sorry. I actually really—"

"Shut up!" she thundered. "I loved you, and you're nothing but a liar. And a murderer?" She looked back at the women behind her. "I'll take care of him." The sky suddenly darkened, casting shadows over the museum as lightening crackled overhead. "You. Don't. Play. With. My. Heart." With every word, a zing of energy hit Jasper. He winced like he was taking a solid punch to his gut, but remained standing.

Angry tears ran down Celeste's cheeks as she pressed both hands out before him, muttering something in . . . French? No, like French, but not exactly. Beams of light, one white, the other red swirled together to create a fiery pink energy that sprang from her palms and ran straight into Jasper's chest.

He struggled against the pressure like he was walking against a strong wind, his face contorted with the effort. He narrowed his eyes, and the pink energy turned red and finally a bright orange.

Alex stared in amazement. His magic curled from his nose in two steady beams of fiery red energy. They coiled in front of him into a ball that he began to mold with his hands. The room was suddenly sticky with humidity and smelled of sulfur. The temperature increased in the room, and everyone, especially Celeste, had sweat rolling down her face. Like a fast ball, he pitched the energy toward Celeste, who screamed when it made impact against her chest.

Her body was engulfed in a red-hot flame of energy. A large purple snake, ethereal and mirage-like, appeared around Celeste's shoulders, wrapping her in a tender embrace and slowly curling around her body, seeming to absorb the brunt of the flames. It slowly lowered Celeste to her knees, on the floor, and then slid away from her and toward Jasper, who stared transfixed, a silly smile on his face.

"Mami Wata, as I live and breathe," he said in whispered awe. "Serpent to serpent, I must tell you how lovely you are."

The snake raised up almost level to his face and hissed a foul smell that enveloped him in a swirl of purple vapor.

He closed his eyes against the heat of the snake's breath and the odor for a moment. "Yes, Mami Wata, yes, I see it, I see it." A moment passed and he opened his eyes. "Thank you, goddess for showing me your long line of priestesses, and I know Celeste is the daughter of your daughter." He looked past the shimmering snake to Celeste, who lay on the floor, still writhing in pain. "Celeste, you have so much potential. I can help you overcome your mermaid side, embrace the serpent within, and help me destroy this mermaid. You're a rare creature, a mixture of both light and dark. Choose the darkness, and I'll show you a world you never even imagined."

Weakly, Celeste shook her head. "We're family," she whispered, then passed out, her body limp on the floor. The snake returned to her body and disappeared.

Alex watched in horror as outside the dark clouds scattered, the thunder and lightning stopped, and sunlight once again poured into the office.

Minka burst into tears, ran to her and sank to her knees, immediately covering Celeste in healing energy.

"Did you kill her?" Alex chucked a burst of white energy his way. Any Mundane would have fallen to the floor, contorted in pain, but Jasper only glanced at her, his nose wrinkled in revulsion.

He caught the ball of energy in his hand, tightened his fist around it until it vanished in a puff of gray smoke. He closed his eyes as if he was listening for something. "No, she'll be fine." His eyes opened. "I can sense her pulse, her heartbeat, her breath. The spirit of Mami Wata is inside of her, healing her from within." He held his palm out, watched as a bright red flame lifted into the air. "But you will not. There's no spirit of the mermaid to come save you—that's not how your magic works." Grinning, he blew the red flame toward her. With his breath, the flame became a torch that rushed forward.

It should've hit her square in the face, but she ducked and caught the flame on her leg.

She let out a yelp of pain and stared at her leg, throbbing in agony as black smoke rose from it.

I'm descended from dragons, he said, his thought hissing its way through her mind. *My element is fire. I grow stronger when fear and anger are near me. Be afraid—I'm feeding off it. I like it.*

Alex folded over, trying to heal herself as fast as possible. It hurt. She was weakened by his attack, and the very act of healing herself made her weaker. And she thought she could hear Athena barking and growling, fighting against her leash, going crazy trying to get lose and inside the museum to help her.

With one hand still hovering over Celeste, Minka reached out to Alex with the other. "Let me help you." She directed a pure white energy toward Alex. The divided effort was quickly draining Minka, who'd grown pale, a sheen of sweat covering her brow.

With a loud gasp, Celeste sat up, panting, grabbing at her chest, her face, her legs. She looked at Minka, then Alex. "I'm okay."

"Thank goodness." Minka exclaimed, before returning to help Alex.

"And that was amazing." Celeste said, her eyes blazing with life. "I've never felt the energy of the goddess in that way—wow!" She breathed deeply before turning back to Jasper.

He looked mildly annoyed. "Oh, goodie. You're awake."

She tossed bursts of pink energy his way.

They fell short, and he laughed at the effort.

"Sorry," she said, turning to Alex and Minka. "I'm still really weak."

Jasper sneered at her. "I see you've made your choice. I really don't want to kill you, Celeste," he said with a bothered expression. "You have such a pretty face."

"Oh no, you don't," Josephine said rushing into the office. "Not my baby girl. Come on, Lidia." She threw a glance at Alex. "Sorry we're late." She tossed her purse onto the floor and aimed her right finger at him, muttering something low and guttural while Lidia helped Minka swiping healing white energy over Celeste to restore her strength, and over Alex to help hasten the healing of her leg.

You called Aunt Lidia? Alex telepathed to Minka, who nodded.

Sorry. She looked embarrassed. *And I called Kamila like you told me to before I came in. They should be here any minute.*

Jasper made a face. "One thing I've always hated about devotees to Mami Wata. You can't make up your mind: Are you good? Or are you bad? We both like snakes, Mrs. Thomas. Why can't we just get along?"

Something sickeningly sweet and purplish-black sprang from Josephine's finger like a long plume of smoke, but it wafted through the air like a slow-moving snake, growing in size and length.

"Josephine," Lidia began in a cautioning voice.

But she shook her head. "Don't worry. I haven't used any black magic this month. I'll be careful."

Alex watched in awe as the wispy purple snake, similar to Celeste's but bigger and stronger looking, moved toward Jasper, floating on the air. It hesitated and then began to curl around his neck. Jasper's hands went to his neck as if could wrench the snake away, but his hands went through the snake. However, the choking and gagging sounds Jasper made were real.

Josephine's gaze was steady, and the string of words, similar to Celeste's, only caused the choking effect on Jasper to worsen, until Celeste climbed to her feet and grabbed her mother's arm. "Mom, please, don't kill him. You're not a murderer."

His face was turning red and was on the way to becoming a dark purple as red veins sprouted in the whites of his eyes, but Josephine refused to lower her arm. "After what he's put you through? What he's done to this town? He killed Neve Ryland. He deserves this and much more."

Alex whipped a vise around Jasper's torso, which he struggled against, until Minka and Lidia added their own strength to the magic, and then he stopped fighting.

"Josephine," Lidia began in a gentle voice, "we've got him. Let go of his throat. He's not going anywhere. And wouldn't it be nice to know he's rotting away in a jail somewhere?"

Finally he stopped fighting against his vise, and Josephine lowered her trembling arm.

Alex heard the sound of running footsteps in the hallways and Kamila entered the office. Shaking her head, she assessed the situation, her nostrils flaring at the thick scent hovering in the air. "Jeesh, this place reeks of magic—and not all good." Her eyes widened in alarm when she saw Jasper's physical condition. "What the heck is going on?"

"He confessed to killing Neve," Alex said. "And he just assaulted Celeste. And me."

"Also," Minka chimed in, "he's a dragon."

Kamila shook her head. "Freaking Dragon Descents," she said as she pulled a set of handcuffs off her belt.

Alex watched with concern. "Is that going to hold him?"

Kamila laughed. "Yeah. These aren't your normal handcuffs.' She held them up for Alex to read the logo etched in the silver bracelets that shone with a blue-black finish in the light.

It read "Wesley Defense."

Alex grinned, shaking her head. *Dylan.* She watched as police flooded the office. But no Jack. She turned to her cousin. "Where is he?"

"Detective Frazier?" Kamila asked, and Alex nodded.

"I'm right here," he said, stepping into the office, his gun drawn and his eyes scanning the room until they landed on Alex.

Kamila stood taller. "It's all under control, sir."

Once Jasper was handcuffed, Kamila grabbed him by the wrists and shoved him hard out of the room. So hard that he stumbled but caught himself on one knee. "That's for messing with my family." She looked at her mother, sister, and cousin. Grinned at Josephine and Celeste.

Then telepathed to them: *Taking him to the Council for a hearing, where they'll shackle him so he can't practice magic, and then I'll bring him to the station so he can get a nice helping of American justice.*

Nodding, Alex suddenly felt light on her feet. She wasn't able to help Neve, but at least her killer would not go free. Until she caught Jack's eye. He didn't look pleased.

He crossed the room to stand before her. "You decided to confront a murderer on your own?"

She turned back to look at her family and friends. "I'm not alone. My family's here."

His gaze was steely. "You know what I mean. When I got the call to come here, I really hoped I wouldn't see you." The vein on his right temple pulsed. "I have to leave for a few days, a special assignment, but when I come back, we need to talk."

He began to turn away, but she grabbed his arm. "You're not breaking up with me, are you?"

"I can't do this now, obviously. I'm working, but this thing where you keep showing up at crime scenes, it can't continue."

From across the room, a crime technician waved him over.

He looked at her. "See you when I get back."

Alex watched him walk away, suddenly feeling deflated. Lidia appeared at her side, wrapping an arm around her. "You okay?"

She nodded. "Yes. Absolutely. Thanks for showing up."

Minka appeared, and Lidia placed one arm around her as well. "That, my dear, is what family is for." She swept a weary but satisfied look around the office. "Now let's go home and have some tea."

Chapter
Twenty-Seven

Dylan smiled as Alex approached him from the opposite end of the boardwalk.

A breeze rolled off the ocean, scenting the air around her with sea salt and whipping her hair around her face.

When she reached him, he greeted her with a chaste kiss on each cheek in European fashion. "I was surprised to get your invitation to join you on the beach. I was hoping I could talk to you."

Alex gazed at the ocean, hands on the boardwalk as she leaned into the breeze. "I think I owe you an apology."

He followed her gaze to the sea. "For?"

She shrugged. "One again thinking you had"—she laughed self-consciously—"evil intentions."

"'Evil' is a strong word." He sighed. "I have nothing but the best of intentions. Bryce too—he's a good guy."

"Tell Bryce I'm sorry I thought he might have . . ." Alex struggled to say the words.

"Killed someone?" He laughed. "Sure, I'll let him know." He shook his head. "Believe it or not, it's fine. He's fine. I think everyone in this town knows you're protective of your family—and that includes Celeste."

"But you"—she grinned, jabbing her finger in the middle of his chest—"I thought you were going to make money off of people—Magicals. I thought you were going to do human testing. Sell bioproducts." She shook her head. "I just couldn't wrap my head around—"

His brow furrowed as he gazed at her. "What could I have possibly done or said to make you think I'd do that?"

"You said you were going to monetize the mermaid gene, the one Bryce's company is researching."

"I never said that. And I *never* mentioned the mermaid gene." He leaned in. "Where did you hear that anyway? That's not common knowledge."

She blinked, staring into his intense chocolate-brown gaze. "Neve told me. Before she . . ."

He frowned, letting his arm drop to his side. "I didn't buy Bryce's company just so I could make money off that research. And I didn't shut down those other companies just to put employees out of business." He closed his eyes and rubbed his forehead. "What kind of monster do you think I am?"

She stared at him. He didn't really want to know what she'd thought of him.

"Why do you constantly think the worst of me?"

Her throat constricted. "I don't know . . . your family? Your history . . ."

He sighed. "I think there's been some sort of mistake."

Alex sighed too. "Possibly. I know you're producing handcuffs that can actually stop Magicals . . ."

"One of the companies that I purchased discovered a mineral-based blend that inhibits the frequencies that magic uses. I purchased the company and shut it down to keep it out of the hands of anyone who might use it for nefarious purposes. Same thing with the mermaid gene research. I own it—that and the database."

Alex's cheeks warmed in embarrassment. "But that's wonderful, Dylan."

"That's just one of many products our defense division has purchased or created. It's Magical and Mundane defense. We supply tools and weapons for Magicals on Mundane law enforcement forces and also for the Council's enforcement wing." He laughed at Alex's expression. "Yes, that's a thing too. You have a lot to learn, Alex. And if you spent more time with me than Detective Jack, I could teach you."

Alex didn't know what to say to that. She'd felt like she made the right choice with Jack.

"There's something I want to show you," Dylan said. "Walk with me to the marina?"

* * *

Fifteen minutes later, Alex was on a Jet Ski with her arms wrapped tightly around Dylan's torso.

She tried not to be afraid. The last time she and Dylan had been in the water together, it was because his sister, Bryn, had created a tidal wave that almost drowned her, and Dylan had used his magic to save her.

"Don't be afraid of the ocean," Dylan told her over his shoulder and the roar of the engine. "You're safe with me."

Alex looked down at the bright yellow life jacket he'd given her at the marina. She'd put it on over a swimsuit and shorts paired with sandals. The water foamed around them and spray kicked up, cooling Alex's skin, which was still heated—whether that was because of the hot summer temperatures or her proximity to Dylan, she couldn't tell.

They were riding across the bay, past the lighthouse keeper's cottage and the lighthouse, which stood tall on the peninsula and further still, by a few hundred yards, to a small uninhabited island, the one she'd seen briefly from the lookout. It was a large mound of sand, a few dunes and barely any vegetation, just a few patches of seagrass here and there. It couldn't have been more than a mile both ways. When they reached land, Alex turned back and looked from where they came.

Dylan pointed. "See there? That's our family homestead. I'm thinking about tearing down the Bennett house and building my own home there." He gave Alex a look she couldn't interpret before pointing farther down the coast. "Public access to the beach . . . and there's downtown."

Alex took off her sandals, rubbed her toes in the sand, and carried her shoes in her hand as Dylan began to walk. "Do you own this island too?" *If you could call it that,* Alex thought.

A lopsided grin appeared on Dylan's face. "Yeah. My dad purchased it years ago. Named it Dylan's Rock," He laughed. "Annoyed the heck out of Bryn."

"But there's nothing here," Alex exclaimed, scrambling to keep up with him as he covered the island in long strides.

His eyes sparkled with mischief. "No?" He waved his hand, and a large shimmery bubble appeared.

Alex looked around in wonder. The iridescent dome, at turns clear and then tinged with blue, green, and purple, covered all but the outer perimeter of the island. Like a magical dome covering a plate of . . . nothing.

Laughing, Dylan extended his arm into the force field, which, like a clear thick jelly, sucked it. "Is this cool or what?"

Alex stared at him in amazement, her heart melting just a bit. She could see the little boy she used to play with when she spent summers here. She'd forgotten the sound of that laugh, the way the darkness of his eyes brightened when he felt joy. He'd laughed like that and smiled like that when they'd played in her aunt's gardens.

"Try it," he said, pointing to the shimmering bubble, his eyes twinkling with mischief. "It doesn't hurt."

"You're using magic?"

"My father's magic. This is all his doing. It doesn't go away just because he died."

She went to his side and stuck her arm inside. The bubble felt warm and slick, almost like nothing at all. "It feels like—"

Dylan winked at her and then simply stepped inside. And then he was gone.

She gasped. Then looked around her. She was all alone. Did he want her to—surely he didn't—

Heart pounding against her chest, she stepped inside. And he was there. Waiting for her. He held his hand out to her. And she took it without hesitation.

"I'm sharing this with you because as a Sobieski, this is your heritage too."

She could now see the island held a small rectangular building made of glass and metallic beams that glistening in the sunlight. Dylan waved his hand, and the door, a large rectangle of glass, slid to the side. They walked inside and Alex gasped. Eyes wide, she turned to Dylan.

"Is that what I think it is?"

He nodded, his face as reverent as hers was shocked.

In the middle of the room, floating in the air but held firmly in place by glowing straps of pulsing blue energy, was the Warsaw Shield.

Chapter Twenty-Eight

"It doesn't look like what I expected," Alex finally said when she could find her voice.

Dylan nodded. "Yeah, I think something was probably lost in translation and through the thousands of years," he chuckled. "But it's understandable."

"Can I?" Alex gestured toward the small round object, a little larger than a dinner plate. It was a perfect circle crafted out of a smooth, shiny black crystal with green veins running through it. A small knob with an oval shape carved into the material protruded from the underside of the mineral, a handle Alex guessed, with an opening for a leather strap so the shield could be worn on the body.

Symbols and some sort of lettering were carved on its face, and they appeared to be illuminated by a pulsing white energy.

Dylan nodded and Alex went to stand directly over the artifact. "It's more like a fancy Frisbee than a shield." She looked at him. "I was imagining something like the Roman soldiers used, or Captain America." She laughed.

"I think the misunderstanding came from the purpose of the object versus the function of the artifact. It is not, in fact, a shield for battle."

Alex nodded, thinking that she understood. "But it . . . creates a shield?" Dylan inclined his head in assent. "It's beautiful," Alex said reverently. The symbols on the shield, she realized, were what Minka had called "mermaid language." At home, they had a sacred crystal bowl etched with the same type of characters, and they were also the same symbols on the Mer at the party.

"One of the companies I purchased is doing research on these symbols. Well, not exactly on this, but on dolphin intelligence. We have an endowed professor of linguistics at Bellamy College, a Magical who has linked our ancient language systems to the communication between dolphins. Of course, ours is much more advanced, but there are connections. He believes the language came from an as-of-yet undiscovered parent language."

It was too much to grasp, really. Yes, Alex knew that dolphins were intelligent animals and that they were used by the military for various types of work. She also knew they were capable of communicating with each other and humans, but this—seeing the actual Warsaw Shield, learning about the language . . . it was a lot. And her head began to hurt.

Dylan turned to her, a look of concern on his face. He reached out to her, his thumb on her cheek, and he slowly dragged it down to her lips before he removed his hand. Peace and calm followed his touch.

"I thought you didn't—"

"I'll do anything to make sure you're okay." His eyes burned with intensity, and Alex had to look away.

"Thank you," she whispered, suddenly overcome with longing to be wrapped up in his embrace. She put space between them because . . . just because.

"It's strange. But since you arrived in town, I've practiced the most magic since I decided against it. You *make* me want to practice magic again."

Alex's throat tightened, but she forced a laugh. "That's weird."

Dylan turned back to the Warsaw Shield. "Say what you want about my sister, but she had the right idea getting our family property back. It was just her means that were—"

"Wicked?"

"Yeah. We grew up with our dad telling us stories about this shield and how one day we'd be the ones to find it. It's why he created the shelter. And it's why I had it brought here."

"It's beautiful," Alex said, unable to stop looking at it.

"And powerful."

"How did you find it? When did you find it?"

"Once I knew the location, I used deep sea mining equipment created by Montgomery's company. I knew purchasing it would put me on his radar, but he's sold the same equipment to other companies, so I hoped he wouldn't realize that I'd actually found it."

"What's so special about his equipment?"

"It's not the equipment per se. It's what it can do. It's created to find a very special mineral. Ozite?"

"I've heard of it. And that's what the shield is made of." Dylan nodded. "What is ozite made of?"

"It's an alloy of diamond, gold, tourmaline, and several minerals created when mollusks and seaweed calcify together. Only certain instruments can find this mixture."

"Jasper said ozite belonged to the Dragons."

Dylan nodded. "Yeah."

"And that he was certain the shield was here. How did you know where to look?"

For a moment he looked ashamed. "We've never been able to locate it before because we didn't know what we were looking for exactly. But Bryn—she's the one that discovered ozite and its properties, and hypothesized that it may be the material the shield was made of."

"How and why could she even make that connection?"

"Our family has been looking for the shield for a very long time, using all of our resources. You will recall that Bryn thought that if she could find the shield for our mother, she would be given the CEO role at the company. But it began long before Bryn. It started with my great-grandfather, who established our company, and I'm carrying on the tradition. We knew what the shield could actually do, knew that the story was that mermen created the shield out of a special mineral found in the Baltic Sea. We reverse-engineered the properties of the shield to narrow down the probable minerals used in the creation and found in a specific area of the world."

"And then, let me guess, Bryn used her . . . charms to get close to the one person in the world who had access to the mineral." Dylan averted his gaze. "So, you knew why Bryn was hanging out with Montgomery. She was working. And working him," Alex continued.

She closed her eyes, thinking. "And that's why she killed Randy Bennett and Edwin Kenley. She knew the shield was somewhere on this land or off the coast of it."

"Once we knew what the shield was made of, we could look for it. My mother used black magic to locate the ozite. We found it right on the edge of our property, in an underwater cave. Whoever stashed it there was smart enough to realize the ocean would be the ideal hiding place for it, as well as the best environment to maintain its structure, since Ozite is only found in the ocean.

"I brought in a team of specialists. Word probably got back to Montgomery—the sea mining world is small really—and they located it, and then I put on some scuba gear and went down with them, followed it back up, and placed a protective spell over it so that no one who was looking for it could find it. But it was vulnerable for a few seconds. And that was all it took for the vultures to descend." He laughed darkly. "Remember when the power went out?"

Alex's head began to pound again, but a feeling of calm quickly washed the pain away. Dylan's magic was still at work in her mind. "How could I forget?"

"We were bringing it up then. The shield is powerful, and it provided a magnetic signature for those few moments for anyone looking for it with the right magical instruments—as well as frying everything and everyone around it. It made some people sick and disoriented, I heard."

"And the cell phones?" Alex asked. "I always thought that was weird. A power outage shouldn't affect cell phone towers."

He nodded. "The shield jammed all cell phone frequencies. It's formidable stuff we're dealing with."

"What does it do?" Alex asked.

"What doesn't it do?" he countered. "It's like an EMF—that's electric and magnetic fields—weapon. It blocks anything: projectiles, frequencies, magnetic waves. And it can create a projected shield of invisibility thousands of miles around it."

"Like around the city of Warsaw?" Alex asked.

He nodded. "The way the Mermaid of Warsaw protected the city was to form a barrier around it in so that nothing harmful could get in."

"Was a magical weapon really necessary, though? Back then it was just armies with their Mundane weapons."

"You think the shield was the only magical weapon in existence? Back then every royal court had a Magical—or magician—as an adviser for personal, governance, and military affairs. If another king wanted to invade, Warsaw had to have the same technology." He quirked an eyebrow. "The only way to fight magic is *with* magic."

Magical weapons.

They were real. When Neve had given that information, it hadn't been disinformation; it had been real. All of her information was real. Alex looked at Dylan. "Thor's hammer?" she began hesitantly.

He grinned. "It's been found. In a lake, I believe. It's not exactly like the one in the movies, but pretty close."

Alex pointed to the shield. "Neve knew?"

The grin slid away. "She knew it was in Bellamy Bay—rather, she had a strong idea it was here, based on her research."

"So, she didn't come here just to paint the mural. She was here on assignment."

He nodded. "Yeah, and she asked me point-blank if it had been discovered. This was a couple weeks before we'd actually found it, and I told her no. But after the power outage, she knew. She said the people she worked with read the heat signature and knew. She told me that she was supposed to tell the organization she worked for where it was, but she didn't want to. And I encouraged her not to tell anyone."

He looked at his feet.

Alex thought she understood the look on his face. "You didn't get her killed."

He winced as if in pain. "I didn't save her life either."

"She never told me who she was working for," he continued, "only that she used her profession as a cover. She told me that when she began, she thought she was doing the right thing helping to bring lost art and history to the world. That's what she considered the Warsaw Shield—a work of art." He ran a hand through his hair. "Later, she discovered that she was helping the bad guys, that they wanted to use these Magical weapons to bully and suppress other countries. She also said that the people she worked for would be very angry if she refused to help them."

"She was working for Jasper. And apparently Montgomery was working for him too."

Dylan sighed, his shoulders slumping as if the weight of the world were on his shoulders, and a part of Alex ached for him.

"Her work sounded fascinating. Did she explain what she did exactly?"

"Yeah. Apparently, she's been working for them—Jasper and his organization—for years. It's a team, I guess, and they used their resources to find out where the weapons were hidden. She'd come in to confirm the location and set up the time for acquisition—her words, not mine. Someone would come in, take the weapon, and then they were off to the next assignment."

Alex thought of the first time she'd seen Neve with Dylan. She'd been watching the news of a Japanese tidal wave and had become upset. She reminded Dylan of that.

"Yeah, she said she was the cause of that wave. She'd created a beautiful mural of the Japanese sea god and the Tide Jewels and brought that chaos to life."

Alex thought back to the list of mythological weapons sent to the blogger. The Tide Jewels was on it. "Someone recently purchased the Tide Jewels and created a tidal wave in Japan with them. The Chinese must've used it as a distraction while they occupied the Senaku Islands," she said.

He nodded. "They've been purchased. And I've seen them. They're exquisite and placed in a tiara. No one seeing them would know what they are. Neve shared the details with me. But after I gave her a tour of my property, she told me she was tired of her life and that she feared adding more pain and suffering to the world. I wasn't sure what she meant. She's an artist, after all, and she created beauty for everyone to share."

Alex thought of the portfolio with the horrific sketches in it. "She wasn't creating beauty; she was creating pain and destruction." She told Dylan about the sketchbook. "I don't think she saw the beauty in her work anymore."

"She told me she was worried about the world she was creating for generations to come, and the part she played in it. She felt she'd made things worse. She worried about karma," he said.

"She was pregnant when she died," Alex said. "I think that's why she didn't want to continue."

Dylan sighed. "That makes sense."

"But what are you going to do with the shield?"

"Keep it safe." He turned his gaze back to the shield. "War is bad—we can all agree to that. But this . . . this is beautiful. It's a part of our heritage, but it can also do some ugly things—in the wrong hands. All mythological weapons can. Have you actually read the accounts of mythological weapons being used? It's brutal. Horrifying."

"But also . . . lucrative?" She frowned at him. "You're not planning on monetizing the mermaid gene, it's this." She turned to look at the shield. "You're in the weapons business now. Mythological weapons."

"There's a hot market for mythological weapons and when I found out that they were being recovered and sold, mostly on the black market, I knew I had to find the Warsaw Shield first. If anyone is going to take ownership' of this artifact, it should be me—someone who will respect the weapon and it's heritage."

Alex's laugh was harsh. "Ever the businessman, aren't we?"

"Don't." He shook his head. "I'm trying to do the right thing. Who would you rather have it? Me or Montgomery?"

"Montgomery? He's after it too?" Alex threw up her hands. "Which of you is the lesser of two evils?"

"Me," he said, frustration edging his voice. "Montgomery is not in Bellamy Bay just so he can fund a mermaid festival. He wants the Shield. He wants to sell the technology to Russia and then maybe China. Iran. He *wants* to sell it to the buyer who promises to cause the most chaos, the most damage."

Something cold slipped down Alex's spine as she looked at Dylan. And that's why Montgomery was spending time with Tegan. He knew the Wesleys were looking for the shield. Montgomery wasn't a Mundane collaborator. Jasper had lied. He was a Dragon Descent. But how did Dylan know that?

"I know," he answered aloud.

"You heard me?" Alex asked surprised.

"Do a better job of guarding your thoughts. You forget to do so when you're emotional."

Alex took a moment to use the technique Minka had shared with her to guard her thoughts.

Dylan grinned. "Better. Now your mind is like Fort Knox as it should be."

Alex rolled her eyes. "How do you know about the Dragons?"

"My mother." He gave her a dark look. "Told me and Bryn about them as children. They were our bedtime stories."

"Your mother told you stories about monsters before bedtime?" Alex stammered.

"They weren't monsters to her." He looked at her, eyes dimmed with sadness.

Alex went back to the shield, holding her hand over it close enough to feel the heat radiating from it. "Who do you want to sell it to?"

"Our government of course. This technology can be used to protect our armed forced, help our allies. Why wouldn't I do that?"

"And that's what you mean by Pro-Tek being set up for the business, having the contacts, the structure in place."

"Yes, that's what I meant."

"How can you sell Magical weapons to Mundanes?"

"There are Magicals in government and Mundanes who know about us and will keep our secrets as long as we're beneficial to them."

"Bryce knows, doesn't he?"

Dylan nodded. "But you don't have to worry about him. He's trustworthy."

She gave him a knowing look. "You have a lot planned for your weapons division, don't you?"

His smile was genuine. "Sky's the limit. We'll be working with the Navy and Marines at Camp Malveaux to develop these technologies."

"You have to let the Council know." she said. "This isn't something you can just keep to yourself."

"I know," he says. "But I think we can both agree there are some dangerous people looking for it. For now, let's just keep it safe here, shall we?"

"It's beautiful." Alex turned to look at the shield. "It's magical."

"You're beautiful," he said, coming to stand behind her so close she could feel the heat from his body. "You're magical."

For a moment, Alex allowed herself to lean into his warmth. And then she stepped away, alarmed at the way he drew her in, the feeling that she should just give in. It reminded her of something. Of someone. The magnetism she'd felt from Montgomery. The magnetism that had bound Celeste to Jasper. She exhaled sharply and put space between them.

He watched her for a moment, his eyes wary. "What is it?"

"Dylan . . ." Her throat was dry. "What kind of Magical are you?"

His jaw hardened. "What do you mean?"

"You're Mer, like me, like my family?"

He averted his gaze, and she saw his Adam's apple move as he swallowed. "How'd you know?" he asked, his voice low.

A pain sliced through her heart. "I know what it feels like now, to be near a Dragon Descent. I saw the way Celeste was irrationally attracted to Jasper, felt a pull toward Montgomery, even though I didn't like him . . . and I feel it now, with you."

He raised his chin and stared at her. "My mother thinks I should be proud of it, our dragon heritage." He shook his head. "But I'm not. And you can see why."

Alex took a step backward, unable to hide the revulsion on her face, and he looked stricken when he saw it.

"I'm only half," he insisted. "My father was Mer, but my mother . . ."

"Is a Dragon Descent." She exhaled slowly. "Well, I guess that makes sense. And Bryn?"

"Takes after our mother. Clearly." He stepped toward her, his arm out to touch her. "You can't hold this against me. Can't you see? I'm at war with myself every single day. I want to be good. I want to be so good." He almost looked like he would cry, and Alex's heart softened just a bit.

"I told you back when we were kids."

"What?"

He nodded. "And you reacted the same way. Revulsion. Disgust. I'd made a mistake. I thought—we'd been playing together all summer, and you were so sweet and trusting, I felt like I could tell you anything. So I did. Told you about the dragons, how much I disliked them . . . Told you about me—"

"But I don't remember anything. I don't recall—" She gasped, her hand going to her mouth. "Dylan, you didn't?"

He turned his back to her, his voice low. "That's why you don't remember practicing magic when you were a child. That's why you don't remember the tricks we did with the water. I wiped your memories so you'd forget about my secret. Only you forgot almost everything about that summer." He turned to face her, his eyes sad. "I'm sorry, Alex. I'm so sorry."

"I don't understand. When I first arrived, you were the one who told me someone had wiped my memories—I thought it was my parents and I was angry with them. But it was you."

His head hung. "I know. It was deceptive. And wrong. I just didn't want you to look at me the way you're looking at me now."

Every time Alex took one step forward with Dylan, he did something to make her take not two, but three steps back. She took a deep calming breath, determined not to respond in the same way she apparently had when she was seven. "At least that solves one mystery: why I can't remember practicing magic as a child."

"Guilty as charged." He turned to face her, looking her squarely in the eyes. "Go ahead. Hate me. I deserve it."

But she shook her head. "I'm not angry, Dylan. Disappointed. Saddened . . . but not angry. You were just a little boy."

The muscles of his face relaxed slightly, and he shook his head slowly. "You're amazing, Alex. Simply amazing. Thank you for understanding."

But Alex didn't feel amazing. She felt torn. Conflicted. She liked Dylan so much, in spite of the fact that every cell in her body told her to run away from him as fast as she could. But she was older now, she couldn't—wouldn't respond the same way. He was half Dragon. Okay. So what? She made herself smile, tried to sound normal. "I'm guessing not practicing magic helps you with your internal conflict?"

He looked relieved and nodded. "Yeah, it just takes the option to fully give in to my reptilian brain off the table."

Alex kept the smile in place, swallowing back the bitter taste on her tongue. "And Montgomery?"

"Is my uncle. My mother's older brother."

Alex took a moment to let this information sink in. "I thought he was Russian."

"My mother is a mix of Polish, Russian, and Welsh. Uncle Montgomery spent a lot of time in Russia after college, reconnecting with family. He owns mines there."

"I get that he wants the shield, but is there another reason he's in town?" She gazed at him, and then she knew. "He wants you to join him?"

"Something like that." His laugh was harsh. "He'd love for Wesley Inc. and Leviathan to merge. But he thinks I'm too soft. Too much like my father and that I've suffered not having a strong male role model in my life. He wants to stick around and be . . . I don't know, a mentor or something to me."

"You don't need to change anything. You are by all accounts a success, Dylan. And I know your mother is proud of you."

"She'd be prouder if I embraced her heritage like Bryn did. For all the good it's done her."

Alex looked at the Warsaw Shield. "And you're trying to protect the Warsaw Shield and other magical weapons from your family and others like him."

"Yes." He bowed his head, suddenly looking very tired.

For an insane second, Alex thought of tiger moms, the super strict mothers who pressured their children to succeed, and wondered about dragon moms. She laughed. Was that a thing too?

Remembering him as the shy little boy who'd played with her. Who'd been afraid to tell his parents he'd asked his chauffeur to stop at her house on the way home from piano lessons so they could play together. He'd been so afraid that he'd never even told her his name. And Alex had wanted to go to him then. But she couldn't. She just couldn't.

He was so, so dangerous for her. "We should go," she finally said, making sure her voice didn't waver or crack.

His gaze seared through her. "You can't tell anyone about this."

"About the shield?"

"About the shield, of course. But I meant about me being a Magical hybrid." He looked stricken. Desperate. "I'm just like all of the other Magicals flying under the radar. Okay? I don't want to be treated differently. Like I'm evil. A monster."

She didn't say anything, and he went her to then, grabbing her in both arms and crushing her against his chest. He rubbed his face against her hair, breathing in the fresh scent of her. The power of his magnetism almost overwhelmed her, and she swayed on her feet, but then she wrenched free, pushing him back.

He stumbled backward only once, hands in the air. "Sorry. Sometimes it just happens. It's a thing—the attraction, the charisma? It's almost like an unconscious spell that I can cast, and I'm constantly having to forcefully, purposely turn it off. Especially with you. I want you"—the words tumbled out of his mouth—"I want you to want me as much as I want you, but it has to be real. I need for it to be real."

Alex could hardly breathe. The air in the room was stifling, and she wanted nothing more than to be held in his arms while he kissed her. But was that really what she wanted? Or was it a trick?

She couldn't look at him. The feeling in her heart . . . it hurt too much. "Please take me home. I won't say anything."

Chapter
Twenty-Nine

The air smelled of cotton candy, buttered popcorn and funnel cakes.

The outdoor portion of the mermaid festival had begun in earnest, and Alex had never seen so many mermaid lovers in one place. The sun was bright and the sky was streaked with puffs of cloud while she managed the Botanika booth. Aunt Lidia and Minka had just stepped away to grab some food.

Children walked by with mermaid and merman face paint, holding Styrofoam shields and swords or giant balloons created to look like pink and purple mermaids. Men on tall stilts, dressed as pirates, stalked the park, much to the children's delight. And on the stage, The Nymphets, a local all-girl rock band, raged about life as a mermaid on land. Several men walked around with accordions, playing Polka music while sporting the traditional dress of shorts, vests, and hats in red, white, and green.

Alex could see the mural from her booth, and as Celeste had predicted, it was a popular spot for photographs and selfies. Customers had been plentiful for the booth, and after four hours they were almost out of their bottled teas, soaps, and candles.

With a pink pouf of cotton candy in hand, Pepper, in a rust-colored dress and heels, skipped over to the Botanika booth, a wide grin on her face as she waited impatiently for Alex to finish a sale. When they left, she shimmied to the table. "You'll never guess what happened to me," she said, as her ponytail swung animatedly from side to side.

Smiling, Alex leaned forward, hands under her chin. "Do tell."

"My news articles on Evelyn Robinson and Jasper Collins were picked up by all the major newspapers in the Carolinas, *and* TV news outlets in Atlanta and Washington, DC, want to interview me about the stor-eees," she sang out. "I'm on my way! If it wasn't for you, I wouldn't have been the first reporter to interview that evil, evil woman and share it with the world. And you were so right about Jasper Collins—he was an arrogant one. All I had to do was play up to his vanity and he told me everything—even though I still feel like he was holding something back. And he was also kind of handsome and intriguing—you know in that sexy psychopath way? Anyway!" She hurried around the table and wrapped her arms around Alex. "I just want to give you the biggest hug, girl."

"Oh, my." Alex laughed, her arms at her sides like a straitjacket while Pepper embraced her.

Pepper finally let go. "I'm actually on my way to the airport, but I had to stop by and let you know personally. My car is waiting, so love you—bye!"

Just as Alex was recovering from Hurricane Pepper, she saw Celeste approaching the table. She wore a festival T-shirt, khaki short shorts that highlighted her toned legs, and high-heeled wedge sandals. Her hair was pulled into a messy bun on the top of her head, and she pushed her mirrored aviator sunglasses onto her forehead when she reached the booth.

"How's your first festival going?"

"It's everything I imagined it to be," Alex replied with a smile. "No issues with the vendors, so I'm pleased."

"Same here. All of the food trucks and food vendors are here and selling as fast as they can prepare the food. No fires." She laughed. "Yet."

"How are you doing? I haven't had a chance to talk to you since—everything happened."

Her smile dropped slightly. "I'm okay."

"You and your mom were amazing by the way. But you use black magic?"

Celeste gave a weak chuckle. "Mami Wata only sees magic and it's neither good or bad. We're taught to use whatever we like from whatever energetic source we choose."

Alex watched her friend, wondering if she felt conflicted about her magic like Dylan. She didn't seem to be. "I noticed your magic was pink? Why is that? Mine is white, and so are Minka's and Aunt Lidia's."

"Because I'm a mix of mermaid, which visually expresses itself as a high vibrating white energy, while Mami Wata's is serpent-like, lower in frequency and red—like Jasper's—like a dragon's."

"Oh." Alex laughed. "I get it: red and white make pink." She had so much to learn. Would she ever feel like she had a handle on the Magical community? When she received one answer, it only created more questions. "You were speaking another language when you worked your magic?"

Celeste smiled. "Haitian Creole."

"Wow. And that snake?"

"Cool, right? Sometimes my magic just appears in that form." She laughed. "Usually when I'm angry."

Alex wasn't a fan of snakes. She tried not to wrinkle her nose in distaste. "Yeah, sure." She looked at her friend. "But if it's so cool, why do you look so sad?"

Celeste smiled, even though her brown eyes were flat. "Not sad, exactly. Disappointed with myself. It's been a busy summer. I dated a murderer who was a Magical incognito, and I couldn't even figure it out, and I was charged with a murder that I didn't do but I thought I did, so a lot got by me. I can't let that happen again. No more time for boyfriends." Her jaw set in a determined line. "I need to be *more*. More focused. More driven."

"You enjoy your work at Wesley?"

Celeste's face brightened with interest. "I'm on a team that's trying to understand the science behind the magic of the weapons we're finding. It's exciting work, Alex."

"Well, there you go. You've got your focus. Your direction. I think you'll be fine," Alex said. "You're definitely on the path to success."

Celeste took a breath, then smiled. "Thanks, that means a lot." She looked down at her phone screen and read a text. "Uh-oh, the pierogi truck is having an emergency. Duty calls." She waved over her shoulder as she trotted off.

*   *   *

For the next thirty minutes, Alex was busy with customers, until all of her soaps and candles were gone. There was a lull in sales, and she allowed herself to relax for a moment, when a shadow was cast over the booth, and Alex looked up. It was Montgomery. Looking summery in a white linen shirt, khaki shorts, and tan sandals. He smiled down at her, dollar bills in hand.

"I'd like a bottle of that Keep Coolade tea I've been hearing so much about."

Alex took his money, and handed him the beverage. He opened it right there and had a swallow. "This is good."

She frowned. "Thanks." And waited for him to leave. When he didn't, she gave him a quizzical look. "You should try the funnel cakes next. They're also great." She pointed to a vendor far, far, away from her booth.

He chuckled. "I might just do that. But I wanted to apologize to you first."

"For?"

"Jasper's behavior. Toward you and the town, generally. When I sent him here—"

"When *you* sent him here?" She crossed her arms. "He made it clear that *he* was the boss, and you took orders from him."

"And that's what was told to The Council, yes?" He chuckled again, a low throaty sound. "True to the end, that one. That was sporting of him."

"You're saying he's not—Neve didn't work for him?"

He held up his hand. "Only the boss wears the ring. I sent him here to do a job, and he went about his task with less finesse than I would've liked." For a moment he looked weary, older. "I told him not to fall in love. It never ends well when they do."

"You knew that he killed Neve?"

"I liked Neve very much. She was one of my best operatives, and an invaluable part of my organization . . . until she was not." He closed his eyes for a moment. "We never discussed her murder, but I had my suspicions. I wasn't pleased," he said mildly. "Not in the least."

Lips pursed, Alex stared at him. Her skin prickled with something . . . Fear? Apprehension? She recalled the revulsion Neve had expressed when she saw news coverage of the tidal wave in Japan. "You sold the Tide Jewels to China?" His expression blanked, but Alex continued. "Knowing they would use it to cause destruction and act as distraction for their military."

"The sale was beneficial to me and my organization."

"Which part? The deaths or the money."

"All of it."

She shot him a look of disbelief. "And this is the same organization you want Minka to work for?"

"Your cousin is interested in helping the environment, so that's what she'd be doing."

"Over my—"

"Please." His smile was pleasant. "It's too beautiful a day for such a weighty topic."

"You want to change the topic? Okay, I have another question for you."

"I'm an open book. Shoot."

"You seem very interested in my family. Why is that?"

"Do I?" He chuckled. "It's not your family, dear. It's you."

"Me?" Alex frowned. "Why me?"

"I heard you looked just like your mother. I wanted to see for myself."

A lump lodged in Alex's throat. "You knew my mother? How? When? Where?"

His smile was gentle. "It was a long time ago. I was sad to hear of her passing, and yes, you look just like her. I wonder . . ."

Alex gritted her teeth. "You wonder what?"

"Oh, nothing."

Neve's words came back to her then: *"There's also the responsibility. The Mermaid of Warsaw had a sword and shield for a reason. To help protect the seas and the coast—that's her domain after all—and any and everything that comes from it."*

Dragons, at least some of them, came from the sea, and they and Montgomery's organization seemed hell-bent on causing destruction. Were mermaids supposed to protect the world from dragons? For a moment, Alex's body tingled with fear.

"Why are you really here, Montgomery?"

He looked around the park filled with tourists and festival-goers. "I'm here to enjoy a summer's day at the beach, just like everyone else. I like this little town. It's absolutely charming."

When he said that last word, "charming," something cold and slippery ran up and down her spine. She looked toward the mural. And she knew without a shadow of a doubt that the serpent sliding in the water underneath the Mermaid of Warsaw was Montgomery. Neve had warned her against him too.

"I have big plans for this town."

Alex rose from her seat then. "Do you?"

"Yes. But don't be alarmed. I don't want to change anything about this place. I just feel like it could be home for me."

"And your kind?"

His shrug was expansive. "Eh."

Lidia and Minka joined her then, coming around the table and standing beside her. Minka's face had been painted as a mermaid in bright shades of pink, purple, and blue. And her brunette curls were streaked with purple and blue.

She looked beautiful, Alex thought. Like a mermaid princess. But the wide grin on her face disappeared when she felt the negative energy hovering around the tent.

"Everything okay, Alex?" Lidia said, a mild look of concern on her face as she handed her a funnel cake covered in powdered sugar and smelling like heaven.

Alex looked up and saw Kamila coming toward them, another kielbasa and roasted potato stick in hand. The feeling of fear and trepidation she'd experienced earlier were gone. Her family was with her, and for some reason, when they were around, she felt fearless. Like she could take on the world.

Or dragons.

She smiled at her aunt. "Yes, I'm fine. Montgomery was just telling me how much he was enjoying the festival."

"That's right. And who doesn't love a mermaid?" Montgomery chuckled, nodding to the women and winking at Minka, who couldn't help but smile in response. "I guess I'll be seeing you then. All of you." He passed Kamila as she arrived at the table.

"What's going on?" she said, handing the stick to Minka. "Take this. It's my third of the day, and I just realized I've hit the kielbasa wall." She made a gagging face. "Not another bite."

Lidia pursed her lips. "There's no such thing as too much kielbasa, my girl." And then she laughed. "What's going on, is that I've got my family together. My girls, all of you." She looked at Alex and grinned. "And it feels good. It feels right, doesn't it?" She playfully shoved Alex aside. "Now you go and enjoy the day. I'm watching the booth for the rest of the day."

Minka grabbed Alex's arm. "This one is getting her face painted."

"No," Alex mock-groaned. "Help me, Kamila."

But Minka wouldn't take no for an answer. "It's one of the few times of the year that we can really be our true selves. Come on— I want to see Alex with a pink and purple glittery mermaid face! Don't you?"

Kamila cocked her head, evaluating Alex's face, and then smiled. "I guess she'd make a good mermaid. What do you say, Alex?"

Laughing, Alex relented. "Let's do it. I'm ready to embrace my inner mermaid." And with a jolt of surprise, Alex realized she really was okay with being a mermaid—whatever that meant and all that it entailed.

With Minka in the middle, she linked arms, Alex and Kamila on either side of her. And Alex smiled. It felt like old times, when both her parents had been alive and she'd stayed in Bellamy Bay for the summers. For just a few moments, they were little girls off for an adventure.

And Alex couldn't have felt happier.